LOVE STORIES

LOVE STORIES

Introduction by
Rosamunde Pilcher

Compiled by
Lynn Curtis

St. Martin's Press
New York

Reader: Diana Vowles
Design: Richard Souper

ISBN 0-312-11847-3

First published in Great Britain by Michael O'Mara Books Limited

Contents

Introduction

As a schoolgirl, over fifty years ago, I was content in thinking that I knew everything that needed to be known about 'love'. This limitless knowledge of the subject was gleaned from the pages of a magazine called *Peg's Paper*, forbidden to our family, but which our housemaid took on a regular basis. She would hide it under the cushion of her basket chair in the kitchen, for fear of being reprimanded by my mother for lowering the 'moral tone' of the household, but, like a true friend, would smuggle this amorous gazette up to the bedroom of my sister and me under the cover of darkness. Many an eye-opening hour was spent with a torch under the bedclothes, with only the interruption of either my sister or me having to scramble to the top of the bed for air.

The formula of these stories seldom changed. Boy meets girl, boy loses girl, boy wins girl. Only the characters came from slightly changing backgrounds . . . sometimes they were dukes and duchesses, or hardworking secretaries wearing dark dresses with fresh touches of white at the throat. Sometimes they were girls with high-flying dreams of becoming ballet dancers, but who, having succumbed to the sting of Cupid's arrow, chose a more humdrum future with the boy next door, he being a faultless young man with blunt features and an open expression, so obviously trustworthy that you wondered why the wretched girl had ever considered going on the stage in the first place.

And then I learned, by chance, what a love story really was. For our English Literature examination at school, we were 'made' to do an in-depth study of Emily Brontë's *Wuthering Heights*. The books issued to everyone in my class were small school editions with red covers and tiny print. I thought, on opening it for the first time, that the only exciting feature about the book was the crack of the newly glued headband, and the smell of the crisp, white paper . . . Homework that night was to read the first ten pages.

Having eaten my supper, and completed the rest of my prep, I climbed into bed with the book, with every expectation of being asleep by the end of the third page . . . I read through the night, and I think it was five o'clock in the morning before I finally fell asleep. This wasn't English Literature. This was love.

When war broke out, my mother's sister, resident in Philadelphia, decided that she must do her bit for the brave British, and rather than send food parcels or clothes ("My dear, we *must* be more original in our thoughts to help you in your hour of need"), she donated to our household an indefinite subscription to the *Ladies Home Journal*. I don't think that any copy of any publication could have been devoured more avidly than was the *LHJ* in our household.

Apart from going to the pictures, where I sat longing to be Deanna Durbin, or howling over Charles Boyer in *Hold Back The Dawn*, it was the monthly arrival of this magazine that became my greatest comfort in dull and dark wartime Britain, opening windows into other worlds that I had either forgotten, or had never known. A beautifully produced magazine, it ran fiction of the highest quality. I read Daphne du Maurier for the first time in its pages, and Elizabeth Goudge, and was also introduced to some of the very best of American writers.

When I started to write my stories, I am afraid they were more of the *Peg's Paper* type, although, I would hope, a little more enterprising. However, as I grew up, married, had children, and felt myself become more qualified in interpreting relationships and feelings, the stories opened and spread their tentacles, covering all aspects of love and liaisons. The love of parents for children, brothers for sisters, grandparents for grandchildren. The love of old people for youth, of youngsters for age, the love of lovers, the love of marriage, the love that isn't love at all, but a mutual respect and affection.

Love does not necessarily have a happy ending, but it can change the colour of the world. With the known quality of the authors that Michael O'Mara Books have selected for this book, I am sure that you will be able to use it as your own personal paintbox.

Rosamunde Pilcher
November 1989

Miss Geraldine Parkington
Catherine Cookson

Though Miss Parkington peered hard through the lead-lighted window of her sitting room, all she could see in the fading afternoon light was the thickly falling snow. It was more than three hours since she had been able to make out the iron gate that led to the road. As for what she had been brought up to think of as the tradesman's entrance, that had disappeared from her view around noon.

What had happened to him? She had never known him miss a day. Mondays, Wednesdays and Fridays, from as far back as '66. Oh, she remembered the year and the first time she had seen him when he came to lay the Cumberland turf lawn that her mother had insisted on having in order to outshine the Baileys' garden next door.

Then after her mother had stopped speaking to the Baileys, she had got him to come back and plant the quick-growing cypress hedge all round. And from then, he had been taken on for three days a week.

Something had happened to him. If humanly possible, he would have been here.

Why, he had even come one snowy Christmas morning to clear the drive so they could get the car out, and her father had said there weren't many men who would do that.

Besides, she wanted to give him his Christmas present.

Until now, she had always given him money. However, there was no thought required in handing someone a few pieces of paper in an envelope, and so she had thought up this . . . wonderful surprise. But then he couldn't take it home tonight—not on his bike; and as she couldn't get the car out . . .

There was a muffled sound coming from the direction of the kitchen. She hurried into the hall, across it, through the kitchen and to the back door. 'Oh, Albert! I'd given you up.'

[9]

'I'm sorry, Miss Parkington. But it's turned out to be one of them days.'

'Oh, you're wet. Come along in; you must have a drink of something hot.'

'Thanks all the same, but I'll get the drive done first.'

'Oh, by the look of it it'll be just as bad again within an hour or so. Come in.'

'But my boots . . . I must take these off,' he laughed, stepping out of his pair of wet wellingtons.

A minute later he was in the kitchen standing before her. He was of the same height as her in his stockinged feet. She had always imagined herself being taller than him; but that had been when she was wearing heels. 'The kettle won't be a minute. Sit down, Albert . . . Have you had trouble of some sort?'

'That's putting it mildly, miss. This morning everybody in my street got a letter from the Authorities. We were informed that we had till the end of January to move to where they had decided: a high-rise block of flats on Market Road. Well, snow or no snow, the whole street was out because—as I think I told you—the last we heard was they were by-passing our road, or what remained of it. And, as I said then, they were really good houses, and it was a shame pulling any of them down. But that was last year; now the plans are changed.

'Anyway, you'd never believe it, Miss Parkington, the whole lot of us stormed the Town Hall. The Big White Chief said he would see two of us in his office, and John Carter and I went in—only to come out half an hour later none the wiser, except that we knew we were beaten before we started.'

As he sighed she brought the teapot to the table and, putting it down none too gently on a tile stand, she exclaimed: 'It's scandalous—utterly scandalous. They are nice houses, and everybody looks after them. Last year the four bottom ones were all painted yellow, doors and windows . . .'

He looked at her. 'I didn't know you got down that way, miss.'

'Well, I sometimes take a short cut when I go to the park . . . well, a sort of short cut. But oh, Albert, won't you hate living in a high-rise flat?'

'I have no intention of living in a high-rise flat, miss. What they're offering me for my house is an absolute disgrace; it'll get me some place, but not into a high-rise flat. Oh no!' His tone was vehement.

And she nodded in agreement, saying: 'I should think not! You've been used to having a garden all your life . . . Will you have another cup of tea?'

'No, miss; no. If you don't mind, I'll get the thick off the drive. But if this keeps up, I doubt if you'll be able to use your car tomorrow; I can see you having to go to your cousin's by rail.'

No sooner had the door closed on him than she rushed to the oven and opened it to look at the beef casserole that was bubbling gently, after which she scurried round the kitchen in preparation.

And in just over twenty minutes the meal was ready and the table laid for two. A jug stood to the side of the stove holding freshly-made custard, and a shop-bought apple pie was being gently warmed through beside it. When the knock came on the back door, she called: 'Come in, Albert.'

'No, miss. I'd better get back; it's coming down thick again.'

'Come in, Albert . . . please.' The last was spoken softly.

Albert Morton looked at the tall grey-haired woman for a moment; then he took off his cap and coat, and stepped out of his wellingtons.

'Look,' she said now, pointing to a pair of slippers, 'do you think you could get into those? My feet are almost as big as yours.'

'Well, I could try!'

'Don't worry about splitting them; they're old ones.'

They both looked down at his feet now and they laughed together when he said: 'Just.'

'You'll stay and have a bite.'

'Oh no, Miss Parkington.'

'Yes, Albert. By the time you get home after trudging those two miles you won't feel like cooking a meal, and the house will be cold; so sit down.' She pointed.

He gave a little shake of his head, but then seated himself at the table; and when she placed the meal before him, he stared down at it before saying: 'My, I've never seen a plate set out like this since my mother went.'

'Well, I don't suppose that'll be as tasty as hers was. But if it does nothing else, it'll fill you up.' When she brought her own plate to the table he made an awkward gesture of half rising from his chair, and she seemed to appreciate this for, smiling, she said: 'We don't stand on ceremony, Albert.'

They started to eat. And their plates were half empty before she spoke again; and then it was about the snow: how long did he think it would last, she asked.

There was no telling, he replied.

After she took away his empty plate, he sat back in his chair, took in a long breath, then said: 'That was a lovely meal indeed. You're a very good cook, miss.'

'I'm glad you enjoyed it, Albert. As for being a good cook, I've had to learn to do a lot of things since Mary left three years ago.'

'Yes, yes.' He nodded. 'It surprised me that you managed it all yourself—the housework and that, and right from the start.'

'Why should it have surprised you all that much, Albert? Librarians are, after all, ordinary women. Most of them in the library have to go home and see to a family.'

'Yes, yes; but somehow . . .'

'You didn't think I was capable?'

'Oh, miss; nothing of the sort. It was just that I thought you being brought up as you were and your mother having two maids all the time and you not having to dirty your hands . . .'

'Oh, Albert—' she gave an impatient toss of her head—'not having to dirty my hands. I dirtied my hands in lots of other ways, if you only but knew.'

He made no reply, just stared at her. Even when she placed the apple pie and custard before him, he still did not make any remark. But once the meal was finished, he rose from the table, saying: 'I'll wash up.'

'You'll do no such thing. But you can dry, if you like.'

So there they stood at the sink: Miss Geraldine Parkington and her gardener Mr. Albert Morton, washing and drying the dishes as if it were a daily occurrence.

'What are you doing over the holidays, Albert?' she asked.

'Oh, the usual: taking a little rest, having a bit of a read. But,' he put in quickly, 'I'll pop over each morning you're away and see everything's all right.'

He had an uncomfortable air about him now as he stood in the middle of the tiled floor: it was as if he was uncertain how to take his leave, until she said: 'I've got a little Christmas box for you, Albert. It's a little different from the usual—you know: the envelope.'

'Oh yes? But there's no need, miss; you pay me well enough.'

'It's on the cold store floor. It's rather heavy. Would you care to lift it up on to the table?'

'Heavy, miss? A present for me?'

'Yes, Albert, a present for you. And it's heavy, but it's not a garden roller!' And now she was pointing to a large cardboard box in the pantry. And as he went to lift it, he twisted round and looked at her in some amazement.

Then, the box on the table, she watched him slit the sticky tape and pull back the half-lids—to look in gaping, silent surprise on twelve bottles.

'Well, I know you like a glass of wine,' she said. 'I remember you talking to Father a long time ago about how you were going to start making home-made wine. Father, too, would have liked to do that, but . . . well . . . Anyway, there you are. But they're not all alike. There's only six table wines; the rest are—' she began to point —'whisky, brandy, port, sherry, rum, and—' she laughed now— 'champagne!'

'What! Why, it . . . it must have cost you the earth, miss.'

'Not as much as you might think, Albert. You see, Mother had a few shares in the Newcastle Brewery, and some weeks ago I was sent a card offering this package at a reduced price to all their shareholders.'

Now she watched him bend forward and rest his forearms on the box's sides. His head was bent over it, and she was looking down on to the thick mop of hair that was still brown at the back.

'Do you think it was silly of me?' The question was tentative.

And it brought him up straight, saying loudly: 'No, no; I think it's marvellous. It's the best present I've ever had in my whole life. And I mean that, honest. It's a gift that . . . well, I wish I could say that'll keep for ever. But I can tell you this, I'll hang on to the empties! Oh, Miss . . . Parkington.'

His hand was outstretched across the bottles, and when she put hers into it he gripped it and shook it, saying: 'Thank you very much. I . . . I wish I was given to making pretty speeches, but I've never had occasion to use them. But now . . . well . . . Look—' he released her hand and pointed to the bottles—'I can't carry this lot with me, can I? One in each pocket would be as much as I would dare to take on the road tonight. So, would you do me the honour of breaking the first one with me?'

'Yes. Yes, Albert, of course I will.' There was a slight break in her voice, and she gulped. 'Which one? What is your favourite?'

'Well, to be truthful, I'm partial to a drop of whisky—especially if I've had a rough day like today and got wet through.'

'A straight whisky it is, then.'

She watched while he opened the bottle; and then laughing like a young girl, she said: 'Oh, the glasses! They're in the cabinet in the sitting room.'

She paused a moment, and now holding out her hand in invitation, she added: 'Come along. Come into the sitting room, Albert. If we're going to drink whisky, let's at least do it in style.'

With the bottle in his hand, Albert stared at the tall figure hurrying from the kitchen; then, as if prodded from behind, he, too, moved into the hall. But here he stopped to glance round him before entering the drawing room.

She was taking down two glasses from a shelf in a small French cabinet standing in a corner of the long room, and she turned and said: 'You haven't been in this room before, have you?'

'No; never, miss. I've seen it through the window. It always did look nice, but it's a beautiful room now. You've altered things?'

'Yes. Yes, I've altered things. This used to be called the drawing room, now I call it the sitting room, because it *is* a sitting room. Sit down, Albert.'

He moved towards an easy chair, and said, indicating his clothes, 'But I've got my working things on; I'll dirty that.'

'Then it will do it good to be dirtied. Sit down.'

There was a puzzled look on his face as he lowered himself on to the yellow satin cushion.

She now took the bottle and, going back to the table, poured out generous measures for them both.

'My! My!' He held up his glass and looked at the golden liquid. 'That's a double and a half, miss!'

'Do you take water?'

'No; I hate drowning anything, from cats to good liquor.'

They chuckled together. Then they sipped at their drinks, and Albert, smacking his lips, said: 'It's a good one . . . malt. It'll help my wellingtons along, this.'

'I'm glad you like it, Albert.' She was smiling at him.

But when he now asked, 'How long will you be away, miss?' her smile disappeared and she hesitated.

'I'm not quite sure, Albert.'

After again sipping at the whisky, she got up and placed some logs on the fire, saying: 'I do love to see a nice blaze.'

'Same here.'

Looking towards him now, she said self-consciously: 'Your glass is empty. Let me have it.'

'Oh no, miss.'

'But it's your whisky.'

'Well, if you say so.' He handed her his glass. And when she again brought him a double measure, he said: 'Aren't you having another yourself, miss?'

'Well . . . not of whisky. Quite candidly, I'm not very fond of it. But I'll tell you what I like, a brandy and port mixed.'

'A brandy and port? . . . Mixed!'

'Oh, yes. It's a marvellous drink—mind, not that I indulge in it much. But you know, when you're feeling low and out of sorts, it's a marvellous reviver. It's like a new kick starter to an old bike.'

After a second's pause, his head went back and the room was filled with a deep rollicking laugh.

Then she, too, was laughing—laughing so much she had to steady herself against the back of the couch. 'New kick starter to an old bike,' he repeated in delight. 'I've never heard that one before.'

'Would you like one, Albert?'

'On top of two doubles, miss? I'll have a job to get on my feet as it is.'

'I'm going to have one.' Her tone was definite.

'Well—' he blinked his wet eyes—'who am I to refuse a . . . kick starter?' And as he tasted the mixture, he added appreciatively: 'I see what you mean, miss. I see what you mean. But it wouldn't take many of these to lay you out on your back.' And immediately seeming to realise the impropriety of his remark, he added quickly: 'I mean, it would go to your head. Then you'd lose your legs.'

'I've never experienced that effect because when I do indulge, it's last thing at night, in bed.'

There followed a short, embarrassed silence during which he took a few more sips of the kick starter. Then looking across at her, he said quietly: 'It surprises me, you know, miss—liquor in this house. Your mother was against it, I think, wasn't she?'

'My mother,' she replied, 'was against everything that tended towards making anybody happy. If Father wanted a drink, he had to have it on the sly. Do you know something, Albert: he had a hell

[15]

of a life. Any pleasure he got he had to steal. He had a woman, you know, in Bog's End. She was a cleaner in his office—nice woman, plump. Mother was skinny, miserably skinny.'

'Did she know?' he asked.

'I don't think so. He was upset when he realised I knew. But I reassured him. And I used to lie for him. Oh, how I loved lying to her. I used to phone her and say I'd met Father and I was going straight from the library to do a show with him. And I used to arrange things to give him a bit of time on his own away from her.'

Her head came up and she looked at him. He was staring unblinkingly at her. 'Do you think I was wicked? Do you think that was a wicked thing to do?'

And he answered emphatically: 'No, I don't. Having known your mother, I don't.'

She nodded, saying: 'You know, Albert, she used to have a special tin mug for you to drink your ten o'clock tea out of. She kept it under the sink. I threw it in the bin one day, and she went for me. "Know your place," she said. "Give others theirs according to their station in life." Oh God, she was a snob . . .'

For a moment there was a telling silence. Then into the quiet he asked, his voice low: 'Why have you never married?' He did not add 'miss' but went on: 'I understand you lost your young man in the War. But you being very presentable and attractive as you were, and still are, I've often wondered . . .'

'Lost my young man in the War? Bosh! That's only what she put about. She wouldn't let a man near me. So after Father died, six years ago, we were stuck alone with each other. She disliked me wholeheartedly, and I returned the compliment. I was fifty-six; she was eighty-four. I told myself I would hang on until she went; with her bad heart it couldn't be all that long. And then I would travel; I was the only relative so the house would be mine, and also the money she had hoarded over her lifetime . . .'

Miss Parkington sat straight up now. 'Well, Albert, I had given notice to the council that I should be leaving at sixty—I'd had enough of libraries and responsibilities—and I told her of this. And I recall how she looked at me as if she could read my mind. And she must have: for when she went, her bequests were staggering. From the cats that you wouldn't drown—' she smiled wanly—'to the church restoration fund, she, being the pious woman that she was, thought of them

[16]

all. I was left with this house and, when all expenses had been paid, one thousand three hundred and fifty pounds.'

'Is that all?'

'Yes; that's all, Albert. That's why I had to let the maids go, pretending I liked housework and wanted to do it myself. And in a strange way I've got to like the chores. Anyway, they fill up the time.'

'But . . . but you kept me on and at full pay.'

'Oh, yes, Albert, I kept you on.'

'But why, when you couldn't afford it . . .?'

She cut in. 'Why?' Then she looked towards the fire as she added: 'Why do we do so many things? Perhaps I'd got used to Mondays, Wednesdays and Fridays. Perhaps because on Tuesdays, Thursdays, Saturdays and Sundays I very rarely see a soul, unless I go out or gaze through the window . . .' Swiftly she changed the subject. 'But you, you've had a very different life, haven't you, Albert?'

'Yes . . . Oh, yes, parentwise you could say. They were the best couple in the world. They kept me at the grammar school until I was seventeen, but then couldn't afford to have me articled.'

'Articled? To whom?'

'An accountant. You had to pay to be articled in those days. Instead, I went into the office as a clerk. I was there three years.'

'You were?'

'Yes.' He smiled broadly. 'Howard and Cape's in the Market Place.'

'Really? But . . . but why didn't you stay on?'

'Well, you see, I got TB and I was advised to work out of doors. Father had always tended our back garden. It was a picture. And he'd had me help him: we worked side by side like buddies . . . always like buddies.' He smiled softly. 'And so, you see, it was an easy step to gardening . . . But you'd never guess what.' He was grinning now. 'Mr Kilbride, from the Hall, has asked me to go there on full time. It's a very nice place.'

'How wonderful,' she said, but her voice sounded wooden. 'You won't be doing odd jobs any more, then, such as coming here?'

'Oh, I haven't taken it yet. I've a lot of thinking to do first.'

There was a pause until she said quietly: 'You were married once, weren't you? And she died.'

'Yes, I was married once.' He drained his glass; then for no reason she could make out he laughed—a loud, short, but mirthless laugh. 'It seems to be a night for spilling the beans, doesn't it? And it's true that

[17]

I was married—but she didn't die; she left me.'

'She left you?'

'Yes. Yes . . . she walked out. I was a very dull fellow then, still am.' His chin jerked upwards. 'The only thing I seem to know anything about is gardening and the odds and ends that I read.'

'She left you?'

'Oh, now, don't look so sad. It was many years ago. I was thirty-two at the time; that was long before I started here. Nobody remembers her. And she did die, but about ten years afterwards. You know how they joke about women going off with the milkman? Well, she went a step higher; she chose the insurance agent.'

She said. 'Oh, Albert. She must have been a fool, and blind, because you must have been such a good-looking man. Oh—' she flapped a hand at him—'that's tactless, isn't it? You are still a good-looking man. But you know what I mean.' She got to her feet and swayed slightly. 'Le . . . let's have another drink.'

'Oh, now, now; they'll be at me with a breathalyser.'

'Well, I'm going to have one. It isn't good to drink alone.'

On her way to the cabinet, she paused and, turning to him, said: 'I found that out, about drinking alone; I stopped it. There's only one way to go when you start to drink alone—down. I stopped it.'

'That was wise.' He walked over, the empty glass in his hand. After she had poured out measures of brandy and port she raised hers, saying: 'Here's to never drinking alone.' He touched her glass with his own, but made no response to her toast.

She stood looking around the room. 'I used to hate this house, but . . . but since it has become mine and I've pushed things around to suit me, I've got to love it. I was born here, you know, Albert; so was my father. His father built it; in fact he built the whole avenue, all fourteen houses. But he left ours with the most ground. They were the cream of the town in those days. They're still in demand. I'll be sorry to leave.'

'You're going to leave?'

'Well, I don't know. It isn't just the money—I can manage to scrape along—it's the loneliness . . . and more so, that feeling of aloneness. Do you know what aloneness is, Albert? No; you wouldn't being brought up with loving parents. And *your* father would have had no need to take another woman, and you'd have had no need to lie.'

'You should take a companion,' he said softly.

She looked towards him. 'Yes,' she said. 'Yes, Albert, I've thought of it a lot these last two years—not just on a Monday, Wednesday and Friday, either. I've thought about it every day in between too . . . Albert . . . will you come and live with me?'

He struggled to rise, gulping at the air. 'Oh. Oh, miss . . .'

'My name's Geraldine. Father called me Gerry. I liked Gerry.'

And now slowly he shook his head as he said: 'You . . . you don't know what you are saying. We've mixed a lot of drink the past hour or two. You . . . you can't mean it. In the morning . . .'

'I do mean it. I've . . . I've always liked you. You . . .' Her voice was breaking. 'You don't like me? I thought you might, a little.'

'Like you? Aw yes, I've always liked you. Yes, I do like you, but . . . but it wouldn't be right. You see, there's a gulf still, no matter what people say.'

'The hell with what people say! I've listened to what people have said all my life: I've had no say in my own life. Now I have. Anyway, Gracie Fields married her gardener. I'm no Gracie Fields, I know.'

'Huh! And I'm no romantic gardener living on the Isle of Capri.'

'You are romantic, Albert. I've always seen you as romantic. You're good-looking. I know your age, but you don't look sixty. Anyway, say you will or you won't.'

'Now . . . now, miss . . .'

'My name is Gerry.'

'Well now, Gerry, sleep on it, eh? I'm not going to take advantage of this . . . this opportunity. I . . . I couldn't live with meself if I did. I'll get home now and I'll be round in the morning.' He went to move from her and stumbled.

She laughed lightly. 'You'll not be able to stand up on the road; and I'll know your answer quicker if you're here in the morning.'

And then the tears were running down her cheeks, and he caught hold of her hands, saying: 'There now. There now.'

'Albert.'

'Yes? Yes, my dear?'

A wide grin spread over her wet face. 'You called me "my dear".'

'Did I? Well, I meant it.'

'Albert.'

'Yes?'

'Stay here tonight. It's all right. It's all right—' she was flapping a hand again—'I've nothing in mind, no, no. But there you are: look at that couch; it's as long as a bed.' She waved towards it. 'I'll get some blankets and you can sleep there.'

'*Not on your life.*'

She became still. Her face was straight; there was pain in her eyes. 'If in the morning you say yes, you will live with me, what difference will one extra night have made—and it spent on the couch? . . . Please, Albert.'

'Oh, God in Heaven!' He now held his brow, pacing the room.

For a moment she stood watching him, her fingers tapping her lips. 'I'll get you some . . . some bl . . . bl . . . blankets.'

He was sitting on the side of the couch when she returned, her outstretched arms holding two blankets and a pillow. 'There you are, then. The quicker you get to sleep, the quicker the morning will come. Good night, Albert.'

The sun was shining; it had stopped snowing; the kitchen was full of light. The table was set for breakfast. He had made the coffee, also the toast; but he didn't know whether to put it on a tray and take it up to her or wait until she came down. The eight o'clock news had just finished, the local announcer saying that the roads had been cleared and this would enable people to do their last-minute Christmas shopping.

He had been up since half-past six. Although he wasn't used to such a mixture as he had imbibed last night, the headache he had woken up with had vanished after he had drunk two cups of black coffee . . .

Before she spoke, he knew she was standing there, and he turned and looked at her downcast figure in the doorway. 'Morning.'

She didn't speak.

'Got a head?'

Still she didn't speak.

'Here, drink this.' He had poured out a coffee, and she took it from him and gulped at the steaming liquid; then pulling the lapels of her dressing-gown together, as if to hide her bare breastbone, she slowly sat down at the table and, resting her head in her hands, she said: 'I'm sorry, Albert. I'm so sorry, and ashamed.'

'Look here. Look at me.'

He had her chin in his hand and had raised her face up to his. 'What are you ashamed of? Being honest? There was a lot of truth spoken last night on both sides, and I thank God for it. Yes, yes, I do. You . . . you won't remember half what you said.'

'Oh, I do; I do remember.'

'Well, then, if you do, you know what I'm talking about. And I'm not going to hold you to anything that you said; but now, solid and sober, I'm going to have my say.' He turned from her and pulled a chair towards the table.

And now they were sitting knee almost touching knee; and, taking her hand, he said: 'You asked me last night if I liked you, and I said yes, I liked you. I didn't say how much because it has come as a surprise: you see, I've more than liked you for a long time. Why do you think I stayed on here working under your mother's airs and graces? You disliked your mother. Well, you weren't the only one. But after your father died I felt you needed someone—no, that wasn't exactly my thought; I only knew I wanted to be here and near you and find out what was going to happen to you. And then when she went and you were on your own . . .

'Oh, the times I've wanted to come here and say, "Would you like to go to the pictures, Miss Parkington?", "Would you like to take a walk, Miss Parkington?", "There's a good show on in Newcastle, Miss Parkington" or "There's a nice country pub I go to on a Friday night, Miss Parkington". Oh, the things I wanted to ask Miss Parkington; the things I wanted to say to her, but hadn't the nerve.

'And then last night Miss Parkington said to me, "Will you come and live with me, Albert?" . . . Don't. Don't hang your head—' his voice was loud—'because as much as you may need me, it's not half as much as I need you . . . and have done for a long, long time, but was such a damn fool I daren't voice it.

'Now, Miss Parkington, look . . . look at me. And oh, don't . . . don't cry. But I must say this to you: I . . . I cannot accept your offer of last night and come and live with you . . .' In the space he allowed himself before going on, he felt the trembling of her hand. 'But what I *shall* ask Miss Parkington is, will she marry me? . . . Oh, my dear! My dear! Don't cry like that. Please don't. Please.'

He had drawn her to her feet; and now, his arms about her and her head on his shoulder, he stroked her hair, repeating: 'There now, my dear. My dear.' Then when her crying didn't subside, he pressed her from him, saying: 'Yes or no? I want a straight answer.'

'Oh, Al . . . Albert.'

He smiled gently now, saying: 'I suppose that means yes. And you know something? I've never been able to stand that name of Albert until last night. Now look,' he added with excitement in his voice, 'come and have some breakfast because we've got a lot to do today. We want a Christmas tree and decorations. I've never had a Christmas tree or decorations since my mother died. And by the way, you'll have to phone that cousin of yours and tell her you're not coming . . .'

And drying her eyes, she said quietly: 'There is no cousin, Albert. I spent my Christmases alone at an hotel in Harrogate.'

'Oh, my dear.' Gently now, he drew her back into his arms, and their gaze held for a second before slowly he placed his lips on hers; then as he felt her body trembling, he held her tightly to him.

'Happy Christmas, Miss Parkington,' he murmured tenderly.

And she replied: 'Happy Christmas, Albert.'

The Chairmender
Guy de Maupassant

I t was towards the end of a dinner-party, given by the Marquis de
Bertran to celebrate the opening of the shooting season. Eleven
sportsmen, eight young women and the local doctor were seated
around the table, which was decorated with fruit and flowers.

The conversation turned on love, and a heated discussion arose on
the eternal question of whether one could really fall in love many
times or only once. Stories were told of some who had only seriously
fallen in love once, and others who had loved often and vehemently.
On the whole, the men maintained that this passion could, like a
disease, attack the same person again and again, and even prove fatal,
if hindered in its course. Although this view could not be disproved,
the ladies, who based their opinion on poetic fancies rather than
observation, held that love, true love, heroic love, could visit
a human being once only; that such love was like a thunderbolt, and
that a heart that had once experienced it was ever afterwards so utterly
devastated, ravaged and consumed, that no other strong passion, or
even passing fancy, could strike root there again. The Marquis, a man
of many love affairs, hotly contested this theory.

'I assure you that one can love time after time with all one's
strength, with all one's soul. You quote examples of people who have
killed themselves for love, as a proof of the impossibility of a second
love, but my answer to that is, that if they had not been so foolish
as to kill themselves, which deprived them of all possibility of another
attack, they would have recovered from the first seizure, and they
would have loved again, and again, to the end of their days. Lovers are
like drunkards. A man who has been drunk will drink again, and a
man who has loved will love again. It is entirely a question of
temperament.'

They referred the dispute to the doctor, who had retired to the country after practising in Paris. They begged him to give his opinion. He had, however, no firm convictions:

'As the Marquis says, it is a question of temperament. But I do know one case of a passion which endured for fifty-five years, without a day's intermission, and ended only with death.'

The Marchioness clapped her hands.

'How beautiful! What a perfect dream to be loved like that! What bliss to live, for fifty-five years, the object of such constant affection! How happy, how exquisitely content with life this man must have been. Who inspired such adoration!'

The doctor smiled:

'You are right on one point, Madam. As you have guessed, the object of this devotion was a man. You know him; it was Monseiur Chouquet, the local chemist. And you knew the woman, too, the old chairmender who used to come every year to the manor house. But I will tell you the story in detail.'

The ladies' enthusiasm suffered a serious blow. They had a look of disgust on their faces, as if they felt that love should confine itself to persons of class and distinction, for in them only could people of quality take a real interest.

'Three months ago,' continued the doctor, 'I was summoned to that old woman's death-bed. She had arrived here the day before in the van, which she lived in and which was drawn by the old nag you have all seen. Her two big black dogs, her friends and protectors, were with her. The priest was already by her side. She appointed us executors of her will and in order to explain her last wishes she told us the whole story of her life. I have never heard anything more unusual or more poignant.

'Her father and mother were chairmenders and she had never lived in a proper house. As a little thing she roamed about, ragged, dirty and uncared for. The family used to stop on the outskirts of villages by the roadside, take the horse out of the van and turn it loose to graze. The dog would curl up and go to sleep, his head on his paws, and the child would tumble about on the grass, while her parents, in the shade of the wayside elms, patched up all the old chairs in the parish. Few words were wasted in that abode on wheels. After a brief discussion as to who should make the round of the houses, shouting the familiar cry: "Chairs to mend", they set to work to plait the straw, sitting opposite each other, or side by side. If the child wandered too far or tried to make friends with some village urchin, her father's angry

[24]

voice recalled her:

' "Come here at once, you little pest!"

'These were the only words of affection she ever heard. As she grew bigger she was sent round to collect chairs that required mending. Eventually in her wanderings, she started to get to know the other youngsters. But then it was the parents of her new friends who roughly called their children away:

' "Come here at once, you young scamp. Don't let me catch you talking to vagabonds."

'Small boys would often throw stones at her. Ladies sometimes gave her pennies which she hoarded carefully.

'One day, when she was eleven years old, the family came to this neighbourhood. At the back of the cemetery she saw young Chouquet, in tears because a playmate had robbed him of a couple of farthings. The little outcast was greatly perturbed by the tears of this small townsman. Her childish mind had supposed that children of his class were always happy and content. She went up to him, and on learning the cause of his trouble, poured into his hands all her savings, seven sous, which he took as a matter of course, wiping away his tears. She was so ecstatically happy that she actually ventured to kiss him and as he was absorbed in the contemplation of the coins, he made no objection. Seeing that he did not shake her off or strike her, she threw her arms round him and kissed him passionately. Then she ran away.

'What was the idea in that poor little head? What was the bond that linked her to that other child? Was it because she had sacrificed to him her whole pitiful little fortune, or because she had given him her first kiss of love? The mystery is one and the same, for children as for grown-ups.

'For months she dreamed of that corner of the cemetery and of that small boy. In the hope of seeing him again, she gradually robbed her parents, pocketing a sou here and there out of sums given her in payment, or entrusted to her for buying food.

'Next time she came, she had two francs in her pocket. But she merely caught a glimpse of the youngster, looking very neat and tidy as she glanced through the windows of his father's drug shop, peering between a big red bottle and a tapeworm in spirits. Dazzled and entranced by the resplendent glory of the coloured water, by the glamour of the glittering phials, she loved him all the more. The memory of him never faded from her mind. Next year when she came upon him behind the school, playing marbles with his friends, she flung herself upon him, clasped him in her arms, and kissed him with such violence that he began to scream with terror. To soothe him, she gave him all the money she had, a veritable fortune, three francs and four sous, at which he stared with wide open eyes. He accepted the money and allowed her to kiss him as much as she pleased.

'For the next four years she poured into his hands all her savings, which he pocketed, conceding kisses as a fair exchange. Once it was thirty sous, once two francs, another time twelve sous—and over this she shed tears of pain and humiliation, but it had been a bad year—finally five francs, a large round coin, which made him laugh with joy.

'He occupied all her thoughts, and he himself awaited her return with a certain impatience, and would come running to her, as soon as he saw her, in a way that made her heart leap with happiness.

'Then he disappeared. He had been sent to school, as she ascertained by skilful questioning. With infinite adroitness, she tried to induce her parents to change the order of their rounds, so that their visits should coincide with the holidays. At last she was successful, but it had cost her a whole year's scheming. Thus two years had elapsed without her seeing him, and she hardly recognised him, he had changed so much. He had grown and had improved in looks, and he was very impressive in a jacket with gold buttons. He pretended not to see her and passed by with his head in the air. She cried for two days and this was the beginning of endless suffering.

'Every year she came back. She passed him in the street without daring to greet him, while he did not deign even to look at her. She loved him to distraction.

' "Doctor," she said to me, "he is the only man I have ever had eyes for in the whole world. I hardly know if the others even exist."

'After her parents' death she carried on their trade, but she now kept two dogs, instead of one, ferocious brutes whom no one would have dared to tackle. One day when she returned to the little town where she had left her heart she saw a young woman coming out of the chemist's shop, leaning on Chouquet's arm. It was his wife. He was married.

'That evening she threw herself into the pond near the Town Hall. A belated reveller fished her out and carried her to the chemist's. Young Chouquet came down in his dressing-gown to attend to her and, without giving any sign of recognition, took off her clothes, and rubbed her, and said severely:

' "You must have been mad. What a silly thing to do!"

'That was enough to restore her. He had spoken to her; it kept her happy for a long time. He declined to accept any remuneration for his services, though she vehemently pressed payment upon him.

'And thus her whole life slipped away. She sat at her chairmending thinking all the while of Chouquet. Every year she saw him through the windows of his shop. She took to buying from him a stock of simple remedies. In this way, she saw him close to, spoke to him, and gave him money as in the old days.

'As I told you before, she died this spring. After telling this pathetic story, she begged me to make over to the man whom she had so faithfully loved, her lifetime savings. She had worked only for him, she said, even going hungry to add to her hoard, so as to make sure that he would think of her at least once more when she was dead. She then gave me two thousand three hundred and twenty-seven francs. The odd twenty-seven francs I left with the priest for funeral expenses, the rest I took away with me as soon as she had breathed her last.

'Next day I went to see the Chouquets. They were seated opposite each other, finishing their luncheon, a fat, red-faced couple, redolent of the drugs they sold, looking important and pleased with life. They invited me to sit down and offered me a liqueur, which I accepted. Then in a voice quivering with emotion I began my story, expecting to move them to tears.

'But as soon as he understood that he had been beloved by that vagabond of a chairmender, Chouquet jumped out of his seat with rage. It was as if she had stolen from him his good name, the esteem of respectable folk, his personal honour, some subtle refinement, which he valued more than life itself. Equally disgusted, his wife could find nothing to say but:

' "That old beggar woman! That old beggar woman!"

'Chouquet was stamping round the table, his skull cap askew over one ear.

' "Did you ever hear the like, Doctor," he broke out. "What a horrible business this is! What on earth am I to do? If I had known this when she was alive I would have had her taken up and sent to jail. And there she should have stayed, I promise you."

'I was thunderstruck at the result of my well-intended effort, and at a loss as to what to say or do. But I had to fulfil my mission. I resumed:

' "She bade me make over to you her savings, amounting to two thousand three hundred francs. But as the story I have told you seems to displease you so much, perhaps this money had better be given to the poor."

'Speechless with surprise, the pair of them stared at me. I took the money from my pockets, a sordid collection of coins of all countries and mintages, gold and copper mixed together, and I asked:

' "What do you think?"

'Madame Chouquet was the first to find words.

' "Well, since it was the woman's last wish . . . I think we can hardly refuse."

'Her husband added, rather shamefacedly:

' "We can always spend it on something for the children."

' "Just as you please," I said drily.

' "Very well," he replied, "as she asked you to, you had better hand it over. We shall find an opportunity of spending it on some deserving object."

'I made over the money, bowed and took my departure.

'Next day Chouquet came to me and said abruptly:

' "I see . . . that woman has left her van here. What are you going to do with it?"

' "Nothing. Take it if you like."

' "Capital. It's just what I wanted for a shed for my kitchen garden."

'As he was going away, I called him back.

' "She has also left her old horse and her two dogs. Do you want them, too?"

'He stood still in surprise.

' "Good Lord, no. What earthly use would they be to me? Do what you like with them."

'He laughed and we shook hands. After all, in a country place, doctor and chemist must remain friends.

'I have kept the dogs. The priest, who has a large courtyard, has the horse. The van is used by Chouquet as a shed and with the money he has bought five shares in a Railway Company.

'That is the only instance of perfect love I have ever known.'

The doctor fell silent. The Marchioness, with tears in her eyes, sighed:

'That proves it. It is only women who know how to love.'

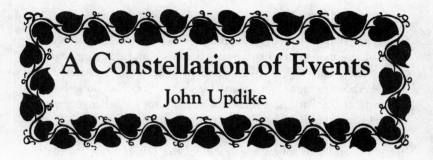

A Constellation of Events
John Updike

T he events felt spaced in a vast deep sky, its third dimension dizzying. Looking back, Betty could scarcely believe that the days had come so close together. But, no, there, flat on the calendar, they were, one after the other—four bright February days.

Sunday, after church, Rob had taken her and the children cross-country skiing. They made a party of it. He called up Evan, because they had discussed the possibility at the office Friday, while the storm was raging around their green-glass office building in Hartford, and she, because Evan, a bachelor, was Lydia Smith's lover, called up the Smiths and invited them, too; it was the sort of festive, mischievous gesture Rob found excessive. But Lydia answered the phone and was delighted. As her voice twittered in Betty's ear, Betty stuck out her tongue at Rob's frown.

They all met at the Patterson's field in their different-coloured cars and soon made a line of dark silhouettes across the white pasture. Evan and Lydia glided obliviously into the lead; Rob and Billy, the son now almost the size of the father, and Fritzie Smith, who in imitation of her mother was quite the girl athlete, occupied the middle distance, the little Smith boy struggling to keep up with this group; and Betty and her baby—poor, bitterly whining, miserably ill-equipped Jennifer—came last, along with Rafe Smith, who didn't ski as much as Lydia and whose bindings kept letting go. He was thinner than Rob, more of a clown, fuller of doubt, hatchet-faced and green-eyed: a sad, encouraging sort of man. He kept telling Jennifer, 'Ups-a-daisy, Jenny, keep in the others' tracks, now you've got the rhythm, oops,' as the child's skis scrambled and she toppled down again. Meanwhile, one of Rafe's feet would have come out of his binding and Betty would have to wait, the others dwindling in the distance into dots.

The fields were immense in their brilliance. Her eyes winced, taking them in. The tracks of their party, and the tracks of the Sno-Cats that had frolicked here in the wake of the storm, scarcely touched the marvellous blankness—slopes up and down, a lone oak on a knoll, rail fences like pencilled hatchings, weathered NO TRESPASSING signs not meant for them. Rob had done business with one of the Patterson sons and would bluff a challenge through; the fields seemed held beneath a transparent dome of Rob's protection. A creek, thawed into audible life, ran where two slopes met. Betty was afraid to follow the tracks of the others here; it involved stepping, in skis, from snowbank to snowbank across a width of icy, confident, secretive water. She panicked and took the wooden bridge fifty yards out of their way. Rafe lifted Jennifer up and stepped across, his binding snapping on the other side but no harm done. The child laughed for the first time that afternoon.·

The sun came off the snow hot; Betty thought her face would get its first touch of tan today, and then it would not be many weeks before cows grazed here again, bringing turds to the mayflowers. Pushing up the slope on the other side of the creek, toward the woods, she slipped backwards and fell sideways. The snow was moist, warm. 'Shit,' she said, and was pleasurably aware of the massy uplifted curve of her hip in jeans as she looked down over it at Rafe behind her, his green eyes sun-narrowed, alert.

'Want to get up?' he asked, and held out a hand, a damp black mitten. As she reached for it, he pulled off the mitten, offering her a bare hand, bony and pink and startling, so suddenly exposed to the air. 'Ups-a-daisy,' he said, and the effort of pulling her erect threw him off balance, and a binding popped loose again. Both she and Jenny laughed this time.

At the entrance of the path through the woods, Rob waited with evident patience. Before he could complain, she did: 'Jennifer is going crazy on these awful borrowed skis. Why can't she have decent equipment like other children?'

'I'll stay with her,' her husband said, both firm and evasive in his way, avoiding the question with an appearance of meeting it, and appearing selfless in order to shame her. But she felt the smile on her face persist as undeniably, as unerasably, as the sun on the field. Rob's face clouded, gathering itself to speak; Rafe interrupted, apologizing, blaming their slowness upon himself and his defective bindings. For a moment that somehow made her shiver inside—perhaps no more than the flush of exertion meeting the chill blue shade of the woods, here at the edge—the two men stood together, intent upon the mechanism, her presence forgotten. Rob found the misadjustment, and Rafe's skis came off no more.

In the woods, Rob and Jennifer fell behind, and Rafe slithered ahead, hurrying to catch up to his children and, beyond them, to his wife and Evan. Betty tried to stay with her husband and child, but they were too maddening—one whining, the other frowning, and neither grateful for her company. She let herself ski ahead, and became alone in the woods, aware of distant voices, the whisper of her skis, the soft companionable heave of her own breathing. Pine trunks shifted about, one behind another and then another, aligned and not aligned, shadowy harmonies. Here and there the trees grew down into the path; a twig touched her eye, so lightly she was surprised to find pain lingering, and herself crying. She came to an open place where paths diverged. Here Rafe was waiting for her; thin, leaning on his poles, he seemed a shadow among others. 'Which way do you think they went?' He sounded breathless and acted lost. His wife and her lover had escaped him.

'Left is the way to get back to the car,' she said.

'I can't tell which are their tracks,' he said.

'I'm sorry,' Betty said.

'Don't be.' He relaxed on his poles, and made no sign of moving. 'Where is Rob?' he asked.

'Coming. He took over dear Jennifer for me. I'll wait, you go on.'

'I'll wait with you. It's too scary in here. Do you want that book?' The sentences followed one another evenly, as if consequentially.

The book was about Jane Austen, by an English professor Betty had studied under years ago, before Radcliffe called itself Harvard. She had noticed it lying on the front seat of the Smiths' car while they were all fussing with their skis, and had exclaimed with recognition, of a sort. In a strange suspended summer of her life, the summer when Billy was born, she had read through all six of the Austen novels, sitting on a sun porch waiting and waiting and then suddenly nursing. 'If you're done with it.'

'I am. It's tame, but dear, as you would say. Could I bring it by tomorrow morning?'

He had recently left a law firm in Hartford and opened an office here in town. He had few clients but seemed amused being idle. There was something fragile and incapable about him. 'Yes,' she said, adding, 'Jennifer comes back from school at noon.'

[31]

And then Jennifer and Rob caught up with them both needing to be placated, and she forgot this shadowy man's promise, as if her mind had been possessed by the emptiness where the snowy paths diverged.

Monday was bright, and the peal at the door accented the musical dripping of the icicles ringing the house around with falling pearls. Rafe was hunched comically under the dripping from the front eaves, the book held dry against his parka. He offered just to hand it to her, but she invited him in for coffee, he seemed so sad, still lost. They sat with the coffee on the sofa, and soon his arms were around her and his lips, tasting of coffee, warm on her mouth and his hands cold on her skin beneath her sweater, and she could not move her mind from hovering, from floating in a golden consciousness of the sun on the floorboards, great slanting splashes of it, rhomboids broken by the feathery silhouettes of her houseplants on the windowsills. From her angle as he stretched her out on the sofa, the shadows of the drips leaped upward in the patches of sun, appearing to defy gravity as her head whirled. She sat up, pushed him off without rebuke, unpinned and repinned her hair. 'What are we doing?' she asked.

'I don't know,' Rafe said, and indeed he didn't seem to. His assault on her had felt clumsy, scared, insincere; he seemed grateful to be stopped. His face was pink, as his hand had been. In the light of the windows behind the sofa his eyes were very green. An asparagus fern hanging there cast a net of shadow that his features moved in and out of as he apologized, talked, joked. 'Baby fat!' he had exclaimed of her belly, having tugged her sweater up, bending suddenly to kiss the crease there, his face thin as a blade, and hot. He was frightened, Betty realized, which banished her own fear.

Gently she manoeuvred him away from her body, out of the door. It was not so hard; she remembered how to fend off boys from the college days his book had brought back to her. In his gratitude he wouldn't stop smiling. She shut the front door. His body as he crossed the melting street fairly danced with relief. And for her, again alone in the empty house, it was as if along with her fear much of her soul had been banished; feeling neither remorse nor expectation, she floated above the patches of sun being stitched by falling drops, among the curved shining of glass and porcelain and aluminium kitchen equipment, in the house's strange warmth—strange as any event seems when only we are there to witness it. Betty lifted her sweater to look at her pale belly. Baby fat. Middle age had softened her middle. But, then, Lydia was an athlete, tom-boyish and lean, swift on skis, with that something Roman and androgynous and enigmatic about her looks. It was what Rafe was used to; the contrast had startled him.

She picked up the book from the sofa. He was one of those men who could read a book gently, so it didn't look read. She surprised herself, in her great swimming calmness, by being unable to read a word.

Tuesday, as they had planned weeks ago, Rob took her to Philadelphia. She had been born there, and he had business there. Taking her along was his tribute, he had made it too plain, to her condition as a bored housewife. Yet she loved it, loved him, once the bumping, humming terror of the plane ride was past. The city in the winter sunlight looked classier and cleaner than she remembered it, her rough and enormous dear drab City of Brotherly Love. Rob was here because his insurance company was helping finance a shopping mall in southern New Jersey; he disappeared into the strangely Egyptian old façade of the Penn Mutual Building—now doubly false, for it had been reconstructed as a historical front on a new skyscraper, a tall box of tinted glass. She wandered window-shopping along Walnut Street until her feet hurt, then took a cab from Rittenhouse Square to the Museum of Art. There was less snow in Philadelphia than in Connecticut; some of the grass beside the Parkway even looked green.

At the head of the stairs inside the museum, Saint-Gaudens's great verdigrised Diana—in Betty's girlhood imagination the statue had been somehow confused with the good witch of fairy stories (only naked, having shed the ball gown and petticoats good witches usually wear, the better to swing her long legs)—still did pose on one tiptoe foot at her shadowy height. But elsewhere within the museum, there were many changes, much additional brightness. The three versions of *Nude Descending a Staircase* and the sadly cracked *Bride Stripped Bare by Her Bachelors, Even* no longer puzzled and offended her. The daring passes into the classic in our very lifetimes, while we age and die. Rob met her, just when he had promised, at three-thirty, amid the Impressionist paintings; her sudden love of him, here in this room of raw colour and light, felt like a melting. She leaned on him, he moved away from her touch, and in her unaccustomed city heels Betty sidestepped to keep her balance.

They had tea in the cafeteria, out of place in their two dark suits among the students and beards and the studied rags that remained of the last decade's revolution. Here, too, the radical had become the comfortable. 'How do you like being back?' Rob asked her.

'It's changed; I've changed. I like it where I am now. You were dear to bring me, though.' She touched his hand, and he did not pull it away on the smooth tabletop, whose white reminded her of snow.

Happiness must have been on her face, glowing like a sunburn, for he looked at her and seemed for an instant to see her. The instant troubled him. Though too heavy to be handsome, he had beautiful eyes, tawny and indifferent like a lion's; they slitted and he frowned in the unaccustomed exercise of framing a compliment. 'It's such a pity,' he said, 'you're my wife.'

She laughed, astonished. 'Is it? Why?'

'You'd make such a lovely mistress.'

'You think? How do you know? Have you ever tried a mistress?' She was so confident of the answer she went on before he could say no. 'Then how do you know I'd make a lovely one? Maybe I'd make an awful one. Shrieking, possessive. Better just accept me as a wife,' she advised complacently. The table was white and cluttered with dirty tea things between them; she could hardly wait until they were home in bed. His lovemaking was like him, firm and tireless, and it always worked. She admired that. Once, she had adored it, until her adoration had seemed to depress him. And something in her now, at this glittering table, depressed him—perhaps the mistress he had glimpsed in her, the mistress that he of all the men in the world was barred from, could never have. She stroked his hand as if in acknowledgement of a shared sorrow. But happiness kept mounting in her, giddy and meaningless, inexplicable, unstoppable, though she saw that on its wings she was leaving Rob behind. And he had never seemed solider or kinder, or she more fittingly, as they rose and paid and left the museum together, his wife.

On the flight back, to calm her terror, she pulled the book from her handbag and read, *As Lionel Trilling was to say in 1957 (before women had risen in their might), 'The extraordinary thing about Emma is that she has a moral life as a man has a moral life'; 'A consciousness is always at work in her, a sense of what she ought to be and do.'*

Rob looked over her shoulder and asked, 'Isn't that Rafe's book?'

'One just like it,' she answered promptly, deceit proving not such a difficult trick after all. 'You must have seen it on the front seat of his car Sunday. So did I, and I found a copy at Wanamaker's this morning.'

'It looks read.'

'I was reading it. Waiting for you.'

His silence she took to be a satisfied one. He rattled his newspaper, then asked, 'Isn't it awfully dry?'

She feigned preoccupation. A precarious rumble changed pitch under her. 'Mmm. Dry but dear.'

'He's a sad guy, isn't he?' Rob abruptly said. 'Rafe.'

'What's sad about him?'

'You know. Being cuckolded.'

'Maybe Lydia loves him all the better for it,' Betty said.

'Impossible,' her husband decreed, and hid himself in the *Inquirer* as the 727, rumbling and shuddering, prepared to crash. She clutched at Rob's arm with that irrational fervour he disliked; deliberately he kept his eyes on the newspaper, shutting her out. Yet in grudging answer to her prayers he brought the plane down safely, with a corner of his mind.

In her dream she was teaching again, and among her students Rafe seemed lost. She had a question for him, and couldn't seem to get his attention, though he was not exactly misbehaving; his back was half turned as he talked to some arrogant skinny girl in the class. . . . It was so exasperating she awoke, feeling empty and slightly scared. Rob was out of the bed. She heard the door slam as he went to work. The children were downstairs quarrelling, a merciless sound as of something boiling over. Wednesday. When she stood, residue of last night's lovemaking slid down the inside of her thigh.

The children gone to school, she moved through the emptiness of the house exploring the realization that she was in love. Like the floorboards, the doorframes, the wallpaper, the fact seemed not so much pleasant as necessary, not ornamental but functional in some way she must concentrate on perceiving. The snow on the roof had all melted; the dripping from the eaves had ceased, and a dry sunlight rested silently on the warm house, the bare street, the speckled rooftops of the town beyond the sunstruck, dirty windows. Valentines the children had brought home from school littered the kitchen counter. The calendar showed the shortest month, a candy box brimming with red holidays. Rafe's office number was newly listed in the telephone book. She dialled it, less to reach him than to test the extent of her emptiness. Alarmingly, the ringing stopped; he answered. 'Rafe?' Her voice surprised him by coming out cracked.

[35]

'Hi, Betty,' he said. 'How was Philly?'

'How did you know I went?'

'Everybody knows. You have no secrets from us.' He stopped joking, sensing that he was frightening her. 'Lydia told me.' Evan had told her; Rob had told him at work. There was a see-through world of love; her bright house felt transparent. 'Was it nice?' Rafe was asking.

'Lovely.' She felt she was defending herself. 'It seemed . . . tamer, somehow.'

'What did you do?'

'Walked around feeling nostalgic. Went to the museum up on its hill. Rob met me there and we had tea.'

'It does sound dear.' His voice, by itself, was richer and more relaxed than his physical presence, his helpless, humiliated clown's air. Her silence obliged him to say more. 'Have you had time to look into the book?'

'I love it,' she said. 'It's so scholarly and calm. I'm reading it very slowly; I want it to last forever.'

'Forever seems long.'

'You want to see me?' Her voice, involuntarily, had thickened.

His answer was as simple and sharp as his green glance when she had exclaimed, 'Shit.' 'Sure,' he said.

'Where? This house feels so conspicuous.'

'Come on down here. People go in and out of the building all day long. There's a hairdresser next to me.'

'Don't you have any clients?'

'Not till this afternoon.'

'Do I dare?'

'I don't know. Do you?' More gently, he added, 'You don't have to *do* anything. You just want to *see* me, right? Unfinished business, more or less.'

'Yes.'

Downtown, an eerie silence pressed through the movement of cars and people. Betty realized she was missing a winter sound from childhood: the song of car chains. Snow tyres had suppressed it. Time suppressed everything, if you waited. Rafe's building was a grim business 'block' built a century ago, when this suburb of Hartford had appeared to have an independent future. An ambitious blazon of granite topped the façade, which might someday be considered historical. The stairs were linoleum and smelled like a rainy-day cloakroom. A whiff of singeing and shampoo came from the door next to his. He was waiting for her in his waiting room, and locked the door. On his sofa, a chill, narrow, and sticky couch of Naugahyde, beneath a wall of leatherbound laws, Rafe proved impotent. The sight of her naked seemed to stun him. Through his daze of embarrassment, he never stopped smiling. And she at him. He was beautiful, so lean and loosely knit, but needed to be nursed into knowing it. 'What do you think the matter is?' he asked her.

'You're frightened,' she told him. 'I don't blame you. I'm a lot to take on.'

He nodded, his eyes less green here in this locked, windowless anteroom. 'We're going to be a lot of trouble, aren't we?'

'Yes.'

'I guess my body is telling us there's still time to back out. Want to?'

On top of the one set of bound statutes, their uniform spines forming horizontal streaks like train windows streaming by, lay a different sort of book, a little paperback. In the dim room, where their nakedness was the brightest thing, she made out the title: *Emma.* She answered, 'No.'

And, though there was much in the aftermath to regret, and a harm that would never cease, Betty remembered these days—the open fields, the dripping eaves, the paintings, the law books—as bright, as a single iridescent unit, not scattered as is a constellation but continuous, a rainbow, a U-turn.

The Kepi
Colette

I f I remember rightly, I have sometimes mentioned Paul Masson, otherwise known as Lemice-Térieux on account of his delight — and his dangerous efficiency — in creating mysteries. As ex-president of the Law Courts of Pondichery, he was attached to the cataloguing section of the Bibliothèque Nationale. It was through him and through the library that I came to know the woman. This is the story of her one and only romantic adventure.

Although Paul Masson was a middle-aged man, and I a very young woman, we established a fairly solid friendship that lasted some eight years. Without being cheerful himself, Paul Masson devoted himself to cheering me up. I think, seeing how very lonely and housebound I was, he was sorry for me, though he concealed the fact. I think, too, that he was proud of being so easily able to make me laugh. The two of us often dined together in the little third-floor flat in the rue Jacob, myself in a dressing gown hopefully intended to suggest Botticelli draperies, he invariably in dusty and correct black. His little pointed beard, slightly reddish, his faded skin and drooping eyelids, his absence of any special distinguishing marks attracted attention like a deliberate disguise. Familiar as he was with me, he avoided using the intimate 'tu', and every time he emerged from his guarded impersonality, he gave every sign of having been extremely well brought up. Never, when we were alone, did he sit down to write at the desk of the man whom I refer to as 'Monsieur Willy' and I cannot remember, over a period of several years, his ever asking me one indiscreet question.

Moreover, I was fascinated by his caustic wit. I admired the way he attacked people on the least provocation, but always in extremely restrained language and without a trace of anger. And he brought up to my third floor flat, not only all the latest Paris gossip, but a series of ingenious lies that I enjoyed as fantastic stories. If he ran into Marcel Schwob, my luck was really in! The two men pretended to hate each other and played a game of insulting each other politely under their breath. The s's hissed between Schwob's clenched teeth; Masson gave little coughs and exuded venom like a malicious old lady. Then they would declare a truce and talk at immense length, and I was stimulated and excited by the battle of wits between those two subtle, insincere minds.

The time off that the Bibliothèque Nationale allowed Paul Masson assured me of an almost daily visit from him but the phosphorescent conversation of Marcel Schwob was a rarer treat. Alone with the cat and Masson, I did not have to talk and this prematurely aged man could relax in silence. He frequently made notes—goodness knows what about—in the pages of a notebook bound in black imitation leather. The fumes from the slow-burning stove lulled us into a torpor; we listened drowsily to the reverberating bang of the street door. Then I would rouse myself to eat sweets or nuts and order my guest to make me laugh. Although he would not admit it to himself he was probably the most devoted of all my friends. I was twenty-two, with a face like an anaemic cat's, and more than a yard and a half of hair that, when I was at home, I let down in a wavy mass that reached to my feet.

'Paul, tell me some lies.'

'Which particular ones?'

'Oh, any old lies. How's your family?'

'Madame, you forget that I'm a bachelor.'

'But you told me . . .'

'Ah yes, I remember. My illegitimate daughter is well. I took her out to lunch on Sunday. In a suburban garden. The rain had plastered big yellow lime leaves on the iron table. She enjoyed herself enormously pulling them off and we ate tepid fried potatoes, with our feet on the soaked gravel . . .'

'No, no, not that, it's sad. I like the lady of the library better.'

'What lady? We don't employ any.'

'The one who you thought was working on a novel about India.'

'She's still labouring over her novelette. Today I've been princely and generous. I've made her a present of baobabs and latonia palms painted from life and thrown in magical incantations, mahrattas, screaming monkeys, Sikhs, saris, and lakhs of rupees.'

Rubbing his dry hands against each other, he added: 'She gets a sou a line.'

'A sou!' I exclaimed. 'Why a sou?'

'Because she works for a chap who gets two sous a line who works for a chap who gets four sous a line, who works for a chap who gets ten sous a line.'

'So what you're telling me isn't a lie, then?'

'All my stories can't be lies,' sighed Masson.

'What's her name?'

'Her Christian name is Marco, as you might have guessed. Women of a certain age, when they belong to the artistic world, have only a few names to choose from, such as Marco, Léo, Ludo, Aldo. It's a legacy from the excellent Madame Sand.'

'Of a certain age? So she's old, then?'

Paul Masson glanced at my face with an indefinable expression. Lost in my long hair, that face became childish again.

'Yes,' he said.

Then he ceremoniously corrected himself: 'Forgive me, I made a mistake. No was what I meant to say. No, she's not old.'

I said triumphantly: 'There, you see! You see it *is* a lie, because you haven't even chosen an age for her!'

'If you insist,' said Masson.

'Or else you're using the name Marco to disguise a lady who's your mistress.'

'I don't need Madame Marco. I have a mistress who is also, thank heaven, my housekeeper.'

He consulted his watch and stood up.

'Do make my excuses to your husband. I must get back or I shall miss the last bus. Concerning the extremely real Madame Marco, I'll introduce you to her whenever you feel inclined.'

He recited, very fast: 'She is the wife of V., the painter, a school friend of mine who's made her abominably unhappy; she has fled from the conjugal establishment where her perfections had rendered her an impossible inmate; she is still beautiful, witty, and penniless; she lives in a boarding house in the rue Demours, where she pays eighty-five francs a month for bed and breakfast; she does writing jobs, anonymous feuilletons, newspaper snippets, addressing envelopes, gives English lessons at three francs an hour, and has never had a lover. You see that this particular lie is as disagreeable as the truth.'

I handed him the little lamp and accompanied him to the top of the stairs. As he walked down them, the tiny flame shone upward on his pointed beard, and tinged its slightly turned-up end red.

When I had had enough of getting him to tell me about Marco, I asked Paul Masson to take me to be introduced to her, instead of bringing her to the rue Jacob. He had told me in confidence that she was about twice my age and I felt it was proper for a young woman to make the journey to meet a lady who was not so young. Naturally, Paul Masson accompanied me to the rue Demours.

The boarding house where Madame Marco V. lived has been pulled down. About 1897, all that this villa retained of its former garden was a euonymus hedge, a gravel path, and a flight of five steps leading up to the door. The moment I entered the hall I felt depressed. Certain kitchen smells, as opposed to cooking smells, are appalling revelations of poverty. On the first floor, Paul Masson knocked on a door and the voice of Madame Marco invited us in. A perfect voice, neither too high nor too low, but gay and well-pitched. What a surprise! Madame Marco looked young, Madame Marco was pretty and wore a silk dress, Madame Marco had pretty eyes, almost black, and wide-open like a deer's. She had a little cleft at the tip of her nose, hair touched with henna and worn in a tight, sponge-like mass on the forehead like Queen Alexandra's and curled short on the nape in the so-called eccentric fashion of certain women painters or musicians.

She called me 'little Madame', indicated that Masson had talked so much about me and my long hair, apologized, without overdoing it, for having no port and no sweets to offer me. With an unaffected gesture, she indicated the kind of place she lived in, and following the sweep of her hand, I took in the piece of plush that hid the one-legged table, the shiny upholstery of the only armchair, and the two little threadbare pancake-cushions of Algerian design on the two other chairs. There was also a little rug on the floor. The mantelpiece served as a bookshelf.

'I've shut the clock up in the cupboard,' said Marco. 'But I swear it deserved it. Luckily, there's another cupboard I can use for my washing things. Don't you smoke?'

I shook my head, and Marco stepped into the full light to put a match to her cigarette. Then I saw that the silk dress was splitting at every fold. What little linen showed at the neck was very white. Marco and Masson smoked and chatted together; Madame Marco had grasped at once that I preferred listening to talking. I forced myself not to look at the wallpaper, with its old-gold and garnet stripes, or at the bed and its cotton damask bedspread.

'Do look at the little painting, over there,' Madame Marco said to me. 'It was done by my husband. It's so pretty that I've kept it. It's that little corner of Hyères, *you* remember, Masson.'

And I looked enviously at Marco, Masson, and the little picture, who had all three been in Hyères. Like most young things, I knew how to withdraw into myself, far away from people talking in the same room, then return to them with a sudden mental effort, then leave them again. Throughout my visit to Marco, thanks to her delicate tact which let me off questions and answers, I was able to come and go without stirring from my chair; I could observe or I could shut my eyes at will. I saw her just as she was and what I saw both delighted and distressed me. Though her features were fine, she had what is called a coarse skin, slightly leathery and masculine, with red patches on the neck and under her ears. But, at the same time, the lively intelligence of her smile was ravishing, as was the shape of her doe's eyes and the unusually proud, yet completely unaffected carriage of her head. She looked less like a pretty woman than like one of those chiseled, clear-cut aristocratic men who adorned the eighteenth century and were not ashamed of being handsome. Masson told me later she was extraordinarily like her grandfather, the Chevalier de St.-Georges, a brilliant forebear who has no place in my story.

We became great friends, Marco and I. And after she had finished her Indian novel—it was rather like *La Femme qui tue*, as specified by the man who got paid ten sous a line—Monsieur Willy soothed Marco's sensitive feelings by asking her to do some research on condition she accepted a small fee. He even consented, when I urgently asked him to, to put in an appearance when she and I had a meal together. I had only to watch her to learn the most impeccable table manners. Monsieur Willy was always professing a love of good breeding and he found something to satisfy it in Marco's charming manners and in her turn of mind, which was urbane but inflexible and slightly caustic. Had she been born twenty years later she would, I think, have made a good journalist. When the summer came, it was Monsieur Willy who proposed taking this extremely pleasant companion, so dignified in her poverty, along with us to a mountain village in Franche-Comté. The luggage she brought with her was heartrendingly light. But at that time, I myself had very little money at my disposal, and we settled ourselves very happily on one upper floor of a noisy inn. The wooden balcony and a wicker armchair were all that Marco needed; she never went for walks. She never wearied of the restfulness, of the vivid purple that evening shed on the mountains, of the great bowls of raspberries. She had travelled and she compared the valleys hollowed out by the twilight with other landscapes. Up there I noticed that the only mail Marco received consisted of picture postcards from Masson and 'Best wishes for a good holiday', also on a postcard, from a fellow ghostwriter at the Bibliothèque Nationale.

As we sat under the balcony awning on those hot afternoons, Marco mended her underclothes. She sewed badly, but conscientiously, and I flattered my vanity by giving her pieces of advice, such as: 'You're using too coarse a thread for fine needles. You shouldn't put blue baby ribbon in chemises, pink is much prettier in lingerie and up against the skin.' It was not long before I gave her others, concerning her face powder, the colour of her lipstick, a hard line she pencilled around the edge of her beautifully shaped eyelids. 'D'you think so? D'you think so?' she would say. My youthful authority was adamant. I took the comb, I made a charming little gap in her tight, sponge-like fringe, I proved expert at softly shadowing her eyes and putting a faint pink glow high up on her cheekbones, near her temples. But I did not know what to do with the unattractive skin of her neck or with a long shadow that hollowed her cheek. That flattering glow I put on her face transformed it so much that I promptly wiped it off again. Using amber powder and being far better fed than in Paris had quite an animating effect. She told me about a journey made a long time ago when, like a good painter's wife, she had followed her husband from Greek village to Moroccan hamlet, washed his brushes, and fried aubergines and pimentos in his oil. She promptly left off sewing to have a cigarette, blowing the smoke out through nostrils as soft as some herbivorous animal's. But she only told me the names of places, not of friends, and spoke of discomforts, not of griefs, so I dared not ask her to tell more. The mornings she spent in writing the first chapters of a new novel, at one sou a line, which was being seriously held up by lack of documentation about the early Christians.

'When I've put in lions in the arena and a golden-haired virgin abandoned to the licentious soldiers and a band of Christians escaping in a storm,' said Marco, 'I shall come to the end of my personal erudition. So I shall wait for the rest till I get back to Paris.'

As I have said: we became great friends. That is, if friendship is confined to a rare smoothness of communication preserved by carefully veiled precautions that blunt all sharp points and angles. All I could do was imitate Marco and her 'well-bred' surface manner. She aroused not the slightest distrust in me. I felt her to be as straight as a die, disgusted by anything that could cause pain, utterly remote from all feminine rivalries. But if love laughs at difference in age, friendship, especially between two women, is more acutely conscious of it. This is particularly true when friendship is just beginning, and wants, like love, to have everything all at once. The country filled me with a terrible longing for running streams, wet fields, active idleness.

'Marco, don't you think it would be marvellous if we got up early tomorrow and spent the morning under the fir trees? There are wild cyclamens and purple mushrooms.'

Marco shuddered, and clasped her little hands together.

'Oh, no! Oh, no! Go off on your own and leave me out of it, you young mountain goat.'

I have forgotten to mention that, after the first week, Monsieur Willy had returned to Paris 'on business'. He wrote me notes, spicing his prose, which derived from Mallarmé and Félix Fénéon, with onomatopoeic words in Greek letters, German quotations, and English terms of endearment.

So I climbed up alone to the firs and the cyclamens. There was something intoxicating to me in the contrast between burning sun and the still-nocturnal cold of the plants growing out of a carpet of moss. More than once, I thought I would not go back for the midday meal. But I did go back, because of Marco, who was savouring the joy of rest as if she had twenty years' accumulated weariness to work off. She used to rest with her eyes shut, her face pale beneath her powder, looking utterly exhausted, as if convalescing from an illness. At the end of the afternoon, she would take a little walk along the road that, in passing through the village, still felt like a delicious, twisting forest path that crunched under one's feet.

You must not imagine that the other 'tourists' were much more active than we were. People of my age will remember that a summer in the country, around 1897, bore no resemblance to the gadabout holidays of today. The most energetic walked as far as a pure, icy, slate-coloured stream, taking with them camp stools, needlework, a novel, a picnic lunch, and useless fishing rods. On moonlit nights, girls and young men would go off in groups after dinner, which was served at seven, wander along the road, then return, stopping to wish each other good night. 'Are you thinking of bicycling as far as Saut-de-Giers tomorrow?' 'Oh, we're not making any definite plans. It all depends on the weather.' The men wore low-cut waistcoats like cummerbunds, with two rows of buttons and sham buttonholes, under a black or cream alpaca jacket, and check caps or straw hats. The girls and the young women were plump and well nourished, dressed in white linen or ecru tussore. When they turned up their sleeves, they displayed white arms, and under their big hats, their scarlet sunburn did not reach as high as their foreheads. Venturesome families went in for what was called 'bathing' and set off in the afternoons to immerse themselves at a spot where the stream broadened out, barely two and a half miles from the village. At night, around the communal dining table, the children's wet hair smelled of ponds and wild peppermint.

One day, so that I could read my mail, which was rich with two letters, an article cut out of *Art et Critique*, and some other odds and ends, Marco tactfully assumed her convalescent pose, shutting her eyes and leaning her head against the padded cushion of the wicker chair. She was wearing the ecru linen dressing gown that she put on to save the rest of her wardrobe when we were alone in our bedrooms or out on the wooden balcony. It was when she had on that dressing gown that she truly showed her age and the period to which she naturally belonged. Certain definite details, pathetically designed to flatter, typed her indelibly, such as a certain deliberate wave in her hair that emphasized the narrowness of her temples, a certain short fringe that would never allow itself to be combed the other way, the carriage of the chin imposed by a high, boned collar, knees that were never parted and never crossed. Even the shabby dressing gown itself gave her away. Instead of resigning itself to the simplicity of a working garment, it was decorated with ruffles of imitation lace at the neck and wrists and a little frill around the hips.

Those tokens of a particular period of feminine fashion and behaviour were just the very ones my own generation was in process of rejecting. The new 'angel' hairstyle and Cléo de Mérode's smooth swathes were designed to go with a boater worn like a halo, shirt blouses in the English style, and straight skirts. Bicycles and bloomers had swept victoriously through every class. I was beginning to be crazy about starched linen collars and rough woollens imported from England. The split between the two fashions, the recent one and the very latest, was too blatantly obvious not to humiliate penniless women who delayed in adopting the one and abandoning the other. Occasionally frustrated in my own burst of clothes-consciousness, I suffered for Marco, heroic in two worn-out dresses and two light blouses.

Slowly, I folded up my letters again, without my attention straying from the woman who was pretending to be asleep, the pretty woman of 1870 or 1875, who, out of modesty and lack of money, was giving up the attempt to follow us into 1898. In the uncompromising way of young women, I said to myself: 'If I were Marco, I'd do my hair like this, I'd dress like that.' Then I would make excuses for her: 'But she hasn't any money. If I had more money, I'd help her.'

Marco heard me folding up my letters, opened her eyes, and smiled. 'Good news?'

'Yes . . . Marco,' I said daringly, 'don't you have your letters sent on here?'

'Of course I do. All the correspondence I have is what you see me get.'

As I said nothing, she added, all in one burst: 'As you know, I'm separated from my husband. V.'s friends, thank heaven, have remained *his* friends and not mine. I had a child, twenty years ago, and I lost him when he was hardly more than a baby. And I've never had a lover. So you see, it's quite simple.'

'Never had a lover . . .' I repeated.

Marco laughed at my expression of dismay.

'Is that the thing that worries you the most? Don't be so upset! That's the thing I've thought about least. In fact I've long ago given up thinking about it at all.'

My gaze wandered from her lovely eyes, rested by the pure air and the green of the chestnut groves, to the little cleft at the tip of her charming nose, to her teeth, a trifle discoloured, but admirably sound and well set.

'But you're very pretty, Marco!'

'Oh!' she said gaily. 'I was even a charmer, once upon a time. Otherwise V. wouldn't have married me. But I'll tell you something, I'm convinced that fate has spared me one great trouble anyway, a temperament. No, no, all that business of blood rushing into the cheeks, upturned eyeballs, palpitating nostrils, I admit I've never experienced it and never regretted not having it. You do believe me, don't you?'

'Yes,' I said mechanically, looking at Marco's florid nostrils.

She laid her narrow hand on mine, with an impulsiveness that did not, I knew, come easily for her.

'A great deal of poverty, my child, and before the poverty the job of being an artist's wife in the most down-to-earth way . . . hard

[46]

manual labour, like being a maid-servant. I wonder where I should have found the time to be idle and well groomed and elegant in secret—in other words, to be someone's romantic mistress.'

She sighed, ran her hand over my hair, and brushed it back from my forehead.

'Why don't you show the top part of your face a little? When I was young, I did my hair like that.'

As I had a horror of having my alley cat's temples exposed, I dodged away from the little hand and interrupted Marco, crying: 'No, you don't! No, you don't! *I'm* going to do *your* hair. I've got a marvellous idea!'

Brief confidences, the amusements of two women shut away from the world, hours that were sometimes like those in a sewing room, sometimes like the idle ones of convalescence—I do not remember that our pleasant holiday produced any genuine intimacy. I was inclined to feel deferential toward Marco, yet, paradoxically, to set hardly any store by her opinions on life and love. When she told me she might have been a mother, I realized that our friendly relationship would never be in the least like my passionate feeling for my real mother, nor would it ever approach the comradeship I should have had with a young woman. But at that time, I did not know any girl or woman of my own age with whom I could share a reckless gaiety, a mute complicity, a vitality that over-flowed in fits of wild laughter, or with whom I could enjoy physical rivalries and rather crude pleasures that Marco's age, her delicate constitution, and her whole personality put out of her range and mine.

We talked, and we also read. I had been an insatiable reader in my childhood. Marco had educated herself. At first, I thought I could delve into Marco's well-stored mind and memory. But I noticed that she replied with a certain lassitude, and as if mistrustful of her own words.

'Marco, why are you called Marco?'

'Because my name is Léonie,' she answered. 'Léonie wasn't the right sort of name for V.'s wife. When I was twenty, V. made me pose in a tasseled Greek cap perched over one ear and Turkish slippers with long turned-up points. While he was painting, he used to sing this old sentimental ballad:

Fair Marco, do you love to dance
In brilliant ballrooms, gay with flowers?

Do you love, in night's dark hours,
Ta ra ra, ta ra ra ra . . .

I have forgotten the rest.'

I had never heard Marco sing before. Her voice was true and thin, clear as the voice of some old men.

'They were still singing that in my youth,' she said. 'Painters' studios did a great deal for the propagation of bad music.'

She seemed to want to preserve nothing of her past but a superficial irony. I was too young to realize what this calmness of hers implied. I had not yet learned to recognize the modesty of renunciation.

Toward the end of our summer holiday in Franche-Comté, something astonishing did, however, happen to Marco. Her husband, who was painting in the United States, sent her, through his solicitor, a cheque for fifteen thousand francs. The only comment she made was to say, with a laugh: 'So he's actually got a solicitor now? Wonders will never cease!'

Then she returned the cheque and the solicitor's letter to their envelope and paid no more attention to them. But at dinner, she gave signs of being a trifle excited, and asked the waitress in a whisper if it was possible to have champagne. We had some. It was sweet and tepid and slightly corked and we only drank half the bottle between us.

Before we shut the communicating door between our rooms, as we did every night, Marco asked me a few questions. She wore an absent-minded expression as she inquired: 'Do you think people will be still wearing those wide-sleeved velvet coats next winter, you know the kind I mean? And where did you get that charming hat you had in the spring—with the brim sloping like a roof? I liked it immensely—on *you*, of course.'

She spoke lightly, hardly seeming to listen to my replies, and I pretended not to realise how deeply she had hidden her famished craving for decent clothes and fresh underlinen.

The next morning, she had regained control of herself.

'When all's said and done,' she said, 'I don't see why I should accept this sum from that . . . in other words, from my husband. If it pleases him at the moment to offer me charity, like giving alms to a beggar, that's no reason for me to accept it.'

As she spoke, she kept pulling out some threads the laundress had torn in the cheap lace that edged her dressing gown. Where it fell open, it revealed a chemise that was more than humble. I lost my temper and I scolded Marco as an older woman might have chided a small girl. So much so that I felt a little ashamed, but she only laughed.

'There, there, don't get cross! Since you want me to, I'll allow myself to be kept by his lordship V. It's certainly my turn.'

I put my cheek against Marco's cheek. We stayed watching the harsh, reddish sun reaching the zenith and drinking up all the shadows that divided the mountains. The bend of the river quivered in the distance. Marco sighed.

'Would it be very expensive, a pretty little corset belt all made of ribbon, with rococo roses on the ends of the suspenders?'

The return to Paris drove Marco back to her novelette. Once again I saw her hat with the three blue thistles, her coat and skirt whose black was faded and pallid, her dark grey gloves, and her schoolgirl satchel of cardboard masquerading as leather. Before thinking of her personal elegance, she wanted to move to another place. She took a year's lease on a furnished flat; two rooms and a place where she could wash, plus a sort of cupboard-kitchen, on the ground floor. It was dark there in broad daylight but the red and white cretonne curtains and bedspread were not too hopelessly shabby. Marco lunched in a little restaurant near the library and had tea and bread-and-butter at home at night except when I managed to keep her at my flat for a meal at which stuffed olives and rollmops replaced soup and roast meat. Sometimes Paul Masson brought along an excellent chocolate 'Quillet' from Quillet's, the cake shop in the rue de Buci.

Completely resigned to her task, Marco had so far acquired nothing except, as October turned out rainy, a kind of rubberized hooded cloak that smelled of asphalt. One day she arrived, her eyes looking anxious and guilty.

'There,' she said bravely, 'I've come to be scolded. I think I bought this coat in too much of a hurry. I've got the feeling that . . . that it's not quite right.'

I was amused by her being as shy as if she were my junior, but I stopped laughing when I had a good look at the coat. An unerring instinct led Marco, so discriminating in other ways, to choose bad material, deplorable cut, fussy braid.

The very next day, I took time off to go out with her and choose a wardrobe for her. Neither she nor I could aspire to the great dress houses, but I had the pleasure of seeing Marco looking slim and years younger in a dark tailor-made and in a navy serge dress with a white front. With the straight little caracul topcoat, two hats, and some underclothes, the bill, if you please, came to fifteen hundred francs: you can see that I was ruthless with the funds sent by the painter V.

I might well have had something to say against Marco's hairstyle. But just that very season, there was a changeover to shorter hair and a different way of doing it, so that Marco was able to look as if she was ahead of fashion. In this I sincerely envied her, for whether I twisted it around my head 'à la Ceres' or let it hang to my skirt hem — 'like a well cord' as Jules Renard said — my long hair blighted my existence.

At this point, the memory of a certain evening obtrudes itself. Monsieur Willy had gone out on business somewhere, leaving Marco, Paul Masson, and myself alone together after dinner. When the three of us were on our own, we automatically became clandestinely merry, slightly childish, and, as it were, reassured. Masson would sometimes read aloud the serial in a daily paper, a novelette inexhaustibly rich in haughty titled ladies, fancy-dress balls in winter gardens, chaises dashing along 'at a triple gallop' drawn by pure-bred steeds, maidens pale but resolute, exposed to a thousand perils. And we used to laugh ourselves silly.

'Ah!' Marco would sigh, 'I shall never be able to do as well as that. In the novelette world, I shall never be more than an amateur.'

'Little amateur,' said Masson one night, 'here's just what you want. I've culled it from the Agony Column: "Man of letters bearing well-known name would be willing to assist young writers of both sexes in early stages career." '

'Both sexes!' said Marco. 'Go on, Masson! I've only got one sex and, even then, I think I'm exaggerating by half.'

'Very well, I will go on,' said Masson. 'I will go on to lieutenant (regular army), garrisoned near Paris, warmhearted, cultured, wishes to maintain correspondence with intelligent, affectionate woman. Very good, but apparently, this soldier does not wish to maintain anything but correspondence. Nevertheless, do we write to him? Let us write. The best letter wins a box of Gianduja Kohler — the nutty kind.'

'If it's a big box,' I said, 'I'm quite willing to compete. What about you, Marco?'

With her cleft nose bent over a scribbling block, Marco was writing already. Masson gave birth to twenty lines in which sly obscenity vied with humour. I stopped after the first page, out of laziness. But how charming Marco's letter was!

'First prize!' I exclaimed.

'Pearls before . . .' muttered Masson. 'Do we send it? Poste Restante, Alex 2, Box 59. Give it to me. I'll see that it goes.'

'After all, he can't come and find me,' said Marco.

When our diversions were over, she slipped on her mackintosh again and put on her narrow hat in front of the mirror. It was a hat I had chosen, which made her head look very small and her eyes very large under its turned-down brim.

'Look at her!' she exclaimed. 'Look at her, the middle-aged lady who corrupts warmhearted and cultured lieutenants!'

With the little oil lamp in her hand, she preceded Paul Masson.

'I shan't see you at all this week,' she told me. 'I've got two pieces of homework to do: the chariot race and the Christians in the lions' pit.'

'Haven't I already read something of the kind somewhere?' put in Masson.

'I sincerely hope you have,' retorted Marco. 'If it hadn't been done over and over again, where should I get my documentation?'

The following week, Masson bought a copy of the paper and with his hard, corrugated nail pointed out three lines in the Agony Column: 'Alex 2 implores author delicious letter beginning "What presumption" to give address. Secrecy scrupulously honoured.'

'Marco,' he said, 'you've won not only the box of Gianduja but also a booby prize in the shape of a first-class mug.'

Marco shrugged her shoulders.

'It's cruel, what you've made me do. He's sure to think he's been made fun of, poor boy.'

Masson screwed up his eyes to their smallest and most inquisitorial.

'Sorry for him already, dear?'

These memories are distant, but clear. They rise out of the fog that inevitably drowns the long days of that particular time, the monotonous amusements of dress rehearsals and suppers at Pousset's, my alternations between animal gaiety and confused unhappiness, the split in my nature between a wild, frightened creature and one with a vast capacity for illusion. But it is a fog that leaves the faces of my friends intact and shining clear.

It was also on a rainy night, in late October or nearly November, that Marco came to keep me company one night; I remember the anthracite smell of the waterproof cape. She kissed me. Her soft nose was wet, she sighed with pleasure at the sight of the glowing stove. She opened her satchel.

'Here, read this,' she said. 'Don't you think he's got a charming turn of phrase, this . . . this ruffianly soldier?'

If, after reading it, I had allowed myself a criticism, I should have said: too charming. A letter worked over and recopied; one draft, two drafts thrown into the wastepaper basket. The letter of a shy man, with a touch of the poet, like everyone else.

'Marco, you mean you actually wrote to him?'

The virtuous Marco laughed in my face.

'One can't hide anything from you, charming daughter of Monsieur de La Palisse! Written? Written more than once, even! Crime gives me an appetite. You haven't got a cake? Or an apple?'

While she nibbled delicately, I showed off my ideas on the subject of graphology.

'Look, Marco, how carefully your "ruffianly soldier" has covered up a word he's begun so as to make it illegible. Sign of gumption, also of touchiness. The writer, as Crépieux-Jamin says, doesn't like people to laugh at him.'

Marco agreed, absentmindedly. I noticed she was looking pretty and animated. She studied herself in the glass, clenching her teeth and parting her lips, a grimace few women can resist making in front of a mirror when they have white teeth.

'Whatever's the name of that toothpaste that reddens the gums, Colette?'

'Cherry something or other.'

'Thanks, I've got it now. Cherry Dentifrice. Will you do me a favour? Don't tell Paul Masson about my epistolary escapades. He'd never stop teasing me. I shan't keep up my relations with the regular army long enough to make myself ridiculous. Oh, I forgot to tell you. My husband has sent me another fifteen thousand francs.'

'Mercy me, be I a-hearing right? as they say where I come from. And you just simply *forgot* that bit of news?'

'Yes, really,' said Marco. 'I just forgot.'

She raised her eyebrows with an air of surprise to remind me delicately that money is always a subject of minor importance.

From that moment, it seemed to me that everything moved very fast for Marco. Perhaps that is due to distance in time. One of my moves—

the first—took me from rue Jacob to the top of the rue de Courcelles, from a dark little cubbyhole to a studio whose great window let in cold, heat, and lots of light. I wanted to show my sophistication, to satisfy my new—and modest—cravings for luxury: I bought white goatskins, and a folding shower bath from Chaboche's.

Marco, who felt at home in dim rooms and in the atmosphere of the Left Bank and of libraries, blinked her lovely eyes under the studio skylight, stared at the white divans that suggested polar bears, and did not like the new way I did my hair. I wore it piled up above my forehead and twisted into a high chignon; this new 'helmet' fashion had swept the hair up from the most modest and retiring napes.

Such a minor domestic upheaval would not have been worth mentioning, except that it explains why for some time, I only had rapid glimpses of Marco. My pictures of her succeeded each other jerkily like the pictures in those children's books that, as you turn the pages fast, give the illusion of continuous movement. When she brought me the second letter from the romantic lieutenant, I had crossed the intervening gulf. As Marco walked into my new, light flat, I saw that she was definitely prettier than she had been the year before. The slender foot she thrust out below the hem of her skirt rejoiced in the kind of shoe it deserved. Through the veil stretched taut over the little cleft at the tip of her nose she stared, now at her gloved hand, now at each unknown room, but she seemed to see neither the one nor the other clearly. With bright patience she endured my arranging and rearranging the curtains: she admired the folding shower bath, which, when erected, vaguely suggested a vertical coffin.

She was so patient and so absentminded that in the end I noticed it and asked her crudely: 'By the way, Marco, how's the ruffianly soldier?'

Her eyes, softened by makeup and shortsightedness, looked into mine.

'As it happens, he's very well. His letters are charming—decidedly so.'

'Decidedly so? How many have you had?'

'Three in all. I'm beginning to think it's enough. Don't you agree?'

'No, since they're charming—and they amuse you.'

'I don't care for the atmosphere of the *poste restante* . . . It's a horrid hole. Everyone there has a guilty look. Here, if you're interested . . .'

She threw a letter into my lap; it had been there ready all the time, folded up in her gloved hand. I read it rather slowly, I was so preoccupied with its serious tone, devoid of the faintest trace of humour.

'What a remarkable lieutenant you've come across, Marco! I'm sure that if he weren't restrained by his shyness . . .'

'His shyness?' protested Marco. 'He's already got to the point of hoping that we shall exchange less impersonal letters! What cheek! For a shy man . . .'

She broke off to raise her veil which was overheating her coarse-grained skin and flushing up those uneven red patches on her cheeks. But nowadays she knew how to apply her powder cleverly, how to brighten the colour of her mouth. Instead of a discouraged woman of forty-five, I saw before me a smart woman of forty, her chin held high above the boned collar that hid the secrets of the neck. Once again, because of her very beautiful eyes, I forgot the deterioration of all the rest of her face and sighed inwardly: 'What a pity . . .'

Our respective moves took us away from our old surroundings and I did not see Marco quite so often. But she was very much in my mind. The polarity of affection between two women friends that gives one authority and the other pleasure in being advised turned me into a peremptory young guide. I decided that Marco ought to wear shorter skirts and more nipped-in waistlines. I sternly rejected braid, which made her look old, colours that dated her, and, most of all, certain hats that, when Marco put them on, mysteriously sentenced her beyond hope of appeal. She allowed herself to be persuaded, though she would hesitate for a moment: 'You think so? You're quite sure?' and glance at me out of the corner of her beautiful eye.

We liked meeting each other in a little tearoom at the corner of the rue de l'Échelle and the rue d'Argenteuil, a warm, poky 'British', saturated with the bitter smell of Ceylon tea. We 'partook of tea', like other sweet-toothed ladies of those far-off days, and hot buttered toast followed by quantities of cakes. I liked my tea very black, with a thick white layer of cream and plenty of sugar. I believed I was learning English when I asked the waitress: 'Edith, please, a little more milk, and butter.'

It was at the little 'British' that I perceived such a change in Marco that I could not have been more startled if, since our last meeting, she had dyed her hair peroxide or taken to drugs. I feared some danger, I imagined that the wretch of a husband had frightened her into his clutches again. But if she was frightened, she would not have had that blank flickering gaze that wandered from table to the walls and was profoundly indifferent to everything it glanced at.

'Marco? Marco?'

'Darling?'

'Marco, what on earth's happened? Have other treasure galleons arrived? Or what?'

She smiled at me as if I were a stranger.

'Galleons? Oh no.'

She emptied her cup in one gulp and said almost in a whisper: 'Oh, how stupid of me, I've burned myself.'

Consciousness and affection slowly returned to her gaze. She saw that mine was astonished and she blushed, clumsily and unevenly, as she always did.

'Forgive me,' she said, laying her little hand on mine.

She sighed and relaxed.

'Oh!' she said. 'What luck there isn't anyone here. I'm a little . . . how can I put it? . . .queasy.'

'More tea? Drink it very hot.'

'No, no. I think it's that glass of port I had before I came here. No, nothing, thanks.'

She leaned back in her chair and closed her eyes. She was wearing her newest suit, a little oval brooch of the 'family heirloom' type was pinned at the base of the high boned collar of her cream blouse. The next moment she had revived and was completely herself, consulting the mirror in her new handbag and feverishly anticipating my questions.

'Ah, I'm better now! It was that port, I'm sure it was. Yes, my dear, port! And in the company of Lieutenant Alexis Trallard, son of General Trallard.'

'Ah!' I exclaimed with relief. 'Is *that* all? You quite frightened me. So you've actually seen the ruffianly soldier? What's he like? Is he like his letters? Does he stammer? Has he got a lisp? Is he bald? Has he a port-wine mark on his nose?'

These and similar idiotic suggestions were intended to make Marco laugh. But she listened to me with a dreamy, refined expression as she nibbled at a piece of buttered toast that had gone cold.

'My dear,' she said at last. 'If you'll let me get a word in edgeways, I might inform you that Lieutenant Trallard is neither an invalid nor a monster. Incidentally, I've known this ever since last week, because he enclosed a photograph in one of his letters.'

She took my hand.

'Don't be cross. I didn't dare mention it to you. I was afraid.'

'Afraid of what?'

'Of you, darling, of being teased a little. And . . . well . . . just simply afraid!'

'But why *afraid*?'

She made an apologetic gesture of ignorance, clutching her arms against her breast.

'Here's the Object,' she said, opening her handbag. 'Of course, it's a very bad snapshot.'

'He's much better looking than the photo . . . of course?'

'Better looking . . . good heavens, he's totally *different*. Especially his expression.'

As I bent over the photograph, she bent over it too, as if to protect it from too harsh a judgment.

'Lieutenant Trallard hasn't got that shadow like a sabre cut on his cheek. Besides, his nose isn't so long. He's got light brown hair and his moustache is almost golden.'

After a silence, Marco added shyly: 'He's tall.'

I realized it was my turn to say something.

'But he's very good-looking! But he looks exactly as a lieutenant should! But what an enchanting story, Marco! And his eyes? What are his eyes like?'

'Light brown like his hair,' said Marco eagerly.

She pulled herself together.

'I mean, that was my general impression. I didn't look very closely.'

I hid my astonishment at being confronted with a Marco whose words, whose embarrassment, whose naïveté surpassed the reactions of the greenest girl to being stood a glass of port by a lieutenant. I could never have believed that this middle-aged married woman, inured to living among bohemians, was at heart a timorous novice. I restrained myself from letting Marco see, but I think she guessed my thoughts, for she tried to turn her encounter, her 'queasiness', and her lieutenant into a joke. I helped her as best I could.

'And when are you going to see Lieutenant Trallard again, Marco?'

'Not for a good while, I think.'

'Why?'

'Why, because he must be left to wear his nerves to shreds in suspense! Left to simmer!' declared Marco, raising a learned fore-finger. 'Simmer! That's my principle!'

We laughed at last; laughed a great deal and rather idiotically. That hour seems to me, in retrospect, like the last halt, the last landing on which my friend Marco stopped to regain her breath. During the days that followed I have a vision of myself writing (I did not sign my work either) on the thin, crackly American paper I liked best of all, and Marco was busy working too, at one sou a line. One afternoon, she came to see me again.

'Good news from the ruffianly soldier, Marco?'

She archly indicated 'Yes' with her chin and her eyes, because Monsieur Willy was on the other side of the glass-topped door. She submitted a sample of dress material which she would not dream of buying without my approval. She was buoyant and I thought that, like a sensible woman, she had reduced Lieutenant Alexis Trallard to his proper status. But when we were all alone in my bedroom, that refuge hung with rush matting that smelled of damp reeds, she held out a letter, without saying a word, and without saying a word, I read it and gave it back to her. For the accents of love inspire only silence and the letter I had read was full of love. Full of serious, vernal love. Why did one question, the very one I should have repressed, escape me? I asked — thinking of the freshness of the words I had just read, of the respect that permeated them — I asked indiscreetly: 'How old is he?'

Marco put her hands over her face, gave a sudden sob, and whispered: 'Oh, heavens! It's appalling!'

Almost at once, she mastered herself, uncovered her face, and scolded herself in a harsh voice: 'Stop this nonsense. I'm dining with him tonight.'

She was about to wipe her wet eyes but I stopped her.

'Let me do it, Marco.'

With my two thumbs, I raised her upper eyelids so that the two tears about to fall should be reabsorbed and not smudge the mascara on her lashes by wetting them.

'There! Wait, I haven't finished.'

I retouched all her features. Her mouth was trembling a little. She submitted patiently, sighing as if I were dressing a wound. To complete everything, I filled the puff in her handbag with a rosier shade of powder. Neither of us uttered a word.

'Whatever happens,' I told her, 'don't cry. At all costs, don't let yourself get tearful.'

She protested at this, and laughed.

'All the same, we haven't got to the scene of the final parting yet!'

I took her over to the best-lighted looking glass. At the sight of her reflection, the corners of Marco's mouth quivered a little.

'Satisfied with the effect, Marco?'

'Too good to be true.'

'Can't ever be too good. You'll tell me what happened? When?'

'As soon as I know myself,' said Marco.

Two days later, she returned, in spite of stormy, almost warm weather that rattled the cowls on the chimney pots and beat back the smoke and fumes of the slow-combustion stove.

'Outdoors in this tempest, Marco?'

'It doesn't worry me a bit, I've got a four-wheeler waiting down there.'

'Wouldn't you rather dine here with me?'

'I can't,' she said, averting her head.

'Right. But you can send the growler away. It's only half past six, you've plenty of time.'

'No, I haven't time. How does my face look?'

'Quite all right. In fact, very nice.'

'Yes, but . . . Quick, be an angel! Do what you did for me the day before yesterday. And then, what's the best thing to receive Alex at home in? Outdoor clothes, don't you think? Anyway, I haven't got an indoor frock that would really do.'

'Marco, you know just as well as I do . . .'

'No,' she broke in, 'I don't know. You might as well tell me I know India because I've written a novelette that takes place in the Punjab. Look, he's sent a kind of emergency supply around to my place—a cold chicken in aspic, champagne, some fruit. He says that, like me, he has a horror of restaurants. Ah, now I think of it, I *ought* to have . . .'

She pressed her hand to her forehead, under her fringe.

'I *ought* to have bought that black dress last Saturday—the one I saw in the secondhand shop. Just my size, with a Liberty silk skirt and a lace top. Tell me, could you possibly lend me some very fine stockings? I've left it too late now to . . .'

'Yes, yes, of course.'

'Thank you. Don't you think a flower to brighten up my dress? No, *not* a flower on the bodice. Is it true that iris is a scent that's gone out of fashion? I'm sure I had heaps of other things to ask you . . . heaps of things.'

Though she was in the shelter of my room, sitting by the roaring stove, Marco gave me the impression of a woman battling with the wind and the rain that lashed the glass panes. I seemed to be watching Marco set off on some kind of journey, embarking like an emigrant. It was as if I could see a flapping cape blowing around her, a plaid scarf streaming in the wind.

Besieged, soon to be invaded. There was no doubt in my mind that an attack was being launched against the most defenceless of creatures. Silent, as if we were committing a crime, we hurried through our beauty operations. Marco attempted to laugh.

'We're trampling the most rigorously established customs underfoot. Normally, it's the oldest witch who washes and decks the youngest for the Sabbath.'

'Ssh, Marco, keep still—I've just about finished.'

I rolled up the pair of silk stockings in a piece of paper, along with a little bottle of yellow chartreuse.

'Have you got any cigarettes at home?'

'Yes. What on earth am I saying? No. But *he'll* have some on him, he smokes Egyptian ones.'

'I'll put four funny little napkins in the parcel, it'll make it more like a doll's tea party. Would you like the cloth too?'

'No, thanks. I've got an embroidered one I bought ages ago in Brussels.'

We were talking in low, rapid whispers, without ever smiling. In the doorway, Marco turned around to give me a long, distracted look out of moist, made-up eyes, a look in which I could read nothing resembling joy. My thoughts followed her in the cab that was carrying her through the dark and the rain, over the puddle-drenched road where the wind blew little squalls around the lampposts. I wanted to open the window to watch her drive away, but the whole tempestuous night burst into the studio and I shut it again on this traveller who was setting off on a dangerous journey, with no ballast but a pair of silk stockings, some pink makeup, some fruit, and a bottle of champagne.

Lieutenant Trallard was still only relatively real to me, although I had seen his photograph. A very French face, a rather long nose, a well-defined forehead, hair *en brosse* and the indispensable moustache. But the picture of Marco blotted out his—Marco all anxious apprehension, her beauty enhanced by my tricks, and breathing fast, as a deer pants when it hears the hooves and clamour of the distant hunt. I listened to the wind and rain and I reckoned up her chances of crossing the sea and reaching port into safety. 'She was very pretty tonight. Provided her lamp with the pleated shade gives a becoming light. This young man preoccupies her, flatters her, peoples her solitude, in a word, rejuvenates her.'

A gust of bad weather beat furiously against the window pane. A little black snake that oozed from the bottom of the window began to creep slowly along. I realized that the window did not shut properly and the water was beginning to soak the carpet. I went off to look for floor cloths and the aid of Maria, the girl from Aveyron who was my servant at that time. On my way, I opened the door to Masson, who had just rung three times.

While he was divesting himself of a limp mackintosh cape that fell dripping on the tiled floor, like a basketful of eels, I exclaimed: 'Did you run into Marco? She's just this minute gone downstairs. She was so sorry not to see you.'

A lie must give off a smell that is apparent to people with sensitive noses. Paul Masson sniffed the air in my direction, curtly wagged his short beard, and went off to join Monsieur Willy in his white study that, with its pretty curtains, beaded mouldings, and small window-panes, rather resembled a converted cake shop.

After that, everything moved very quickly for Marco. She came back, after that stormy night, but she didn't confide in me probably because somebody else was there. That particular day, my impatience to know was restrained by the fear that her confidence might yield something that would have slightly horrified me; there was an indefinable air of furtiveness and guilt about her whole person. At least, that is what I *think* I remember. My memories, after that, are much more definite. How could I have forgotten that Marco underwent a magical transformation, the kind of belated, embarrassing puberty that fools nobody. She reacted violently to the slightest stimulus. A thimbleful of Frontignac set her cheeks and her eyes ablaze. She laughed for no reason, stared blankly into space, was incessantly digging out her powder puff and her mirror. Everything was in overdrive. I could not long put off the 'Well, Marco?' she must be waiting for.

One clear, biting winter night, Marco was with me. I was stoking up the stove. She kept her gaze fixed on its mica window and did not speak.

'Are you warm enough in your little flat, Marco? Does the coal grate give enough heat?'

She smiled vaguely, as if at a deaf person, and did not answer. So I said at last: 'Well, Marco? Contented? Happy?'

It was the last, the most important word, I think, that she pushed away with her hand.

'I did not believe,' she said, very low, 'that such a thing could exist.'

'What? Happiness?'

She flushed here and there, in dark, fiery patches. I asked her—it was my turn to be naïve: 'Then why don't you look more pleased?'

'Can one rejoice over something terrible, something that's so . . . so like an evil spell?'

I secretly permitted myself the thought that to use such a grim and weighty expression was, as the saying goes, to clap a very large hat on a very small head, and I waited for her next words. But none came. At this point, there was a brief period of silence. I saw nothing wrong in Marco's keeping quiet about her love affair: it was rather the love affair itself that I resented. I thought—unjust as I was and unmindful of her past—that she had been very quick to reward a casual acquaintance, even if he were an officer, a general's son, and had golden brown hair into the bargain.

The period of reserve was followed by the season of unrestricted joy. Happiness, once accepted, is seldom reticent; Marco's, as it took firm root, was not very vocal but expressed itself in the usual boring way. I knew that, like every other woman, she had met a man 'absolutely unlike anyone else' and that everything he did was a source of abundant delight to his dazzled mistress. I was not allowed to remain ignorant about Alexis's 'lofty soul' or 'cast-iron body'. Marco did not, thank heaven, belong to that tribe who boastfully whisper precise details—the sort of female I call a Madame-how-many-times. Nevertheless, by looking confused or by spasms of perturbed reticence, she had a mute way of conveying things I would rather not have known.

This virtuous victim of belated love and suddenly awakened sensuality did not submit all at once to blissful immolation. But she could not escape the usual snares of her new condition, the most unavoidable of which is eloquence, both of speech and gesture.

The first few weeks made her thin and dry-lipped, with feverish, glittering eyes. 'A Rops!' Paul Masson said behind her back. 'Madame Dracula,' said Monsieur Willy, going one better. 'What the devil can our worthy Marco be up to, to make her look like that?'

Masson screwed up his little eyes and shrugged one shoulder. 'Nothing,' he said coldly. 'These phenomena belong to neurotic

[61]

simulation, like imaginary pregnancy. Probably, like many women, our worthy Marco imagines she is the bride of Satan. It's the phase of infernal joys.'

I thought it detestable that either of her two friends should call Madame V. 'our worthy Marco.' Nor was I any more favourably impressed by the icily critical comments of these two disillusioned men, especially on anything concerning friendship, esteem, or love.

Then Marco's face became irradiated with a great serenity. As she regained her calm, she gradually lost the fevered flitter of a lost soul and put on a little flesh. Her skin seemed smoother, she had lost the breathlessness that betrayed her nervousness and her haste. Her slightly increased weight slowed down her walk and movements; she smoked cigarettes lazily.

'New phase,' announced Masson. 'Now she looks like the Marco of the old days, when she'd just got married to V. It's the phase of the odalisque.'

I now come to a period when, because I was travelling and working more, I saw Marco only at intervals. I dared not drop in on her without warning, for I dreaded I might encounter Lieutenant Trallard, only too literally in undress, in the minute flat that had nothing in the way of an entrance hall. What with teas put off and appointments broken, fate kept us apart, till at last it brought us together again in my studio, on a lovely June day that blew warm and cool breezes through the open window.

Marco smelled delicious. She was wearing a brand-new black dress with white stripes, and was all smiles. Her romantic love affair had already been going on for eight months. She looked so much fatter to me that the proud carriage of her head no longer preserved her chin line and her waist, visibly compressed, no longer moved flexibly inside the petersham belt, as it had done last year.

'Congratulations, Marco! You look marvellously well!'

Her long deer's eyes looked uneasy.

'You think I've got plump? Not too plump, I hope?'

She lowered her lids and smiled mysteriously. 'A little extra flesh does make one's breasts so pretty.'

I was not used to that kind of remark from her and I was the one who felt embarrassed, frankly, as embarrassed as if Marco—that very Marco who used to barricade herself in her room at the country inn, crying: 'Don't come in, I'll slip on my dressing gown!'—had deliberately stripped naked in the middle of my studio drawing room.

The next second, I told myself I was being ungenerous and unfriendly, that I ought to rejoice wholeheartedly in Marco's happiness. To prove my goodwill, I said gaily: 'I bet, one of these days, when I open the door to you, I'll find Lieutenant Trallard in your wake! I'm too magnanimous to refuse him a cup of tea and a slice of bread and cheese, Marco. So why not bring him along next time?'

Marco gave me a sharp look that was like a total stranger's. Quickly as she averted it, I could not miss the virulent, suspicious glance that swept over me, over my smile and my long hair, over everything that youth lavishes on a face and body of twenty-five.

'No,' she said.

She recovered herself and looked back at me with her usual doe-like gentleness.

'It's too soon,' she said gracefully. 'Let's wait till the "ruffianly soldier" deserves such an honour!'

But I was appalled at having caught, in one look, a glimpse of a primitive female animal, black with suspicion, hostility, and possessive passion. For the first time, we were both aware of the difference in our ages as something sharp, cruel, and irremediable. It was the difference in age, revealed in the depths of a beautiful velvety eye, that falsified our relationship and disrupted our old bond. When I saw Marco again after the 'day of the look' and I inquired after Lieutenant Trallard, the new-style Marco, plump, white, calm—almost matriarchal—answered me in a tone of false modesty, the tone of a greedy and sated proprietress. I stared at her, stupefied, looking for all the things of which voracious, unhoped-for love had robbed her. I looked in vain for her elegant thinness, for the firmness of her slender waist, for her rather bony, well-defined chin, for the deep hollows in which the velvety, almost black eyes used to shelter . . . Realizing that I was registering the change in her, she renounced the dignity of a well-fed sultana and became uneasy.

'What can I do about it? I'm putting on weight.'

'It's only temporary,' I said. 'Do you eat a lot?'

She shrugged her thickened shoulders.

'I don't know. Yes. I *am* more greedy, that's a fact, than . . . Than before. But I've often seen you eat enormously and *you* don't put on weight!'

To exonerate myself, I made a gesture to signify that I couldn't help this. Marco stood up, planted herself in front of the mirror, clutched her waist tightly with both hands, and kneaded it.

'Last year, when I did that, I could feel myself positively melting away between my two hands.'

'Last year you weren't happy, Marco.'

'Oh, so that's it!' she said bitterly.

She was studying her reflection at close quarters as if she were alone. The addition of some few pounds had turned her into another woman, or rather another type of woman. The flesh was awkwardly distributed on her lightly built frame. 'She's got a behind like a cobbler's,' I thought. In my part of the country, they say that the cobbler's behind gets fat from sitting so much but develops a square shape. 'And, in addition, breasts like jellyfish, very broad and decidedly flabby.' For even if she is fond of her, a woman always judges another woman harshly.

Marco turned around abruptly.

'What was that?' she asked.

'I didn't say anything, Marco.'

'Sorry. I thought you did.'

'If you really want to fight against a tendency to put on flesh . . .'

'*Tendency*,' Marco echoed, between her teeth. 'Tendency is putting it mildly.'

'. . . why don't you try Swedish gymnastics? People are talking a lot about them.'

She interrupted me with a gesture of intolerant refusal.

'Or else cut out breakfast? In the morning don't have anything but unsweetened lemon juice in a glass of water.'

'But I'm hungry in the morning!' cried Marco. 'Everything's different, do realize that! I'm hungry, I wake up thinking of fresh butter—and thick cream—and coffee, and ham. I think that, after breakfast, there'll be luncheon to follow and I think of . . . of what will come after luncheon, the thing that kindles this hunger again—and all these cravings I have now that are so terribly fierce.'

Dropping her hands that had been harshly pummelling her waist and bosom, she challenged me in the same querulous tone: 'But really, could *I* ever have foreseen . . .'

Her voice changed. 'He actually says that I make him so happy.'

I could not resist putting my arms around her neck.

'Marco, don't worry about so many things! What you've just said explains everything, justifies everything. Be happy, Marco, make him happy and let everything else go!'

We kissed each other. She went away reassured, swaying on those

unfamiliar broadened hips. Soon afterward, Monsieur Willy and I
went off to Bayreuth and I did not fail to send Marco a great many
picture postcards, covered with Wagnerian emblems entwined with
leitmotifs. As soon as I returned, I asked Marco to meet me at our
tearoom. She had not grown any thinner nor did she look any
younger. Where others develop curves and rotundity, Marco's fleshi-
ness tended to be square.

'And you haven't been away from Paris at all, Marco? Nothing's
changed?'

'Nothing, thank God.'

She touched the wood of the little table with the tip of her finger to
avert ill luck. I needed nothing but that gesture to tell me that Marco
still belonged, body and soul, to Lieutenant Trallard. Another, no less
eloquent sign was that Marco only asked me questions of pure
politeness about my stay in Bayreuth—moreover, I guessed she did not
even listen to my answers.

She blushed when I asked her, in my turn: 'What about work,
Marco? Any novelettes on the stocks for next season?'

'Oh, nothing much,' she said in a bored voice. 'A publisher wants a
novel for children of eight to fourteen. As if that was up my street!
Anyway . . .'

A gentle, cowlike expression passed over her face like a cloud and
she closed her eyes.

'Anyway, I feel so lazy . . . oh, so lazy!'

When Masson, informed of our return, announced himself with his
usual three rings, he hastened to tell me he knew 'all' from Marco's
own lips. To my surprise, he spoke favourably of Lieutenant Trallard.
He did not take the line that he was a tenth-rate gigolo or a drunkard
destined to premature baldness or a garrison-town Casanova. On the
other hand, I thought he was decidedly harsh about Marco and even
more cold than harsh.

'But, come now, Paul, what are you blaming Marco for in this
affair?'

'Nothing,' said Paul Masson.

'And they're madly happy together, you know!'

'Madly strikes me as no exaggeration.'

He gave a quiet little laugh that was echoed by Monsieur Willy.
Despicable sniggers that made fun of Marco and myself, and were
accompanied by blunt opinions and pessimistic predictions, formu-
lated with complete assurance and indifference, as if the romance that

lit up Marco's Indian summer were no more than some stale bit of gossip.

'Physically,' Paul Masson said, 'Marco *had* reached the phase known as the brewer's dray horse. When a gazelle turns into a brood mare, it's a bad lookout for her. Lieutenant Trallard was perfectly right. It was Marco who compromised Lieutenant Trallard.'

'Compromised? You're crazy, Masson! Honestly, the things you say.'

'My dear girl, a child of three would tell you, as I do, that Marco's first, most urgent duty was to remain slender, charming, elusive, a twilight creature beaded with raindrops, not to be bursting with health and frightening people in the streets by shouting: "I've done it! I've done it! I've . . ." '

'Masson!'

My blood was boiling; I flogged Masson with my rope of hair. I understood nothing of that curious kind of severity only men display toward an innocence peculiar to women. I listened to the judgments of these two on the 'Marco case', judgments that admitted not one extenuating circumstance, as if they were lecturing on higher mathematics.

'She *wasn't* up to it,' decreed one of them. 'She fondly supposed that being the forty-six-year-old mistress of a young man of twenty-five was a delightful adventure.'

'Whereas it's a profession,' said the other.

'Or rather, a highly skilled sport.'

'No. Sport is an unpaid job. But she wouldn't even understand that her one and only hope is to break it off.'

I had not yet become inured to the mixture of affected cynicism and literary paradox by which, around 1900, intelligent, bitter, frustrated men maintained their self-esteem.

September lay over Paris, a September of fine, dry days and crimson sunsets. I sulked over being in town and over my husband's decision to cut short my summer holiday. One day, I received an express letter that I stared at in surprise, for I did not know Marco's writing well. The handwriting was regular but the spaces between the letters betrayed emotional agitation. She wanted to talk to me. I was in, waiting for her, at the hour when the red light from the setting sun tinged the yellow-curtained windowpane with a vinous flush. I was pleased to see there was no outward trace of disturbance about her. As if there were no other possible subject of conversation, Marco announced at once: 'Alex is going off on a mission.'

'On a mission? Where to?'

'Morocco.'

'When?'

'Almost at once. Perhaps in a week's time. Orders from the War Office.'

'And there's no way out of it?'

'His father, General Trallard . . . yes, if his father intervened personally, he might be able . . . But he thinks this mission—incidentally, it's quite a dangerous one—is a great honour. So . . .'

She made a little, abortive gesture and fell silent, staring into vacancy. Her heavy body, her full, pale cheeks and stricken eyes made her look like a tragedy queen.

'Does a mission take a long time, Marco?'

'I don't know—I haven't the faintest idea. He talks of three or four months, possibly five.'

'Now, now, Marco,' I said gaily. 'What's three or four months? You'll wait for him, that's all.'

She did not seem to hear me. She seemed to be attentively studying a purple-ink cleaner's mark on the inside of her glove.

'Marco,' I risked, 'couldn't you go over there with him and live near him?'

The moment I spoke, I regretted it. Marco, with trunks full of dresses, Marco as the European favourite, or else Marco as the native wife going in for silver bangles, couscous, and fringed scarves. The pictures my imagination conjured up made me afraid—afraid for Marco.

'Of course,' I hastily added, 'that wouldn't be practical.'

Night was falling and I got up to give us some light, but Marco restrained me.

'Wait,' she said. 'There's something else. I'd rather not talk to you about it here. Will you come to my place tomorrow? I've got some good China tea and some little cakes from the boulevard Malesherbes.'

'Of course I'd love to, Marco! But . . .'

'I'm not expecting anyone tomorrow. Do come, you might be able to do me a great service. Don't put on the light, the light in the hall is all I need.'

Marco's little 'furnished suite' had changed too. An arrangement of curtains on a wooden frame behind the entrance door provided it with a substitute for a hall. The brass bedstead had become a divan-bed and various new pieces of furniture struck me quite favourably, as did some Oriental rugs. A garlanded Venetian glass over the mantelpiece reflected some red and white dahlias. In the scent that pervaded it, I recognized Marco's married, if I can use the expression, to another, full-bodied fragrance.

The second, smaller room served as a bathroom; I caught sight of a zinc bathtub and a kind of shower arrangement fixed to the ceiling. I made, as I came in, some obvious remark such as: 'How nice you've made it, Marco!'

The stormy, precociously cold September day did not penetrate into this confined dwelling, whose thick walls and closed windows kept the air perfectly still. Marco was already busy getting tea, setting out our two cups and our two plates. 'She's not expecting anyone,' I thought. She offered me a saucer full of greengages while she warmed the teapot.

'What beautiful little hands you have, Marco!'

She suddenly knocked over a cup, as if the least unexpected sound upset the conscious control of her movements. We went through that pretence of a meal that covers and puts off the embarrassment of explanations, rifts, and silences; nevertheless, we reached the moment when Marco had to say what she wanted to say. It was indeed high time; I could see she was almost at the end of her tether. We instinctively find it odd, even comic, when a plump person shows signs of nervous exhaustion and I was surprised that Marco could be at once so buxom and in such a state of collapse. She pulled herself together; I saw her face, once again, look like a noble warrior's. The cigarette she avidly lit after tea completed her recovery. The glint of henna on her short hair suited her.

'Well,' she began in a clear voice, 'I think it's over.'

No doubt she had not planned to open with those words, for she stopped, as if aghast.

'Over? Why, what's over?'

'You know perfectly well what I mean,' she said. 'If you're at all fond of me, as I think you are, you'll try and help me, but . . . All the same, I'm going to tell you.'

Those were almost her last coherent words. In putting down the story that I heard, I am obliged to cut out all that made it, in Marco's version, so confused and so terribly clear.

She told it as many women do, going far back, and irrelevantly, into the past of what had been her single, dazzling love affair. She kept on repeating herself and correcting dates: 'So it must have been Thursday, December 26. What *am* I saying? It was a Friday, because we'd been to Prunier's to have a fish dinner. He's a practising Catholic and abstains on Fridays.'

Then the detailed minuteness of the story went to pieces. Marco lost the thread and kept breaking off to say, 'Oh well, no point in going over that' or 'Goodness, I can't remember where I'd got to!' and interlarding every other sentence with 'You know.' Grief drove her to violent gesticulation: she kept smiting her knees with the palm of her hand and flinging her head back against the chair cushions.

All the time she was running on with the prolixity and banality that give all lovers' laments a family likeness, accompanying certain indecent innuendoes with a pantomime of lowering her long eyelids. I felt completely unmoved. I was conscious only of a longing to get away and even had to keep clenching my jaws to repress nervous yawns. I found Marco all too tiresomely like every other woman in love; she was also taking an unconscionably long time to tell me how all this raving about a handsome young soldier came to end in disaster—a disaster, of course, totally unlike anyone else's; they always are.

'Well, one day . . .' said Marco, at long last.

She put her elbows on the arms of her chair. I imitated her and we both leaned forward. Marco broke off her confused jeremiad and I saw a gleam of awareness come into her soft, sad eyes, a look capable of seeing the truth. The tone of her voice changed too, and I will try to summarize the dramatic part of her story.

In the verbosity of the early stage, she had not omitted to mention the 'madness of passion', the fiery ardour of the young man who would impetuously rush through the half-open door, pull aside the curtain, and, from there, make one bound onto the divan where Marco lay awaiting him. He could not endure wasting time in preliminaries or speeches. Impetuosity has its own particular ritual. Marco gave me to understand that, more often than not, the lieutenant, his gloves, and his peaked cap were all flung down haphazardly on the divan. Poetry and sweet nothings only came afterward. At this point in her story, Marco made a prideful pause and turned her gaze toward a bevelled, nickel-plated photograph frame. Her silence and her gaze invited me to various conjectures, and perhaps to a touch of envy.

'Well, so one day . . .' said Marco.

A day of licence, definitely. One of those rainy Paris days when a mysterious damp that dulls the mirrors and a strange craving to fling off clothes incited lovers to shut themselves up and turn day into night. 'One of those days,' Marco said, 'that are the perdition of body and soul . . .' I had to follow my friend and to imagine her—she forced me to—half naked on the divan bed, emerging from one of those ecstasies that were so crude and physical that she called them 'evil spells'. It was at that moment that her hand, straying over the bed, encountered the peaked forage cap known as a kepi and she yielded to one of those all too-typical feminine reflexes; she sat up in her crumpled chemise, planted the kepi over one ear, gave it a roguish little tap to settle it, and hummed:

With bugle and fife and drum
The soldiers are coming to town . . .

'Never,' Marco told me, 'never have I seen anything like Alex's face. It was . . . incomprehensible. I'd say it was hideous, if he weren't so handsome . . . I can't tell you what my feelings were . . .'

She broke off and stared at the empty divan-bed.

'What happened then, Marco? What did he say?'

'Why, nothing. I took off the kepi, I got up, I tidied myself, we had some tea. In fact, everything passed off just as usual. But since that day I've two or three times caught Alex looking at me with that face again and with such a very odd expression in his eyes. I can't get rid of the idea that the kepi was fatal to me. Did it bring back some unpleasant memory? I'd like to know what *you* think. Tell me straight out, don't hedge.'

Before replying, I took care to compose my face; I was so terrified it might express the same horror, disapproval, and disgust as Lieutenant Trallard's. Oh, Marco! In one moment I destroyed you, I wept for you—I saw you. I saw you just as Alexis Trallard had seen you. My contemptuous eyes took in the slack breasts and the slipped shoulder straps of the crumpled chemise. And the leathery, furrowed neck, the red patches on the skin below the ears, the chin left to its own devices and long past hope . . . And that groove, like a dried-up river, that hollows the lower eyelid after making love, and that vinous, fiery flush that does not cool off quickly enough when it burns on an ageing face. And crowning all that, the kepi! The kepi—with its stiff lining and its jaunty peak, slanted over one roguishly winked eye.

With bugle and fife and drum . . .

'I know very well,' went on Marco, 'that between lovers, the slightest thing is enough to disturb a magnetic atmosphere . . . I know very well . . .'

Alas! What did she know?

'And after that, Marco? What was the end?'

'The end? But I've told you all there is to tell. Nothing else happened. The mission to Morocco turned up. The date's been put forward twice. But that isn't the only reason I've been losing sleep. Other signs . . .'

'What signs?'

She did not dare give a definite answer. She put out a hand as if to thrust away my question and averted her head.

'Oh, nothing, just . . . just differences.'

She strained her ears in the direction of the door.

'I haven't seen him for three days,' she said. 'Obviously he has an enormous amount to do getting ready for this mission. All the same . . .'

She gave a sidelong smile.

'All the same, I'm not a child,' she said in a detached voice. 'In any case, he writes to me. Express letters.'

'What are his letters like?'

'Oh, charming, of course, what else would they be? He may be very young but *he's* not quite a child either.'

As I had stood up, Marco suddenly became anguished and humble and clutched my hands.

'What do you think I ought to do? What *does* one do in these circumstances?'

'How can I possibly know, Marco? I think there's absolutely nothing to be done but to wait. I think it's essential, for your own dignity.'

She burst into an unexpected laugh.

'My dignity! Honestly, you make me laugh! My dignity! Oh, these young women.'

I found her laugh and her look equally unbearable.

'But Marco, you're asking my advice—I'm giving it to you straight from the heart.'

She went on laughing and shrugging her shoulders. Still laughing, she brusquely opened the door in front of me. I thought that she was going to kiss me, that we should arrange another meeting, but I had hardly got outside before she shut the door behind me without saying anything beyond: 'My dignity! No, really, that's *too* funny!'

If I stick to facts, the story of Marco is over. Marco had had a lover; Marco no longer had a lover. Marco had brought down the sword of Damocles by putting on the fatal kepi, and at the worst possible moment. At the moment when the man is a melancholy, still-vibrating harp, an explorer returning from a promised land, half glimpsed but not attained, a lucid penitent swearing 'I'll never do it again' on bruised and bended knees.

I stubbornly insisted on seeing Marco again a few days later. I knocked and rang at her door, which was not opened. I went on and on, for I was aware of Marco there behind it, solitary, stony, and fevered. With my mouth to the keyhole, I said: 'It's Colette', and Marco opened the door. I saw at once that she regretted having let me in. With an absentminded air, she kept stroking the loose skin of her small hands, smoothing it down toward the wrist like the cuff of a glove. I did not let myself be intimidated; I told her that I wanted her to come and dine with me at home that very night and that I wouldn't take no for an answer. And I took advantage of my authority to add: 'I suppose Lieutenant Trallard has left?'

'Yes,' said Marco.

'How long will it take him to get over there?'

'He isn't *over there*,' said Marco. 'He's at Ville d'Avray, staying with his father. It comes to the same thing.'

When I had murmured 'Ah!' I did not know what else to say.

'After all,' Marco went on, 'why shouldn't I come and have dinner with you?'

I made exclamations of delight, I thanked her. I behaved as effusively as a grateful fox terrier, without, I think, quite taking her in. When she was sitting in my room, in the warmth, under my lamp, in the glare of all that reflected whiteness, I could measure not only Marco's decline in looks but a kind of strange reduction in her. A diminution of weight—she was thinner—a diminution of resonance—she talked in a small, indistinct voice. She must have forgotten to feed herself, and taken things to make herself sleep.

Masson came in after dinner. When he found Marco there, he showed as much apprehension as his illegible face could express. He gave her a crab-like sidelong bow.

'Why, it's Masson,' said Marco indifferently. 'Hello, Paul.'

They started up an old cronies' conversation, completely devoid of interest. I listened to them and I thought that such a string of bromides ought to be as good as a sleeping draught for Marco. She left early and Masson and I remained alone together.

'Paul, don't you think she looks ill, poor Marco?'

'Yes,' said Masson. 'It's the phase of the priest.'

'Of the . . . *what?*'

'The priest. When a woman, hitherto extremely feminine, begins to look like a priest, it's the sign that she no longer expects either kindness or ill treatment from the opposite sex. A certain yellowish pallor, something melancholy about the nose, a pinched smile, falling cheeks: Marco's a perfect example. The priest, I tell you, the priest.'

He got up to go, adding: 'Between ourselves, I prefer that in her to the odalisque.'

In the weeks that followed, I made a special point of not neglecting Marco. She was losing weight very fast indeed. It is difficult to hold on to someone who is melting away, it would be truer to say consuming herself. She moved house, that is to say, she packed her trunk and took it off to another little furnished flat. I saw her often, and never once did she mention Lieutenant Trallard. Then I saw her less often and the coolness was far more on her side than on mine. She seemed to be making a strange endeavour to turn herself into a shrivelled little old lady. Time passed . . .

'But, Masson, what's happened to Marco? It's ages since . . . Have *you* any news of Marco?'

'Yes,' said Masson.

'And you haven't told me anything!'

'You haven't asked me anything.'

'Quick, where is she?'

'Almost every day at the Nationale. She's translated an extraordinary series of articles about the Ubangi from English into French. As the manuscript is a little short to make a book, she's making it longer at the publisher's request, and she's documenting herself at the library.'

'So she's taken up her old life again,' I said thoughtfully. 'Exactly as it was before Lieutenant Trallard . . .'

'Oh, no,' said Masson. 'There's a tremendous change in her existence?'

'What change? Really, one positively has to drag things out of you?'

'Nowadays,' said Masson, 'Marco gets paid two sous a line.'

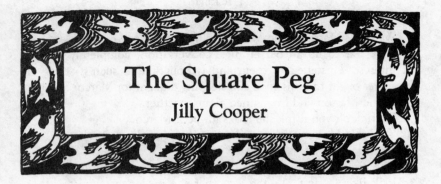

The Square Peg

Jilly Cooper

Clutching her parcels, Penny charged through the front door, skilfully avoided a workman on a ladder, but cannoned straight into the Sales Manager coming out of the Board Room with an important client. Gibbering apologies, she raced upstairs, tiptoed past the Personnel Officer's room, and eased herself stealthily into her office.

Miss Piggott, the Managing Director's senior secretary, looked at her watch in disapproval. 'It's nane minutes past three,' she said in her ultra refined voice. 'Don't you think you're sailin' a bit close to the wind?'

'Oh gosh, Miss Piggott, I'm sorry,' said Penny, who was the Managing Director's junior secretary, 'but I saw this divine dress and then I found these shoes to match in a sale, and then in the same sale, I saw these garden scissors. I thought you might like them.'

Miss Piggott's disapproving face softened. 'That was very thoughtful of you, Penny. How much do Ay owe you?'

'Nothing, it's a present.' Penny kicked off her shoes, and collapsed into a chair, scattering parcels among the debris on her desk. 'I bought some éclairs, three in fact, in case *he*—' she pointed contemptuously at the door leading off their office—'gets back in time.'

'He's back,' said Miss Piggott. 'He's been ringing you since two o'clock.'

Penny went pale. 'Mr. McInnes is back already? My goodness, is he in a foul mood?'

'A've known him more accommodatin',' said Miss Piggott with a sniff.

'Oh dear,' sighed Penny, tugging a comb through her dark red curls, 'I do wish darling Mr. Fraser was still here. Everything was so much nicer then.'

Mr. Fraser had run the London office of Joshua McInnes Inc. with bumbling but good-natured incompetence; and immediately he had retired last autumn, old Joshua McInnes, who had been viewing the situation from across the Atlantic with increasing dismay, had sent his younger son, Jake, to sort out the muddle.

At first the London office hadn't known what had hit them. Young Jake McInnes went through every department with a tooth-comb, and for six months everyone had shivered in their shoes. Then gradually they began to realise things were running far more smoothly. Orders poured in and the factory had enough work in hand for three years.

People stopped flattening themselves against the wall whenever Jake McInnes walked down the passage. Everyone settled down — everyone except Penny, that is, for she was catastrophically inefficient.

Mr. Fraser had kept her as a kind of office pet. He had found her useful at remembering birthdays and knowing which of the telephonist's grandchildren was down with the measles. Occasionally he had given her letters, which he always signed without bothering to read.

'Penny's beautiful and she keeps me young,' he had insisted every time Miss Payne from Personnel had agitated for her dismissal. 'She makes a good cup of coffee, and she keeps the flowers in the conference room looking simply wonderful.'

But now Mr. Fraser had gone, and Jake McInnes had taken his place, and everyone was laying bets on how much longer Penny could possibly last.

The day Penny had decided to make her shopping expedition, Jake McInnes had not been expected back until late afternoon.

'Hello, Mr. McInnes, did you have a super time?' she asked nervously as she went into his office.

Jake McInnes looked her up and down for a minute, taking in the white silk shirt, the vestigial scarlet skirt over long brown legs. 'Sit down,' he said icily.

Jake McInnes was a powerfully built man in his late twenties, with thick hair, deep-set eyes the colour of mahogany, and a very square jaw. With that nasty smile playing round his mouth, he looks more like a Sicilian bandit than an American businessman, thought Penny.

They glared at each other across the vast desk.

'It's twenty minutes after three. I thought your lunch break ran from twelve-thirty to one-thirty,' he said.

'I'm sorry,' mumbled Penny, 'but I saw this perfectly marvellous dress, and then . . .'

'I don't want any excuses,' he snapped. 'I've told Miss Payne to dock two hours' pay from your salary this week.' He picked up her folder. 'You must have been busy while I was away, these letters are beautifully typed.'

'Oh good,' said Penny, beaming at him.

'It's a pity,' he continued softly, 'that they bear absolutely no relation to what I dictated.'

Penny flinched as though he'd struck her.

'Don't you do shorthand?' he asked.

'Not a lot,' admitted Penny, 'but my longhand's terribly fast, so I can get the gist of things. Mr Fraser never complained,' she added defiantly.

'That doesn't surprise me,' said Jake McInnes.

For the next half-hour he went through each letter like an examination paper, until every shred of her self-confidence was ripped to pieces. Then he tore the letters up and dropped them into the wastepaper basket.

Scarlet in the face, Penny got to her feet.

'And another thing,' he added, 'next time you make reservations at a hotel, book single rooms. I don't like arriving in the middle of the night to find I'm expected to share a double bed with Mr. Atwater.'

Penny went off into a peal of laughter, which she quickly stifled when she saw the expression of disapproval on his face.

'And one last thing,' he added, as she went out of the door. 'Put your shoes on when you come in here.'

'Was he fraightfully angry?' asked Miss Piggott.

'He wasn't pleased,' sighed Penny.

Valerie from the typing pool had just arrived with the tea. She took a cup into Jake McInnes's office, and returned a few seconds later with starry eyes.

'Isn't he beautiful,' she said to Penny. 'The way he looks at you. Not that I stand a chance when you think of all those sophisticated women who come and pick him up from Reception. That Mrs. Ellerington last week looked just like a film star. Still, there's no harm in hoping, is there?'

'You need your head examined,' said Penny shortly.

Valerie bridled and glanced at the photograph over Penny's desk of a young man whose startlingly blond good looks were somewhat obscured by a long, motheaten beard.

'Oh well, since you fancy those drippy lefties with dirty fingernails, I don't suppose you would go for Mr. McInnes,' she said sarcastically.

'Francis doesn't have dirty fingernails,' snapped Penny. 'And don't you dare mention him in the same breath as Jake McInnes. Francis is so gentle and sweet and unaggressive.'

'He wasn't so unaggressive when he broke that placard over the policeman's head in Trafalgar Square during that Disarmament Rally,' observed Miss Piggott.

'That's different,' said Penny scornfully. 'Francis was just showing how deeply he feels about non-violence.'

'Funny way of showing it,' said Miss Piggott, who disapproved of Francis not so much for his politics or his appearance, as for the casual way he treated Penny.

At that moment the telephone rang. Penny swooped on it. 'Hello . . . I mean Mr. McInnes's office. Francis! Darling! Is it really you? How lovely to hear your voice.' She made a triumphant face at Valerie and Miss Piggott.

Half an hour later, she reluctantly put down the receiver, gave an ecstatic shudder and buried her face in her hands. 'He rang,' she said simply.

'So Ay noticed,' said Miss Piggott. 'Mr. McInnes did, too. He came in twice and went out looking like a thundercloud.'

'To hell with Mr. McInnes,' said Penny. 'Oh Miss Piggott, Francis still loves me. I thought he was cooling off. There's a demo on Saturday and he wants me to join him.'

Thrilled by this evidence of Francis's continuing interest she wandered off to the typing pool to give Valerie the third éclair as a peace offering.

During the next fortnight Penny tried very hard to be more efficient, but she dropped enough bricks to build her own office block. She booked tables at the wrong restaurants, arranged meetings for the wrong days, and spilled a cup of tea over Miss Piggott's electric typewriter. She also got more and more depressed because Francis hadn't rung her, her only comfort being that he had promised to take her to the theatre the following Thursday.

Thursday dawned. Having washed her hair that morning, Penny arrived later than usual at the office. Jake McInnes sent for her immediately. 'Penny,' he said wearily.

'Oh golly, what have I done now?'

'Remember last week I wrote two letters, one to my father saying Atkinsons' were playing hard to get, but I thought we'd clinch the deal with them by the end of the month; and the other letter to Atkinsons' playing it very, very cool?'

'Yes,' said Penny. 'You signed them both.'

'And you put them into the wrong envelopes. Now get out, just get out. And I don't want to talk to Emma McBride if she rings.'

Towards the end of the morning, Penny's telephone rang.

'Can I speak to Jake?' said a soft, smoky voice.

Oh goodness, thought Penny, which one did he say he didn't want to talk to? 'Who's that speaking,' she said cautiously.

'It's a personal call,' murmured the voice.

Penny had a brainwave. 'How's your little dog?' she asked.

'He's fine, Penny, just fine.'

It must be Mrs. Ellerington, who had a peke. Penny decided to throw herself on her mercy. 'Well, Mrs. Ellerington, Mr. McInnes said he specially didn't want to talk to someone, but I can't remember who it was; you or Emma McBride, or it might have been Mrs. Lusty. I'd ask him, but he's so mad at me this morning. You haven't fallen out with him lately, have you?'

'No, but I'm just about to.' The smoky voice had hardened. 'I think you'd better put me through.'

Two minutes later, Jake McInnes came out of his office. It was the first time he'd really lost his temper with Penny and it was the most terrifying thing that had ever happened to her.

'And take down that photograph of your boyfriend,' he shouted finally. 'This is an office not a film studio.'

'Well Ay never,' said Miss Piggott, as he slammed the door behind him. 'Ay've never known him fly off the handle like that before. Perhaps he is keen on that Mrs. Ellerington after all!'

'I think I'd better look for another job,' said Penny listlessly, unpinning Francis's photograph.

'It might be advisable; have a look in the newspaper,' said Miss Piggott. She brandished a toothbrush. 'Well, Ay'm off to the dentist. Ay shan't be back.'

'Bye. Hope it doesn't hurt too much,' said Penny, who was already poring over the Situations Vacant column.

Nothing really took her fancy, until she suddenly read:

'*Managing Director requires highly intelligent, hardworking secretary/*

personal assistant. Meticulous shorthand and typing essential. Salary £8000 upwards for the right person. Apply Box 9873.'

The salary was almost twice what she was getting at the moment, and Penny thought of all the clothes she could buy. Her two cats could have liver every day.

The letter of application took her only a few minutes. She saw her new boss as a younger version of Mr. Fraser, kindly and appreciative, just waiting for someone to bring sunshine into his life. She told him all about her troubles with Jake McInnes, and gave a much embellished version of her own career. Very pleased with herself, she sealed the letter and delivered it to the newspaper office by hand during her lunch hour.

Late that afternoon, Jake McInnes faced one of the toughest battles of his career. He lounged, outwardly relaxed, at the end of the long Board Room table. On either side of him sat the Board, all distinguished Englishmen, many years his senior. He was outlining the reforms he intended to make; reforms which, he must make them see, were desirable in themselves, and not just proof that, as his father's son, he was trying to throw his weight about in the London office of the firm.

Gradually as the meeting progressed, he felt he was winning the battle, antagonism was dwindling, and he was even getting a few laughs. He had just moved on to the subject of delivery, when Charles Atwater, the Sales Director, suddenly wondered if he was seeing things. For through the thickening cigar smoke, from the direction of the door, loped a rabbit. Hastily he put on his spectacles. Yes, it was a rabbit.

'Look,' he nudged the Director of Public Relations beside him.

'Good God,' said the Director of Public Relations, clapping his hands over his eyes, and resolving to give up heavy business lunches.

Jake McInnes looked in their direction. 'Have you anything to add, Charles?'

Mr. Atwater roared with laughter and pointed to the rabbit which had reached Jake McInnes's chair.

Pandemonium broke out.

'Good God, it's a rabbit.'

'Tally ho, after it, boys.'

'Perhaps it wants a seat on the Board.'

'Is that your own hare, or is it a wig? Ho, ho, ho.'

They are like a crowd of schoolboys, thought Jake McInnes, trying hard to keep his temper.

'How did it get in here?' said Mr. Atwater.

'I think I know,' said Jake McInnes, picking up the panic-stricken animal. 'If you'll excuse me a minute, gentlemen.'

He found Penny on her knees by the filing cabinet.

She looked up, cheeks red, a large smudge on her nose. 'Oh,' she said, a happy smile breaking over her face, 'you've found him. I was terrified he might have escaped into the street.'

Words failed Jake McInnes, as Penny took the rabbit from him, crooning, 'There, there, poor little love, were you frightened then?'

'Penny,' he said, 'where did you get it from?'

Penny's eyes filled with tears. 'From the market. He was the last one. The man said he'd go in the pot if no-one bought him.'

A faint smile flickered across Jake McInnes's face. 'Well, you'd better go and buy him a hutch, hadn't you?'

'It's Thursday,' said Penny. 'I haven't got any money left.'

Jake McInnes took out his wallet and handed her twenty pounds. 'Go round to the pet shop now. And I want all those letters finished by the time I come out of the meeting,' he added.

Half an hour later, the rabbit was happily installed in a smart, blue hutch, nibbling at some lettuce, and Penny was busily typing when the telephone rang. It was Francis.

'Darling,' cried Penny, 'what a treat. I am going to see you later, aren't I?' (Silly to let anxiety creep into her voice.)

Francis's voice was sulky with embarrassment. 'I can't make it after all,' he said.

'Oh, why not? You promised,' wailed Penny.

Francis explained that he had this picket duty . . .

'Well, I'll come too,' said Penny.

'No, no,' said Francis much too quickly. 'It's only a small picket.'

Penny panicked. 'I don't believe you. You've found someone else. It's that horrible blonde,' she choked. 'Oh Francis, I can't bear it.'

'Well, you'll just have to lump it,' said Francis. 'I'll give you a ring sometime.' The receiver clicked.

Penny's world seemed to be crumbling round her. In one day, she'd virtually lost her job, and had certainly lost her boyfriend. 'No-one loves me,' she said. 'No-one wants me, and I've got a bed-sitter, two cats and now a rabbit to support. Oh Francis!'

She ripped the letter she was typing out of her machine and put in a fresh sheet.

'*Darling, darling,*' she typed frenziedly. '*I'm so frightfully sorry. I didn't mean to disbelieve you, I was just so disappointed—*'

A shadow fell across the page. Penny leant quickly forward to hide what she was typing.

'What the hell are you doing?' Jake McInnes's voice was like a rifle shot. Penny burst into tears. She laid her head among the papers on her desk and sobbed. Jake McInnes did nothing, he just sat on the edge of Miss Piggott's desk, drawing on his cigar, waiting for her to stop.

'I'm so sorry,' she said eventually.

'What's the matter?' he said. 'Is it the boyfriend?'

Penny nodded dolefully. 'He's not going to take me out tonight after all. I think he's found another girl, an awful blonde with a forty-inch placard.'

Jake McInnes examined his fingernails. 'Well, as we both appear to have been stood up this evening . . .'

'Oh no,' said Penny in horror. 'Not you too—not Mrs Ellerington. Was she furious about that telephone call?'

'She wasn't "fraightfully accommodating", as our Miss Piggott would say.'

Penny began to giggle.

'And as I was saying,' he went on, 'as we've both got nothing better to do, I suggest we sort out this mess.' He pointed to the chaos which spread in a ten-foot radius round Penny's desk. 'Now which is your in-tray?'

'Well, those two tables over there,' said Penny, wondering what terrible skeletons were going to come tumbling out of the cupboard.

In the end, she rather enjoyed herself. Jake McInnes had obviously decided to be nice, and she found lots of things she thought she'd lost: her passport, several cleaning tickets and a bar of chocolate.

Two hours later, the tables, desks and surrounding filing cabinets were cleared and Penny was shoving paper into a sack.

'Miss Piggott will have a shock in the morning,' she said happily.

'Just try and keep it like this,' said Jake McInnes. 'Now I think we both deserve some dinner.'

'I've got stacks of food at home,' said Penny.

'I know, half a packet of fish fingers in the icebox. Stop being silly, and go and fix your face.'

Penny was appalled when she took a look at herself in the mirror.

Crying had devastated her make-up and there was a large smudge on her nose. Hastily she repaired the damage.

Jake McInnes took her to a very smart restaurant.

'Your usual table, Mr. McInnes,' said the waiter, leading them to a discreet corner. Penny wondered how often Jake McInnes had sat there, lavishing wine and compliments on the lovely Clare Ellerington.

Jake ordered drinks, and with them the waiter brought a dish of radishes, which Penny longed to pocket for the rabbit.

'It's so lovely being hungry for a change,' she said. 'I'm so overwhelmed by Francis that I can never eat a thing when he's around. I'm afraid he has definitely gone off me. I should have realised it when he started putting second class stamps on his letters instead of first class ones.'

The waiter arrived with avocado pear for Penny and oysters for Jake. For a few minutes they ate in silence, then Penny noticed that a beautiful woman at the next table was staring at Jake. How odd, she thought, and had a good look at Jake herself, taking in the breadth of the shoulders, the strong, well-shaped hands, the thick black hair. Suddenly he glanced up and caught her staring at him.

'Well?' he demanded, just like he did in the office.

Penny blushed. 'I was just thinking that you're very attractive.'

'You shouldn't say so in such a surprised tone, it isn't very flattering.'

'Well—I mean—all the typing pool are besotted with you, but, of course, I'm immune because I'm in love with Francis. And I'm never attracted to people who bully me,' she added.

'That's blackmail,' said Jake McInnes. 'From now on, have I got to put up with your crumby typing, just so you'll like me?'

'Oh no,' said Penny, 'I've decided I like you anyway, after this evening—in fact I like you very much.'

He looked at her for a long time, his eyes moving over her face. 'That makes me feel as though I've just won the Nobel Peace Prize,' he said slowly.

Penny stared back at him, unable to tear her eyes away, the colour mounting in her cheeks. The waiter arriving with their second course brought them both back to earth.

'Goodness, it looks delicious,' said Penny, picking up her fork.

'Mr. McInnes,' she said in a small voice five minutes later, looking down at her untouched plate, 'I'm terribly sorry, but I don't think I can eat this. I can't think what's happened . . . I was so hungry, and now I'm not, and it was so expensive . . .'

'It's all right,' he said gently. 'It doesn't matter.' And as he smiled at her she noticed the tired lines round his eyes, as though he hadn't been getting enough sleep lately. Suddenly she felt shy of him, and in the car going home, she sat as far away as possible with the rabbit hutch between them.

He didn't attempt to kiss her, as he delivered her to the door. 'Go to bed early,' he said. 'It might get you in on time in the morning.'

Back to square one, thought Penny—but she didn't go to bed. She wandered round her room, chattering to the rabbit and the two cats, drinking cups of coffee, and determinedly thinking how very much better-looking Francis was than Jake McInnes. She didn't attempt to localise the vague happiness which was stealing over her.

'Hello, Miss Piggott,' Penny said dreamily next morning. 'How was the dentist?'

'Fraightful,' said Miss Piggott. 'He was drillin' away for hours. Mr. McInnes wants to see you.'

'I thought he might,' said Penny, drenching herself with Miss Dior.

'Ay should watch your step if Ay were you. He seems a bit taight-lipped,' warned Miss Piggott.

Jake McInnes's face was quite expressionless when Penny went into the room. She beamed at him. 'The rabbit's very well,' she said. 'He ate lots of—'

'Sit down,' snapped Jake McInnes. 'You'd better explain this letter.' He held two pieces of paper between finger and thumb.

'Oh goodness, have I put my foot in something else?' sighed Penny.

'I think I'll read it to you,' he said silkily.

'*Dear Sir*, it begins. *In answer to your advertisement for a secretary/personal assistant, I feel I have the ideal qualifications for the job.*'

'Oh,' said Penny, interested. 'Are you getting another secretary? It will be a terrible squash with me and Miss Piggott and her.'

'It goes on,' said Jake McInnes, '*I relish hard work, and my aim in life is to find a job that I can really get my teeth into!*'

'I should hire her,' said Penny. 'She sounds jolly keen.'

'You would? Well, listen to this then. *I am meticulously accurate in every way and used to acting on my own initiative.*'

Horror crept into Penny's face. 'Oh no,' she whispered, 'it can't be.'

'Now it really begins to get interesting,' he said softly. '*My reason for leaving my present job is that the Managing Director (a wonderful man) was recently replaced by a director from the parent company in America. To be quite frank, this director is one of the most tyrannical individuals you could care to meet. He has already fired dozens of my colleagues—dear people who have given many years of service to the firm. I live in dread that I may be the next to go, as he bullies me unmercifully and makes my life a misery.'*

Penny buried her face in her hands.

He looked at her sternly. 'You could be prosecuted for writing that letter,' he said. 'It's complete libel from start to finish. A good thing I got in early, and no-one else saw it.'

'I'm sorry,' muttered Penny. 'Truly I am.'

'So you should be.' Then to her amazement he threw back his head and roared with laughter. 'Used to acting on your own initiative, meticulously accurate . . . Penny, Penny . . .' He wiped his streaming eyes.

Tears of mortification welled up in Penny's eyes. 'How was I to know it was you lurking behind a box number? And then being so sweet to me last night, when all the time you were looking for someone else to fill my job. Of all the mean, cruel . . .'

'Tyrannical things to do,' said Jake McInnes, still laughing.

'I'm going,' sobbed Penny. 'I'm walking out of your hateful firm right now.'

She leapt to her feet, but before she reached the door, he caught her by the arm. 'Easy now, before you go charging out of my life, just read this memo. It came from Public Relations this morning.'

Penny looked at it suspiciously.

'*Dear Jake,*' she read. '*Thanks for your letter. Just to confirm that we can fit in your leggy red-head any time you choose to release her—particularly if she's as ravishing as you say. There's a vacancy on the copy side now, and she can do the occasional shift in reception. Best wishes, Jim Stokely.*'

Penny put the memo down on his desk. 'You arranged to have me transferred,' she said slowly.

He nodded. 'So I can get some work done during the day, and some sleep at night. I thought you might do rather well in Public Relations with that fertile imagination.'

Penny was still staring at him in bewilderment. 'Ravishing and distracting,' she said quietly. 'You're not just trying to get rid of me?'

He shook his head ruefully. 'I spent most of last night thinking about you; seeing you cuddling that rabbit, I realised you were wasted as a secretary. You ought to be living in the country looking after a houseful of animals and babies and one very lucky man.'

'I only wrote that letter because I was mad at you,' said Penny. 'I thought that you loathed me.'

'Loathed you! I've been hooked ever since I walked into old Fraser's office for the first time. It was in the middle of the afternoon, and you were painting your nails with the radio on, and the sun was streaming through your hair.'

He was coming towards her, and the expression on his face made Penny back away from him until she was trapped against his desk. He took her into his arms.

'Oh, we can't,' she said in confusion. 'Not here.'

'Why not?' said Jake McInnes. 'I'm the boss around here.' And he kissed her very hard.

'Oh my goodness,' said Penny, very pink and glowing. 'I don't think I do want to marry Francis after all.'

'And I don't think I can afford to have you sabotaging my public relations company either; you'd be much better going into private relations with me. We'll discuss it over lunch.'

Still with his arm round her, he leant across and pressed the intercom switch. 'Miss Piggott, I'm going to lunch, and I won't be back this afternoon. You're in sole charge of the office. Hire and fire at will.'

'But, Mr. McInnes,' Miss Piggott's anguished voice echoed inter-communally over the room, 'you've got a meetin'.'

'Cancel it, I've got a meeting of my own lined up.'

He released the switch and turned his attention to Penny.

'But Mr. McInnes,' said Miss Piggott, charging into the room like a herd of buffaloes, 'Ay don't think Ay can contact the people comin' to the meetin' in taime.'

She broke off suddenly as she saw Penny in Jake McInnes's arms. 'Craikey,' she said.

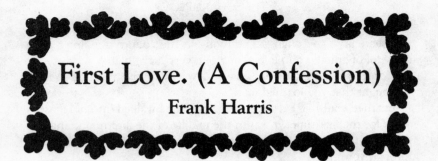

First Love. (A Confession)

Frank Harris

My boyhood and youth were passed in Brighton. I entered the College there as a boy of ten, and went through every class on the Modern side in the usual seven years. I only tell this to show that from the beginning my father intended me to go into business, and that I was not particularly clever at books. I loved football as much as I hated French, and I learned more of 'fives' in half an hour than I knew of German after eight years' teaching. In fact, if it had not been for mathematics I should not have got my 'remove' each year regularly as I managed to do. There were lots of fellows who could beat my head off at learning; but there were very few as strong or as good at games, and I'd have been Captain of the School if Wilson, who was one of the best 'bats' of his day (he played afterwards for the 'Gentlemen'), had not been a contemporary of mine. I was not bad-looking either. I do not mean I was handsome or anything of that sort; but I was tall and dark, and my features were fairly regular, and, as I had more of a moustache than almost any fellow in the school, I rather fancied myself.

After leaving Brighton College, my father got me a clerkship with Lawrence, Loewenthall and Co., stockbrokers, of Copthall Court. My father was rector of a Brighton parish, and knew Mr. Lawrence, who came regularly to his church. The two old boys were great 'pals', because, as my father said, they were both Protestants and not Catholics in disguise; but I always thought that my father's liking for Mr. Lawrence's port and Mr. Lawrence's respect for my father's birth and learning had more to do with their mutual esteem. However that may be, old Lawrence gave me a good start and I turned it to account. From the first I took to business. The school work at Latin and Greek had had no meaning for me; but in the City the tangible results of energy and skill were always before me, interesting me in spite of myself, and exciting me to do my best. And rivalry soon came to lend another spur. In Throgmorton Street my chief competitors were young German Jews, keen as mustard in everything relating to business, and preternaturally sharp in scenting personal profit. Their acuteness and boldness fascinated me: I went about with them a good deal, picked up conversational German without much effort, and soon learned from my mentors how fortunes were to be made. A little group of us pooled our savings, and began to speculate and, after a succession of gains and losses which about balanced themselves, turned our tens into hundreds over a 'slump' in American rails. Our success was due to Waldstein—the Julius Waldstein who has since made a great fortune, and whom I should like to write about some day or other, as I look upon him as the first financial genius of the age. But now I must get on with my story. It was a remark I made after this lucky 'deal' that drew Mr. Lawrence's attention to me and gave me my first step up in the house. I had gone into his private room with some transfers to be signed. He was reading a letter; in the middle of it he rang for the managing clerk, and asked him:

'How are Louisvilles going?'

'I'll see,' was the reply; and in a minute or two old Simkins returned with:

'Steady at 48.'

I could not help muttering, 'They'll be steadier at 35.'

'What do you know about it?' asked Lawrence, with an air of amused surprise. His tone put me on my mettle, and I laid my reasons, or rather Waldstein's, before him, and he soon saw that I knew what I was talking about. A year afterwards I, too, was a managing clerk and a member of the Stock Exchange; and from that time on have never found it very difficult to lay by something each year. It's curious, too, how the habit of saving grows on one—but I am forgetting my story.

As I became interested in my work and confident of success I wanted someone to talk to, to brag to if the truth must be told, and life, I have noticed, generally furnishes us with the opportunity of gratifying our desires. I still kept up the custom of going home to Brighton from Saturday till Monday. And one Sunday, coming out of church, my sister introduced me to some people whom I took to immediately, Mrs. and Miss Longden. Mabel Longden was tall and good-looking, but too dark for my taste. Still, we chummed at once, and perhaps got along together better than if we had fallen in love at first sight—a thing, by the way, which I have never believed in.

Mrs. Longden was the widow of a major in the army, and lived in a small house in Kemp Town. She had only a hundred a year or so beyond her pension, and her one ambition in life was to keep herself and her two daughters like ladies. Her love of gentility was so passionate that when the rumour got about that she was the daughter of a small tradesman, everyone believed it. Mabel had a sister whom I have not mentioned yet, perhaps because I saw little of her for some time, and the little I saw did not interest me. She could not have been more than thirteen or fourteen years of age when I first met her, and she seemed to me an ordinary schoolgirl—all ribs and ankles. Her face was not even pretty; the eyes were all right, greyish and large, but the nose was inclined to be thick and the oval of the face was too narrow; the jaws seemed pinched in, and this peculiarity gave her an uncomfortably sharp look. She was a strange child in every way, and I did not like her. I remember the first time I really noticed her. I had been talking to Mabel about business; telling her how I had nabbed a fellow who had tried to cheat me, when suddenly I looked up and found Blanche gazing at me. As our eyes met she looked away quickly, and then got up and went out of the room, leaving me under the impression that she disapproved of me, or did not like what I had been saying. I put this down to 'cheek' that deserved to be snubbed; but she never gave me the opportunity of snubbing her; she seemed rather to avoid me.

A few weeks later I was waiting one afternoon in the little parlour. Mabel had gone up to dress to go out with me, when suddenly Blanche came into the room with her cheeks aglow, crying, 'Where's Mother?' She had been skating, and her sparkling eyes and rich colour so improved her that I exclaimed, 'Why, Blanche, you're quite pretty!' I suppose the astonishment in my voice was rather marked; for as I looked her eyes grew indignant; the colour in her cheeks flamed from pink to scarlet, and she turned and stalked out of the room with her chin in the air. An absurd child; she annoyed without interesting me, and I resolved to take no further notice of her.

It was easy to keep that resolution; for about this time my companionship with Mabel became close: we began to spoon in fact, and soon tried to believe ourselves very much in love with each other. But there was always something lacking in our intimacy, and now, looking back, I see that there was no real bond between us, and I begin to suspect that kisses often stand youth in lieu of sympathy. For even if I would, I really could not tell much of my flirtation with

Mabel Longden. She was good to look at and good to be with, too uniformly sweet-tempered ever to have cared much about me, I imagine; but I knew nothing of her true character and temperament; for love was not in her, love with its terrible need of self-betrayal. There were moments, it is true, when we seemed drawn together, moments when her eyes sought mine with timid abandonment, and when pride in her looks and pity of her weakness grew in me to unselfish tenderness; but there was no enduring strength in the feeling, no roots of life in it, and a few days' separation chilled us both. I am glad now to think that the play was pure comedy on both sides, though at the time I was often vaguely disappointed with our aloofness from one another, and tried by dwelling on her beauty to bring myself to the passionate ardour I ought to have felt for her. Mabel never really loved me at all; at the height of our intimacy I noticed that she used to lead me on to talk of the fortune I should make, and the great house we should have and the horses and carriages, and it seems to me now, though I am half ashamed to say it, that it was some picture in her mind of dress and jewellery and distinction which made her try to like me. In any case the matter is not worth thinking about any longer, and I only mention it now because it belongs to my story.

I had known Mabel Longden for nearly two years, and for six or eight months had spent three-fourths of the time I passed in Brighton with her, when I called early one Saturday evening and found that she was out. I was a little hurt—more in vanity than in affection, I think—and disappointed, which I took to be a proof of feeling, whereas it was merely the result of baulked habit. True, I was later than usual, much later in fact; but then my father had kept me talking of my younger brother Tom, and I had bought tickets for the theatre to make up for my late coming. I found it difficult to disguise my bad humour when I was told that Mabel had gone out for the evening and would probably not be home till eleven.

'You see,' said Mrs. Longden apologetically, 'you never sent her word, and I presume she thought you were not coming at all.' While she was speaking, my eyes, wandering about in hesitation and annoyance, suddenly caught sight of an expression of indignant contempt on Blanche's face as she sat looking into the fire.

'But what am I to do with these tickets?' I asked, in helpless irritation. As I spoke Blanche kicked the fender and got up hastily, and an idea came into my head.

'Would you let me take Blanche?' And I turned to Mrs. Longden.

'Yes,' said Mrs. Longden after a moment's hesitation, only to be noticed because of her unvarying suavity; 'yes, certainly; and I think Blanche would enjoy it. She loves music.'

'Well, Blanche?' I asked; but there was no need of an answer, for the girl's eyes were dancing.

'Oh,' she said in a low voice, as if to excuse her joy, 'it is "Le Nozze di Figaro" isn't it? And I love music, and Titiens and Trebelli are both in it. Oh,' and she drew in her breath with delight and clasped her hands, 'it *is* kind of you!'

'What will you wear, dear?' asked her mother, and the girl's face fell so lugubriously that I could not help laughing. 'Anything will do: we must start at once,' I said, and bustled them both upstairs. I like music as much as most people, but I like, too, to talk between the acts, and my companion that night was more than silent; still Titiens was very good in spite of her bulk, and Trebelli the most enchanting page that was ever seen. When she sang 'Voi che sapete' with that angelic voice of hers, I was carried off my feet.

As she finished the song my companion gave a queer, little, hysterical squeak that turned all eyes upon her. I saw that the child was overwrought; her face was pale and pinched, and the eyes blazing, so I whispered, 'Let us go, Blanche, eh?'

'Oh, no!' she said. 'No! It is too beautiful—please don't go.'

'If we stay,' I insisted, 'you mustn't cry out: the people are all looking at you.'

'What do the people matter?' she snapped, and then, pleadingly, 'Please, let me listen.' Of course there was nothing more to be said, and we stayed to the end.

It was a fine night, and we walked home together, Blanche taking my arm.

'Are you glad I took you?' I asked, feeling that I should like her to thank me; she pressed my arm. But I wanted to talk, so I went on:

'You liked the play, didn't you?' That started her off; she was so excited with enthusiasm and admiration that she talked like one out of breath.

'The music,' she said, 'was divine; so beautiful, it hurt. I ache with it still. I can never forget it.'

I laughed at her exaggerations, and brought her down to common sense, and then she began to attack the play.

'It was beastly,' if you please; 'all falsehood and deceit and cheating. I hope life isn't like that,' she burst out, 'if it is, I shall hate it. How could Mozart have given that perfect music to those horrid words and horrid people? How could he?'

There seemed to be some sense in what she said, but as I knew very little about it, I preferred to change the subject. And then the conversation died away.

When we reached her house I left her at the door. Somehow or other I did not feel inclined to go and make up my little difference with Mabel. It seems to me now as if our estrangement began that evening; but, indeed, I did not trouble much about it, either then or later. And it was not any affection for Blanche that put Mabel out of my head: no, the child excited my curiosity, and that was all; she was evidently clever, and I liked that; but she was so intensely emotional, which seemed odd rather than pleasant to me.

For some weeks I did not call at the Longdens, and when I called I noticed that Mabel was affected in manners and speech. Her coldness I didn't mind; in fact, I felt relieved by it; but her graceful poses and little slang phrases of gentility seemed ridiculous to me. I wondered that I had never been disagreeably impressed by them before. I felt too, that they were characteristic of her; she was affected and vain. I did not want to be alone with her, and though we spent several afternoons together I maintained my attitude of polite carelessness. Mabel scarcely seemed to notice my change of manner; she was often out when I called, and I fell upon the idea of asking Blanche to accompany us whenever Mabel happened to go out with me. At first Blanche used to refuse point blank; but as I returned to the charge she consented now and then, evidently in accord with her sister; indeed, Mabel often pressed her to say 'Yes'.

I remember one Saturday evening taking them both to dine at Mutton's. We had a private room and the best dinner the place could afford; for success and Waldstein's example were teaching me to be extravagant in such matters. The week had been a red-letter one for me; I had cleared a thousand pounds in it and naturally was cock-a-hoop, though I did not conceal from myself, or even from the Longdens, that my success was due to Waldstein. In fact, towards the end of the dinner I set his whole plan before them and gave all his reasons for the course he took. Before I had got half through the story it was impossible not to notice that Blanche was my only listener. Mabel made polite exclamations of attention at the proper places; but she was manifestly rather bored by the account, whereas Blanche asked about everything she didn't understand, and appeared to be really engrossed by the dramatic elements in the struggle for wealth. Piqued by Mabel's manner, I did my best to interest Blanche and succeeded, I suppose, for Mabel at length left the table and took to drumming on the window pane to show her impatience.

'I must go!' she exclaimed at last. 'I expect Captain Burroughs to call this evening to try over a song with me, and I don't want to be late.' After that there was nothing left for us but to put on our wraps and go. I had met Captain Burroughs at the Longdens more than once, but had not paid much attention to him. He was an ordinary-looking man, I thought, with nothing particular about him except that he was well set-up and had large blue eyes. Now as Mabel spoke his image came before me, and I understood that he was good-looking, that she thought him exceedingly attractive, and had more than consoled herself with his courtship for my inattention. Perhaps even she had begun to go her own way before I had thought of going mine. Yes, she had; a hundred little signs unnoticed at the time assured me that she had. The discovery relieved and pleased me greatly; I grew excited and felt quite cordial to her. She was a fine girl after all, and deserved a handsome husband like Burroughs. Was it this elation or the wine I had drunk that made me act as I did? I don't know; the bare facts are not flattering to me, but I'll set them down. Mabel went out of the room first, as if in a hurry to get to her Captain; she disappeared just as I took up Blanche's jacket to help her on with it. As the young girl swung round before me I noticed for the first time that she had a figure, a figure that promised to be a very pretty one, and after putting on her jacket I could not help taking her slender waist in my hands. Of course I said something to cover my action: 'Go along, let us catch Mabel,' or something of that sort; but the words died on my lips, for she turned abruptly and faced me with an imperative: 'Don't!'

'Go along,' I repeated awkwardly, 'you're only a child.'

She moved away haughtily, without a word, and followed her sister downstairs.

The cab was waiting for us, and as soon as we were seated in it I forced a conversation with Mabel on the subject of her song and Captain Burroughs' voice.

After this incident Blanche avoided me persistently. At first, feeling rather uncomfortable, I was not at all sorry to get out of a complete explanation. But as the feeling of shame wore off I began to contrive opportunities of being alone with her. 'I don't care for her,' I used to say to myself, 'but I don't want her to think me a howling cad.' But though I did not care for her she was in my thoughts a good deal, and knew how to pique my vanity at least by continually avoiding me. She was more successful in this than she could have been a few months before; for now I never went to the house without finding Burroughs in the little parlour on the ground floor, filling the place I had formerly occupied beside Mabel. In fact, about this time Mrs. Longden confided to me that the pair were engaged, and when I congratulated Mabel I noticed that she was prettier and less affected than I had ever imagined she could be. Love is like youth for hiding faults and enhancing merits. After this event my chances of meeting Blanche alone became too slight to be worth the risk of disturbing the lovers, and so I gave up going to the house at all regularly. Mere chance soon helped me where purpose had failed. One afternoon late, as I reached the house I found the servant at the door, who told me that everyone was out except Miss Blanche. I was very glad to hear it. Blanche was in the parlour alone, and as I entered she stood up hastily, and returned my greeting with a cold 'I'll see if Mother or Mabel is in.' But I stopped in front of the door, and said:

'Won't you speak to me, Blanche? If I've offended you, I beg your pardon. Forgive me, and let us be friends again.' I caught myself speaking with an intensity far greater than I had thought of using; and, as her face did not relax and she kept her eyes obstinately bent on the ground, I began again with an extraordinary eagerness:

'Why will you bear malice? I had no idea you could be so cross. Just remember what a great talk we had that night, and forgive me.' Still the same silence and little downcast face, scarcely to be seen in the gathering shadows. I began again: 'Really, Blanche, you ought to be ashamed of yourself. It is childish to sulk so: yes, childish,' I repeated, for she had looked up at last. 'If you were older you would know that every woman forgives when the man apologises and asks for pardon.' She looked me straight in the face, but said nothing. Had I excited myself by my own pleading, or what was it? I don't know; but I began again in a different tone:

'Upon my word, if you won't speak, I'll treat you like the little girl you are, and kiss you into a good temper.'

'You daren't,' she said, and stood rigidly.

'You mustn't dare me,' I cried, and I threw my left arm round her waist and held her face to mine with my right hand. At first she struggled desperately, and writhed so that I could hardly hold her. Then gradually I overcame her struggles, and kissed her again and again. I shall never be able to describe the strange, keen pleasure I took in the touch of her lips; nor the intimate, intense delight it gave me to hold her tender, panting form against my breast in the darkness. Whilst I was still embracing and kissing her, the idea came to me that her resistance had become merely formal; that she was not trying to avoid my lips. At once conscience smote me, and I felt that I had been a brute. No sort of excuse for me— none. I pulled myself together, and stopped kissing her. Then I began pleading again.

'Little Blanche, have you forgiven me? Are we friends again? Won't you speak to me now?' And I laid my cheek to hers: the girl's face was wet, and I realised with a pang that she was crying silently. This was worse than I had feared. I was genuinely grieved.

'Oh Blanche,' I exclaimed, 'if you knew how sorry I am! Please don't cry; I didn't mean to hurt you; I'm so sorry—what am I to do? I'll never, never forgive myself.' As I began to speak she slipped from my arms and went to the door.

'Blanche,' I went on—for I couldn't let her go like that—'you must hate me to leave me so; won't you say you'll forgive me, please?' She paused, holding the door ajar; then I heard her say in a little subdued voice:

'There's nothing to forgive,' and then, 'It wasn't your fault,' and the door closed behind her quickly, leaving me in the dark, half penitent and half in doubt as to her meaning, though the tone of her voice had partially reassured me.

After she left me I seemed to be possessed by a demon of unrest. Up and down the parade I tramped reproaching myself for what I had done. I had no business to kiss her. It was a shame. I felt very clearly that kisses meant infinitely more to her than they did to her sister. What was I to do? I didn't love her, and yet I had never kissed anyone with such passion. She was an inscrutable mystery to me. Why had she cried? Did she dislike me? Had she grown tired of struggling, or merely affected to struggle, wishing all the time to be kissed? This flattering hypothesis seemed to be true; but, if true, why had she begun to cry? And if she had cried out of vexation, why did she say that there was nothing to forgive, and that it wasn't my fault? I couldn't read the riddle; and it was too fascinating to leave unread. I wanted to return to the house to see her if but for a moment, but that went against my pride. I resolved to write to her. The girl was a mystery, and the mystery had an attraction for me that I could not account for or explain. That night I went up to my little bedroom and sat down to write to her. I soon found that the task was exceedingly difficult. At one moment I was writing as if I loved her, and the next I was warning her that I did not love her yet. At length I began to quiet myself: 'Why write at all?' But I couldn't leave her without a word, and so I decided at last to write just a brief note, saying how grieved I should be to hurt or offend her in any way, and declaring that I would call next Saturday afternoon as soon as I reached Brighton. I began 'Dear little Blanche,' and ended up with 'I shall think of you all through the week; yours, Will Rutherford.'

The week passed much as other weeks had passed, with this difference however, that from Monday I began to look forward more and more eagerly to seeing Blanche again. I did not write this to her in the meantime, partly out of prudence, partly out of the wish to tell it to her when we met. As soon as I reached Brighton on the Saturday I hurried off to the Longdens. The mother met me in the parlour.

'Where's Blanche?' I asked, gaily.

'Blanche!' repeated Mrs. Longden, with a slight tone of surprise; 'she has gone into the country to stay with some friends.'

'Into the country,' I muttered, in confusion; 'where to?'

'Near Winchester,' came the calm reply.

'But did she leave no message for me—no letter?'

'Not that I'm aware of,' replied Mrs. Longden smilingly; 'I didn't even know that you took interest enough in each other to write or send messages.'

And that was all. I left the house more bewildered than ever; but my pride was up in arms, and I resolved to put Blanche out of my mind completely. That seemed easy enough at first; but with time it became increasingly difficult. The mystery puzzled me more and more, and the abrupt parting piqued my curiosity. As the weeks passed and I recalled all our meetings and what she had said, I began to see that she was very intelligent and very ingenuous. At length I couldn't stand it any longer; so I wrote to her, telling her how constantly I thought of her, and begging her to let me see her. I took the letter to Mrs. Longden, who promised to forward it, with a request to Blanche to answer it, and next week Mrs. Longden showed me the end of a letter Blanche had written to her: 'I received the letter you sent me; please tell him there's no answer. I have nothing to say.'

I had gone as far as my pride would allow. From that day I never went near the Longdens, but gave myself up to work, and gradually the fascination of business took hold of me once again. Four or five years later I married and bought a little country place near Winchester. A year or so afterwards I took my wife to a ball given by the officers of the —— Hussars, who were quartered in the Cathedral city. I knew a good many people and, as I liked dancing, prepared to enjoy myself; feeling sure that my wife would be well taken care of. After the second or third dance a Captain Wolfe came up to me and said, 'You're in luck, my friend; I'm going to introduce you to the belle of the ball.' With some laughing protestation I followed him and he presented me by simply saying, 'This is Mr. Rutherford.'

The girl certainly deserved his praise; she was one of those astoundingly pretty girls one sees now and then in England and nowhere else in the world. I cannot describe her except by saying that she was above the middle height and of a very perfect round figure, with the most beautiful face I have ever seen.

'Pardon me,' I said, 'but Captain Wolfe forgot to tell me your name.'

'Don't you know it?' she asked, while her blue eyes danced with amusement.

'No,' I replied, 'how should I? I have never seen you before.'

I spoke with absolute conviction.

'What a bad compliment—to forget me and deny me! Aren't you ashamed of yourself?' and she pouted adorably.

'The best of compliments,' I retorted warmly; 'the certainty that if I had ever seen you I could never have forgotten you.'

She swept me a low curtsy, and then, with sudden gravity, 'Allow me to introduce myself, Miss Blanche Longden that was, now Miss Longden.'

I was dumbfounded. The grace, the charm, the self-possession, I could understand, even the fine figure: but not the change in face. Blanche's nose had been rather heavy and shapeless, and now it was daintily cut; the pointed chin was rounded, the oval of the face had filled out, the eyes had surely grown darker, the complexion that had been muddy was now dazzling; but even these extraordinary changes did not account for her beauty. I was lost in wonder.

She laughed in a pleased way at my embarrassment:

'You don't recognise me even now?'

'No,' I confessed ruefully. 'You are altogether changed: even your voice has improved beyond recognition.'

'Let us sit down,' she said, 'and talk, if you have this dance free;' and I sat down, careless whether I was free or not. At last I should get the mystery solved. What did we talk about? At first the usual things. Her sister, I learned, was married and had three children. She was in India now with her husband, and Mrs. Longden, in Brittany, was taking care of the little ones. At last I put my question:

'Why did you go away from Brighton, and never answer my letters?'

'I did answer them. Mother told me she showed you my answer.'

'That was no answer. You have no idea how disappointed and hurt I was; how grieved over your silence.' I could not help being much more intense with this girl than I had any right to be. 'But tell me why you left me so, and I'll forgive you.'

She seemed to consider, and then:

'I don't know; there *was* nothing to be said;' and then, 'You are married, aren't you?' I nodded; she went on: 'I want to know your wife; you must introduce me.'

'With pleasure,' I replied: 'but my answer; you will explain the mystery now.'

'But you must have understood?'

'No; I did not, I assure you, and even now I can't make out why you acted as you did.'

'How strange!' And she laughed, looking away from me. On reflection afterwards, it seemed to me that this laughter of hers was a trifle forced; but I may be mistaken. At the time I didn't remark the false note. 'How strange!' she repeated; and then, with sudden gravity. 'Shall I dot the "is" and cross the "ts" for you, and confess? I wonder will it be good for my soul. The truth is very simple, and yet very hard to tell. I loved you. Oh! as a child, of course, I mean, but with an ideal passion. You never guessed it? I'm glad. Do you know, I think it began that night at the theatre. You won something of the charm of that fatal music that seemed to me the voice of my soul's desire. It transformed me; the tide of it swept through me, and ebbed and flowed in me, and bore me away out upon it till the sweet tears scalded my eyes and made my heart ache. After that my guard broke down before you; the way was open and you took possession of the empty throne. How I loved you! I invested you with every grace and every power; you were the lay figure and I the artist. Forgive me, I don't mean to hurt you; but that's the truth. You brought the wild fresh air of struggle and triumph into our close narrow life, and I made a hero of you, that was all.

'I think I began by pitying you; even in short frocks some of us are mothers. I saw that Mabel didn't love you and was indignant with her.

After seeing her with you my heart has ached for you, and I've gone out of the room hating her make-believe of love and stopped in the hall to talk to your coat. How I used to kiss and stroke it and put my cheek against it and whisper sweet things to it! "Tell him, dear coat," I used to say, "that I love him, and he mustn't be sad or lonely. Tell him—tell him that I love him." I used to believe that unconsciously you must receive some comfort from those assurances.

'Do you remember the dinner when you touched me? I stopped you; I was so glad at heart that I had to pretend to be angry for fear you'd understand. And that afternoon when you kissed me; I provoked it— on purpose? I don't know. I do know that I resisted as long as I could, and when I could resist no longer, *you stopped*. How the passion of shame hurt me then! I thought I should die of it, and then I thought of the sweet unknown affection I had been giving you—all past and at an end—and the tears came. . . . Well, there's my confession. You see now that I could not answer your letters. I had to win back self-respect, and I did.'

There; that's all the story. I know I've told it badly, but I've done my best. What did I say to her? I played the fool. I could find nothing sensible to say; I held my head in my hands and muttered:

'And now?'

'And now,' she repeated, smiling through wet eyes, 'I'm grown up and you're married, and I want to know your wife.'

'And that's all?' I blundered on.

'All?' she said; 'all—and enough too, I should think.' Her voice had changed and grown hard; even as a girl she was quick-tempered: 'Do you know I look at you and can't tell what possessed me, what I could have seen in you? You're not even like the mental picture I had made of you. I don't know how I could have dressed you up in those heroic vestments. When I look at you I wonder at myself. I must really ask your wife what she sees in you. I must—'

At last I came to sense; the beautiful play was over, and I had offended her; but she had gone too far in punishment: the words came to me:

'If you go on hurting me, I shall think you are daring me again.'

The blood surged to the roots of her hair; she rose and took the arm of a man who had just come up, and vanished from my sight; and with her going romance died out of my life, and the grey walls of the ordinary shrank round and hemmed me in for ever.

In the years that have elapsed since, my business instincts have often forced me to try and strike a balance: I was richer by a wonderful memory and poorer by the sense of incalculable loss. Sometimes I try to console myself with the thought that perhaps that is all life holds, even for the luckiest of us.

Kiss Me Again, Stranger
Daphne du Maurier

I looked around for a bit, after leaving the army and before settling down, and then I found myself a job up Hampstead way, in a garage it was, at the bottom of Haverstock Hill near Chalk Farm, and it suited me fine. I'd always been one for tinkering with engines, and in REME that was my work and I was trained to it—it had always come easy to me, anything mechanical.

My idea of having a good time was to lie on my back in my greasy overalls under a car's belly, or a lorry's, with a spanner in my hand, working on some old bolt or screw, with the smell of oil about me, and someone starting up an engine, and the other chaps around clattering their tools and whistling. I never minded the smell or the dirt. As my old Mum used to say when I'd be that way as a kid, mucking about with a grease can, 'It won't hurt him, it's clean dirt,' and so it is, with engines.

The boss at the garage was a good fellow, easy-going, cheerful, and he saw I was keen on my work. He wasn't much of a mechanic himself, so he gave me the repair jobs, which was what I liked.

I didn't live with my old Mum—she was too far off, over Shepperton way, and I saw no point in spending half the day getting to and from my work. I like to be handy, have it on the spot, as it were. So I had a bedroom with a couple called Thompson, only about ten minutes' walk away from the garage. Nice people, they were. He was in the shoe business, cobbler I suppose he'd be called, and Mrs Thompson cooked the meals and kept the house for him over the shop. I used to eat with them, breakfast and supper—we always had a cooked supper—and being the only lodger I was treated as family.

I'm one for routine. I like to get on with my job, and then when the day's work's over settle down to a paper and a smoke and a bit of music on the wireless, variety or something of the sort, and then turn in early. I never had much use for girls, not even when I was doing my time in the army. I was out in the Middle East, too, Port Said and that.

No, I was happy enough living with the Thompsons, carrying on much the same day after day, until that one night, when it happened. Nothing's been the same since. Nor ever will be. I don't know . . .

The Thompsons had gone to see their married daughter up at Highgate. They asked me if I'd like to go along, but somehow I didn't fancy barging in, so instead of staying home alone after leaving the garage I went down to the picture palace, and taking a look at the poster saw it was cowboy and Indian stuff—there was a picture of a cowboy sticking a knife into the Indian's guts. I like that—proper baby I am for westerns—so I paid my one and twopence and went inside. I handed my slip of paper to the usherette and said, 'Back row, please,' because I like sitting far back and leaning my head against the board.

Well, then I saw her. They dress the girls up no end in some of these places, velvet tams and all, making them proper guys. They hadn't made a guy out of this one, though. She had copper hair, page-boy style I think they call it, and blue eyes, the kind that look short-sighted but see further than you think, and go dark by night, nearly black, and her mouth was sulky-looking, as if she was fed up, and it would take someone giving her the world to make her smile. She hadn't freckles, nor a milky skin, but warmer than that, more like a peach, and natural too. She was small and slim, and her velvet coat—blue it was—fitted her close, and the cap on the back of her head showed up her copper hair.

I bought a programme—not that I wanted one, but to delay going in through the curtain—and I said to her, 'What's the picture like?'

She didn't look at me. She just went on staring into nothing, at the opposite wall. 'The knifing's amateur,' she said, 'but you can always sleep.'

I couldn't help laughing. I could see she was serious though. She wasn't trying to have me on or anything.

'That's no advertisement,' I said. 'What if the manager heard you?'

Then she looked at me. She turned those blue eyes in my direction, still fed-up they were, not interested, but there was something in them I'd not seen before, and I've never seen it since, a kind of laziness like someone waking from a long dream and glad to find you there. Cat's eyes have that gleam sometimes, when you stroke them, and they purr and curl themselves into a ball and let you do anything you want. She looked at me this way a moment, and there was a smile lurking somewhere behind her mouth if you gave it a chance, and tearing my slip of paper in half she said, 'I'm not paid to advertise. I'm paid to look like this and lure you inside.'

She drew aside the curtains and flashed her torch in the darkness. I couldn't see a thing. It was pitch black, like it always is at first until you get used to it and begin to make out the shapes of the other people sitting there, but there were two great heads on the screen and some chap saying to the other, 'If you don't come clean I'll put a bullet through you,' and somebody broke a pane of glass and a woman screamed.

'Looks all right to me,' I said, and began groping for somewhere to sit.

She said, 'This isn't the picture, it's the trailer for next week,' and she flicked on her torch and showed me a seat in the back row, one away from the gangway.

I sat through the advertisements and the news reel, and then some chap came and played the organ, and the colours of the curtains over the screen went purple and gold and green—funny, I suppose they think they have to give you your money's worth—and looking around I saw the house was half empty—and I guessed the girl had been right, the big picture wasn't going to be much, and that's why nobody much was there.

Just before the hall went dark again she came sauntering down the aisle. She had a tray of ice-creams, but she didn't even bother to call them out and try and sell them. She could have been walking in her sleep, so when she went up the other aisle I beckoned to her.

'Got a sixpenny one?' I said.

She looked across at me. I might have been something dead under her feet, and then she must have recognized me, because that half-smile came back again, and the lazy look in the eye, and she walked round the back of the seats to me.

'Wafer or cornet?' she said.

I didn't want either, to tell the truth. I just wanted to buy something from her and keep her talking.

'Which do you recommend?' I asked.

She shrugged her shoulders. 'Cornets last longer,' she said, and put one in my hand before I had time to give her my choice.

'How about one for you too?' I said.

'No thanks,' she said, 'I saw them made.'

And she walked off, and the place went dark, and there I was sitting with a great sixpenny cornet in my hand looking a fool. The damn thing slopped all over the edge of the holder, spilling on to my shirt, and I had to ram the frozen stuff into my mouth as quick as I could for fear it would all go on my knees, and I turned sideways, because someone came and sat in the empty seat beside the gangway.

I finished it at last, and cleaned myself up with my pocket handkerchief, and then concentrated on the story flashing across the screen. It was a western all right, carts lumbering over prairies, and a train full of bullion being held to ransom, and the heroine in breeches one moment and full evening dress the next. That's the way pictures should be, not a bit like real life at all; but as I watched the story I began to notice the whiff of scent in the air, and I didn't know what it was or where it came from, but it was there just the same. There was a man to the right of me, and on my left were two empty seats, and it certainly wasn't the people in front, and I couldn't keep turning round and sniffing.

I'm not a great one for liking scent. It's too often cheap and nasty, but this was different. There was nothing stale about it, or stuffy, or strong; it was like the flowers they sell up in the West End in the big flower shops before you get them on the barrows—three bob a bloom sort of touch, rich chaps buy them for actresses and such—and it was so darn good, the smell of it there, in that murky old picture palace full of cigarette smoke, that it nearly drove me mad.

At last I turned right round in my seat, and I spotted where it came from. It came from the girl, the usherette; she was leaning on the back board behind me, her arms folded across it.

'Don't fidget,' she said. 'You're wasting one and twopence. Watch the screen.'

But not out loud, so that anyone could hear. In a whisper, for me alone. I couldn't help laughing to myself. The cheek of it! I knew where the scent came from now, and somehow it made me enjoy the picture more. It was as though she was beside me in one of the empty seats and we were looking at the story together.

When it was over, and the lights went on, I saw I'd sat through the last showing and it was nearly ten. Everyone was clearing off for the night. So I waited a bit, and then she came down with her torch and started squinting under the seats to see if anybody had dropped a glove or a purse, the way they do and only remember about it after-wards when they get home, and she took no more notice of me than if

I'd been a rag which no one would bother to pick up.

I stood up in the back row, alone—the house was clear now—and when she came to me she said, 'Move over, you're blocking the gangway,' and flashed about with her torch, but there was nothing there, only an empty packet of Player's which the cleaners would throw away in the morning. Then she straightened herself and looked me up and down, and taking off the ridiculous cap from the back of her head that suited her so well she fanned herself with it and said, 'Sleeping here tonight?' and then went off, whistling under her breath, and disappeared through the curtains.

It was proper maddening. I'd never been taken so much with a girl in my life. I went into the vestibule after her, but she had gone through a door to the back, behind the box-office place, and the commissionaire chap was already getting the doors to and fixing them for the night. I went out and stood in the street and waited. I felt a bit of a fool, because the odds were that she would come out with a bunch of others, the way girls do. There was the one who had sold me my ticket, and I dare say there were other usherettes up in the balcony, and perhaps a cloak-room attendant too, and they'd all be giggling together, and I wouldn't have the nerve to go up to her.

In a few minutes, though, she came swinging out of the place alone. She had a mac on, belted, and her hands in her pockets, and she had no hat. She walked straight up the street, and she didn't look to right or left of her. I followed, scared that she would turn round and see me off, but she went on walking, fast and direct, staring straight in front of her, and as she moved her copper page-boy hair swung with her shoulders.

Presently she hesitated, then crossed over and stood waiting for a bus. There was a queue of four or five people, so she didn't see me join the queue, and when the bus came she climbed on to it, ahead of the others, and I climbed too, without the slightest notion where it was going, and I couldn't have cared less. Up the stairs she went with me after her, and settled herself in the back seat, yawning, and closed her eyes.

I sat myself down beside her, nervous as a kitten, the point being that I never did that sort of thing as a rule and expected a rocket, and when the conductor stumped up and asked for fares I said,' Two sixpennies, please,' because I reckoned she would never be going the whole distance and this would be bound to cover her fare and mine too.

He raised his eyebrows—they like to think themselves smart, some of these fellows—and he said, 'Look out for the bumps when the driver changes gear. He's only just passed his test.' And he went down the stairs chuckling, telling himself he was no end of a wag, no doubt.

The sound of his voice woke the girl, and she looked at me out of her sleepy eyes, and looked too at the tickets in my hand—she must have seen by the colour they were sixpennies—and she smiled, the first real smile I had got out of her that evening, and said without any sort of surprise, 'Hullo, stranger.'

I took out a cigarette, to put myself at ease, and offered her one, but she wouldn't take it. She just closed her eyes again, to settle herself to sleep. Then, seeing there was no one else to notice up on the top deck, only an Air Force chap in the front slopped over a newspaper, I put out my hand and pulled her head down on my shoulder, and got my arm round her, snug and comfortable, thinking of course she'd throw it off and blast me to hell. She didn't though. She gave a sort of laugh to herself, and settled down like as if she might have been in an armchair, and she said, 'It's not every night I get a free ride and a free pillow. Wake me at the bottom of the hill, before we get to the cemetery.'

I didn't know what hill she meant, or what cemetery, but I wasn't going to wake her, not me. I had paid for two sixpennies, and I was darn well going to get value for my money.

So we sat there together, jogging along in the bus, very close and very pleasant, and I thought to myself that it was a lot more fun than sitting at home in the bed-sit reading the football news, or spending an evening up Highgate at Mr and Mrs Thompson's daughter's place.

Presently I got more daring, and let my head lean against hers, and tightened up my arm a bit, not too obvious-like, but nicely. Anyone coming up the stairs to the top deck would have taken us for a courting couple.

Then, after we had had about fourpenny-worth, I got anxious. The old bus wouldn't be turning round and going back again, when we reached the sixpenny limit; it would pack up for the night, we'd have come to the terminus. And there we'd be, the girl and I, stuck out somewhere at the back of beyond, with no return bus, and I'd got about six bob in my pocket and no more. Six bob would never pay for a taxi, not with a tip and all. Besides, there probably wouldn't be any taxis going.

What a fool I'd been not to come out with more money. It was silly, perhaps, to let it worry me, but I'd acted on impulse right from the start, and if only I'd known how the evening was going to turn out I'd have had my wallet filled. It wasn't often I went out with a girl, and I hate a fellow who can't do the thing in style. Proper slap-up do at a Corner House—they're good these days with that help-yourself service—and if she had a fancy for something stronger than coffee or orangeade, well, of course as late as this it wasn't much use, but nearer home I knew where to go. There was a pub where my boss went, and you paid for your gin and kept it there, and could go in and have a drink from your bottle when you felt like it. They have the same sort of racket at the posh night clubs up West, I'm told, but they make you pay through the nose for it.

Anyway, here I was riding a bus to the Lord knows where, with my girl beside me—I called her 'my girl' just as if she really was and we were courting—and bless me if I had the money to take her home. I began to fidget about, from sheer nerves, and I fumbled in one pocket after another, in case by a piece of luck I should come across a half-crown, or even a ten-bob note I had forgotten all about, and I suppose I disturbed her with all this, because she suddenly pulled my ear and said, 'Stop rocking the boat.'

Well, I mean to say . . . It just got me. I can't explain why. She held my ear a moment before she pulled it, like as though she were feeling the skin and liked it, and then she just gave it a lazy tug. It's the kind of thing anyone would do to a child, and the way she said it, as if she had known me for years and we were out picnicking together, 'Stop rocking the boat.' Chummy, matey, yet better than either.

'Look here,' I said, 'I'm awfully sorry, I've been and done a darn silly thing. I took tickets to the terminus because I wanted to sit beside you, and when we get there we'll be turned out of the bus, and it will be miles from anywhere, and I've only got six bob in my pocket.'

'You've got legs, haven't you?' she said.

'What d'you mean, I've got legs?'

'They're meant to walk on. Mine were,' she answered.

Then I knew it didn't matter, and she wasn't angry either, and the evening was going to be all right. I cheered up in a second, and gave her a squeeze, just to show I appreciated her being such a sport—most girls would have torn me to shreds—and I said, 'We haven't passed a cemetery, as far as I know. Does it matter very much?'

'Oh, there'll be others,' she said. 'I'm not particular.'

I didn't know what to make of that. I thought she wanted to get out at the cemetery stopping point because it was her nearest stop for home, like the way you say, 'Put me down at Woolworth's' if you live handy. I puzzled over it for a bit, and then I said, 'How do you mean, there'll be others? It's not a thing you see often along a bus route.'

'I was speaking in general terms,' she answered. 'Don't bother to talk, I like you silent best.'

It wasn't a slap on the face, the way she said it. Fact was, I knew what she meant. Talking's all very pleasant with people like Mr and Mrs Thompson, over supper, and you say how the day has gone, and one of you reads a bit out of the paper, and the other says, 'Fancy, there now,' and so it goes on, in bits and pieces, until one of you yawns, and somebody says, 'Who's for bed?' Or it's nice enough with a chap like the boss, having a cuppa mid-morning, or about three when there's nothing doing, 'I'll tell you what I think, those blokes in the government are making a mess of things, no better than the last lot,' and then we'll be interrupted with someone coming to fill up with petrol. And I like talking to my old Mum when I go and see her, which I don't do often enough, and she tells me how she spanked my bottom when I was a kid, and I sit on the kitchen table like I did then, and she bakes rock cakes and gives me peel, saying, 'You always were one for peel.' That's talk, that's conversation.

But I didn't want to talk to my girl. I just wanted to keep my arm round her the way I was doing, and rest my chin against her head, and that's what she meant when she said she liked me silent. I liked it too.

One last thing bothered me a bit, and that was whether I could kiss her before the bus stopped and we were turned out at the terminus. I mean, putting an arm round a girl is one thing, and kissing her is another. It takes a little time as a rule to warm up. You start off with a long evening ahead of you, and by the time you've been to a picture or a concert, and then had something to eat and to drink, well, you've got yourselves acquainted, and it's the usual thing to end up with a bit of kissing and a cuddle, the girls expect it. Truth to tell, I was never much of a one for kissing. There was a girl I walked out with back home, before I went into the army, and she was quite a good sort. I liked her. But her teeth were a bit prominent, and even if you shut your eyes and tried to forget who it was you were kissing, well, you knew it was her, and there was nothing to it. Good old Doris from next door. But the opposite kind are even worse, the ones that grab you and nearly eat you. You come across plenty of them, when you're in uniform. They're much too eager, and they muss you about, and you get the feeling they can't wait for a chap to get busy about them. I don't mind saying it used to make me sick. Put me dead off, and that's a fact. I suppose I was born fussy. I don't know.

But now, this evening in the bus, it was all quite different. I don't know what it was about the girl—the sleepy eyes, and the copper hair, and somehow not seeming to care if I was there yet liking me at the same time; I hadn't found anything like this before. So I said to myself, 'Now, shall I risk it, or shall I wait?' and I knew, from the way the driver was going and the conductor was whistling below and saying 'goodnight' to the people getting off, that the final stop couldn't be far away; and my heart began to thump under my coat, and my neck grew hot below the collar—darn silly, only a kiss you know, she couldn't kill me—and then . . . It was like diving off a spring-board. I thought, 'Here goes,' and I bent down, and turned her face to me, and lifted her chin with my hand, and kissed her good and proper.

Well, if I was poetical, I'd say what happened then was a revelation. But I'm not poetical, and I can only say that she kissed me back, and it lasted a long time, and it wasn't a bit like Doris.

Then the bus stopped with a jerk, and the conductor called out in a sing-song voice, 'All out, please.' Frankly, I could have wrung his neck.

She gave me a kick on the ankle. 'Come on, move,' she said, and I stumbled from my seat and racketed down the stairs, she following behind, and there we were, standing in a street. It was beginning to rain too, not badly but just enough to make you notice and want to turn up the collar of your coat, and we were right at the end of a great wide street, with deserted unlighted shops on either side, the end of the world it looked to me, and sure enough there was a hill over to the left, and at the bottom of the hill a cemetery. I could see the railings and the white tombstones behind, and it stretched a long way, nearly half-way up the hill. There were acres of it.

'God darn it,' I said, 'is this the place you meant?'

'Could be,' she said, looking over her shoulder vaguely, and then she took my arm. 'What about a cup of coffee first?' she said.

First . . .? I wondered if she meant before the long trudge home, or was this home? It didn't really matter. It wasn't much after eleven. And I could do with a cup of coffee, and a sandwich too. There was a stall across the road, and they hadn't shut up shop.

We walked over to it, and the driver was there too, and the

conductor, and the Air Force fellow who had been up in front on the top deck. They were ordering cups of tea and sandwiches, and we had the same, only coffee. They cut them tasty at the stalls, the sandwiches, I've noticed it before, nothing stingy about it, good slices of ham between thick white bread, and the coffee is piping hot, full cups too, good value, and I thought to myself 'Six bob will see this lot all right.'

I noticed my girl looking at the Air Force chap, sort of thoughtful-like, as though she might have seen him before, and he looked at her too. I couldn't blame him for that. I didn't mind either; when you're out with a girl it gives you a kind of pride if other chaps notice her. And you couldn't miss this one. Not my girl.

Then she turned her back on him, deliberate, and leant with her elbows on the stall, sipping her hot coffee, and I stood beside her doing the same. We weren't stuck up or anything, we were pleasant and polite enough, saying good evening all round, but anyone could tell that we were together, the girl and I, we were on our own. I liked that. Funny, it did something to me inside, gave me a protective feeling. For all they knew we might have been a married couple on our way home.

They were chaffing a bit, the other three and the chap serving the sandwiches and tea, but we didn't join in.

'You want to watch out, in that uniform,' said the conductor to the Air Force fellow, 'or you'll end up like those others. It's late too, to be out on your own.'

They all started laughing. I didn't quite see the point, but I supposed it was a joke.

'I've been awake a long time,' said the Air Force fellow. 'I know a bad lot when I see one.'

'That's what the others said, I shouldn't wonder,' remarked the driver, 'and we know what happened to them. Makes you shudder. But why pick on the Air Force, that's what I want to know?'

'It's the colour of our uniform,' said the fellow. 'You can spot it in the dark.'

They went on laughing in that way. I lighted up a cigarette, but my girl wouldn't have one.

'I blame the war for all that's gone wrong with the women,' said the coffee-stall bloke, wiping a cup and hanging it up behind. 'Turned a lot of them barmy, in my opinion. They don't know the difference between right or wrong.'

' 'Tisn't that, it's sport that's the trouble,' said the conductor. 'Develops their muscles and that, what weren't never meant to be developed. Take my two youngsters, f'r instance. The girl can knock the boy down any time, she's a proper little bully. Makes you think.'

'That's right,' agreed the driver, 'equality of the sexes, they call it, don't they? It's the vote that did it. We ought never to have given them the vote.'

'Garn,' said the Air Force chap, 'giving them the vote didn't turn the women barmy. They've always been the same, under the skin. The people out East know how to treat 'em. They keep 'em shut up, out there. That's the answer. Then you don't get any trouble.'

'I don't know what my old woman would say if I tried to shut her up,' said the driver. And they all started laughing again.

My girl plucked at my sleeve and I saw she had finished her coffee. She motioned with her head towards the street.

'Want to go home?' I said.

Silly. I somehow wanted the others to believe we were going home. She didn't answer. She just went striding off, her hands in the pockets of her mac. I said goodnight, and followed her, but not before I noticed the Air Force fellow staring after her over his cup of tea.

She walked off along the street, and it was still raining, dreary somehow, made you want to be sitting over a fire somewhere snug, and when she had crossed the street, and had come to the railings outside the cemetery she stopped, and looked up at me, and smiled.

'What now?' I said.

'Tombstones are flat,' she said, 'sometimes.'

'What if they are?' I asked, bewildered-like.

'You can lie down on them,' she said.

She turned and strolled along, looking at the railings, and then she came to one that was bent wide, and the next beside it broken, and she glanced up at me and smiled again.

'It's always the same,' she said. 'You're bound to find a gap if you look long enough.'

She was through that gap in the railings as quick as a knife through butter. You could have knocked me flat.

'Here, hold on,' I said, 'I'm not as small as you.'

But she was off and away, wandering among the graves. I got through the gap, puffing and blowing a bit, and then I looked around, and bless me if she wasn't lying on a long flat gravestone, with her arms under her head and her eyes closed.

Well, I wasn't expecting anything. I mean, it had been in my mind to see her home and that. Date her up for the next evening. Of course, seeing as it was late, we could have stopped a bit when we came to the doorway of her place. She needn't have gone in right away. But lying there on the gravestone wasn't hardly natural.

I sat down, and took her hand.

'You'll get wet lying there,' I said. Feeble, but I didn't know what else to say.

'I'm used to that,' she said.

She opened her eyes and looked at me. There was a street light not far away, outside the railings, so it wasn't all that dark, and anyway in spite of the rain the night wasn't pitch black, more murky somehow. I wish I knew how to tell about her eyes, but I'm not one for fancy talk. You know how a luminous watch shines in the dark. I've got one myself. When you wake up in the night, there it is on your wrist, like a friend. Somehow my girl's eyes shone like that, but they were lovely too. And they weren't lazy cat's eyes any more. They were loving and gentle, and they were sad, too, all at the same time.

'Used to lying in the rain?' I said.

'Brought up to it,' she answered. 'They gave us a name in the shelters. The dead-end kids, they used to call us, in the war days.'

'Weren't you never evacuated?' I asked.

'Not me,' she said. 'I never could stop any place. I always came back.'

'Parents living?'

'No. Both of them killed by the bomb that smashed my home.' She didn't speak tragic-like. Just ordinary.

'Bad luck,' I said.

She didn't answer that one. And I sat there, holding her hand, wanting to take her home.

'You been on your job some time, at the picture-house?' I asked.

'About three weeks,' she said. 'I don't stop anywhere long. I'll be moving on again soon.'

'Why's that?'

'Restless,' she said.

She put up her hands suddenly and took my face and held it. It was gentle the way she did it, not as you'd think.

'You've got a good kind face. I like it,' she said to me.

It was queer. The way she said it made me feel daft and soft, not sort of excited like I had been in the bus, and I thought to myself, well, maybe this is it, I've found a girl at last I really want. But not for an evening, casual. For going steady.

'Got a bloke?' I asked.

'No,' she said.

'I mean, regular.'

'No, never.'

It was a funny line of talk to be having in a cemetery, and she lying there like some figure carved on the old tombstone.

'I haven't got a girl either,' I said. 'Never think about it, the way other chaps do. Faddy, I guess. And then I'm keen on my job. Work in a garage, mechanic you know, repairs, anything that's going. Good pay. I've saved a bit, besides what I send my old Mum. I live in digs. Nice people, Mr and Mrs Thompson, and my boss at the garage is a nice chap too. I've never been lonely, and I'm not lonely now. But since I've seen you, it's made me think. You know, it's not going to be the same any more.'

She never interrupted once, and somehow it was like speaking my thoughts aloud.

'Going home to the Thompsons is all very pleasant and nice,' I said, 'and you couldn't wish for kinder people. Good grub too, and we chat a bit after supper, and listen to the wireless. But d'you know, what I want now is different. I want to come along and fetch you from the cinema, when the programme's over, and you'd be standing there by the curtains, seeing the people out, and you'd give me a bit of a wink to show me you'd be going through to change your clothes and I could wait for you. And then you'd come out into the street, like you did tonight, but you wouldn't go off on your own, you'd take my arm, and if you didn't want to wear your coat I'd carry it for you, or a parcel maybe, or whatever you had. Then we'd go off to the Corner House or some place for supper, handy. We'd have a table reserved—they'd know us, the waitresses and them; they'd keep back something special, just for us.'

I could picture it too, clear as anything. The table with the ticket on 'Reserved'. The waitress nodding at us, 'Got curried eggs tonight.' And we going through to get our trays, and my girl acting like she didn't know me, and me laughing to myself.

'D'you see what I mean?' I said to her. 'It's not just being friends, it's more than that.'

I don't know if she heard. She lay there looking up at me, touching my ear and my chin in that funny, gentle way. You'd say she was sorry for me.

'I'd like to buy you things,' I said, 'flowers sometimes. It's nice to see a girl with a flower tucked in her dress, it looks clean and fresh. And for special occasions, birthdays, Christmas, and that, something you'd seen in a shop window, and wanted, but hadn't liked to go in and ask the price. A brooch perhaps, or a bracelet, something pretty. And I'd go in and get it when you weren't with me, and it'd cost much more than my week's pay, but I wouldn't mind.'

I could see the expression on her face, opening the parcel. And she'd put it on, what I'd bought, and we'd go out together, and she'd be dressed up a bit for the purpose, nothing glaring I don't mean, but something that took the eye. You know, saucy.

'It's not fair to talk about getting married,' I said, 'not in these days, when everything's uncertain. A fellow doesn't mind the uncertainty, but it's hard on a girl. Cooped up in a couple of rooms maybe, and queueing and rations and all. They like their freedom, and being in a job, and not being tied down, the same as us. But it's nonsense the way they were talking back in the coffee stall just now. About girls not being the same as in the old days, and the war to blame. As for the way they treat them out East—I've seen some of it. I suppose that fellow meant to be funny, they're all smart Alicks in the Air Force, but it was a silly line of talk, I thought.'

She dropped her hands to her side and closed her eyes. I was getting quite wet there on the tombstone. I was worried for her, though she had her mac of course, but her legs and feet were damp in her thin stockings and shoes.

'You weren't ever in the Air Force, were you?' she said.

Queer. Her voice had gone quite hard. Sharp, and different. Like as if she was anxious about something, scared even.

'Not me,' I said, 'I served my time with REME. Proper lot they were. No swank, no nonsense. You know where you are with them.'

'I'm glad,' she said. 'You're good and kind. I'm glad.'

I wondered if she'd known some fellow in the RAF who had let her down. They're a wild crowd, the ones I've come across. And I remembered the way she'd looked at the boy drinking his tea at the stall. Reflective, somehow. As if she was thinking back. I couldn't expect her not to have been around a bit, with her looks, and then brought up to play about the shelters, without parents, like she said. But I didn't want to think of her being hurt by anyone.

'Why, what's wrong with them?' I said. 'What's the RAF done to you?'

'They smashed my home,' she said.

'That was the Germans, not our fellows.'

'It's all the same, they're killers, aren't they?' she said.

I looked down at her, lying on the tombstone, and her voice wasn't hard any more, like when she'd asked me if I'd been in the Air Force, but it was tired, and sad, and oddly lonely, and it did something queer to my stomach, right in the pit of it, so that I wanted to do the darndest silliest thing and take her home with me, back to where I lived with Mr and Mrs Thompson, and say to Mrs Thompson—she was a kind old soul, she wouldn't mind—'Look, this is my girl. Look after her.' Then I'd know she'd be safe, she'd be all right, nobody could do anything to hurt her. That was the thing I was afraid of suddenly, that someone would come along and hurt my girl.

I bent down and put my arms round her and lifted her up close.

'Listen,' I said, 'it's raining hard. I'm going to take you home. You'll catch your death, lying here on the wet stone.'

'No,' she said, her hands on my shoulders, 'nobody ever sees me home. You're going back where you belong, alone.'

'I won't leave you here,' I said.

'Yes, that's what I want you to do. If you refuse I shall be angry. You wouldn't want that, would you?'

I stared at her, puzzled. And her face was queer in the murky old light there, whiter than before, but it was beautiful, Jesus Christ, it was beautiful. That's blasphemy. But I can't say it no other way.

'What do you want me to do?' I asked.

'I want you to go and leave me here, and not look back,' she said, 'like someone dreaming, sleep-walking, they call it. Go back walking through the rain. It will take you hours. It doesn't matter, you're young and strong and you've got long legs. Go back to your room, wherever it is, and get into bed, and go to sleep, and wake and have your breakfast in the morning, and go off to work, the same as you always do.'

'What about you?'

'Never mind about me. Just go.'

'Can I call for you at the cinema tomorrow night? Can it be like what I was telling you, you know . . . going steady?'

She didn't answer. She only smiled. She sat quite still, looking in my face, and then she closed her eyes and threw back her head and said, 'Kiss me again, stranger.'

I left her, like she said. I didn't look back. I climbed through the railings of the cemetery, out on to the road. No one seemed to be about, and the coffee stall by the bus stop had closed down, the boards were up.

I started walking the way the bus had brought us. The road was straight, going on for ever. A High Street it must have been. There were shops on either side, and it was right away north-east of London, nowhere I'd ever been before. I was proper lost, but it didn't seem to matter. I felt like a sleep-walker, just as she said.

I kept thinking of her all the time. There was nothing else, only her face in front of me as I walked. They had a word for it in the army, when a girl gets a fellow that way, so he can't see straight or hear right or know what he's doing; and I thought it a lot of cock, or it only happened to drunks, and now I knew it was true and it had happened to me. I wasn't going to worry any more about how she'd get home; she'd told me not to, and she must have lived handy, she'd never have ridden out so far else, though it was funny living such a way from her work. But maybe in time she'd tell me more, bit by bit. I wouldn't drag it from her. I had one thing fixed in my mind, and that was to pick her up the next evening from the picture palace. It was firm and set, and nothing would budge me from that. The hours in between would just be a blank for me until ten p.m. came round.

I went on walking in the rain, and presently a lorry came along and I thumbed a lift, and the driver took me a good part of the way before he had to turn left in the other direction, and so I got down and walked again, and it must have been close on three when I got home.

I would have felt bad, in an ordinary way, knocking up Mr Thompson to let me in, and it had never happened before either, but I was all lit up inside from loving my girl, and I didn't seem to mind. He came down at last and opened the door. I had to ring several times before he heard, and there he was, grey with sleep, poor old chap, his pyjamas all crumpled from the bed.

'Whatever happened to you?' he said. 'We've been worried, the wife and me. We thought you'd been knocked down, run over. We came back here and found the house empty and your supper not touched.'

'I went to the pictures,' I said.

'The pictures?' He stared up at me, in the passage-way. 'The pictures stop at ten o'clock.'

'I know,' I said, 'I went walking after that. Sorry. Goodnight.'

And I climbed up the stairs to my room, leaving the old chap muttering to himself and bolting the door, and I heard Mrs Thompson calling from her bedroom, 'What is it? Is it him? Is he come home?'

I'd put them to trouble and to worry, and I ought to have gone in there and then and apologized, but I couldn't somehow, it wouldn't have come right; so I shut my door and threw off my clothes and got into bed, and it was like as if she was with me still, my girl, in the darkness.

They were a bit quiet at breakfast the next morning, Mr and Mrs Thompson. They didn't look at me. Mrs Thompson gave me my kipper without a word, and he went on looking at his newspaper.

I ate my breakfast, and then I said, 'I hope you had a nice evening up at Highgate?' and Mrs Thompson, with her mouth a bit tight, she said, 'Very pleasant, thank you, we were home by ten,' and she gave a little sniff and poured Mr Thompson out another cup of tea.

We went on being quiet, no one saying a word, and then Mrs Thompson said, 'Will you be in to supper this evening?' and I said, 'No, I don't think so. I'm meeting a friend,' and then I saw the old chap look at me over his spectacles.

'If you're going to be late,' he said, 'we'd best take the key for you.'

Then he went on reading his paper. You could tell they were proper hurt that I didn't tell them anything, or say where I was going.

I went off to work, and we were busy at the garage that day, one job after the other came along, and any other time I wouldn't have minded. I liked a full day and often worked overtime, but today I wanted to get away before the shops closed; I hadn't thought about anything else since the idea came into my head.

It was getting on for half past four, and the boss came to me and said, 'I promised the doctor he'd have his Austin this evening, I said you'd be through with it by seven-thirty. That's OK, isn't it?'

My heart sank. I'd counted on getting off early, because of what I wanted to do. Then I thought quickly that if the boss let me off now, and I went out to the shop before it closed, and came back again to do the job on the Austin, it would be all right, so I said, 'I don't mind working a bit of overtime, but I'd like to slip out now, for half an hour, if you're going to be here. There's something I want to buy before the shops shut.'

He told me that suited him, so I took off my overalls and washed and got my coat and I went off to the line of shops down at the bottom of Haverstock Hill. I knew the one I wanted. It was a jeweller's, where

Mr Thompson used to take his clock to be repaired, and it wasn't a place where they sold trash at all, but good stuff, solid silver frames and that, and cutlery.

There were rings, of course, and a few fancy bangles, but I didn't like the look of them. All the girls in the NAAFI used to wear bangles with charms on them, quite common it was, and I went on staring in at the window and then I spotted it, right at the back.

It was a brooch. Quite small, not much bigger than your thumbnail, but with a nice blue stone on it and a pin at the back, and it was shaped like a heart. That was what got me, the shape. I stared at it a bit, and there wasn't a ticket to it, which meant it would cost a bit, but I went in and asked to have a look at it. The jeweller got it out of the window for me, and he gave it a bit of a polish and turned it this way and that, and I saw it pinned on my girl, showing up nice on her frock or her jumper, and I knew this was it.

'I'll take it,' I said, and then asked him the price.

I swallowed a bit when he told me, but I took out my wallet and counted the notes, and he put the heart in a box wrapped up careful with cotton wool, and made a neat package of it, tied with fancy string. I knew I'd have to get an advance from the boss before I went off work that evening, but he was a good chap and I was certain he'd give it to me.

I stood outside the jeweller's, with the packet for my girl safe in my breast pocket, and I heard the church clock strike a quarter to five. There was time to slip down to the cinema and make sure she understood about the date for the evening, and then I'd beat it fast up the road and get back to the garage, and I'd have the Austin done by the time the doctor wanted it.

When I got to the cinema my heart was beating like a sledge-hammer and I could hardly swallow. I kept picturing to myself how she'd look, standing there by the curtains going in, with the velvet jacket and the cap on the back of her head.

There was a bit of a queue outside, and I saw they'd changed the programme. The poster of the western had gone, with the cowboy throwing a knife in the Indian's guts, and they had instead a lot of girls dancing, and some chap prancing in front of them with a walking-stick. It was a musical.

I went in, and didn't go near the box office but looked straight to the curtains, where she'd be. There was an usherette there all right, but it wasn't her. This was a great tall girl, who looked silly in the clothes, and she was trying to do two things at once — tear off the slips of tickets as the people went past, and hang on to her torch at the same time.

I waited a moment. Perhaps they'd switched over positions and my girl had gone up to the circle. When the last lot had got in through the curtains and there was a pause and she was free, I went up to her and I said, 'Excuse me, do you know where I could have a word with the other young lady?'

She looked at me. 'What other young lady?'

'The one who was here last night, with copper hair,' I said.

She looked at me closer then, suspicious-like.

'She hasn't shown up today,' she said. 'I'm taking her place.'

'Not shown up?'

'No. And it's funny you should ask. You're not the only one. The police was here not long ago. They had a word with the manager, and the commissionaire too, and no one's said anything to me yet, but I think there's been trouble.'

My heart beat different then. Not excited, bad. Like when someone's ill, took to hospital, sudden.

'The police?' I said. 'What were they here for?'

'I told you, I don't know,' she answered, 'but it was something to do with her, and the manager went with them to the police station, and he hasn't come back yet. This way, please, circle on the left, stalls to the right.'

I just stood there, not knowing what to do. It was like as if the floor had been knocked away from under me.

The tall girl tore another slip off a ticket and then she said to me, over her shoulder, 'Was she a friend of yours?'

'Sort of,' I said. I didn't know what to say.

'Well, if you ask me, she was queer in the head, and it wouldn't surprise me if she'd done away with herself and they'd found her dead. No, ice-creams served in the interval, after the news reel.'

I went out and stood in the street. The queue was growing for the cheaper seats, and there were children too, talking, excited. I brushed past them and started walking up the street, and I felt sick inside, queer. Something had happened to my girl. I knew it now. That was why she had wanted to get rid of me last night, and for me not to see her home. She was going to do herself in, there in the cemetery. That's why she talked funny and looked so white, and now they'd found her, lying there on the gravestone by the railings.

If I hadn't gone away and left her she'd have been all right. If I'd stayed with her just five minutes longer, coaxing her, I'd have got her round to my way of thinking and seen her home, standing no nonsense, and she'd be at the picture palace now, showing the people to their seats.

It might be it wasn't as bad as what I feared. It might be she was found wandering, lost her memory and got picked up by the police and taken off, and then they found out where she worked and that, and now the police wanted to check up with the manager at the cinema to see if it was so. If I went down to the police station and asked them there, maybe they'd tell me what had happened, and I could say she was my girl, we were walking out, and it wouldn't matter if she didn't recognize me even, I'd stick to the story. I couldn't let down my boss, I had to get that job done on the Austin, but afterwards, when I'd finished, I could go down to the police station.

All the heart had gone out of me, and I went back to the garage hardly knowing what I was doing, and for the first time ever the smell of the place turned my stomach, the oil and the grease, and there was a chap roaring up his engine, before backing out his car, and a great cloud of smoke coming from his exhaust, filling the workshop with stink.

I went and got my overalls, and put them on, and fetched the tools, and started on the Austin, and all the time I was wondering what it was that had happened to my girl, if she was down at the police station, lost and lonely, or if she was lying somewhere . . . dead. I kept seeing her face all the time like it was last night.

It took me an hour and a half, not more, to get the Austin ready for the road, filled up with petrol and all, and I had her facing outwards to the street for the owner to drive out, but I was all in by then, dead tired, and the sweat pouring down my face. I had a bit of a wash and put on my coat, and I felt the package in the breast pocket. I took it out and looked at it, done so neat with the fancy ribbon, and I put it back again, and I hadn't noticed the boss come in—I was standing with my back to the door.

'Did you get what you wanted?' he said, cheerful-like and smiling.

He was a good chap, never out of temper, and we got along well.

'Yes,' I said.

But I didn't want to talk about it. I told him the job was done and the Austin was ready to drive away. I went to the office with him so that he could note down the work done, and the overtime, and he offered me a fag from the packet lying on his desk beside the evening paper.

'I see Lady Luck won the three-thirty,' he said. 'I'm a couple of quid up this week.'

He was entering my work in his ledger, to keep the pay-roll right.

'Good for you,' I said.

'Only backed it for a place, like a clot,' he said. 'She was twenty-five to one. Still, it's all in the game.'

I didn't answer. I'm not one for drinking, but I needed one bad, just then. I mopped my forehead with my handkerchief. I wished he'd get on with the figures, and say goodnight, and let me go.

'Another poor devil's had it,' he said. 'That's the third now in three weeks, ripped right up the guts, same as the others. He died in hospital this morning. Looks like there's a hoodoo on the RAF.'

'What was it, flying jets?' I asked.

'Jets?' he said. 'No, damn it, murder. Sliced up the belly, poor sod. Don't you ever read the papers? It's the third one in three weeks, done identical, all Air Force fellows, and each time they've found 'em near a graveyard or a cemetery. I was saying just now, to that chap who came in for petrol, it's not only men who go off their rockers and turn sex maniacs, but women too. They'll get this one all right though, you see. It says in the paper they've a line on her, and expect an arrest shortly. About time too, before another poor blighter cops it.'

He shut up his ledger and stuck his pencil behind his ear.

'Like a drink?' he said. 'I've got a bottle of gin in the cupboard.'

'No,' I said, 'no, thanks very much. I've . . . I've got a date.'

'That's right,' he said, smiling, 'enjoy yourself.'

I walked down the street and bought an evening paper. It was like what he said about the murder. They had it on the front page. They said it must have happened about two a.m. Young fellow in the Air Force, in north-east London. He had managed to stagger to a call-box and get through to the police, and they found him there on the floor of the box when they arrived.

He made a statement in the ambulance before he died. He said a girl called to him, and he followed her, and he thought it was just a bit of love-making—he'd seen her with another fellow drinking coffee at the stall a little while before—and he thought she'd thrown this other fellow over and had taken a fancy to him, and then she got him, he said, right in the guts.

It said in the paper that he had given the police a full description of her, and it said also that the police would be glad if the man who had been seen with the girl earlier in the evening would come forward to help in identification.

I didn't want the paper any more. I threw it away. I walked about the streets till I was tired, and when I guessed Mr and Mrs Thompson had gone to bed I went home, and groped for the key they'd left on a piece of string hanging inside the letterbox, and I let myself in and went upstairs to my room.

Mrs Thompson had turned down the bed and put a thermos of tea for me, thoughtful-like, and the evening paper, the late edition.

They'd got her. About three o'clock in the afternoon. I didn't read the writing, nor the name or anything. I sat down on my bed, and took up the paper, and there was my girl staring up at me from the front page.

Then I took the package from my coat and undid it, and threw away the wrapper and the fancy string, and sat there looking down at the little heart I held in my hand.

When Love Isn't Enough
Stella Whitelaw

The girl came timidly into the hairdressing salon. She stopped, just inside the entrance, obviously self-conscious in her badly-fitting, mud-coloured coat, her long, brown hair hanging limply round her shoulders.

Janice walked briskly out of her office into the salon, just in time to see the girl wavering on the verge of escape. She called over to one of the juniors.

'How many times must I tell you about incoming clients! Take their coats at once, then seat them at the shampoo counter. Don't ignore them! Make them feel welcome! It's most important.'

'Yes, Miss Prescott. Sorry, Miss Prescott.'

Janice ran a well-manicured finger down the appointments list. Yes, this mud-coloured girl was for her. A Miss Marlowe. That was a new name. Every week brought a few more clients. It was very satisfying. When the holiday trade started they would have to stay open late in the evenings. . . .

The girl was brought over to her, her head swathed in a soft towel. Janice took a comb and scissors out of the pocket of her lilac smock, unwound the towel and combed a few strands tentatively.

'How would you like your hair done?' she enquired.

'I don't know, really.' The girl was nervous. 'I always look so awful . . . I don't care what you do with it!'

Janice lifted a long strand experimentally and looked at the girl's face in the mirror. She could not help looking at herself at the same time. What a contrast! Her new, ash-mink rinse was stunning, perfect with her English rose colouring. She looked again at the mouse who sat so unhappily in front of the mirror as if she were waiting at the dentist's. . . .

'It ought to be cut,' Janice said firmly. 'You've got split ends. And

[122]

it'll give your hair more body. Perhaps we could get rid of this centre parting. It's not fashionable now. . . .'

'Anything,' the girl said desperately. 'Anything to make me look different!'

Miss Marlowe watched silently as Janice snipped away at the wet hair. 'It's terribly important to me,' she began to say.

Janice smothered a sigh. She knew what was coming. But it was part of her job to listen sympathetically. Clients liked to talk.

'You see,' the girl went on, 'I've got to make someone notice me.'

'A boyfriend?' Janice pulled the setting trolley towards her and began to roll up the hair with quick, neat movements.

The girl flushed. 'No. I wish he was! He's my boss. He's marvellous. But he's engaged to this awful woman.'

Janice raised a beautifully arched eye-brow. 'Aren't you wasting your time, then, if he's going to be married?'

'I don't think they'll ever get married. She doesn't really love him,' Miss Marlowe said with conviction. 'She treats him so badly. Breaks dates, keeps him waiting. Treats him like a servant. She's just so selfish! I've heard them have terrible arguments on the telephone, but he's much too kind a person to break it off, even though she's making him miserable.'

'Perhaps he likes being miserable.'

'Oh, no!' The girl looked shocked. 'Surely being in love should make you happy?'

She's in love with him herself, thought Janice, slipping the last clip into place. She patted the bristling, rollered head. 'Number four drier for Miss Marlowe,' she said to the junior waiting at her side with net and ear-pads.

Janice went back to her tiny office and poured herself some coffee from her electric percolator. She seemed to live on coffee. She picked up a sheaf of sketches. She had to decide on the styles they would demonstrate at the new Spa Hotel on Saturday evening. There was a school-leaver coming for an interview later on and there was still a pile of invoices to check. There seemed no end to the work she had to do.

Janice sighed. It was no good. She would have to put Tony off and take the invoices home to her flat to do.

Her coffee grew cold as she went through the drawings, and made a list of equipment to take over to the hotel. Perhaps Tony wouldn't mind helping her move it on Saturday in his car.

She was only half listening as she rolled up her next client's hair. There were so many things to think about in running her own business. For three years now she'd been running it, and she reckoned she'd done pretty well for a girl who'd left school with only 'O' levels. First her training, then gaining experience in different salons, all leading to the moment when she felt she was ready to launch into business on her own.

'But it's too big a risk,' Tony had said, when she had told him about the old, odd-shaped empty shop at the end of the promenade. 'You'll be bankrupt in six months.'

'I'm determined to have a real career,' said Janice, who had already decided. 'This is my chance.'

'Miss Marlowe is dry now, Miss Prescott.'

'Thank you, June. Put Mrs. Nichols under six, please.'

Miss Marlowe sat sipping coffee, her cheeks pink and shiny, her unpinned hair bobbing round her head in stiff, fat curls. 'Will it really look all right?' she asked anxiously.

'Of course,' said Janice, taking two clean brushes out of the sterilising cabinet. 'Wait and see. You'll knock spots off his other woman.'

'Oh no, I couldn't compete with her. Not with her looks! She's terribly glamorous!'

'You've seen her, then?'

'Only once, quite briefly, when she was getting into his car. Her hair's a gorgeous golden-red, piled into complicated curls. She's really stunning.'

Janice paused in her brushing and caught her own startled eyes in the mirror. The reflected face stared back as if she were a stranger. Behind, vaguely, the white salon—the assistants in lilac, the juniors in pale yellow, the delicate colours fluttering in the mirror like a bank of sweet peas. . . .

Miss Marlowe's voice came back to her '. . . he's never really noticed me. It's just "Good morning, Miss Marlowe", "Will you do this letter, Miss Marlowe?" I could be a piece of office furniture for all the interest he takes in me.'

'What made you decide on this sudden transformation?' Janice asked. 'Tired of waiting?'

'No, it's not that. I'd wait for ever!' The girl was starry-eyed.

'But something's happened, and she's going to spoil his whole life. He's been offered a partnership in a business up North, in Yorkshire. It's a marvellous opportunity, but he's going to turn it down.' The girl looked indignant. 'And why? Because this selfish woman won't go with him.'

Janice forced herself to concentrate on the head in front of her, coaxing stray strands into shape with an old-fashioned hairpin. She lightly lacquered the arrangement. 'How's that, Miss Marlowe?' Janice held a hand mirror at an angle.

'Why, it's lovely,' said Miss Marlowe, surprised at the new elfin-looking creature that smiled back at her.

She pressed 10p into Janice's hand. 'I'm so grateful to you. You've done marvels. Now, the rest is up to me!'

Janice held the coin uneasily. The girl was paying at the reception desk, going out through the door, her face radiant.

'Here, June!' Janice called over the junior who had done the shampoo. 'Miss Marlowe left this for you.'

Tony agreed to help move the equipment needed for the demonstration over to the Spa Hotel during Saturday lunchtime. It took several journeys as Janice decided to include hairpiece and wig care as an afterthought.

Janice got back into Tony's car and checked her list again. He looked wearily at his watch, his kind eyes clouded.

'It's too late to eat anywhere now,' he said.

'I couldn't eat anything, anyway,' said Janice, sitting back and closing her eyes. 'But you need something.'

'Hairdressing demonstrations don't affect me emotionally,' said Tony with a wry smile. 'So I'm still hungry. Got time for a sandwich somewhere?'

Janice shook her head. 'I can't be late back. I've a client at two o'clock. Sorry.'

'What about dinner after the show?'

'I don't know—I'll see. I might be too tired.'

'You've got to eat. I'll pick you up, anyway.'

The demonstration had all the appearance of success. It created interest, relieved a dull Saturday evening and Janice was showered with congratulations.

'I only hope they mean what they say, and book an appointment,' Janice said wearily, sipping a sherry in the bar with Tony afterwards.

'I think you're wasting your time doing this,' Tony said impatiently. 'If a woman has decided to have her hair done, she'll have it done, whether you've shown her the latest styles or not.'

'Trade slackens off in the winter. You know how dead everything is . . . I'm sure it helps to give the local ladies some ideas, and a little glamour.'

'I'm glad surveying isn't seasonal. . . .' Tony's voice trailed away. He was silent for a moment and Janice knew what he was thinking. The Yorkshire Dales were reflected in his grey eyes.

'Still hankering after that job?' Janice asked. 'But do you think you'd be happy up North, among those strangers?'

'I wouldn't be among strangers, if you came with me.'

Janice stifled a sigh. 'Please don't let's go over that again! We'll only have an argument and I'm much too tired.'

'It's got to be settled. They wrote to me again, renewing the offer. It's such a chance, Janice. To start as my own boss. Surely you, of all people, can understand that?' he urged.

'Of course I can,' she said angrily. 'But that doesn't give you the right to make me give up my business just to move with you. How would you like it if I made you move just when you were making a success of things?'

'But if we love each other. . . .'

'It's got nothing to do with love!' cried Janice.

'Ssh! Darling—people are looking.'

Janice got up quickly from the bar, snatched her coat and handbag and dashed out of the hotel. Then she walked briskly over to the sea wall and leant against it. The sound of the sea pounded in her aching head. There were no bright lights in this town in the winter. The sea front looked gloomy and neglected. Bits of waste paper flattened themselves against the stones of the wall, then hurled themselves into the air and fell into the dark water below.

She heard footsteps behind her. It was Tony. He came and stood beside her. Then, gently, he took her in his arms and kissed her. His warm embrace was reassuring, yet Janice pulled herself away, a worried look on her face. She looked at him steadily.

'Have you got a girl called Marlowe in your office?' she asked.

'Yes. She's one of the typists. Why?' Tony looked surprised.

'She came in the other day to have her hair done,' Janice stated.

'And I suppose she went out looking like another Prescott special. Somehow, you manage to take away all the character from an individual. The women coming out of your shop all look the same,' he said harshly.

'How unfair!' Janice flamed. 'And it's not a shop! It's a salon. Oh, my hair!' Her hands went up to protect her coiffure from the wind.

Tony turned on his heel. 'You're obsessed with hair, that's your trouble!'

He disappeared into the darkness. In disbelief, she heard the sound of his car starting up. She stood there, shaken. Tony had never left her just like that before. It was so unlike him. . . .

It wasn't far to walk to her little flat at the back of the town. She even went out of her way so that she could pass her hairdressing salon, to admire for the hundredth time the way the signwriter had scrawled 'janice' with a small 'j'.

Tonight she stood looking at the shop with a fierce, possessive pride. 'I won't give it up!' she said aloud. 'I won't!'

On Monday morning, Janice wrote to Tony, breaking off their engagement. Her heart ached as she posted the letter. If only they had got married in those first magical months of falling in love when everything had seemed so simple and straightforward.

Miss Marlowe came in during the following week, wearing a new, and more becoming, blue suit. Her cheeks were flushed. 'Can you fit me in?' she asked tentatively. 'I haven't an appointment.'

Later, when Janice was rolling up her hair, the girl came out of her rosy day-dream and spoke suddenly.

'You remember that man I told you about?'

'Your boss?' Janice's voice wasn't quite steady.

'His engagement is off. I've just found out. She's given him up at last!'

'Oh!' Janice was careful not to look in the mirror.

'And he's taking this wonderful job up North.'

'When does he go?'

'I don't know. Why?'

'Well, you'll have to hurry, won't you? If he's leaving the district.'

'I see what you mean.' Miss Marlowe smiled happily. 'But it's all right. I've offered to work late tonight, to help him—and he's going to take me out to dinner afterwards. Isn't that wonderful?'

Janice controlled her expression. It hurt her that Tony had consoled himself so quickly. And with one of her Prescott specials, as he had so critically put it.

But her own solace lay close at hand. Next door, in fact. Janice had heard a rumour that the shop premises next to hers would soon be vacant. It was a sweet shop, and trade had been declining for a long time.

In the event of the premises becoming vacant, Janice had it all worked out. She would expand her business. A comb-out bar—season tickets for regulars—a cosmetic counter where clients could experiment with new products—all these dreams could come true if she doubled the size of her salon.

Miss Marlowe now booked regular appointments. But she stopped talking about her private life, and wore a quiet smile that said more than any words. Janice noticed the new clothes and new self-confidence, and drew her own conclusions.

Rumour became fact, and when the shop next door became vacant, Janice flew to her bank manager to make arrangements to take over the lease. As she came out of the bank, surprised at how simple it had all been, she almost bumped into Tony.

'Oh! Hallo.'

'Janice!'

'I hear I have to congratulate you,' she said quickly.

'On what?'

For a moment Janice was tempted to mention Miss Marlowe. 'On the new partnership. I hear you are going to take it, after all. I'm so glad. It's a wonderful opportunity for you.'

'You didn't think so once,' he said briefly.

It was like talking to a stranger. The traffic moved noisily up and down the High Street; they were jostled by shoppers on the pavement; but they stood looking at each other, coolly, as if they had never been in love at all.

'I'm taking over the lease of the shop next to the salon,' she went on, determined to get some response. 'Expanding. . . .'

'My turn to congratulate.' But his face was a blank.

'It's going to be chaos,' she prattled brightly. 'And a lot of work. The builders will be knocking through an archway. There's new plumbing, and oh, so many things to arrange—'

'Then you must be very busy,' he interrupted. 'I won't detain you. Good luck with the new premises!'

She stared after him as he hurried away, his tall, familiar figure quickly swallowed up by the shoppers. She wanted to run after him, to tell him how much she loved him, but her pride, and her own plans, stopped her. And she knew that if she tried to prevent him from taking this partnership, he would regret it all his life. He needed the chance. But it was a horrible feeling to be left, mid-sentence, on the pavement.

It's my own fault, thought Janice, sadly. If only I were more like Miss Marlowe, adoring and subservient. But I'm not, and I can't change myself.

When Miss Marlowe came in for her next appointment, Janice could not bring herself to do her hair. For the first time in her career, she pleaded a headache and asked Josie, her best assistant, to take over. Janice sipped coffee in her office, going through all the plans and estimates, the figures swimming round in her head.

'Another wedding for us!' Josie popped her head round the door. 'Bride and two bridesmaids. Saturday fortnight.'

'Is—is it Miss Marlowe?'

'How did you guess?'

Janice tried to sound bright. 'You should know! When you're doing people's hair, they don't leave you much to guess at!'

No long engagement this time, thought Janice, her throat tight. He wasn't going to make the same mistake a second time. No waiting for love to take second place.

The arrival of the builders created more chaos than Janice had ever imagined. They tramped in and out, leaving trails of plaster and icy blasts coming through the open door. Dust settled everywhere, despite the protective tarpaulins hanging across the hole being knocked through the wall. The workmen plodded through the salon, their faces hardly concealing their amusement. The clients were less amused and tried to hide behind their magazines.

The new equipment was delivered promptly. Grey swivel arm-chairs, a battery of primrose-coloured hoods, more delicate trellis work, contemporary dressing-out mirrors and sleek, modern wall lighting. A roll of top-quality grey carpet lay snugly against the far wall, waiting to be laid in the new reception area when it was finished.

It was all very modern, in good taste, and very expensive.

Janice sat late at her desk that evening, doing the weekly accounts and pay packets. It was a long job and she preferred to do it when all the girls had gone home.

The telephone rang in reception, and Janice wondered who could be phoning so late.

'Janice Hairdressing,' she said crisply.

'Hallo—this is Mrs. Ellen Parker. I'm a resident at the Spa Hotel. I remember you did a very interesting demonstration here some time ago.'

Janice looked at her watch. It was ten past six. Didn't the old dear realise they were closed?

'I was wondering,' Mrs. Parker meandered on, 'if you could do my hair.'

'Of course!' Janice said, opening the appointment book. 'When would you like to come?'

'Oh, I'm afraid you misunderstood me. I can't come in. I've got arthritis. I'd like you to come here, if that's possible.'

'I'm sorry,' Janice said. 'I don't do any private work.'

'Oh what a pity. . . .' the elderly voice was full of disappointment. 'I was so looking forward to having my hair done professionally again. It's years since I've been able to get out. And my grandson is coming down this weekend—I didn't want him to think I've let myself go.'

Janice thought quickly as the woman chattered on. Business had been down this week. Her clients didn't like the workmen staring at them. Her flat was cold and lonely. She might just as well go and do this old lady's hair.

'I have some accounts to finish first,' Janice said. 'Would it be all right to come at eight this evening?'

'That would be splendid! Oh my dear, how kind of you!'

After putting her accounts straight, Janice packed a hand dryer and a selection of small rollers—old hair was usually very fine. As she came out of the salon she was almost bowled over by the strong wind which had suddenly sprung up from the direction of the sea. It tore at her clothes and whipped her scarf across her face. She struggled to lock the shop door, and a breaker crashed against the sea wall, sending spray up about twelve feet high. Janice dodged the curtain of water as the wind flung the spray across the road.

What a night! She hoped there were no boats out there. The roar of the waves was deafening.

Janice was glad to reach the centrally-heated foyer of the Spa Hotel. Mrs. Parker turned out to be a bright seventy-year-old who insisted that 'the poor child' should have some coffee first. 'I should never have asked you to come—it's such dreadful weather—and your coat's soaked!'

Janice found herself dressing Mrs. Parker's hair. The old lady was full of lively reminiscences and was only too glad to have a new audience.

'I'll come again,' said Janice. 'Any time. It's no trouble.' Mrs. Parker beamed.

The bedroom windows were rattling furiously. Janice looked out into the dark and fastened her coat round her neck. There seemed to be a lot of activity out there — lights, people, cars. . . . Whatever was going on? Someone was using a loud hailer, but the words were lost.

'Good night, Mrs. Parker. Have a lovely weekend with your grandson,' Janice smiled.

'Good night, my dear! And thank you so much. . . .'

Janice hurried out. She had an uneasy feeling that something was very wrong. Then she saw police cars and policemen looming up in the dark. Barriers were set up, and water was swirling across the road, dark and glistening like oil. The sea was crashing with mighty roars, sounding nearer than ever. Water lapped over her boots.

'You can't go there, Miss! Sea wall's been breached,' said a burly policeman. 'Flooding's a foot deep further down.'

'But I *must* get through,' Janice insisted. 'My shop. . . .'

'All the shops along the front are flooded. The fire engine's pumping them out now.'

'My shop!' Janice cried. She thought of the new grey carpet, the new equipment stacked on the floor, waiting to be fitted. She pushed through the growing crowds of sightseers.

'Please let me through!' she implored. 'My shop's been damaged. I must try and save something. . . .'

Walls of water reared up out of the maddened sea and thundered against the breached concrete.

Janice ran, half-blinded by the rain and spray, looking for someone in charge. She found a fire officer, his dark face drenched with spray.

'My shop's in the promenade,' she said in an urgent voice. 'Can you let me through? I must try and put sandbags or something. . . .'

'Steady on, Miss. You can't do that. The sea's still running high. Flooding's a foot deep. It's very dangerous.'

'Your shop's got a boat in the window,' said a man nearby.

Janice stared at the speaker in disbelief.

'Tossed through the window like a toy,' he went on. 'What a mess! The mast smashed through a desk. I saw it all. Cor! I thought, what's that boat doing there in the window!' He went on cheerfully, as his audience grew, 'I saw this boat, large as life. . . .'

The fire officer looked anxiously at Janice's ashen face. 'Yacht pulled its anchor,' he confirmed. 'Lucky no one was in it. Best wait till morning, Miss.'

A boat in her window. . . . She could feel the muddy water swirling round her ankles. A foot of sea water. Tears mingled with the rain and spray.

'I want to see it,' Janice said.

'Sorry, Miss. My orders are—'

'Janice! Are you all right? I saw the light on earlier. I knew you usually did your accounts late. . . .' Tony's voice was strained. His jacket was wet through. He hadn't even stopped to put on a raincoat.

'There's a boat in my window!' She stared at him, her eyes dull with shock. Her carefully pinned coiffure was blown about and tangled strands of hair were plastered across her face like silver. Tears and spray had washed off her make-up, leaving her face childlike.

'Don't despair. You'll start again,' he soothed.

'How can I?' she cried desperately, 'I thought I was so efficient, and yet I wasn't even properly insured! Funny, isn't it? I forgot to increase the premium to cover the new shop and the new equipment. . . .'

'There, there. It doesn't matter.' He was rocking her gently in his arms. 'You're safe, that's the main thing.'

He held her until she stopped trembling, and then he began to walk her away from the crowds and the scene of destruction.

'But what about Miss Marlowe?' she asked, many hours later, when they were both warm and dry in her flat.

'What about Miss Marlowe?' He looked at her blankly.

'She's in love with you, isn't she? You're going out together, aren't you?' Janice spoke carefully, not wanting to be hurt any more.

Tony grinned into the firelight. 'Funny sort of love,' he said. 'She's getting married to one of the draughtsmen in the office! I did take her out once, but it wasn't very successful—I couldn't stop thinking about you.'

'Oh, Tony. . . .' Janice's voice was shaking with relief. 'And all the time I thought I had been making her beautiful for you!'

'I guess that proves something, although I'm not quite sure what,' he said, taking her hand very gently.

'I hope it proves that I love you,' Janice said in a low voice. 'Please, forgive me, Tony—I really do love you.'

He tilted her chin and smiled at her vulnerable, rain-washed face.

'There's a lot of hair needs doing in Yorkshire,' he suggested.

'I don't think I could face starting again,' she faltered. She searched his face and knew that she must never lose him again. From now on, Tony came first.

But a new salon—in Yorkshire. When she felt strong again, when she felt able to plan, and fight and work. . . .

Tony looked into her hopeful eyes and guessed her thoughts.

'But this time, it'll be different,' he said firmly. 'This time you'll be with me.'

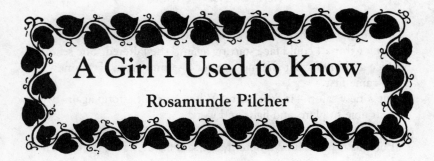

A Girl I Used to Know

Rosamunde Pilcher

The cable-car, at ten o'clock in the morning, was as crammed with humanity as a London bus at rush-hour. Grinding, swaying slightly, it mounted, with hideous steadiness, up into the clear, blindingly bright air, high over the snow-fields and scattered chalets of the valley. Behind them, the village sank away—houses, shops, hotels clustered around the main street. Far below lay great tracts of glittering snow, blue-shadowed beneath random stands of fir. Ahead and above it climbed—it gave Jeannie vertigo just to think about it—towards the distant peak piercing the dark-blue sky like a needle of ice . . .

The peak. The Kreisler. Just below it stood the sturdy wooden buildings of the upper cable station, the complex of the restaurant. The face of this edifice was one enormous window, flashing signals of reflected sunshine, and overhead fluttered the flags of many nations. Both the cable-car station and the restaurant had seemed, from the village, as distant as the moon, but now, with every moment, they drew closer.

Jeannie swallowed. Her mouth felt dry, her stomach tight with apprehension. Pressed into a corner of the cable-car, she turned her head to look for Alistair, but he and Anne and Colin had become separated from her in the rush to get on board, and he was away over on

[134]

the other side. Easy to spot, because he was so tall, his profile blunt and handsome. She willed him to turn and catch her eye, to give her a smile of reassurance, but all his concentration was for the mountain, for the morning's run down the Kreisler and back into the village.

Last night, as the four of them had sat in the bar of the hotel, she had said, "I won't come." There was dancing going on and a jolly band in lederhosen.

"But of course you must. That was the whole point of your coming on holiday, so that we could all ski together. It's no fun if you spend the whole time rabbiting around on the nursery slopes."

"I'm not good enough."

"It's not difficult. Just long. We'll take it at your speed."

That was even worse. "I'll hold you back."

"Don't be so self-abasing."

"I don't want to come."

"You're not frightened, are you?"

She was, but she said, "Not really. Just frightened of spoiling it for you."

"You won't spoil it." He sounded marvellously certain of this, just as he was marvellously certain of himself. He seemed not to know the meaning of physical fear, and so was unable to recognize it in another person.

"But . . ."

"Don't argue any more. Don't talk about it. Come and dance."

Now, crammed into a corner of the cable-car, she decided that he had forgotten her existence. She sighed, and turned back to the window to view the void, the impossible, dizzying height. Far, far below, the skiers were already moving down the pistes, tiny antlike creatures drawing trails in the virgin snow, flying down the slopes back to the village. It looked so easy. That was the horrible thing, it looked so easy. But for Jeannie it was almost impossibly difficult. *Bend the knees*, the instructor had told her. *Weight on the outside leg.*

Weight on the outside leg. I mustn't forget. Weight on the outside leg. I can do it. I have to do it. Relax. Bend the knees. Weight on the outside leg.

They had arrived. One moment swinging in the clear air and the brilliant sunshine, the next clanking into the shadowed gloom of the cable-car terminal. They stopped with a jerk. The doors opened, everybody flooded out. Up here it was degrees colder. Icicles festooned the exit door, and there was the crunch of frozen snow underfoot. Jeannie was the last to emerge, and by the time she did this, the first ones out were already away, down the mountain, anxious not to waste a moment of the morning, reluctant to spend even five minutes in the warmth of the restaurant, with a mug of hot chocolate or a steaming glass of glühwein.

"Come on, Jeannie."

Alistair and Colin and Anne already had their skis on, their goggles pulled down over their eyes, the three of them itching to be off. Her feet felt like lead in the heavy boots, slipping and stumbling across the snow. The cold stung her cheeks, filled her lungs with painfully icy air.

"Here, come on, I'll help you."

Somehow, she reached Alistair's side, dropped her skis. He stooped to help her, snapping on the bindings. Lumbered with the weight of the skis she felt even more incapable, helpless.

"All right?"

She could not even speak. Colin and Anne, taking her silence for assent, smiled cheerfully, gave her a wave with their ski poles, and were gone. A smooth push sent them over the brow of the slope, and they disappeared, with a hiss of snow, into the glittering infinity of space that lay beyond.

"Just follow me," Alistair told her. "It'll be fine." And then he, too, was gone.

Just follow me. It was Alistair, and she would have followed him anywhere, but this was an impossibility. Impossible to do anything but simply stand there, quaking. In her wildest imaginings she had never thought up such horror as this. Shivering with cold and fright, there was a moment when she wondered if she was actually going to be sick. But the moment passed, and she was still standing there, and in place of panic came, slowly, a calm resolution.

She was not going to ski down the Kreisler. She was going to take off her skis and go into the restaurant and sit down and get warm and have a hot drink. Then, like any old lady, she would clamber into the cable-car and go back that way, on her own, to the village. Alistair would be furious, but she was beyond caring. The others would think nothing of her, but that had ceased to matter. She was hopeless. A funk. She couldn't ski and never would. At the first possible opportunity, she would get herself to Zurich, get herself on a plane, and go home.

Having faced up to this, everything suddenly became quite easy. She took off her skis and carried them back to the restaurant and stuck them in the snow, along with the ski poles. She went up the wooden steps and through the heavy glass doors. Here was warmth, the smell of pine and wood-smoke and cigars and coffee. She bought herself a cup of coffee and took it to an empty table and sat down. The coffee steamed, fragrant and comforting. She pulled off her woollen hat and shook out her hair and felt as though she were taking off some hideous disguise and was herself again. Putting her hands around the blissful warmth of the coffee mug, she decided that she would concentrate on this moment of total relief and not think one moment ahead. Most specially, she would not think about Alistair. She would not think about losing him . . .

"Is anybody joining you?"

The question came out of nowhere. Startled, Jeannie looked up, saw the man standing across the table from her, and realized, after a second's blankness, that he was talking to her.

"No. Nobody."

"Then would you mind if I did?"

She was astonished, but endeavored to hide her astonishment. "No . . . of course not . . ." There was no question of being chatted up, because he was a quite elderly man, obviously British, and perfectly presentable. Which made his unexpected appearance all the more surprising.

He too had a cup of coffee in his hand. He set it down on the table and pulled out a chair and settled himself. She saw his very blue eyes, his thinning grey hair. He wore a navy-blue anorak with a scarlet sweater beneath it. His skin was very brown, netted with wrinkles, and he had the weather-beaten appearance of a man who has spent most of his life in the open air.

He said, "It's a beautiful morning."

"Yes."

"There was a fall of snow at two o'clock in the morning. Quite a heavy one. Did you know that?"

She shook her head. "No. I didn't know."

He watched her, his bright eyes unblinking. He said, "I've been sitting by the table in the window. I saw what happened."

Jeannie's heart sank. "I . . . I don't understand." But of course, she understood only too well.

"Your friends went off without you." He made it sound like an accusation, and Jeannie instantly sprang to their defence.

"They didn't mean to. They thought I was going to follow."

"Why didn't you?"

A number of likely fibs sprang to mind. *I like to ski alone. I wanted a cup of coffee. I'm waiting till they come up again on the cable-car, and then we'll all go down together in time for lunch.*

But those blue eyes were not to be lied to. She said, "I'm afraid."

"Of what?"

"Of heights. Of skiing. Of making a fool of myself. Of spoiling their fun for them."

"Haven't you skied before?"

"Not before this holiday. We've been here for a week and I've spent all that time on the nursery slopes with an instructor, trying to get the hang of it."

"And have you?"

"Sort of. But I think I'm uncoordinated or something. Or else just plain chicken. I mean, I can get down the slopes and turn corners and stop, and things like that, but I'm never sure when I'm not going to fall flat on my back, and then I get nervous and I tense up, and then of course I usually do fall. It's a vicious circle. And I'm frightened of heights as well. Even coming up on the cable-car I found terrifying."

He did not comment on this. "Your friends, I take it, are all fairly expert?"

"Yes, they've been skiing together for a long time. Alistair used to come out here with his parents when he was a little boy. He loves the village, and he knows all the runs like the back of his hand."

"Is Alistair *your* friend?"

She felt embarrassed. "Yes."

"Is he the reason you came in the first place?"

"Yes." He smiled. Suddenly, it was easy to talk, as it is easy to confide in a stranger met by chance in a train, knowing that you will never see that particular stranger again. "It's funny, we have everything in common, and we get on so well, and we laugh at the same things . . . but now there's this. I always knew that if I really wanted to be with him, and part of his life, I'd have to ski, because it's the one thing he really loves to do. And I've always been apprehensive about it, because, like I said, I'm the most uncoordinated person in the world. I used to go to dancing classes when I was a little girl, and I could never even tell my left foot from my right.

But I thought perhaps skiing would be different, and that it would be something I'd be able to do. So when Alistair suggested we all come out together, I jumped at the chance to prove that I *could*. And I thought it would be fun . . . like the advertisements for winter holidays. You know, jolly fun in the snow, and the whole business not much more demanding than a game of tennis. I never imagined being put on a mountain the height of this one, and being expected to actually ski down it."

"Does Alistair know how you feel about all this?"

"It's hard to make him understand. And I don't want him to think that I'm not enjoying myself."

"But you're not."

"No. I'm hating it. Even the evenings and the fun we have then are spoiled, because all the time I'm thinking about what I've got to make myself do the next day."

"When you've finished that cup of coffee, how are you going to get back to the village?"

"I thought on the cable-car."

"I see." He considered this, and then said, "Let's both have another cup of coffee and talk things over."

Jeannie couldn't think what there could possibly be to talk over, but the idea of another cup of coffee was a good one, and so she said, "All right."

He took their cups and went to the bar, and came back with them, steaming and refilled. As he sat again, he said, "You know, you remind me, quite extraordinarily, of a girl I used to know. She looked rather like you, and she talked with your voice. And she was just as frightened as you were."

"What happened to her?" Stirring her coffee, Jeannie tried to turn the whole thing into a joke. "Did she go down in the cable-car, and then fly home in disgrace? Because I think that's what's going to happen to me."

"No, she didn't do that. She found someone who understood and was prepared to give her a little help and encouragement."

"I need more than that. I need a miracle."

"Don't underestimate yourself."

"I'm a coward."

"That's nothing to be ashamed of. It isn't brave to do something that you're not afraid of. But it's very brave to face up to something which frightens you paralytic."

As he was saying this, the door of the restaurant opened and a man appeared, looked about him, and then came across the room towards them. Reaching their table, he stopped, respectfully removing his woollen hat.

"Herr Commander Manleigh."

"Hans! What can I do for you?"

The man spoke in German, and Jeannie's companion replied in the same language. They talked for a moment, and then the problem, whatever it was, was apparently solved. The man bowed to Jeannie, made his farewells, and took himself off.

"What was all that about?" she asked.

"That's Hans from the cable-car. Your young man telephoned up from the village to find out what had happened to you. He thought you might have had a fall. Hans came to find you, he recognized you from your friend's description."

"What did you say?"

"I said to tell him not to worry. We'll be down in our own time."

"We?"

"You and I. But not in the cable-car. We're doing the Kreisler run together."

"I can't."

He did not contradict her. Instead, after a thoughtful pause, he asked, "Are you in love with this young man?"

She had never actually considered this before. Not seriously. But all at once, faced with the question, she knew the truth. "Yes," she told him.

"Do you want to lose him?"

"No."

"Then come with me. Now. Right away. Before either of us has time to change our minds."

Outside again, it was still just as cold, but the sun was climbing into the sky, and the icicles that festooned the balcony of the restaurant and the doorways of the cable house were already beginning to thaw and drip. Jeannie pulled on her hat and her gloves, retrieved her skis, fastened the bindings, took a ski pole in either hand. Her new friend was ready before her, and waiting, and together they moved across the beaten, rutted snow to the verge of the slope where the piste, like a silver ribbon, wound away down the snowfields before them. The village, reduced by distance to toy size, lay deep in the valley, and beyond again, the further mountains, ranges of them, shone and glittered like glass.

She said, for the first time, "It's so beautiful."

"Enjoy the beauty. That is one of the joys of skiing. Having time to stop and stare. And this is a magical day. Now. Are you ready to go?"

"As ready as I'll ever be."

"Then shall we make a start?"

"Before we do, can I ask you one thing?"

"What's that?"

"The girl you told me about. The one who was as scared as I am. What happened to her?"

He smiled. "I married her," he said, and then he was gone, gently, smoothly, down the slope, traversing a ridge, turning, sailing away in the other direction.

Jeannie took a deep breath, set her teeth, pushed with her ski poles and followed him.

At first, she was as stiff and awkward as she had ever been, but every moment that passed increased her confidence. Three turns and she hadn't fallen. Her blood quickened, her body warmed, she could actually feel her muscles relax. There was sunshine on her face and the cool rush of clean air, sparkling, crisp as chilled wine. There was the sweet hiss of her own skis in the snow, the gathering sense of speed, the rasp of steel edges on ice as she manoeuvred a tricky corner.

He was never far ahead. Every so often, he would stop to wait for her and let her get her breath. Sometimes the way ahead needed a little explanation. "It's a narrow track through the woods," he would say. "Let your skis run in the tracks that other skiers have made, and then you'll be quite safe." Or, "The piste circles the edge of the mountain here, but it's not as dangerous as it looks."

He made her feel that nothing could be too difficult or frightening if he was there, leading the way. As they sank down into the valley, the terrain altered. There were bridges to be crossed, and open farm gateways through which they hurtled.

And then, all at once, long before she had expected it, they were in familiar territory, at the top of the nursery slopes, and so the finish of the run was child's play compared with what had gone before. Jeannie came down these slopes, on which she had unhappily struggled for seven solid days, with a flourish of speed, and a sensation of elation and achievement that she had never known before in her life. She had done it. She had come down the Kreisler. She had done it.

It was over. The slope levelled out by the ski-school hut and the little café where she had gone each day for a comforting mug of hot chocolate. Here, he waited for her, relaxed and smiling, delighted as she was, and yet obviously amused by her own delight.

She stopped alongside him, pushed up her goggles and laughed up into his face. "I thought it was going to be horrible and it was *heavenly.*"

"You did very well."

"I didn't fall once. I don't understand it."

"You only fell because you were nervous. Now you will never fall for that reason again."

"I can't thank you enough."

"You don't have to thank me. I enjoyed it. And if I'm not mistaken, I think that's your young man come to claim you."

Jeannie turned and saw that it was indeed Alistair, emerging from the door of the café, down the wooden steps and across the snow towards them. His face was filled with a marvellous relief, and the smile he had for her, a congratulation in itself.

"You made it, Jeannie. Well done, my darling." He enfolded her in a huge bear-hug. "I watched you coming down the last bit of the nursery slope, and you were really good." And then, across her head, her eyes met those of the man who had come to her rescue. Jeannie looked up and saw another expression cross his handsome features—the same respect and reverence that had shown on the face of the cable-car man when he had come to deliver Alistair's message.

"Commander Manleigh." If he had been wearing a hat, he would surely have removed it. "I didn't realize it was you. I didn't even know you were out here." The two men shook hands. "How are you, sir?"

"All the better for having met your charming young lady. I'm sorry, I don't know your name."

"Alistair Hansen. I used to watch you skiing when I was a boy. I had great photographs of you pinned up all over my bedroom walls."

"Well, it's very nice to meet you."

"It was good of you to come down with Jeannie."

"Hans at the cable-car station gave me your message."

"I was half-way down the piste before I realized that she wasn't behind me, and by then it was too late to make my way back."

"I found her in the restaurant. She was feeling a bit cold, so she went to get herself a hot drink. We got talking."

"I was afraid she'd fallen. Had visions of her coming down the mountain on the blood-wagon."

Commander Manleigh stooped and loosened his bindings and stepped out of his skis. Shouldering them, he stood erect. He smiled. "Given a little encouragement, young man, she won't let you down. Now I must be off. Goodbye, Jeannie, and good luck."

"Goodbye, and thank you again for being so kind."

He slapped Alistair across the shoulder. "Take good care of her," he told him, and then turned and walked away from them, a tall grey-haired man on his own. A strangely solitary figure in the crowded street.

Jeannie was taking off her own skis. "Who is he?" she wanted to know.

"Bill Manleigh. Come on, let's go and have a drink."

"But who's Bill Manleigh?"

"I can't believe you've never heard of him. A famous fellow. One of the best skiers we've ever produced. When he grew too old to race, he became a coach for the Olympic team. So you see, my darling, you came down the Kreisler with a champion."

"I didn't know that. I only know that he was terribly kind. And Alistair, it wasn't because I was cold that I went into the restaurant, it was because I was too frightened to follow you. You might as well know."

"You should have told me."

"I couldn't. I just stood there, being terrified, and then I knew I hadn't the nerve to make the run. And I was drinking coffee and he came and talked to me. And he didn't tell me anything about himself at all. Not at all." She thought about this. "Except that he was married."

Alistair lifted her skis onto his shoulder, and took her hand in his other hand. Together, they made their way towards the little café. "Yes, he was," he told her. "To a lovely girl. I used to watch them ski together, and think that they must be the most glamorous couple in the world. They were always such good friends, always laughing together. As though they didn't need anybody but each other."

"You talk as though it's all in the past."

"It is." They had reached the wooden building, and Alistair paused to ram her skis into the snow. "She died last summer. She was drowned. I read about it in the papers. They were sailing with friends in Greece, and there was some ghastly misadventure. He was devastated, and now he must be so lonely without her." Jeannie looked down the street, the way that he had gone, but he had been swallowed up in the cheerful crowds of holiday-makers, and there was no sign of him. *He must be so lonely.* For a terrible moment, she thought that she was going to cry. A lump swelled in her throat, and her eyes misted with ridiculous tears. Such a kind man. She would probably never see him again, and yet she owed him an immeasurable debt. She would never forget him. "But I don't suppose," Alistair went on, "that he would have said anything to you about that."

You remind me, quite extraordinarily, of a girl I used to know.

Going hand in hand with him up the wooden steps that led to the café door, she realized that she wasn't going to cry after all. "No," she said. "No, he didn't say anything."

Joe Johnson

H.E. Bates

J oe Johnson, who never hurt a soul, wore white overalls in summer
and extra-weight woollens in winter, and in very cold weather a
kind of Balaclava helmet. For some years he had kept an open-
fronted fruit shop with a small trade in flowers. In winter it was often
so bitterly cold in the unprotected shop that Joe, having once put on
the Balaclava helmet, was afraid of leaving it off again for fear of
catching cold in his ears. One spring he began to notice a young girl
who went by the shop two or three times a day. She had bright,
careless black eyes.

Up to about that time the shop was doing well. 'Eat More Fruit', the
notices said. 'Say it with Flowers.' At the week-ends Joe took a risk on
specialities that were just out of season, asparagus, peaches, roses and
such things. It was a luxury trade, but there were always customers. It
had not always been so. For five years Joe had been in the street trade,
pushing a barrow; for nearly another ten still in the street trade, with
a horse and cart. He had struggled up. Now he was heard to complain
of 'the caterpillarists of the trade'. He would say, 'Take bananas.
Bananas are a monopoly. If they wasn't a monopoly they'd be four a
penny. It's the caterpillarists. They keep you down.' Apart from this
he was well satisfied with himself. He was a man of forty who did not
know what it was to be unhappy except when he caught cold in his
ears.

All that spring the young girl went by the shop. The weather was
warm and Joe put on his white overalls. Tulips stood in vases among
the first boxes of hot-house tomatoes and Joe stood in front of the
fruit, passing the time of day with people he knew.

The only person who passed regularly by the shop and to whom he
never spoke was the young girl. When she came along something in
him went cold and contracted; he began trembling and picked up a

tomato or an apple and hastily rubbed it with a cloth. He wanted to look at her, but his eyes remained downcast. Always, after she had gone, he would look up; his blood would run hot and the palms of his hands were greasy with sweat.

This repeated phase of emotion astonished and baffled him. He felt himself rock on his feet, slightly giddy, whenever he saw her coming. He went through this same state of feeling four times a day. She went by at nine in the morning, and back at the lunch-hour; she went by again about two o'clock, and back again about five. One morning he was delayed down at the banana depot; the fruit had not arrived. When he reached the shop it was nine-thirty and he knew that the girl had gone. For some time he felt ill, with a clot of nausea and disappointment in his throat, and all that day he complained of 'the caterpillarists, who think you got all day to wait. The caterpillarists, who keep you down'.

One morning as the girl came by she lifted her bright casual eyes and looked at the shop. Among the fruit stood a vase of red carnations. He saw her eyes rest on it, hesitate for a moment, and then swing away. Almost as soon as she had gone he got on the telephone and ordered six dozen red carnations.

When they came he arranged them in big conspicuous bunches along the front of the shop. When she came past at the lunch-hour it was as he hoped. Seeing the flowers, she was held in a moment of agreeable surprise. In that moment, too, she must have caught sight of his transfixed and in some way transfigured face. And as if she saw the meaning of the face and the flowers she stopped and spoke.

'Nice,' she said.

'Very nice. Fresh in too,' he said. 'Fresh in.'

'Do they smell?'

'Oh! Yes,' he said. 'Yes, they smell. Clove-scented. See.' He picked up a vase and held it down towards her face. She took a deep breath, and he said: 'Nice, ain't it? You like the colour?'

'Well, yes, and no.'

His heart beat heavily. 'No?'

'Well, really they're not my colour,' she said. 'I like pale pink. The sort of shell-pink sort. Powder pink.'

'I know,' he said. 'I know. I can get 'em if you like 'em.'

'Well—'

'I tell you what,' he said. 'I'll get a few in. If you like 'em, have 'em. If you don't, it's all right, it don't matter.'

When she came back that afternoon he had the pale pink carnations tied in a cover of tissue paper, but now he did not wait for her to speak. 'I'd like to make a present of them,' he said.

'Oh! But that's very nice of you,' she said, as if taking it for granted.

Under the pressure of great embarrassment he gave her the flowers, and then stood locking and unlocking his empty hands.

'It's all right. I like doing it,' he said. 'I just like doing it.'

'Well—'

'I just hope you like them, that's all,' he said. 'I just hope they're the right colour.'

'Thanks,' she said. 'You've got a nice little shop here.'

'Yes?' he said. 'You think it's all right?'

'Lovely.'

'Bit of a struggle at first,' Joe said. 'But I got over that.'

'Well, thanks for the carnations,' she said.

'That's all right, it's nothing,' Joe said. 'Any time you want something particular and you don't see it, just ask. I can get it. It's no trouble. Anything. Any time.'

'I'll remember,' she said.

As the days of the spring went past she would remember it quite often. When strawberries were five shillings a pound, Joe had a punnet put away for her at the back of the shop. Soon there were long pink stalks of gladioli, early Napoleon cherries. Joe talked to her every day.

These things were presents. At first, when she tried to pay, he said, 'I couldn't. Not from you. I couldn't take money from you.' After that she did not offer to pay; it became as if she expected these things.

Joe, discovering that she worked in a printing works office, wondered what she did with her evenings. A terrible sickness of fear took hold of him when he thought that she might have boy-friends, young men of her own age. A sense of heavy embarrassment depressed him when he remembered how old he was. He felt among other things that there were between them awful spaces of age that could never be made up.

He began to be stupefied by a great sense of devotion. After the shop was shut at night he went into one of the two rooms at the back. He would lie down on the bed or the sofa and think of her. In anxiety he would rub over his face his large clammy hands that smelt of fruit. Late at night he would remember that he had not made up the books for the day. He would get out the books and try to enter up the figures. It was no good. The anxiety of thinking of her, of wanting her, jumbled his brain. He would realize finally that he was hungry. He would go down into the shop and bring back handfuls of fruit. Lying in bed, eating it, he would look up at the stars and try to measure what he felt and wanted and feared.

'I'm surprised you don't have a car,' she said. 'With your business.'

'I'm getting one,' he said. 'There's a fellow trying to do a deal with me. Keeps bothering me every time I see him.'

He wondered why he had not thought of it before. That evening, instead of sitting behind the shop, he went round to the nearest garage and bought a secondhand coupé for two hundred and thirty-five pounds, taking an evening's driving lesson at the same time. On other evenings he took more lessons; by the week-end he could drive.

Polished up, the car stood outside the shop. Because it was Saturday there were many customers. To Joe they were momentarily of no importance. The girl came and stood for a long time by the car, her manner idle and cool. As Joe stood talking to her, turning his back on the shop, a few customers walked away.

'What about a drive now?' Joe said. 'Just when you like. You just say when.'

'Well, what's wrong with this afternoon?'

'But I got the shop,' he said. 'I don't shut.'

'Oh! Well—!'

'It's Saturday, you see, it's Saturday—'

'I know it's Saturday. But you said any time. You shouldn't say any time if you don't mean it.'

'All right, all right,' he said, 'I do mean it. I can shut. I can go. I'm sorry. I meant any time. Where can I meet you?'

'Pick me up outside the post office at two,' she said.

Joe drove the car to the post office about a quarter to two. The girl did not come until almost three. Dispirited and nervous, Joe was afraid of reminding her she was late. It was a warm day and the coupé was stuffy from standing in the sun. Joe wore a brown suit and a trilby to match. 'Take your hat off,' the girl said. She put the side window down. 'It's so hot and you look so much better with it off.'

Joe put his hat in the back seat. Though he was pleased, he was afraid also of catching cold in his ears.

All that afternoon he felt emotion simmering like something about to boil in his throat. Eyes hard on the road, he was aware of the girl as something not quite positive. Fear of her being bored made him talk a lot. He wondered why he had not thought of a car before, why such days as this had never happened. As he looked at the sun on the young corn and the cherry orchards, it seemed to him that life, in a way to him not fully expressible, was only just beginning.

The girl did not like the country. 'Another time let's run down to the sea.'

'That's sixty miles,' Joe said.

'Well, the sea won't come to us, will it?' she said.

After that, on Sundays, they drove to the sea. Joe brought with him baskets of fruit, which they ate as they drove along or as they sat on the beach, watching the sea. Later they had lunch at one of the hotels on the sea-front. Joe was aware of these visits costing him money. In the past he had straightened up the weekly accounts on Sundays. Now he left them. They would do some other time. Life was beginning and he did not care.

Yet in a strange way the girl did not come to life. It seemed to him that she remained shut away from him, in a cool compartment of youth. He felt that he could not touch her. He used her Christian name, Myra, uneasily, with a sense of sharp embarrassment. It was almost three weeks before he took her with great clumsiness into his arms and kissed her. 'You don't mind?' he said when it was done. 'You don't mind?'

'Well, I like that!' she said.

Presently he rushed forward in a series of heavy attacks, caressing her body with his large uneasy hands. After a week or so of this the girl began to hold him away, slightly mocking.

'Kiss me,' Joe would say. 'Kiss me.'

'I just kissed you.'

'Again. Come on, again.'

'You'll wear it out,' she would say. 'You'll make it stale.'

'No,' Joe would say. 'It'll never be stale. It'll never wear out. Not what I feel for you. It never will. My God, no.'

'You've got it bad,' she would say.

Sometimes she held away altogether. The more she held away the more deeply he felt he wanted her. Her lips became small and hard in resistance. He wanted to break them down. With his eager fleshy lips he tried to drive response and warmth into her mouth; his hands wandered over her body.

'Oh, stop mauling me,' she would say. 'For God's sake stop mauling me.'

'I love you,' he would say. 'I want you.'

'Well, if you do that's not the way to get me!'

'I'll buy you something nice.'

'I don't want anything nice. Let me alone, that's all.'

'Let you alone? You mean not come out with you?'

'I don't know!' she would say. 'I don't care!'

The next time he saw her Joe would have a little present for her: chocolates, a bottle of expensive perfume. Once he dared to buy her a silk house-gown. After these gifts she would be more warm towards him. 'I like nice things,' she would say. 'I'd love to be able to dress well.'

In the car Joe caught a slight cold in his ears. 'You're like me,' she said. 'You feel the cold quickly. All last winter I was perished. Before next winter I want to get a good thick warm coat.'

Joe told her soon how he would like to buy her a coat: not an ordinary coat, not a tweed or even a camel-hair, but a fur coat. He did not mind how much the coat cost. Thirty or forty pounds, perhaps. He did not mind. Only, by means of it, he felt that he could break down the cool resistances, the slight barrier of mockery that kept him apart from her.

Soon after the excitement of the fur coat had passed Joe discovered that the shop accounts, neglected for nearly three months, were in a mess. He told the girl how, for two or three evenings at least, he must stay at home and straighten things out.

'I thought you were taking me out?' she said.

'But just this once. Just for a night or two.'

'Just this once my foot. You either want to take me out or you don't. You can do the books when you get home. Who do you think I am?'

When she spoke to him like this he was pained and felt quite small. Pain and love and fear would drive him to do as she asked. In the evenings that were now growing dark a little earlier, he would still drive with her down to the sea. It was a long way and by the time he got back to the shop it was too late and he was too tired to touch the accounts. A great fear of losing her began to make him spend money recklessly. 'Let's have a good time,' he would say. 'Let's have a good time!' From a few gay evenings by the sea, under the heavy August stars, among the holiday crowds, he extracted from her momentary concessions of tenderness. They went to dances that were hot and crowded and where they drank champagne. For a little while the dark sea itself would seem to him to have the appearance of wine, glowing softly. Next day he would feel old.

Now, too, he began to be more worried about the accounts and the weekly takings. The shutting of the shop on Saturday afternoons, in the face of the weekend trade, was a bad thing. Many customers had gone away and not come back. He tried to confide to the girl, vainly, what was on his mind.

'All you talk about is bananas,' she said.

He decided to cut out the luxury trade. In a few days he saw the effect on his better-class customers, who dropped away. One day a woman remarked tartly, 'When I come for a pound of apples I don't expect an exhibition of spooning.'

To the girl he tried to conceal his dismay by anger. 'Snobs! That's what they are. Because I won't give 'em credit. That's how they treat you. She's one of these caterpillarists. Treat you like dirt.'

'Oh, stop worrying,' she said.

'You never sympathize,' he said. He felt that he needed guidance and confidence.

'Sympathize?' she said. 'You want me to cry on your neck?'

A day or two later she did not keep the evening appointment. He wandered idly round the streets, looking for her, trying to think. After some hours he went back home and sat in the room above the shop. A huge sense of oppression held him immobile by the window. For some time he sat there looking down at the street, not thinking or moving, and then at last he saw her, walking on the opposite pavement with a stranger. As he saw her he felt his whole body rock, so that he trembled heavily on his feet.

When she came by the shop in the morning she did not stop. Joe walked desperately after her, beseeching her to tell him what it was all about, uselessly lifting his hands. She raised her small hard face, expressing weariness.

'You just make me tired, that's all,' she said.

In the evening he waited outside the office where she worked. Coming out, she walked straight past him. Again he hurried after her.

She turned angrily on him. 'For God's sake don't keep following me!'

'I want you. I got to talk to you. What's wrong?'

'Nothing.'

'What have I done?'

'Nothing.'

'There must be something. It just can't happen like this. You just can't go.'

'I tell you there's nothing!' she said, 'and I'm going. That's all.'

After that, whenever he got the opportunity, he would wait for her in the street. Raising his large hands in a hopeless sort of way, he would run after her. He began to close the shop a few minutes before five in the evening, so that he could meet her outside the office.

'Can't you take no for an answer?' she would shout at him.

'No.'

'Well then, learn! Because it's the only answer you'll get!'

Gradually there was roused in him a sense of deep cold anger that began to vent itself on the customers. He began to be annoyed when they squeezed the hearts of cabbages or tested the ripeness of plums and pears. In resentment he put up a large notice in the shop. 'Don't handle the goods! It's unhygienic!'

'What's the reason for that?' a woman asked.

'A lot of people have got dirty hands, that's all!'

The trade of the shop fell rapidly away. It was almost October; the days were cooler. People did not like standing outside the shop, in the wind, to be told that they had dirty hands. When Joe came to straighten up the accounts that had been left for so long he got up and walked about the room, hitting his forehead with his hands.

His anger broke down into despondency. What he felt about the girl, what he had felt about her since first seeing her go past the shop with her bright careless eyes, was not changed. When he saw her in the street, from a distance, or thought of her, he experienced the rush of trembling tenderness that made him rock on his feet.

By the time he had given up the shop and had decided to go back to the street trade, with a horse and cart, it was late November. He once saw the girl in the fur coat. She walked softly, small bright eyes glittering above the brown fur, like a cat that watches people. Seeing her, he remembered with an acute, blinding pain, the days of the summer.

As he drove round the back streets of the town with the small cart and its boxes of fruit and vegetables and occasional flowers, he caught cold in his ears through forgetting his Balaclava helmet. The pain drove through his head, breaking down his nerves. But beside the pain of frustration and the everlasting feeling of tenderness for which there was no outlet it seemed a little thing.

'I see you're back, Joe,' the people said. 'Given up the shop, after all.'

'Yes,' he would say. 'Yes.'

For a moment he would be at a loss to explain his return.

And then, finding an explanation that had nothing to do with the frustration, the tenderness or the pain, he would raise his heavy hands and let them fall again.

'It's the caterpillarists, you see,' he would explain. 'It's the caterpillarists. There's no room for a man like me.'

Snowstorm

Jean Stubbs

The Friday before Christmas, as Sarah came out of the new office block into the new traffic complex, snow began to fall. She pushed up the collar of her coat and nestled her chin in the soft fur. Time was on her side for once. In fact if she found a taxi now, she could catch the fast train home and eat well in the Greek restaurant round the corner at a reasonable hour—instead of drinking whisky while she cooked scrambled eggs in her flat at eleven o'clock.

She was very slim, very smart with her swaggering boots and scarlet coat. She walked with authority. Her leather brief-case bespoke a woman of business. Her pale hair shone and was beautifully cut. She had made up her face carefully and well. The effect was elegant, expensive and impersonal.

Swifter and thicker whirled the flakes. Standing on the edge of the whitening pavement, peering into the blur of traffic, she felt like the little figure at the centre of a child's glass snowstorm.

The city held her earliest adult memories. She had spent her student years here, experienced her first love affair. From here she had set foot on the first important rung of the monetary ladder, up which she now mounted steadily. Yet in all those seven years she had never been back.

Strange that business had now brought her here unexpectedly, at the same time of year that she and Kit Nicolson first met. Stranger still that the new office should be so close to the square in which she and he had lived . . .

Never look back, she told herself. And summoned a taxi, which drove blindly past.

As if, she thought, I didn't exist.

And this was strange, too: for she divided people into those who could find a taxi and those who could not. She had always been able to spirit them up. Kit Nicholson, on the other hand, might signal from the kerb forever without anyone paying the slightest attention to him.

It was our differences which brought us together, she remembered, and our differences which drove us apart. Not that it matters now, seven years later. Not a bit. I've come a long way since then.

Taxi after taxi bowled heedlessly past. In a while she crossed two traffic islands, which hadn't existed in her day, and stood on the opposite side to change her luck.

Here they had done their shopping on a Saturday morning, coming out of the elegant decay of Dover Square into this little row of shops which was the focal point of their local community. She was surprised they had survived. She would have expected to see a big stationer's, a unisex hairdresser's, a supermarket, a Wimpy Bar, a computer shop.

Relics of time past, The Copper Kettle still stood next door to May's Grocer's, which was also a greengrocer's and a sub-post office. The launderette still had no more than four machines, and one of them was 'Out of Order' as usual. There was Jarvis's off-licence, whose dry white wine had made their teeth ache, and Marilyn's Ladies Stylist with two torrid dryers. And there behind her, Burnett's Newsagent and Tobacconist's who advertised the neighbourhood's wants and wares in a side window.

That December day, years ago, Kit Nicholson had walked up and stood there beside her, hands thrust deep into his duffel-coat pockets, collar pulled high against the winter weather. He was seeking exactly what she sought: a room to let, at a price which students on a grant might afford. And as their eyes hunted in pairs through lost dogs, second-hand furniture and free kitchens, there it had been in the bottom left-hand corner.

'Furnished apartment, with kitchenette and use of bathroom. £5 a week. Contact Mrs Palfrey, 10 Dover Square, after 6 p.m.'

The clock of St Martin's Church chimed four. Four o'clock on a cold white afternoon. The traffic was veiled in snow, already slowing to a crawl, and not a taxi in sight. Softer and thicker came the falling snow. Now her fashionable boots left prints on the pavement. White flakes turned her fur collar to feathers.

'You won't get a taxi here, dear,' said a stout woman, laden with bags of Christmas shopping. 'Try farther down.'

So farther down she went, and spied a taxi in a side-street, but someone else stepped into it. She found another on the corner of a little park, but the driver said he was going home. Then she turned down here and up there until she lost her way and knew the train had gone. Stopping to draw breath, defeated, she laid one hand on the iron railings—and so looked up into the windows of the room on the first floor which had been briefly and intensely their world.

Whoever owned the house still kept the communal dustbins outside, overflowing, and prey to stray cats. In high summer the battered bins used to be abuzz with flies. Today, she noticed, the snow covered them kindly.

Slowly she walked up the path. The front door stood slightly ajar. A sleepwalker, she stepped inside the hall and knocked tentatively.

'Come in! It's not locked!' cried a familiar voice.

And there was the old girl herself, not a wrinkle different, in one of her coquettish frilled tea-gowns with georgette sleeves. Her lifestyle had not changed. Sandwiches sat on a chipped plate, a fresh pot of coffee steamed on the tray. For the millionth time she was consulting the Tarot cards.

'It's Sarah, Mrs Palfrey. Sarah Clough.'

Absorbed in her task, the old lady seemed unsurprised: talking to the cards rather than to Sarah.

'Hello, dear. Long time no see. How many years is it? Well, never mind. Sit down there, near me.'

Her poise deserting her, Sarah removed two cats and several newspapers from the chair indicated.

She murmured: 'I can't believe it. I thought you must be . . .'

'Dead?' said Mrs Palfrey shrewdly. 'Not a bit of it. I wasn't that ancient. It was just that both of you were so young. Tell me, what sign were you? I forget.'

'Leo, Mrs Palfrey.'

'Oh, yes: the noble ruler. Knew what you wanted and went for it. Good job, good clothes, good food, a good address. In short—' with a flourish of the sleeves—'la dolce vita! Well—' turning and looking at her for the first time—'is life sweet for you, Sarah?'

'In some ways. Yes.'

'High on luxury and a bit short on love?'

Sarah was silent, nursing a cat, her head bent.

'A married man,' said Mrs Palfrey, reading her face, 'must always spend Christmas with his family. That's an unspoken rule, you know.'

'We will have Christmases together,' said Sarah stubbornly.

'Oh no, you won't,' said Mrs Palfrey. 'He's had enough of marriage.

He wants things the way they are! Gemini?' she added. 'I thought so. They do like a flirtation. Now the other one, that nice lad who used to mend the fuses for me . . .'

'Kit Nicolson.'

'Yes, Kit—he was Aquarius, an oddball. He liked his freedom. Plenty of talent and no compromise. You loved order and he liked adventure. That's always tricky.'

'Salad days!' said Sarah, and tried to smile.

'Halcyon days! Nothing like them before or since, I'll be bound. He was air and you were ballast. Put the two together and you could make a beautiful balloon. But you weren't old enough to know that, or experienced enough to work it out!'

Sarah inclined her head over the cat. The train was pulling out of the station and heading for somewhere she called home, but she'd known no home since this one.

'The room's vacant. Do you want to see it? The cleaning lady did it this morning. You won't mind if I don't come with you? All them stairs. It's me heart. I'll see you again when you come down.'

She spoke to Sarah now as she had spoken to them both then. Together she and Kit had mounted the shabby staircase, each determined not to give in to the other, to let Mrs Palfrey decide which of them should have the room.

The room was very large and gracious. The long faded curtains had been lovely in their day. The long windows looked out on to Dover Square dressed in its winter white. An arch divided one half of the room from the other. Beyond lay the kitchenette which must have been a converted clothes cupboard. Still, it had a very old small gas stove at one end, a minute porcelain sink at the other, and shelves all round which a tall man might reach if he stretched. The shared bathroom was on another landing.

'With a geyser which either trickles or explodes,' said Kit, experienced in such matters.

His dark-blue eyes were perceptive, his mouth sensitive. He had forgotten to comb his dark hair. His clothes seemed to have been thrown on rather than selected. She decided he could be chivalrous.

'It would mean all the difference in the world to me, to have this room,' Sarah had said honestly, unfairly. 'I need privacy.'

He gauged her too, not as a pretty girl but as a fellow being.

'Same here,' he said simply. 'I need personal space.'

A student's world of communal living, inadequate lodgings and prying landladies lay behind the pair of them.

Then he added: 'I suppose we're both in the same boat. If we understand what's involved, then perhaps we could share. Strictly person to person.' He became practical. 'Look. This room has been two rooms in its time. These panels are folding doors. They might unfold again.'

Suddenly business-like, Sarah assessed the situation.

'One of us would have a sofa to sleep on and a view of Dover Square. The other would have the bed and easy access to the kitchen.'

'I don't cook much,' said Kit, anxious to set obstacles aside.

She thought that he didn't look as though he ate much, either, but did not say so. Personally, she enjoyed food and cooked well. 'We *could* sort it out, I suppose,' she said.

'I tell you what. I'll borrow an oil-can from mad Madame Sosostris downstairs, and see if I can coax the hinges!' he cried.

Several minutes later they trundled the doors together and converted the apartment into two separate rooms. They wiped their hands and grinned at each other in triumph.

'That garden-shed's in a right old muddle,' he said. 'There's no handyman about the house, that's for sure. If I offered to make myself useful—did a bit of rewiring, mowed the jungle—I reckon the old girl would turn a blind eye to our domestic arrangements. I daresay no-one will believe the truth of them, but that's our business.'

'Oh, but what would my parents say?' Sarah asked, appalled.

'Where do they live?' he replied briskly.

'About two hundred miles away.'

He smiled a lovely smile, which Sarah answered. Then he said: 'So do mine. We can work something out if they ever visit us.'

'Well, okay. If you truly *mean* person to person. If you ask her.'

The sixth and the eleventh stairs still creaked, and Sarah pressed them again out of sheer nostalgia. She drew a deep breath. She opened the door and looked into the aftermath of a celebration.

Clearly, Mrs Palfrey's cleaning lady had skipped this room. The curtains were still closed. The Woolworth chandelier sparkled cheerfully up against the ceiling. No-one had washed up the wine glasses or removed the bottle of Chablis. The remnants of a picnic supper were still on the green baize card-table in front of the cold gas fire. Over the fire-guard hung a string of translucent soapy beads. A man's watch was spread out neatly on the green marble mantelshelf.

So deeply had the room experienced its tenants that they seemed only to have left it for a moment. Their vitality lingered in the air and made her feel a trespasser, made her heart ache. Sarah turned on her heel to go, and stopped, remembering the beads.

'I bought them because I saw you coveting them!' Kit said, trying to sound amusing and nonchalant.

'But you couldn't afford to buy *sausages* yesterday, so how can you buy these today?' she cried. 'Oh, but they're so beautiful! How did you know I wanted them so much? You shouldn't have known!'

'Shall I fasten them on?' he asked shyly.

Equally shy, she nodded. In the closeness and silence her senses were heightened. She could feel the warmth of him, hear the sounds of his body. He held his breath in concentration. His fingertips brushed her neck and the brush felt like a burn.

'There!' said Kit. 'That's worth more than a packet of bangers!'

The girl stared into the enormous mirror over the fireplace, and saw that she was beautiful. And the boy's image stared humbly back, a little awed that he had created this moment.

'Never given a woman jewellery before,' he mumbled.

The word 'jewellery' amused her, for if the opals had been real they would have cost a ransom. She swung round, laughing. Then felt ashamed, and bowed her head. As though she had given him permission, he parted the curtain of her long pale hair, and kissed her for the very first time.

Disturbed, Sarah thrust the curtains back to scatter memories with light, but the room would not give up its past. The unmade bed in the room's other half showed signs of occupation by two people.

'Thank God we're living in sin now. Those sofa springs were lethal,' said Kit, that first morning.

His clothes and hers hung on the brass rail at the end. Had she really worn green and red striped tights? Yes, long ago. Books which she had forgotten lay on the window-seat. His and hers. In the cupboard which they called the kitchen were their dishes, showing signs of egg and bacon fried in butter.

In its passion to remember everything the room had jumbled its seasons. A crimson rose he bought for her birthday lived again in the green tumbler. The front window-sill was banked with snow. In the back garden daffodils grew. The calendar said October.

Sarah came full circle in front of the spotted mirror, and saw the man in the doorway staring at her and their ghostly room, incredulous. They spoke to each other as if they had never been away.

'So we were as important as this to the old girl,' Kit said, looking slowly round. 'She must have cracked up.'

'It isn't that at all,' cried Sarah. 'Look out of the windows!' And she pulled him by the sleeve, just as she used to do.

'Good God, Sarah!' said Kit, clearly shaken.

'And how did you happen to arrive here just now?'

'I was here for an interview, but the buses seem to have disappeared and I kept wandering down the wrong streets.'

'I'm not exactly afraid,' said Sarah, 'but what can we do to get back? Oh, Kit, is Mrs Palfrey real?'

'Let's go downstairs and see.'

'We're going to The Copper Kettle to talk,' she informed their faithful room gently.

'It might not exist, either,' said Kit, 'but the together bit seems to be what they're after.'

He saw the beads. 'Want me to fasten them?' he asked cautiously.

'There's no need,' she answered. 'I always wear them.'

And she opened her fine fur collar to show him the string he gave her all those years ago.

'Of course,' said Kit, smiling, knowing her weaknesses. 'No-one would imagine that they weren't real opals. On *you*.'

[160]

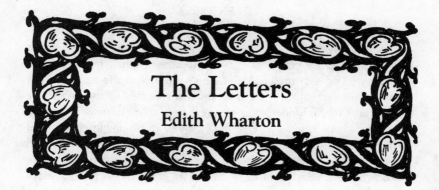

The Letters

Edith Wharton

Up the hill from the station at St. Cloud, Lizzie West climbed in the cold spring sunshine. As she breasted the incline, she noticed the first waves of wisteria over courtyard railings and the highlights of new foliage against the walls of ivy-matted gardens; and she thought again, as she had thought a hundred times before, that she had never seen so beautiful a spring.

She was on her way to the Deerings' house in a street near the hilltop, and every step was dear and familiar to her. She went there five times a week to teach little Juliet Deering, the daughter of Mr. Vincent Deering, the distinguished American artist. Juliet had been her pupil for two years, and day after day, during that time, Lizzie West had mounted the hill in all weathers; sometimes with her umbrella bent against the rain, sometimes with her frail cotton parasol unfurled beneath a fiery sun, sometimes with the snow soaking through her boots or a bitter wind piercing her thin jacket, sometimes with the dust whirling about her and bleaching the flowers of the poor little hat that *had* to 'carry her through' till next summer.

At first the ascent had seemed tedious enough, as dull as the trudge to her other lessons. Lizzie was not a heaven-sent teacher; she had no born zeal for her calling, and though she dealt kindly and dutifully with her pupils, she did not fly to them on winged feet. But one day something had happened to change the face of life, and since then the climb to the Deering house had seemed like a dream flight up a heavenly stairway.

Her heart beat faster as she remembered it—no longer in a tumult of fright and self-reproach, but softly, happily, as if brooding over a possession that none could take from her.

It was on a day of the previous October that she had stopped, after Juliet's lesson, to ask if she might speak to Juliet's papa. One had

[161]

always to apply to Mr. Deering if there was anything to be said about the lessons. Mrs. Deering lay on her lounge upstairs, reading relays of dog-eared novels, the choice of which she left to the cook and the nurse, who were always fetching them for her from the *cabinet de lecture*; and it was understood in the house that she was not to be 'bothered' about Juliet. Mr. Deering's interest in his daughter was fitful rather than consecutive; but at least he was approachable, and listened sympathetically, if a little absently, stroking his long fair moustache, while Lizzie stated her difficulty or put in her plea for maps or copybooks.

'Yes, yes—of course—whatever you think right,' he would always assent, sometimes drawing a five-franc piece from his pocket, and laying it carelessly on the table, or oftener saying, with his charming smile: 'Get what you please, and just put it on your account, you know.'

But this time Lizzie had not come to ask for maps or copybooks, or even to hint, in crimson misery—as once, poor soul, she had had to do—that Mr. Deering had overlooked her last little account—had probably not noticed that she had left it, some two months earlier, on a corner of his littered writing table. That hour had been bad enough, though he had done his best to carry it off gallantly and gaily; but this was infinitely worse. For she had come to complain of her pupil; to say that, much as she loved little Juliet, it was useless, unless Mr. Deering could 'do something', to go on with the lessons.

'It wouldn't be honest—I should be robbing you; I'm not sure that I haven't already,' she half laughed, through mounting tears, as she put her case. Little Juliet would not work, would not obey. Her poor little drifting existence floated aimlessly between the kitchen and the *lingerie*, and all the groping tendrils of her curiosity were fastened about the life of the backstairs.

It was the same kind of curiosity that Mrs. Deering, overheard in her drug-scented room, lavished on her dog-eared novels and on the 'society notes' of the morning paper; but since Juliet's horizon was not yet wide enough to embrace these loftier objects, her interest was centred in the anecdotes that Céleste and Suzanne brought back from the market and the library. That these were not always of an edifying nature the child's artless prattle too often betrayed; but unhappily they occupied her fancy to the complete exclusion of such nourishing items as dates and dynasties, and the sources of the principal European rivers.

At length the crisis became so acute that poor Lizzie felt herself bound to resign her charge or ask Mr. Deering's intervention; and for Juliet's sake she chose the harder alternative. It *was* hard to speak to him not only because one hated to confess one's failure, and hated still more to ascribe it to such vulgar causes, but because one blushed to bring them to the notice of a spirit engaged with higher things. Mr. Deering was very busy at that moment: he had a new picture 'on'. And Lizzie entered the studio with a flutter of one profanely intruding on some sacred rite; she almost heard the rustle of retreating wings as she approached.

And then—and then—how differently it had all turned out! Perhaps it wouldn't have, if she hadn't been such a goose—she who so seldom cried, so prided herself on a stoic control of her little twittering cageful of 'feelings'. But if she had cried, it was because he had looked at her so kindly, and because she had nevertheless felt him so pained and shamed by what she said. The pain, of course, lay for both in the implication behind her words—in the one word she left unspoken. If little Juliet was as she was, it was because of the mother upstairs—the mother who had given the child her frivolous impulses, and grudged her the care that might have corrected them. The case so obviously revolved in its own vicious circle that when Mr. Deering had murmured, 'Of course if my wife were not an invalid,' they both turned with a spring to the flagrant 'bad example' of Céleste and Suzanne, fastening on that with a mutual insistence that ended in his crying out: 'All the more, then, how can you leave her to them?'

'But if I do her no good?' Lizzie wailed; and it was then that, when he took her hand and assured her gently, 'But you do, you do!'—it was then that, in the traditional phrase, she 'broke down', and her poor little protest quivered off into tears.

'You do *me* good, at any rate—you make the house seem less like a desert,' she heard him say; and the next moment she felt herself drawn to him, and they kissed each other through her weeping.

They kissed each other—there was the new fact. One does not, if one is a poor little teacher living in Mme. Clopin's *Pension Suisse* at Passy, and if one has pretty brown hair and eyes that reach out trustfully to other eyes—one does not, under these common but defenceless conditions, arrive at the age of twenty-five without being now and then kissed—waylaid once by a noisy student between two doors, surprised once by one's grey-bearded professor as one bent over the 'theme' he was correcting—but these episodes, if they tarnish the surface, do not reach the heart; it is not the kiss endured, but the kiss returned, that lives. And Lizzie West's first kiss was for Vincent Deering.

As she drew back from it, something new awoke in her—something deeper than the fright and the shame, and the penitent thought of Mrs. Deering. A sleeping germ of life thrilled and unfolded, and started out to seek the sun.

She might have felt differently, perhaps—the shame and penitence might have prevailed—had she not known him so kind and tender, and guessed him so baffled, poor and disappointed. She knew the failure of his married life, and she divined a corresponding failure in his artistic career. Lizzie, who had made her own faltering snatch at the same laurels, brought her thwarted proficiency to bear on the question of his pictures, which she judged to be remarkable, but suspected of having somehow failed to affirm their merit publicly. She understood that he had tasted an earlier moment of success: a *mention*, a medal, something official and tangible; then the tide of publicity had somehow set the other way, and left him stranded in a noble isolation. It was incredible that any one so naturally eminent and exceptional should have been subject to the same vulgar necessities that governed her own life, should have known poverty and obscurity and indifference. But she gathered that this had been the case, and felt that it formed the miraculous link between them. For through what medium less revealing than that of shared misfortune would he ever have perceived so inconspicuous an object as herself? And she recalled now how gently his eyes had rested on her from the first—the grey eyes that might have seemed mocking if they had not seemed so gentle.

She remembered how kindly he had met her the first day, when Mrs. Deering's inevitable headache had prevented her receiving the new teacher. Insensibly he had led Lizzie to talk of herself and his questions had at once revealed his interest in the little stranded compatriot doomed to earn a precarious living so far from her native shore. Sweet as the moment of unburdening had been, she wondered afterward what had determined it; how she, so shy and sequestered, had found herself letting slip her whole poverty-stricken story, even to the avowal of the ineffectual 'artistic' tendencies that had drawn her to Paris, and had then left her there to the dry task of tuition. She wondered at first, but she understood now; she understood everything after he had kissed her. It was simply because he was as kind as he was great.

She thought of this now as she mounted the hill in the spring sunshine, and she thought of all that had happened since. The intervening months, as she looked back at them, were merged in a vast golden haze, through which here and there rose the outline of a shining island. The haze was the general enveloping sense of his love, and the shining islands were the days they had spent together. They had never kissed again under his own roof. Lizzie's professional honour had a keen edge, but she had been spared the necessity of making him feel it. It was of the essence of her fatality that he always 'understood' when his failing to do so might have imperilled his hold on her.

But her Thursdays and Sundays were free, and it soon became a habit to give them to him. She knew, for her peace of mind, only too much about pictures, and galleries and churches had been the one outlet from the greyness of her personal conditions. For poetry, too, and the other imaginative forms of literature, she had always felt more than she had hitherto had occasion to betray; and now all these folded sympathies shot out their tendrils to the light. Mr. Deering knew how to express with unmatched clearness the thoughts that trembled in her mind: to talk with him was to soar up into the azure on the outspread wings of his intelligence, and look down, dizzily yet clearly, on all the wonders and glories of the world. She was a little ashamed, sometimes, to find how few definite impressions she brought back from these flights; but that was doubtless because her heart beat so fast when he was near, and his smile made his words seem like a long quiver of light. Afterward, in quieter hours, fragments of their talk emerged in her memory with wondrous precision, every syllable as minutely chiseled as some of the delicate objects in crystal or ivory that he pointed out in the museums they frequented. It was always a puzzle to Lizzie that some of their hours should be so blurred and others so vivid.

She was reliving all these memories with unusual distinctness, because it was a fortnight since she had seen her friend. Mrs. Deering, some six weeks previously, had gone to visit a relative at St. Raphael; and, after she had been a month absent, her husband and the little girl had joined her. Lizzie's adieux to Deering had been made on a rainy afternoon in the damp corridors of the Aquarium at the Trocadéro. She could not receive him at her own *pension*. That a teacher should be visited by the father of a pupil, especially when that father was still, as Madame Clopin said, *si bien*, was against that lady's austere

Helvetian code. And from Deering's first tentative hint of another solution Lizzie had recoiled in a wild flurry of all her scruples. He took her 'No, no, *no!*' as he took all her twists and turns of conscience, with eyes half tender and half mocking, and an instant acquiescence which was the finest homage to the 'lady' she felt he divined and honoured in her.

So they continued to meet in museums and galleries, or to extend, on fine days, their explorations to the suburbs, where now and then, in the solitude of grove or garden, the kiss renewed itself, fleeting, isolated, or prolonged in a shy pressure of the hand. But on the day of his leave-taking the rain kept them under cover; and as they threaded the subterranean windings of the Aquarium, and Lizzie gazed unseeingly at the grotesque faces glaring at her through walls of glass, she felt like a drowned wretch at the bottom of the sea, with all her sunlit memories rolling over her like the waves of its surface.

'You'll never see him again—never see him again,' the waves boomed in her ears through his last words; and when she had said goodbye to him at the corner, and had scrambled, wet and shivering, into the Passy omnibus, its grinding wheels took up the derisive burden—'Never see him, never see him again.'

All that was only two weeks ago, and here she was, as happy as a lark, mounting the hill to his door in the fresh spring sunshine! So weak a heart did not deserve such a radiant fate; and Lizzie said to herself that she would never again distrust her star.

The cracked bell tinkled sweetly through her heart as she stood listening for Juliet's feet. Juliet, anticipating the laggard Suzanne, almost always opened the door for her governess, not from any eagerness to hasten the hour of her studies, but from the irrepressible desire to see what was going on in the street. But doubtless on this occasion some unusually absorbing incident had detained the child belowstairs; for Lizzie, after vainly waiting for a step, had to give the bell a second twitch. Even a third produced no response, and Lizzie, full of dawning fears, drew back to look up at the house. She saw that the studio shutters stood wide, and then noticed, without surprise, that Mrs. Deering's were still unopened. No doubt Mrs. Deering was resting after the fatigue of the journey. Instinctively Lizzie's eyes turned again to the studio window; and as she looked, she saw Deering approach it. He caught sight of her, and an instant later was at the door. He looked paler than usual, and she noticed that he wore a black coat.

'I rang and rang—where is Juliet?' she asked.

He looked at her gravely; then, without answering, he led her down the passage to the studio, and closed the door when she had entered.

'My wife is dead—she died suddenly ten days ago. Didn't you see it in the papers?' he said.

Lizzie, with a cry, sank down on the rickety divan propped against the wall. She seldom saw a newspaper, since she could not afford one for her own perusal, and those supplied to the *Pension* Clopin were usually in the hands of its more privileged lodgers till long after the hour when she set out on her morning round.

'No; I didn't see it,' she stammered.

Deering was silent. He stood twisting an unlit cigarette in his hand, and looking down at her with a gaze that was both constrained and hesitating.

She, too, felt the constraint of the situation, the impossibility of finding words which, after what had passed between them, should seem neither false nor heartless: and at last she exclaimed, standing up: 'Poor little Juliet! Can't I go to her?'

'Juliet is not here. I left her at St. Raphael with the relations with whom my wife was staying.'

'Oh,' Lizzie murmured, feeling vaguely that this added to the difficulty of the moment. How differently she had pictured their meeting!

'I'm so—so sorry for her!' she faltered.

Deering made no reply, but, turning on his heel, walked the length of the studio and halted before the picture on the easel. It was the landscape he had begun the previous autumn, with the intention of sending it to the Salon that spring. But it was still unfinished— seemed, indeed, hardly more advanced than on the fateful October day when Lizzie, standing before it for the first time, had confessed her inability to deal with Juliet. Perhaps the same thought struck its creator, for he broke into a dry laugh and turned from the easel with a shrug.

Under his protracted silence Lizzie roused herself to the fact that, since her pupil was absent, there was no reason for her remaining any longer; and as Deering approached her she rose and said with an effort: 'I'll go, then. You'll send for me when she comes back?'

Deering still hesitated, tormenting the cigarette between his fingers. 'She's not coming back—not at present.'

Lizzie heard him with a drop of the heart. Was everything to be changed in their lives? Of course; how could she have dreamed it would be otherwise? She could only stupidly repeat: 'Not coming back? Not this spring?'

'Probably not, since our friends are so good as to keep her. The fact is, I've got to go to America. My wife left a little property, a few pennies, that I must go and see to—for the child.'

Lizzie stood before him, a cold knife in her breast. 'I see—I see,' she reiterated, feeling all the while that she strained her eyes into utter blackness.

'It's a nuisance, having to pull up stakes,' he went on, with a fretful glance about the studio.

She lifted her eyes to his face. 'Shall you be gone long?' she took courage to ask.

'There again—I can't tell. It's all so mixed up.' He met her look for an incredibly long strange moment. 'I hate to go!' he murmured abruptly.

Lizzie felt a rush of moisture to her lashes, and the familiar wave of weakness at her heart. She raised her hand to her face with an instinctive gesture, and as she did so he held out his arms.

'Come here, Lizzie!' he said.

And she went—went with a sweet wild throb of liberation, with the sense that at last the house was his, that *she* was his, if he wanted her; that never again would that silent presence in the room above constrain and shame her rapture.

He pushed back her veil and covered her face with kisses. 'Don't cry, you little goose!' he said.

That they must see each other before his departure, in some place less exposed than their usual haunts, was as clear to Lizzie as it appeared to be to Deering. His expressing the wish seemed, indeed, the sweetest testimony to the quality of his feeling, since, in the first weeks of the most perfunctory widowhood, a man of his stamp is presumed to abstain from light adventures. If, then, he wished so much to be quietly and gravely with her, it could be only for reasons she did not call by name, but of which she felt the sacred tremor in her heart; and it would have seemed to her vain and vulgar to put forward, at such a moment, the conventional objections with which such little exposed existences defend the treasure of their freshness.

In such a mood as this, one may descend from the Passy omnibus at the corner of the Pont de la Concorde (she had not let him fetch her in a cab) with a sense of dedication almost solemn, and may advance to meet one's fate, in the shape of a gentleman of melancholy elegance, with an auto taxi at his call, as one has advanced to the altar steps in some girlish bridal vision.

Even the experienced waiter ushering them into an upper room of the quiet restaurant on the Seine could hardly have supposed their quest for privacy to be based on the familiar motive, so soberly did Deering give his orders, while his companion sat small and grave at his side. She did not, indeed, mean to let her distress obscure their hour together: she was already learning that Deering shrank from sadness. He should see that she had courage and gaiety to face their coming separation, and yet give herself meanwhile to this completer nearness; but she waited as always for him to strike the opening note.

Looking back at it later, she wondered at the sweetness of the hour. Her heart was unversed in happiness, but he had found the tone to lull her fears, and make her trust her fate for any golden wonder. Deepest of all, he gave her the sense of something tacit and established between them, as if his tenderness were a habit of the heart hardly needing the support of outward proof.

Such proof as he offered came, therefore, as a kind of crowning luxury, the flowering of a profoundly rooted sentiment; and here again the instinctive reserves and defences would have seemed to vulgarize what his confidence ennobled. But if all the tender casuistries of her heart were at his service, he took no grave advantage of them. Even when they sat alone after dinner, with the lights of the river trembling through their one low window, and the rumour of Paris enclosing them in a heart of silence, he seemed, as much as herself, under the spell of hallowing influences. She felt it most of all as she yielded to the arm he presently put about her, to the long caress he laid on her lips and eyes: not a word or gesture missed the note of quiet understanding, or cast a doubt, in retrospect, on the pact they sealed with their last look.

That pact, as she reviewed it through a sleepless night, seemed to have consisted mainly, on his part, in pleadings for full and frequent news of her, on hers in the promise that it should be given as often as he wrote to ask it. She did not wish to show too much eagerness, too great a desire to affirm and define her hold on him. Her life had given her a certain acquaintance with the arts of defence: girls in her situation were supposed to know them all, and to use them as occasion called. But Lizzie's very need of them had intensified her disdain. Just because she was so poor, and had always, materially, so to count her change and calculate her margin, she would at least know the joy of emotional prodigality, and give her heart as recklessly as the rich their millions. She was sure now that Deering loved her, and if he had seized the occasion of their farewell to give her some definitely worded sign of his feeling—if, more plainly, he had asked her to marry him— his doing so would have seemed less a proof of his sincerity than of his suspecting in her the need of such a warrant. That he had abstained seemed to show that he trusted her as she trusted him, and that they were one most of all in this complete security of understanding.

She had tried to make him guess all this in the chariness of her promise to write. She would write; of course she would. But he would be busy, preoccupied, on the move: it was for him to let her know when he wished a word, to spare her the embarrassment of ill-timed intrusions.

'Intrusions?' He had smiled the word away. 'You can't well intrude, my darling, on a heart where you're already established to the complete exclusion of other lodgers.' And then, taking her hands, and looking up from them into her happy dizzy eyes: 'You don't know much about being in love, do you, Lizzie?' he laughingly ended.

It seemed easy enough to reject this imputation in a kiss; but she wondered afterward if she had not deserved it. Was she really cold and conventional, and did other women give more richly and recklessly? She found that it was possible to turn about every one of her reserves and delicacies so that they looked like selfish scruples and pretty pruderies, and at this game she came in time to exhaust all the resources of casuistry.

Meanwhile the first days after Deering's departure wore a soft refracted light like the radiance lingering after sunset. *He*, at any rate, was taxable with no reserves, no calculations, and his letters of farewell, from train and steamer, filled her with long murmurs and echoes of his presence. How he loved her, how he loved her—and how he knew how to tell her so!

She was not sure of possessing the same gift. Unused to the expression of personal emotion, she wavered between the impulse to pour out all she felt and the fear lest her extravagance should amuse or even bore him. She never lost the sense that what was to her the central crisis of experience must be a mere episode in a life so predestined as his to romantic incidents. All that she felt and said would be subjected to the test of comparison with what others had already given him: from all quarters of the globe she saw passionate missives winging their way toward Deering, for whom her poor little swallow flight of devotion could certainly not make a summer. But such moments were succeeded by others in which she raised her head and dared affirm no woman had ever loved him just as she had, and that none, therefore, had probably found just such things to say to him. And this conviction strengthened the other less solidly based belief that *he* also, for the same reason, had found new accents to express his tenderness, and that the three letters she wore all day in her shabby blouse, and hid all night beneath her pillow, not only surpassed in beauty, but differed in quality from, all he had ever penned for other eyes.

They gave her, at any rate, during the weeks that she wore them on her heart, sensations more complex and delicate than Deering's actual presence had ever produced. To be with him was always like breasting a bright rough sea that blinded while it buoyed her; but his letters formed a still pool of contemplation, above which she could bend, and see the reflection of the sky, and the myriad movements of the life that flitted and gleamed below the surface. The wealth of this hidden life— that was what most surprised her! She had had no inkling of it, but had kept on along the narrow track of habit, like a traveller climbing a road in a fog, and suddenly finding himself on a sunlit crag between leagues of sky and dizzy depths of valley. And the odd thing was that all the people about her—the whole world of the Passy *pension*— seemed plodding along the same dull path, preoccupied with the pebbles underfoot, and unaware of the glory beyond the fog!

There were hours of exultation, when she longed to cry out to them what one saw from the summit—and hours of abasement, when she asked herself why *her* feet had been guided there, while others, no doubt as worthy, stumbled and blundered in obscurity. She felt, in particular, an urgent pity for the two or three other girls at Mme. Clopin's—girls older, duller, less alive than she, and by that very token more thrown upon her sympathy. Would they ever know? Had they ever known? Those were the questions that haunted her as she crossed her companions on the stairs, faced them at the dinner table, and listened to their poor pining talk in the dimly lit slippery-seated *salon*. One of the girls was Swiss, another English; a third, Andora Macy, was a young lady from the Southern States who was studying French with the ultimate object of imparting it to the inmates of a girls' school at Macon, Georgia.

Andora Macy was pale, faded, immature. She had a drooping accent, and a manner which fluctuated between arch audacity and fits of panicky hauteur. She yearned to be admired, and feared to be insulted; and yet seemed wistfully conscious that she was destined to miss both these extremes of sensation, or to enjoy them only in the experiences of her more privileged friends.

It was perhaps for this reason that she took a tender interest in Lizzie, who had shrunk from her at first, as the depressing image of her own probable future, but to whom she now suddenly became an object of sentimental pity.

Miss Macy's room was next to Miss West's, and the Southerner's knock often appealed to Lizzie's hospitality when Mme. Clopin's early curfew had driven her boarders from the *salon*. It sounded thus one evening, just as Lizzie, tired from an unusually long day of tuition, was in the act of removing her dress. She was in too indulgent a mood to withhold her 'Come in', and as Miss Macy crossed the threshold, Lizzie felt that Vincent Deering's first letter—the letter from the train—had slipped from her bosom to the floor.

Miss Macy, as promptly aware, darted forward to recover it. Lizzie stooped also, instinctively jealous of her touch; but the visitor reached the letter first, and as she seized it, Lizzie knew that she had seen whence it fell, and was weaving round the incident a rapid web of romance.

Lizzie blushed with annoyance. 'It's too stupid, having no pockets! If one gets a letter as one is going out in the morning, one has to carry it in one's blouse all day.'

Miss Macy looked at her fondly. 'It's warm from your heart!' she breathed, reluctantly yielding up the missive.

Lizzie laughed, for she knew it was the letter that had warmed her heart. Poor Andora Macy! *She* would never know. Her bleak bosom would never take fire from such a contact. Lizzie looked at her with kind eyes, chafing at the injustice of fate.

The next evening, on her return home, she found her friend hovering in the entrance hall.

'I thought you'd like me to put this in your own hand,' Andora whispered significantly, pressing a letter upon Lizzie. 'I couldn't *bear* to see it lying on the table with the others.'

It was Deering's letter from the steamer. Lizzie blushed to the forehead, but without resenting Andora's divination. She could not have breathed a word of her bliss, but she was not sorry to have it guessed, and pity for Andora's destitution yielded to the pleasure of using it as a mirror for her own abundance.

Deering wrote again on reaching New York, a long fond dissatisfied letter, vague in its indication to his own projects, specific in the expression of his love. Lizzie brooded over every syllable till they formed the undercurrent of all her waking thoughts, and murmured through her midnight dreams; but she would have been happier if they had shed some definite light on the future.

That would come, no doubt, when he had had time to look about and got his bearings. She counted up the days that must elapse before she received his next letter, and stole down early to peep at the papers, and learn when the next American mail was due. At length the happy date arrived, and she hurried distractedly through the day's work, trying to conceal her impatience by the endearments she bestowed upon her pupils. It was easier, in her present mood, to kiss them than to keep them at their grammars.

That evening, on Mme. Clopin's threshold, her heart beat so wildly that she had to lean a moment against the doorpost before entering. But on the hall table, where the letters lay, there was none for her.

She went over them with an impatient hand, her heart dropping down and down, as she had sometimes fallen down an endless stairway in a dream—the very same stairway up which she had seemed to fly when she climbed the long hill to Deering's door. Then it struck her that Andora might have found and secreted her letter, and with a spring she was on the actual stairs, and rattling Miss Macy's door handle.

'You've a letter for me, haven't you?' she panted.

Miss Macy enclosed her in attenuated arms. 'Oh, darling, did you expect another?'

'Do give it to me!' Lizzie pleaded with eager eyes.

'But I haven't any! There hasn't been a sign of a letter for you.'

'I know there is. There *must* be,' Lizzie cried, stamping her foot.

'But, dearest, I've *watched* for you, and there's been nothing.'

Day after day, for the ensuing weeks, the same scene re-enacted itself with endless variations. Lizzie, after the first sharp spasm of disappointment, made no effort to conceal her anxiety from Miss Macy, and the fond Andora was charged to keep a vigilant eye upon the postman's coming and to spy on the *bonne* for possible negligence or perfidy. But these elaborate precautions remained fruitless, and no letter from Deering came.

During the first fortnight of silence, Lizzie exhausted all the ingenuities of explanation. She marvelled afterward at the reasons she had found for Deering's silence: there were moments when she almost argued herself into thinking it more natural than his continuing to write. There was only one reason which her intelligence rejected; and that was the possibility that he had forgotten her, that the whole episode had faded from his mind like a breath from a mirror. From that she resolutely averted her thoughts, conscious that if she suffered herself to contemplate it, the motive power of life would fail, and she would no longer understand why she rose in the morning and lay down at night.

If she had had leisure to indulge her anguish she might have been unable to keep such speculations at bay. But she had to be up and working: the *blanchisseuse* had to be paid, and Mme. Clopin's weekly bill, and all the little 'extras' that even her frugal habits had to reckon with. And in the depths of her thought dwelt the dogging fear of illness and incapacity, goading her to work while she could. She hardly remembered the time when she had been without that fear; it was second nature now, and it kept her on her feet when other incentives might have failed. In the blankness of her misery she felt no dread of death; but the horror of being ill and 'dependent' was in her blood.

In the first weeks of silence she wrote again and again to Deering, entreating him for a word, for a mere sign of life. From the first she had shrunk from seeming to assert any claim on his future, yet in her bewilderment she now charged herself with having been too possessive, too exacting in her tone. She told herself that his fastidiousness shrank from any but a 'light touch', and that hers had not been light enough. She should have kept to the character of the 'little friend', the artless consciousness in which tormented genius may find an escape from its complexities; and instead, she had dramatized their relation, exaggerated her own part in it, presumed, forsooth, to share the front of the stage with him, instead of being content to serve as scenery or chorus.

But though, to herself, she admitted, and even insisted on, the episodical nature of the experience, on the fact that for Deering it could be no more than an incident, she was still convinced that his sentiment for her, however fugitive, had been genuine.

His had not been the attitude of the unscrupulous male seeking a vulgar 'advantage'. For a moment he had really needed her, and if he was silent now, it was perhaps because he feared that she had mistaken the nature of the need, and built vain hopes on its possible duration.

It was of the essence of Lizzie's devotion that it sought, instinctively, the larger freedom of its object; she could not conceive of love under any form of exaction or compulsion. To make this clear to Deering became an overwhelming need, and in a last short letter she explicitly freed him from whatever sentimental obligation its predecessors might have seemed to impose. In this communication she playfully accused herself of having unwittingly sentimentalized their relation, affecting, in self-defence, a retrospective astuteness, a sense of the impermanence of the tenderer sentiments, that almost put Deering in the position of having mistaken coquetry for surrender. And she ended, gracefully, with a plea for the continuance of the friendly regard which she had 'always understood' to be the basis of their sympathy. The document, when completed, seemed to her worthy of what she conceived to be Deering's conception of a woman of the world—and she found a spectral satisfaction in the thought of making her final appearance before him in this distinguished character. But she was never destined to learn what effect the appearance produced; for the letter, like those it sought to excuse, remained unanswered.

The fresh spring sunshine which had so often attended Lizzie West on her dusty climb up the hill of St. Cloud, beamed on her, some two years later, in a scene and a situation of altered import.

Its rays, filtered through the horse chestnuts of the Champs Elysées, shone on the gravelled circle about Laurent's restaurant; and Miss West, seated at a table within that privileged space, presented to the light a hat much better able to sustain its scrutiny than those which had shaded the brow of Juliet Deering's instructress.

Her dress was in keeping with the hat, and both belonged to a situation rife with such possibilities as the act of a leisurely luncheon at Laurent's in the opening week of the Salon. Her companions, of both sexes, confirmed this impression by an appropriateness of attire and an ease of manner implying the largest range of selection between the forms of Parisian idleness; and even Andora Macy, seated opposite, as in the place of co-hostess or companion, reflected, in coy greys and mauves, the festal note of the occasion.

This note reverberated persistently in the ears of a solitary gentleman straining for glimpses of the group from a table wedged in the remotest corner of the garden; but to Miss West herself the occurrence did not rise above the usual. For nearly a year she had been acquiring the habit of such situations, and the act of offering a luncheon at Laurent's to her cousins, the Harvey Mearses of Providence, and their friend Mr. Jackson Benn, produced in her no emotion beyond the languid glow which Mr. Benn's presence was beginning to impart to such scenes.

'It's frightful, the way you've got used to it,' Andora Macy had wailed, in the first days of her friend's transfigured fortunes, when Lizzie West had waked one morning to find herself among the heirs of an ancient miserly cousin whose testamentary dispositions had formed, since her earliest childhood, the subject of pleasantry and conjecture in her own improvident family. Old Hezron Mears had never given any sign of life to the luckless Wests; had perhaps hardly been conscious of including them in the carefully drawn will which, following the old American convention, scrupulously divided his millions among his kin. It was by a mere genealogical accident that Lizzie, falling just within the golden circle, found herself possessed of a pittance sufficient to release her from the prospect of a long grey future in Mme. Clopin's *pension*.

The release had seemed wonderful at first; yet she presently found that it had destroyed her former world without giving her a new one. On the ruins of the old *pension* life bloomed the only flower that had ever sweetened her path; and beyond the sense of present ease, and the removal of anxiety for the future, her reconstructed existence blossomed with no compensating joys. She had hoped great things from the opportunity to rest, to travel, to look about her, above all, in various artful feminine ways, to be 'nice' to the companions of her less privileged state; but such widenings of scope left her, as it were, but the more conscious of the empty margin of personal life beyond them. It was not till she woke to the leisure of her new days that she had the full sense of what was gone from them.

Their very emptiness made her strain to pack them with transient sensations: she was like the possessor of an unfurnished house, with random furniture and bric-a-brac perpetually pouring in 'on approval'. It was in this experimental character that Mr. Jackson Benn had fixed her attention, and the languid effort of her imagination to adjust him to her taste was seconded by the fond complicity of Andora, and by the smiling approval of her cousins. Lizzie did not discourage these attempts: she suffered serenely Andora's allusions to Mr. Benn's infatuation, and Mrs. Mears's boasts of his business standing. All the better if they could drape his narrow square-shouldered frame and round unwinking countenance in the trailing mists of sentiment: Lizzie looked and listened, not unhopeful of the miracle.

'I never saw anything like the way these Frenchmen stare! Doesn't it make you nervous, Lizzie?' Mrs. Mears broke out suddenly, ruffling her feather boa about an outraged bosom. Mrs. Mears was still in that stage of development when her countrywomen taste to the full the peril of being exposed to the gaze of the licentious Gaul.

Lizzie roused herself from the contemplation of Mr. Benn's round baby cheeks and the square blue jaw resting on his perpendicular collar. 'Is someone staring at me?' she asked.

'Don't turn round, whatever you do! There—just over there, between the rhododendrons—the tall blond man alone at that table. Really, Harvey, I think you ought to speak to the headwaiter, or something, though I suppose in one of these places they'd only laugh at you,' Mrs. Mears shudderingly concluded.

Her husband, as if inclining to this probability, continued the undisturbed dissection of his chicken wing, but Mr. Benn, perhaps conscious that his situation demanded a more punctilious attitude, sternly revolved upon the parapet of his high collar in the direction of Mrs. Mears's glance.

'What, that fellow all alone over there? Why, *he's* not French; he's an American,' he then proclaimed with a perceptible relaxing of the muscles.

'Oh!' murmured Mrs. Mears, as perceptibly disappointed, and Mr. Benn continued: 'He came over on the steamer with me. He's some kind of an artist—a fellow named Deering. He was staring at *me*, I guess: wondering whether I was going to remember him. Why, how d'e do? How are you? Why, yes, of course; with pleasure—my friends, Mrs. Harvey Mears—Mr. Mears; my friends, Miss Macy and Miss West.'

'I have the pleasure of knowing Miss West,' said Vincent Deering with a smile.

Even through his smile Lizzie had seen, in the first moment, how changed he was; and the impression of the change deepened to the point of pain when, a few days later, in reply to his brief note, she granted him a private hour.

That the first sight of his writing—the first answer to her letters—should have come, after three long years, in the shape of this impersonal line, too curt to be called humble, yet revealing a consciousness of the past in the studied avoidance of its language! As she read, her mind flashed back over what she had dreamed his letters would be, over the exquisite answers she had composed above his name. There was nothing exquisite in the lines before her; but dormant nerves began to throb again at the mere touch of the paper he had touched, and she threw the note into the fire before she dared to reply to it.

Now that he was actually before her again, he became, as usual, the one live spot in her consciousness. Once more her tormented self sank back passive and numb, but now with all its power of suffering mysteriously transferred to the presence, so known yet so unknown, at the opposite corner of her hearth. She was still Lizzie West, and he was still Vincent Deering; but the Styx rolled between them, and she saw his face through its fog. It was his face, really, rather than his words, that told her, as she furtively studied it, the tale of failure and discouragement which had so blurred its handsome lines. She kept, afterward, no precise memory of the details of his narrative: the pain it evidently cost him to impart it was so much the sharpest fact in her new vision of him. Confusedly, however, she gathered that on reaching America he had found his wife's small property gravely impaired; and that, while lingering on to secure what remained of it, he had contrived to sell a picture or two, and had even known a moment of success, during which he received orders and set up a studio. Then the tide had ebbed, his work had remained on his hands, and a tedious illness, with its miserable sequel of debt, soon wiped out his advantage. There followed a period of eclipse, during which she inferred that he had tried his hand at diverse means of livelihood, accepting employment from a fashionable house decorator, designing wallpapers, illustrating magazine articles, and acting for a time—she dimly understood—as the social tout of a new hotel desirous of advertising its restaurant. These disjointed facts were strung on a slender thread of personal allusions—references to friends who had been kind (jealously, she guessed them to be women), and to enemies who had schemed against him. But, true to his tradition of 'correctness', he carefully avoided the mention of names, and left her imagination to grope dimly through a crowded world in which there seemed little room for her small shy presence.

As she listened, her private grievance vanished beneath the sense of his unhappiness. Nothing he had said explained or excused his conduct to her; but he had suffered, he had been lonely, had been humiliated, and she felt, with a fierce maternal rage, that there was no possible justification for any scheme of things in which such facts were possible. She could not have said why: she simply knew that it hurt too much to see him hurt.

Gradually it came to her that her absence of resentment was due to her having so definitely settled her own future. She was glad she had decided—as she now felt she had—to marry Jackson Benn, if only for the sense of detachment it gave her in dealing with Vincent Deering. Her personal safety insured her the requisite impartiality, and justified her in lingering as long as she chose over the last lines of a chapter to which her own act had fixed the close. Any lingering hesitations as to the finality of this decision were dispelled by the need of making it known to Deering: and when her visitor paused in his reminiscences to say, with a sigh, 'But many things have happened to you too,' the words did not so much evoke the sense of her altered fortunes as the image of the suitor to whom she was about to entrust them.

'Yes, many things; it's three years,' she answered.

Deering sat leaning forward, in his sad exiled elegance, his eyes gently bent on hers; and at his side she saw the form of Mr. Jackson Benn, with shoulders preternaturally squared by the cut of his tight black coat, and a tall shiny collar sustaining his baby cheeks and hard blue chin. Then the vision faded as Deering began to speak.

'Three years,' he repeated musingly. 'I've so often wondered what they'd brought you.'

She lifted her head with a blush, and the terrified wish that he should not—at the cost of all his notions of correctness—lapse into the blunder of becoming 'personal'.

'You've wondered?' she smiled back bravely.

'Do you suppose I haven't?' His look dwelt on her. 'Yes, I dare say that *was* what you thought of me.'

She had her answer pat—'Why, frankly, you know, I *didn't* think of you at all.' But the mounting tide of her memories swept it indignantly away. If it was his correctness to ignore, it could never be hers to disavow!

'*Was* that what you thought of me?' she heard him repeat in a tone of sad insistence; and at that, with a lift of her head, she resolutely answered: 'How could I know what to think? I had no word from you.'

If she had expected, and perhaps almost hoped, that this answer would create a difficulty for him, the gaze of quiet fortitude with which he met it proved that she had underestimated his resources.

'No, you had no word. I kept my vow,' he said.

'Your vow?'

'That you *shouldn't* have a word—not a syllable. Oh, I kept it through everything!'

Lizzie's heart was sounding in her ears the old confused rumour of the sea of life, but through it she desperately tried to distinguish the still small voice of reason.

'What was your vow? Why shouldn't I have had a syllable from you?'

He sat motionless, still holding her with a look so gentle that it almost seemed forgiving.

Then, abruptly, he rose, and crossing the space between them, sat down in a chair at her side. The movement might have implied a forgetfulness of changed conditions, and Lizzie, as if thus viewing it, drew slightly back; but he appeared not to notice her recoil, and his eyes, at last leaving her face, slowly and approvingly made the round of the small bright drawing room. 'This is charming. Yes, things *have* changed for you,' he said.

A moment before, she had prayed that he might be spared the error of a vain return upon the past. It was as if all her retrospective tenderness, dreading to see him at such a disadvantage, rose up to protect him from it. But his evasiveness exasperated her, and suddenly she felt the desire to hold him fast, face to face with his own words.

Before she could repeat her question, however, he had met her with another.

'You *did* think of me, then? Why are you afraid to tell me that you did?'

The unexpectedness of the challenge wrung a cry from her. 'Didn't my letters tell you so enough?'

'Ah—your letters—' Keeping her gaze on his with unrelenting fixity, she could detect in him no confusion, not the least quiver of a nerve. He only gazed back at her more sadly.

'They went everywhere with me—your letters,' he said.

'Yet you never answered them.' At last the accusation trembled to her lips.

'Yet I never answered them.'

'Did you ever so much as read them, I wonder?'

[180]

All the demons of self-torture were up in her now, and she loosed them on him as if to escape from their rage.

Deering hardly seemed to hear her question. He merely shifted his attitude, leaning a little nearer to her, but without attempting, by the least gesture, to remind her of the privileges which such nearness had once implied.

'There were beautiful, wonderful things in them,' he said, smiling.

She felt herself stiffen under his smile. 'You've waited three years to tell me so!'

He looked at her with grave surprise. 'And do you resent my telling you, even now?'

His parries were incredible. They left her with a sense of thrusting at emptiness, and a desperate, almost vindictive desire to drive him against the wall and pin him there.

'No. Only I wonder you should take the trouble to tell me, when at the time—'

And now, with a sudden turn, he gave her the final surprise of meeting her squarely on her own ground.

'When at the time, I didn't? But how *could* I—at the time?'

'Why couldn't you? You've not yet told me.'

He gave her again his look of disarming patience. 'Do I need to? Hasn't my whole wretched story told you?'

'Told me why you never answered my letters?'

'Yes—since I could only answer them in one way: by protesting my love and my longing.'

There was a pause, of resigned expectancy on his part, on hers of a wild, confused reconstruction of her shattered past. 'You mean, then, that you didn't write because—'

'Because I found, when I reached America, that I was a pauper: that my wife's money was gone, and that what I could earn—I've so little gift that way!— was barely enough to keep Juliet clothed and educated. It was as if an iron door had been locked and barred between us.'

Lizzie felt herself driven back, panting, on the last defences of her incredulity. 'You might at least have told me—have explained. Do you think I shouldn't have understood?'

He did not hesitate. 'You would have understood. It wasn't that.'

'What was it then?' she quavered.

'It's wonderful you shouldn't see! Simply that I couldn't write you *that*. Anything else—not *that*!'

'And so you preferred to let me suffer?'

There was a shade of reproach in his eyes. 'I suffered too,' he said.

It was his first direct appeal to her compassion, and for a moment it nearly unsettled the delicate poise of her sympathies, and sent them trembling in the direction of scorn and irony. But even as the impulse rose it was stayed by another sensation. Once again, as so often in the past, she became aware of a fact which, in his absence, she always failed to reckon with; the fact of the deep irreducible difference between his image in her mind and his actual self—the mysterious alteration in her judgment produced by the inflections of his voice, the look of his eyes, the whole complex pressure of his personality. She had phrased it once, self-reproachfully, by saying to herself that she 'never could remember him'—so completely did the sight of him supersede the counterfeit about which her fancy wove its perpetual wonders. Bright and breathing as that counterfeit was, it became a figment of the mind at the touch of his presence, and on this occasion the immediate result was to cause her to feel his possible unhappiness with an intensity beside which her private injury paled.

'I suffered horribly,' he repeated, 'and all the more that I couldn't make a sign, couldn't cry out my misery. There was only one escape from it all—to hold my tongue, and pray that you might hate me.'

The blood rushed to Lizzie's forehead. 'Hate you—you prayed that I might hate you?'

He rose from his seat, and moving closer, lifted her hand in his. 'Yes, because your letters showed me that if you didn't, you'd be unhappier still.'

Her hand lay motionless, with the warmth of his flowing through it, and her thoughts, too—her poor fluttering stormy thoughts—felt themselves suddenly penetrated by the same soft current of communion.

'And I meant to keep my resolve,' he went on, slowly releasing his clasp. 'I meant to keep it even after the random stream of things swept me back here, in your way; but when I saw you the other day I felt that what had been possible at a distance was impossible now that we were near each other. How could I see you, and let you hate me?'

He had moved away, but not to resume his seat. He merely paused at a little distance, his hand resting on a chair back, in the transient attitude that precedes departure.

Lizzie's heart contracted. He was going, then, and this was his farewell. He was going, and she could find no word to detain him but the senseless stammer: 'I never hated you.'

He considered her with a faint smile. 'It's not necessary, at any rate, that you should do so now. Time and circumstances have made me so harmless—that's exactly why I've dared to venture back. And I wanted to tell you how I rejoice in your good fortune. It's the only obstacle between us that I can't bring myself to wish away.'

Lizzie sat silent, spellbound, as she listened, by the sudden evocation of Mr. Jackson Benn. He stood there again, between herself and Deering, perpendicular and reproachful, but less solid and sharply outlined than before, with a look in his small hard eyes that desperately wailed for re-embodiment.

Deering was continuing his farewell speech. 'You're rich now—you're free. You will marry.' She saw him holding out his hand.

'It's not true that I'm engaged!' she broke out. They were the last words she had meant to utter; they were hardly related to her conscious thoughts; but she felt her whole will gathered up in the irrepressible impulse to repudiate and fling away from her forever the spectral claim of Mr. Jackson Benn.

It was the firm conviction of Andora Macy that every object in the Vincent Deerings' charming little house at Neuilly had been expressly designed for the Deerings' son to play with.

The house was full of pretty things, some not obviously applicable to the purpose; but Miss Macy's casuistry was equal to the baby's appetite, and the baby's mother was no match for them in the art of defending her possessions. There were moments, in fact, when she almost fell in with Andora's summary division of her works of art into articles safe or unsafe for the baby to lick, or resisted it only to the extent of occasionally substituting some less precious, or less perishable, object for the particular fragility on which her son's desire was fixed. And it was with this intention that, on a certain spring morning—which wore the added lustre of being the baby's second birthday—she had murmured, with her mouth in his curls, and one hand holding a bit of Chelsea above his clutch: 'Wouldn't he rather have that beautiful shiny thing in Aunt Andora's hand?'

The two friends were together in Lizzie's morning room—the room she had chosen, on acquiring the house, because, when she sat there, she could hear Deering's step as he paced up and down before his easel in the studio she had built for him. His step had been less regularly audible than she had hoped, for, after three years of wedded bliss, he had somehow failed to settle down to the great work which was to result from that state; but even when she did not hear him she knew that he was there, above her head, stretched out on the old divan from St. Cloud, and smoking countless cigarettes while he skimmed the morning papers; and the sense of his nearness had not yet lost its first keen edge of wonder.

Lizzie herself, on the day in question, was engaged in a more arduous task than the study of the morning's news. She had never unlearned the habit of orderly activity, and the trait she least understood in her husband's character was his way of letting the loose ends of life hang as they would. She had been disposed to ascribe this to the chronic incoherence of his first *ménage*; but now she knew that, though he basked under her beneficent rule, he would never feel any impulse to further its work. He liked to see things fall into place about him at a wave of her wand; but his enjoyment of her household magic in no way diminished his smiling irresponsibility, and it was with one of its least amiable consequences that his wife and her friend were now dealing.

Before them stood two travel-worn trunks and a distended portmanteau, which had shed their heterogeneous contents over Lizzie's rosy carpet. They represented the hostages left by her husband on his somewhat precipitate departure from a New York boarding house, and redeemed by her on her learning, in a curt letter from his landlady, that the latter was not disposed to regard them as an equivalent for the arrears of Deering's board.

Lizzie had not been shocked by the discovery that her husband had left America in debt. She had too sad an acquaintance with economic strain to see any humiliation in such accidents; but it offended her sense of order that he should not have liquidated his obligation in the three years since their marriage. He took her remonstrance with his usual good humour, and left her to forward the liberating draft, though her delicacy had provided him with a bank account which assured his personal independence. Lizzie had discharged the duty without repugnance, since she knew that his delegating it to her was the result of his indolence and not of any design on her exchequer. Deering was not dazzled by money; his altered fortunes had tempted him to no excesses: he was simply too lazy to draw the check, as he had been too lazy to remember the debt it cancelled.

'No, dear! No!' Lizzie lifted the Chelsea higher. 'Can't you find something for him, Andora, among that rubbish over there? Where's the beaded bag you had in your hand? I don't think it could hurt him to lick that.'

Miss Macy, bag in hand, rose from her knees, and stumbled across the room through the frayed garments and old studio properties. Before the group of mother and son she fell into a rapturous attitude.

'Do look at him reach for it, the tyrant! Isn't he just like the young Napoleon?'

Lizzie laughed and swung her son in air. 'Dangle it before him, Andora. If you let him have it too quickly, he won't care for it. He's just like any man, I think.'

Andora slowly lowered the bag till the heir of the Deerings closed his masterful fist upon it. 'There—my Chelsea's safe!' Lizzie smiled, setting her boy on the floor, and watching him stagger away with his booty.

Andora stood beside her, watching too. 'Do you know where the bag came from, Lizzie?'

Mrs. Deering, bent over a pile of discollared shirts, shook an inattentive head. 'I never saw such wicked washing! There isn't one that's fit to mend. The bag? No: I've not the least idea.'

Andora surveyed her incredulously. 'Doesn't it make you utterly miserable to think that some woman may have made it for him?'

Lizzie, still bowed in scrutiny above the shirts, broke into a laugh. 'Really, Andora, really! Six, seven, nine; no, there isn't even a dozen. There isn't a whole dozen of *anything*. I don't see how men live alone.'

Andora broodingly pursued her theme. 'Do you mean to tell me it doesn't make you jealous to handle these things of his that other women may have given him?'

Lizzie shook her head again, and, straightening herself with a smile, tossed a bundle in her friend's direction. 'No, I don't feel jealous. Here, count these socks for me, like a darling.'

Andora moaned 'Don't you feel *anything at all?*' as the socks landed in her hollow bosom; but Lizzie, intent upon her task, tranquilly continued to unfold and sort. She felt a great deal as she did so, but her feelings were too deep and delicate for the simplifying processes of speech. She only knew that each article she drew from the trunks sent through her the long tremor of Deering's touch. It was part of her wonderful new life that everything belonging to him contained an infinitesimal fraction of himself—a fraction becoming visible in the warmth of her love as certain secret elements become visible in rare intensities of temperature. And in the case of the objects before her, poor shabby witnesses of his days of failure, what they gave out acquired a special poignancy from its contrast to his present cherished state. His shirts were all in round dozens now, and washed as carefully as old lace. As for his socks, she knew the pattern of every pair, and would have liked to see the washerwoman who dared to mislay one, or bring it home with the colors 'run'! And in these homely tokens of his well-being she saw the symbol of what her tenderness had brought him. He was safe in it, encompassed by it, morally and materially, and she defied the embattled powers of malice to reach him through the armour of her love. Such feelings, however, were not communicable, even had one desired to express them: they were no more to be distinguished from the sense of life itself than bees from the lime blossoms in which they murmur.

'Oh, do *look* at him, Lizzie! He's found out how to open the bag!'

Lizzie lifted her head to look a moment at her son, throned on a heap of studio rubbish, with Andora before him on adoring knees. She thought vaguely 'Poor Andora!' and then resumed the discouraged inspection of a buttonless white waistcoat. The next sound she was conscious of was an excited exclamation from her friend.

'Why, Lizzie, do you know what he used the bag for? To keep your letters in!'

Lizzie looked up more quickly. She was aware that Andora's pronoun had changed its object, and was now applied to Deering. And it struck her as odd, and slightly disagreeable, that a letter of hers should be found among the rubbish abandoned in her husband's New York lodgings.

'How funny! Give it to me, please.'

'Give it to Aunt Andora, darling! Here—look inside, and see what else a big, big boy can find there! Yes, here's another! Why, why—'

Lizzie rose with a shade of impatience and crossed the floor to the romping group beside the other trunk.

'What is it? Give me the letters, please.' As she spoke, she suddenly recalled the day when, in Mme. Clopin's *pension*, she had addressed a similar behest to Andora Macy.

Andora lifted to her a look of startled conjecture. 'Why, this one's never been opened! Do you suppose that awful woman could have kept it from him?'

Lizzie laughed. Andora's imaginings were really puerile! 'What awful woman? His landlady? Don't be such a goose, Andora. How can

[186]

it have been kept back from him, when we've found it among his things?'

'Yes; but then why was it never opened?'

Andora held out the letter, and Lizzie took it. The writing was hers; the envelope bore the Passy postmark; and it was unopened. She looked at it with a sharp drop of the heart.

'Why, so are the others—all unopened!' Andora threw out on a rising note; but Lizzie, stooping over, checked her.

'Give them to me, please.'

'Oh, Lizzie, Lizzie—' Andora, on her knees, held back the packet, her pale face paler with anger and compassion. 'Lizzie, they're the letters I used to post for you—the letters he never answered! *Look!*'

'Give them back to me, please.' Lizzie possessed herself of the letters.

The two women faced each other, Andora still kneeling, Lizzie motionless before her. The blood had rushed to her face, humming in her ears, and forcing itself into the veins of her temples. Then it ebbed, and she felt cold and weak.

'It must have been some plot—some conspiracy,' Andora cried, so fired by the ecstasy of invention that for the moment she seemed lost to all but the aesthetic aspect of the case.

Lizzie averted her eyes with an effort, and they rested on the boy, who sat at her feet placidly sucking the tassels of the bag. His mother stooped and extracted them from his rosy mouth, which a cry of wrath immediately filled. She lifted him in her arms, and for the first time no current of life ran from his body into hers. He felt heavy and clumsy, like some other woman's child; and his screams annoyed her.

'Take him away, please, Andora.'

'Oh, Lizzie, Lizzie!' Andora wailed.

Lizzie held out the child, and Andora, struggling to her feet, received him.

'I know just how you feel,' she gasped, above the baby's head.

Lizzie, in some dark hollow of herself, heard the faint echo of a laugh. Andora always thought she knew how people felt!

'Tell Marthe to take him with her when she fetches Juliet home from school.'

'Yes, yes.' Andora gloated on her. 'If you'd only give way, my darling!'

The baby, howling, dived over Andora's shoulder for the bag.

'Oh, *take* him!' his mother ordered.

Andora, from the door, cried out: 'I'll be back at once. Remember, love, you're not alone!'

But Lizzie insisted, 'Go with them—I wish you to go with them,' in the tone to which Miss Macy had never learned the answer.

The door closed on her reproachful back, and Lizzie stood alone. She looked about the disordered room, which offered a dreary image of the havoc of her life. An hour or two ago, everything about her had been so exquisitely ordered, without and within: her thoughts and her emotions had all been outspread before her like jewels laid away symmetrically in a collector's cabinet. Now they had been tossed down helter-skelter among the rubbish there on the floor, and had themselves turned to rubbish like the rest. Yes, there lay her life at her feet, among all that tarnished trash.

She picked up her letters, ten in all, and examined the flaps of the envelopes. Not one had been opened—not one. As she looked, every word she had written fluttered to life, and every feeling prompting it sent a tremor through her. With vertiginous speed and microscopic distinctness of vision she was reliving that whole period of her life, stripping bare again the ruin over which the drift of three happy years had fallen.

She laughed at Andora's notion of a conspiracy—of the letters having been 'kept back'. She required no extraneous aid in deciphering the mystery: her three years' experience of Deering shed on it all the light she needed. And yet a moment before she had believed herself to be perfectly happy! Now it was the worst part of her pain that it did not really surprise her.

She knew so well how it must have happened. The letters had reached him when he was busy, occupied with something else, and had been put aside to be read at some future time—a time which never came. Perhaps on the steamer, even, he had met 'someone else'—the 'someone' who lurks, veiled and ominous, in the background of every woman's thoughts about her lover. Or perhaps he had been merely forgetful. She knew now that the sensations which he seemed to feel most intensely left no reverberations in his memory—that he did not relive either his pleasures or his pains. She needed no better proof than the lightness of his conduct toward his daughter. He seemed to have taken it for granted that Juliet would remain indefinitely with the friends who had received her after her mother's death, and it was at Lizzie's suggestion that the little girl was brought home and that they had established themselves at Neuilly to be near her school. But Juliet once with them, he became the model of a tender father, and Lizzie wondered that he had not felt the child's absence, since he seemed so affectionately aware of her presence.

Lizzie had noted all this in Juliet's case, but had taken for granted that her own was different; that she formed, for Deering, the exception which every woman secretly supposes herself to form in the experience of the man she loves. She had learned by this time that she could not modify his habits; but she imagined that she had deepened his sensibilities, had furnished him with an 'ideal'—angelic function! And she now saw the fact of her letters—her unanswered letters— having on his own assurance, 'meant so much' to him, had been the basis on which this beautiful fabric was reared.

There they lay now, the letters, precisely as when they had left her hands. He had not had time to read them; and there had been a moment in her past when that discovery would have been to her the sharpest pang imaginable. She had travelled far beyond that point. She could have forgiven him now for having forgotten her; but she could never forgive him for having deceived her.

She sat down, and looked again about the room. Suddenly she heard his step overhead, and her heart contracted. She was afraid that he was coming down to her. She sprang up and bolted the door; then she dropped into the nearest chair, tremulous and exhausted, as if the act had required an immense effort. A moment later she heard him on the stairs, and her tremor broke into a fit of shaking. 'I loathe you—I loathe you!' she cried.

She listened apprehensively for his touch on the handle of the door. He would come in, humming a tune, to ask some idle question and lay a caress on her hair. But no, the door was bolted; she was safe. She continued to listen, and the step passed on. He had not been coming to her, then. He must have gone downstairs to fetch something— another newspaper, perhaps. He seemed to read little else, and she sometimes wondered when he had found time to store the material that used to serve for their famous 'literary' talks. The wonder shot through her again, barbed with a sneer. At that moment it seemed to her that everything he had ever done and been was a lie.

She heard the house door close, and started up. Was he going out? It was not his habit to leave the house in the morning.

She crossed the room to the window, and saw him walking, with a quick decided step, between the lilacs to the gate. What could have called him forth at that unusual hour? It was odd that he should not have told her. The fact that she thought it odd suddenly showed her how closely their lives were interwoven. She had become a habit to him, and he was fond of his habits. But to her it was as if a stranger had opened the gate and gone out. She wondered what he would feel if he knew that she felt *that*.

'In a hour he will know,' she said to herself, with a kind of fierce exultation; and immediately she began to dramatize the scene. As soon as he came in she meant to call him up to her room and hand him the letters without a word. For a moment she gloated on the picture; then her imagination recoiled. She was humiliated by the thought of humiliating him. She wanted to keep his image intact; she would not see him.

He had lied to her about her letters—had lied to her when he found it to his interest to regain her favour. Yes, there was the point to hold fast. He had sought her out when he learned that she was rich. Perhaps he had come back from America on purpose to marry her; no doubt he had come back on purpose. It was incredible that she had not seen this at the time. She turned sick at the thought of her fatuity and of the grossness of his arts. Well, the event proved that they were all he needed. . . . But why had he gone out at such an hour? She was irritated to find herself still preoccupied by his comings and goings.

Turning from the window, she sat down again. She wondered what she meant to do next. . . . No, she would not show him the letters; she would simply leave them on his table and go away. She would leave the house with her boy and Andora. It was a relief to feel a definite plan forming itself in her mind—something that her uprooted thoughts could fasten on. She would go away, of course; and meanwhile, in order not to see him, she would feign a headache, and remain in her room till after luncheon. Then she and Andora would pack a few things, and fly with the child while he was dawdling about upstairs in the studio. When one's house fell, one fled from the ruins: nothing could be simpler, more inevitable.

Her thoughts were checked by the impossibility of picturing what would happen next. Try as she would, she could not see herself and the child away from Deering. But that, of course, was because of her nervous weakness. She had youth, money, energy: all the trumps were on her side. It was much more difficult to imagine what would become of Deering. He was so dependent on her, and they had been so happy together! It struck her as illogical and even immoral, and yet she knew he had been happy with her. It never happened like that in novels:

happiness 'built on a lie' always crumbled, burying the presumptuous architect beneath its ruins. According to the laws of fiction, Deering, having deceived her once, would inevitably have gone on deceiving her. Yet she knew he had not gone on deceiving her. . . .

She tried again to picture her new life. Her friends, of course, would rally about her. But the prospect left her cold; she did not want them to rally. She wanted only one thing—the life she had been living before she had given her baby the embroidered bag to play with. Oh, why had she given him the bag? She had been so happy, they had all been so happy! Every nerve in her clamoured for her lost happiness, angrily, irrationally, as the boy had clamoured for his bag! It was horrible to know too much; there was always blood in the foundations. Parents 'kept things' from children—protected them from all the dark secrets of pain and evil. And was any life livable unless it were thus protected? Could anyone look in the Medusa's face and live?

But why should she leave the house, since it was hers? Here, with her boy and Andora, she could still make for herself the semblance of a life. It was Deering who would have to go; he would understand that as soon as he saw the letters.

She saw him going—leaving the house as he had left it just now. She saw the gate closing on him for the last time. Now her vision was acute enough: she saw him as distinctly as if he were in the room. Ah, he would not like returning to the old life of privations and expedients! And yet she knew he would not plead with her.

Suddenly a new thought seized her. What if Andora had rushed to him with the tale of the discovery of the letters—with the 'Fly, you are discovered!' of romantic fiction? What if he *had* left her for good? It would not be unlike him, after all. For all his sweetness he was always evasive and inscrutable. He might have said to himself that he would forestall her action, and place himself at once on the defensive. It might be that she *had* seen him go out of the gate for the last time.

She looked about the room again, as if the thought had given it a new aspect. Yes, this alone could explain her husband's going out. It was past twelve o'clock, their usual luncheon hour, and he was scrupulously punctual at meals, and gently reproachful if she kept him waiting. Only some unwonted event could have caused him to leave the house at such an hour and with such marks of haste. Well, perhaps it was better that Andora should have spoken. She mistrusted her own courage; she almost hoped the deed had been done for her. Yet her next sensation was one of confused resentment. She said to herself,

'Why has Andora interfered?' She felt baffled and angry, as though her prey had escaped her. If Deering had been in the house she would have gone to him instantly and overwhelmed him with her scorn. But he had gone out, and she did not know where he had gone, and oddly mingled with her anger against him was the latent instinct of vigilance, the solicitude of the woman accustomed to watch over the man she loves. It would be strange never to feel that solicitude again, never to hear him say, with his hand on her hair: 'You foolish child, were you worried? Am I late?'

The sense of his touch was so real that she stiffened herself against it, flinging back her head as if to throw off his hand. The mere thought of his caress was hateful; yet she felt it in all her veins. Yes, she felt it, but with horror and repugnance. It was something she wanted to escape from, and the fact of struggling against it was what made its hold so strong. It was as though her mind were sounding her body to make sure of its allegiance, spying on it for any secret movement of revolt. . . .

To escape from the sensation, she rose and went again to the window. No one was in sight. But presently the gate began to swing back, and her heart gave a leap—she knew not whether up or down. A moment later the gate opened to admit a perambulator, propelled by the nurse and flanked by Juliet and Andora. Lizzie's eyes rested on the familiar group as if she had never seen it before, and she stood motionless, instead of flying down to meet the children.

Suddenly there was a step on the stairs, and she heard Andora's knock. She unbolted the door, and was strained to her friend's emaciated bosom.

'My darling!' Miss Macy cried. 'Remember you have your child—and me!'

Lizzie loosened herself. She looked at Andora with a feeling of estrangement which she could not explain.

'Have you spoken to my husband?' she asked, drawing coldly back.

'Spoken to him? No.' Andora stared at her, surprised.

'Then you haven't met him since he went out?'

'No, my love. Is he out? I haven't met him.'

Lizzie sat down with a confused sense of relief, which welled up to her throat and made speech difficult.

Suddenly light seemed to come to Andora. 'I understand, dearest. You don't feel able to see him yourself. You want me to go to him for you.' She looked eagerly about her, scenting the battle. 'You're right, darling. As soon as he comes in, I'll go to him. The sooner we get it over, the better.'

She followed Lizzie, who had turned restlessly back to the window. As they stood there, the gate moved again, and Deering entered.

'There he is now!' Lizzie felt Andora's excited clutch upon her arm. 'Where are the letters? I will go down at once. You allow me to speak for you? You trust my woman's heart? Oh, believe me, darling,' Miss Macy panted, 'I shall know exactly what to say to him!'

'What to say to him?' Lizzie absently repeated.

As her husband advanced up the path she had a sudden vision of their three years together. Those years were her whole life; everything before them had been colourless and unconscious, like the blind life of the plant before it reaches the surface of the soil. The years had not been exactly what she had dreamed; but if they had taken away certain illusions they had left richer realities in their stead. She understood now that she had gradually adjusted herself to the new image of her husband as he was, as he would always be. He was not the hero of her dreams, but he was the man she loved, and who had loved her. For she saw now, in this last wide flash of pity and initiation, that, as a comely marble may be made out of worthless scraps of mortar, glass, and pebbles, so out of mean mixed substances may be fashioned a love that will bear the stress of life.

More urgently, she felt the pressure of Miss Macy's hand.

'I shall hand him the letters without a word. You may rely, love, on my sense of dignity. I know everything you're feeling at this moment!'

Deering had reached the doorstep. Lizzie watched him in silence till he disappeared under the projecting roof of the porch; then she turned and looked almost compassionately at her friend.

'Oh, poor Andora, you don't know anything—you don't know anything at all!' she said.

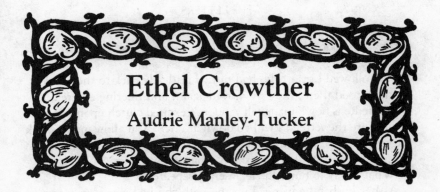

Ethel Crowther

Audrie Manley-Tucker

Ethel walked into our lives out of the rosy calm of a June evening in 1940. It was just after six o'clock, so we had made our beds — which we were not allowed to do earlier in the day. The mattress and pillow, the gritty-feeling blankets and calico sheets, had to be folded into a neat bundle on the iron-framed bed in our barrack room.

We sat on our beds, cleaning our buttons, heads bent in fierce concentration. The buttons had to shine like the spurious gold they were; our shoes had to be polished, our hair must never touch our collars. Five of us, on an AA Gun Site in the mellow English countryside, lived by those stern rules, following a daily ritual of cleaning and hair cutting.

Our stockings had long since washed to an unbecoming shade of banana, which set us apart from raw newcomers with their khaki-coloured hosiery. We were nineteen years old, Nora and I, innocent and fresh as starched muslin and spring sunshine. We worked with men; we believed we had touched the heights of sophistication, because we drank beer (rarely, hating it) and smoked cigarettes (dubiously). We had once heard a four-letter word used by one of the men who manned the four guns on the site, and we were not sure of its exact meaning. We followed the parental injuction: 'never above the knee or below the waist' but agreed, in private, that there were times when we almost forgot to check straying hands.

I had been none-too-chastely kissed by moonlight on occasions and believed that something vital was missing from my life. The War was something that concerned us only when we heard sirens wail their laments for cities soon to be lost under a hail of bombs. We took cover in routine drill when our guns began to shout back at formations of German planes; we were proud that our guns sent several of them hurtling off the coast into the waters of the English Channel. It was all a game, faintly spiced with danger. We were no more callous than the rest of our generation—just impossibly young and unaware.

One man had gone from our battery to join a regiment fighting in France. He had returned that afternoon, gaunt and stubble-chinned, with red-rimmed eyes; wearing only underpants beneath a crumpled greatcoat and carrying enough ammunition to fight a war alone. He had been borne off to the cookhouse and given audience as though he had arrived from another planet; we thought it must be very thrilling to be a minor hero from a film called *Dunkirk*.

I had only just returned from leave, with purchases about which Nora voiced grave suspicions. Why did I need two pairs of artificial silk knickers, one pink, one white, each with a butterfly embroidered near the knee elastic?

'I don't like khaki issue baggy bloomers,' I objected.

'But who sees your knickers?'

'No one, of course,' I said.

I had also bought perfume; heady and sweet, one shilling and three-pence for a small bottle. What was wrong with lavender water? she demanded.

She made me feel depraved; I was delighted; and into this calm contentment walked Ethel; standing in the open doorway of the hut, the ATS Sergeant fussing behind her.

The Sergeant was middle-aged and maternal; thrush-shaped, being plump of body, skinny of leg, with a vast, pillow-like bosom towards which many a soldier had cast a longing eye.

'Now girls. This is Private Ethel Crowther. She'll be sharing Private Bran's room. Show her where to put her things and make her feel at home.'

She nodded at us, smiled, and hurried away to supper in the Sergeants' Mess. We looked kindly upon Ethel, because she was going to share with Bran, not occupy the empty bed in our room. Bran snored, never brushed out her elaborately waved and curled hair, and washed, skimpily, only under protest once each week.

'In there,' we said to Ethel.

The room was identical to ours; two iron beds, two grey steel lockers and two wooden chairs.

Ethel put down her suitcases and kitbag; she surveyed the scene, hands on hips, lower lip thrust out, as though she was making some kind of assessment.

She was short and square. Her face was pale and solemn, though there was a sensuous fullness about her mouth; her large brown eyes were alert and watchful.

We said that we hoped she'd like being here, and then went back to our button-cleaning. We heard her moving about and unpacking. Presently, she came back, tunic and button-stick in hand, and sat down on the end of my bed.

She looked at the sleeves of our tunics, innocent of any decoration except the prized aeroplane-descending-in-flames flash that we wore so proudly.

'How long do you think it will be before I get any stripes?' she asked briskly.

Out of the pin-drop silence, we eyed her in outraged disbelief.

'How long have you been in the ATS?' we wanted to know.

'Just finished my training.'

'We've been here a year.'

She was not chilled by my frosty voice; she smiled, brightly.

'I shall work hard. I want to get on, not be an Officers' Mess Orderly all my life.'

We looked and listened in utter disgust. She was as brassy as the buttons she was polishing so assiduously. She was cocksure and cool as she had no right to be with the colour of her stockings testifying to her newness. She would creep; she would walk primly along the thin, straight lines of the Rules; never sneak out to dances in town with a dress hidden under her greatcoat and a pair of precious silk stockings in her pocket; nor sneak in at five minutes past eleven, knowing that Sergeant Johnson was a sound sleeper, who trusted her charges to be in by ten-thirty.

'What's your job?' Ethel asked.

'We're shorthand typists in the Battery Office.' I tried to make it sound as though the social gulf between us was a thousand miles wide.

'I'm studying shorthand,' she announced. 'You'll be able to help me. I've brought my Pitman's. Perhaps I could practise on your typewriter in the evenings.'

'Oh no, you couldn't,' Nora said firmly. 'The Battery Major wouldn't allow it.'

Her look said: we'll see.

I was apprehensive. Our world was no longer safe, with Ethel storming the ramparts. She asked plenty of questions about the Battery, the jobs we all did. We answered her with the minimum of information. She finished cleaning all her brassware and went to her room.

'What a cheek!' we raged quietly to one another. 'Thinking she'd be promoted over us. Who wants stripes, anyway? All that responsibility and actually having to behave!'

We knocked on her door, en route for the NAAFI, to know if she wanted anything.

She was sitting up in bed, in her striped issue pyjamas, the blue Shorthand Instruction book in front of her. The quality of her smile intimated that, if we applied ourselves as diligently as she did, we would be wearing more than flashes on our arms at this moment.

We went on our way, giggling. At ten o'clock, when we returned to our hut, the two telephonists who shared the third room still weren't back from the town. They were sisters who made up a foursome with two of the Gunners.

In her single room, a discreet distance from ours, Sergeant Johnson slept dreamlessly. We could hear Ethel speaking words aloud as she worked through lists of grammalogues and contractions. We weren't in bed when the Bugler sounded lights out. Who cared? Only Saint Ethel, who promptly closed her shorthand book and snapped off her light; Bran was on leave.

Daily, Ethel eroded any latent goodwill we might have entertained for her. She asked permission to borrow a typewriter for an hour in the evenings; and permission was given by Major Hart with open approval for such a desire to Get On.

I was furious. The Major was a bachelor, good-looking, nicely remote and pleasantly friendly at the same time. I absolutely adored him, silently and secretly. He had black hair, blue eyes, a voice that made me feel weak and helpless. His home was in London, and if he entertained girlfriends there, when he was on leave, none of us ever knew. The faint air of mystery added to his enchantment.

Sergeant Johnson, who knew everything about the Rules and nothing about psychology, constantly held Ethel up as a Shining Example to Us All.

Ethel seemed unmoved by it all. We alternately ignored her, or tried to cut her down to size. She remained pleasant in the face of the sarcasm that we passed off as wit. She never visited the NAAFI nor showed any save a platonic interest in the men around her. Every night she was in bed early, with books spread around her.

'You ought to have some relaxation,' said Sergeant Johnson.

'This is relaxation, honestly. I love books. Of all kinds!'

We soon discovered that she was a walking encyclopaedia, a rich mine of information on dozens of subjects. She would bounce into the Office with a message and stay long enough to air her knowledge to the male staff. She even had the freedom of the Holy of Holies, where the Major spent part of each day and to which we were summoned at intervals with our notebooks and pencils.

'Crowther,' the Major would say, 'how many cubic inches in a cubic foot?'

'One thousand, seven hundred and twenty-eight, sir.'

She bounced back with the right answer and he laughed, approvingly. It was his approval that made me hate her, not her knowledge.

'Isn't she clever?' said the Lance-Bombardier admiringly.

'Why don't you cultivate her? She might teach you something,' I said bitterly.

'Who, me?' he said. 'No fear. I prefer my girls good-looking.'

Thus mollified, I went out with him that evening. I had a marvellous time. Poor Ethel Crowther, I thought. I felt magnanimous enough to stop by her open door and bid her goodnight, on my return. Her smile was warm and surprised.

'What are you reading?' I asked.

'Egyptology. Fascinating. You have no idea. Makes a change from studying shorthand, and it might come in useful.'

Ethel, I reflected, would hoard scraps of knowledge as some people hoarded scraps of material to make a patchwork quilt.

I listened to Bran's bubbling snores, and said: 'How can you study with that noise going on all the time?'

'It doesn't bother me. There's three of us to a room, at home. I used to put cotton wool in my ears.'

'Where's home?'

'Halifax.'

We had never bothered to ask Ethel about her home; she never mentioned it when she returned from leave, though she always seemed to have enjoyed herself.

She steadfastly refused to come to any of the NAAFI dances with us. Not that we made too many overtures of friendship. She spoiled everything by charting her progress aloud to us each week; each week, it seemed, she was so many light years nearer promotion. She exasperated us by being a walking book of knowledge, by her eagerness to fill gaps in our minds—and there were many— by sticking to the rules and being anxious to please everyone.

She never made much impression on Bran, who had other fish to fry. We thought it was cook-house fare that was thickening Bran's waistline so rapidly; we didn't imagine that her increasing girth was connected with the quiet little soldier who was suddenly posted to another Unit.

'Bran's going to have a baby, Nora! Isn't that awful? They've sent her home and she'll be discharged. She's nearly seven months and she can't marry him, because he's got a wife.'

Nora gave me a long, unsmiling look that said: that's what comes of not wearing issue clothes. Bran liked French knickers and look where it landed her.

You don't believe me? I swear it's all perfectly true. It was nineteen hundred and forty, the end of the Last Age of Innocence.

There was no one available to replace Bran. Ethel liked having a room to herself. To us, it was an unfair privilege.

So life went on: we laughed at the thought of bossy know-all Ethel, being kissed, having her hand held; we looked knowingly at one another when she insisted casually that she was only interested in men as good friends.

Then Lieutenant Butterby was posted to our Battery.

Charles Butterby was a neat little man, dapper and efficient, shy with women. He never put a foot wrong and knew the correct procedure for everything. He spent a great deal of time studying.

He liked Ethel, and admired her brain. When he told her so, she looked at him adoringly.

Ethel put steel curling pins in her straight hair each night; Ethel put powder on her nose and experimented with pale lipstick.

'Lieutenant Butterby,' Nora and I said to one another.

'She's never been out with him; she still goes to bed with a good book every night,' I said.

'Bet she'll come to the next NAAFI dance!' Nora whispered.

Nevertheless, we weren't looking forward to this particular dance. A detachment of WRNS had been invited to even up the number of females. They were always allowed to wear civilian clothes when they went to off-duty social functions. What chance did we have, in thick skirts, heavy shoes and khaki shirts? Sergeant Johnson was adamant.

We knew the regulations. The WRNS were nothing to do with us.
'You going?' we asked Ethel.
'I might,' she said.

Ethel had changed, subtly, since she discovered that Lieutenant
Butterby shared her interests in the mysteries of Ancient Egypt.
I often came upon them in odd corners, deep in discussions about
Gods and Goddesses, royal Pharaohs and dusty tombs. The Shorthand
Instructor lay at the back of her locker. She no longer spanned
the keys painstakingly to produce a correct version of 'the quick brown
fox jumps over the lazy dog'; nor did she seem so interested in the
possibility of one day sewing a set of stripes on her sleeves.

The NAAFI dance would follow its usual routine. There would be
an amateur local band, plus Sergeant Fielder crooning grittily into the
microphone. The Major would appear, have a drink with the Sergeant
Major, smile at us all and disappear without dancing. I lived in hopes.

Ethel walked between us to the NAAFI hall. She was tense and
stiff-kneed. Her hair had frizzed and she had bought a new shade of
lipstick, plum-coloured, accenting her pallor.

As soon as she stood blinking under the bright lights I knew that
the evening was going to be disastrous.

Cruelly, we left her to her own devices. She glanced hopefully at
Charles Butterby, who was talking to a golden-haired WRN Petty
Officer. I glanced at the Major, who smiled and nodded, making my
heart do a dozen double-somersaults. I sighed, and looked for the
Lance-Bombardier.

Two dances later, I saw Ethel. She was being partnered by Charles
Butterby, who had the air of a man facing the firing squad.

He was a marvellous dancer. Ethel, however, had two left feet.
How could we have guessed?

She was heavy and awkward, stumbling over feet, stepping on toes,
bumping into other couples. Charles Butterby must have apologised
to every couple on the floor, as they went on their unhappy way, Ethel
clutching him as if he were a lifeline in a hostile sea.

The Major had left. Ethel's partner sent imploring glances towards
the band, as though silently willing them to bring the dance to an
end, releasing him from the purgatory of amused side-glances and
giggles.

Ethel had let us down in front of everyone. No one could possibly
be as stupid about feet as she was pretending to be. She must know

how to dance; the rest of us knew.

There was a crash as Ethel collided with a chair and over-balanced. In a silence, Charles Butterby helped her to her feet.

He then made his escape with all possible speed, in the direction of the golden-haired Wren. It never occurred to me, at the time, that his action was unkind and discourteous, nor that Ethel coped much better, saying goodnight to us all, adding that she didn't think dancing was much in her line.

There was a light under her door when we arrived back that evening. It was eleven o'clock; we had been allowed an extension.

'Come in!' Ethel called briskly. She was sitting up in bed, pyjamas buttoned to her neck, face scrubbed clean under its frizz of hair. The look she gave me had some of the patronage I had been used to showing her. 'I don't care for dances,' she announced, making it sound as though only the stupid danced away hours that could be used in efforts to better themselves.

I said nothing. I didn't know what I had intended to say. . . .

'Switch off the light, please,' she added. As she turned her head away, I saw that her cheeks were blotched, her nose pink at the tip as though she had been crying. It made her seem plainer than ever.

For the first time, I thought: she uses her knowledge as the rest of us use feminine charm and cosmetics. What else was there for the Ethel Crowthers of this world? Surely she didn't have to be so lumpish and frumpish?

I was in the Office when she came in, next morning. Charles Butterby was there. He looked sheepishly at her.

'You shouldn't have dashed off so fast last night,' he said. 'Wanted to have a chat about the book you lent me.'

'A NAAFI dance isn't really the place for a literary discussion, is it, sir?'

I was pleased to see him look steam-rollered.

They had no more long discussions. Ethel rejected my belated overtures of friendship because she suspected they were motivated by pity. The one person she seemed to be at ease with was Major Hart. They had a kind of quiz-team for two, each sharpening their brains on the other. . . .

'You made a mistake, sir, about the quotation from *As You Like It*.'

'All right, Crowther. Not much of a mistake, anyway. Not even worth a drink!'

His voice would be full of laughter. So far as I knew he never bought her a drink, nor took any notice of her outside the office. I suspected that she preferred things that way, nice and neat and tidy.

Some months later, the whole Regiment was ordered overseas. They left the ATS behind. We were split up, and sent to other Units in the Command; we were tragic and tearful, knowing that life could never again be the same; then we settled down happily enough, to grow up.

I didn't see Ethel again; until today.

I heard that she passed her Proficiency Test to become a Clerk, Grade One, and I was pleased for her. I thought that we could have been more understanding and tried harder with her. I wondered what became of her, after the war was over.

Nora married a Canadian serviceman and went to live in Toronto. Do you remember butterflies on your knickers, she wrote, and perfume and poor old Bran, and that dimwit, Ethel Crowther?

I married a farmer and went to live in Gloucestershire. I didn't come to London very much in the years that followed — we had three children in quick succession and a farm that took a long time to get unsteadily on its feet. It was mostly mud and gumboots in the winter, rather like the Gun Site; and it was hard work all the year round.

Yesterday, I came to visit my youngest daughter, and decided to do some shopping before I went home; so that was how I almost walked into Ethel, outside Selfridges in Oxford Street.

Ethel recognised me first. She called my name in glad surprise.

She hadn't grown chic or slim or beautiful though she was less square, more nicely rounded. A plump little woman, bright-eyed, a contented look to her soft, full mouth. She wore the minimum of make-up and she was hatless, her short, fine hair blowing all ways in the October wind. An unspectacular woman, not likely to be noticed in a crowd. Yet she had something: serenity.

We were pigs, I thought soberly. Like a crowd of children, ringing around the odd one out in the school playground, hostile and scornful. Ethel, with her plainness, her two left feet, her neat notebook full of hieroglyphics and her easy way with the Major.

She laughed, and said: 'Gosh, it's thirty-seven years! How young we were. You haven't changed!'

'You have. What happened to you?'

'Someone sent me to an Officer Selection Board. I was lucky!'

'Lucky? How?'

'Well, it was a forty-eight hour thing, all sorts of tests, including an impromptu talk on any subject we chose. I opted for five minutes on the Pharaohs. Hang it all, I'd read enough about them, when I wanted a change from shorthand. The Officer in charge of the Board was mad keen on Egyptian History and I'll swear it was her recommendation that got me through.'

'So you got more than the stripes you wanted?'

She laughed, without rancour.

'Yes. It had never occurred to me to aim that high. I must have been awful, that time I was with you. A prig. I envied you both so much; you had it all put together properly, as they say: the looks, the know-how. I was scared of everything, then, except facts and figures.'

'Did you get married?' I asked.

'Oh yes, I met up with him again, in Brussels, at the end of the war. I was a Captain, then.'

Again. I was glad it had turned out right for her, though Charles Butterby didn't deserve her.

'Here he is, now.'

I watched him stride towards her through the knots of people. He hadn't changed that much, except that the grey in his hair made him look distinguished. He was still the tall, handsome man he had been in his bachelor days; he had the same easy walk, the self-confidence, the smile. All the things that had made him as terrifyingly attractive to me as he was out of reach. Major Hart. Ethel's husband.

He saw her and smiled. I saw the way she looked back at him, and suddenly remembered a non-existent appointment that couldn't wait another second.

I hurried away; there was no point in seeing him.

So now I know what became of Ethel Crowther. I no longer need to feel guilty about her, as I have done all these years.

The guilt has been a good and useful thing; making me do things I didn't want to do, and knew that I should. Preventing me from doing things I'd have regretted. A one-woman psychology course in how to understand other people; even though I didn't pass with distinction, I scraped through, and the memory of Ethel was the best tutor I could have had.

I'm going to miss feeling guilty about her.

The Curious Courtship of Mrs Blishen

Judy Gardiner

Mrs Blishen of The Mount, Barton Drive, had been living neatly alone ever since death in the form of a strangulated hernia had deprived her of Mr Blishen, Estate Agent and Valuer. Life was calm and pleasingly routine with bridge on Tuesdays, shampoo-and-set on Wednesdays and a woman to do the rough on Mondays and Fridays, and would most likely have remained that way if it hadn't been for the appearance of the toothbrush.

As toothbrushes go, it was in no way exceptional. The handle was sober blue and the bristles white and evenly spaced. There was nothing exceptional about it at all, other than the fact that it appeared uninvited in the bathroom tumbler next to the toothbrush belonging to Mrs Blishen.

Noticing it for the first time she stood motionless, one hand on the light switch, blinking slowly and trying to remember the last occasion on which anyone stayed with her. No-one had stayed with her since the funeral, three years ago. And the toothbrush, she was prepared to swear, had not been there on the previous day. Thoughtfully she went across to it, scrutinising it without touching it. Mrs Ouse must have decided that her own needed replacing and had put it there in readiness, but prolonged inspection proved that this could not have been so, for at the base of the bristles was a slight but unmistakable smudge of toothpaste. The brush had already been used.

Recoiling sharply, Mrs Blishen retraced her steps to the bedroom and sat down at the dressing table, where the mirror reflected a puzzled woman of forty-seven with well-cut hair and nostrils that quivered very slightly. She looked round the room. Quietly elegant in apricot and shadowed green, its smoothly draped bed, fitted clothes cupboards, fragrant hairbrushes and immaculately stoppered scent bottles indicated an owner fastidious to the point of fussiness, while the Monet reproduction over the bedside table spoke of a fondness for nature when tempered with decent restraint. It was scarcely the milieu of a woman accustomed to finding a strange toothbrush gate-crashing her bathroom tumbler.

She decided to leave it there until the following day, but when she asked Mrs Ouse whether she could explain its appearance Mrs Ouse swore that she had never seen it before in her life.

'What you want me to do—chuck it out?'

'Yes,' said Mrs Blishen. 'No. On second thoughts, leave it where it is.'

So the toothbrush remained in the bathroom tumbler while Mrs Blishen awaited further developments. If it had cheated rationality by appearing unbidden from nowhere, there was no reason to suppose that it wouldn't disappear in the same way and during the course of the following few days Mrs Blishen watched it closely. Sometimes she watched it furtively, from the corner of her eye, as she tweaked at a strand of her crisp hair in front of the mirror or pretended to search in the cabinet for an aspirin. At other times she pounced suddenly, snapping on the light and drawing in her breath with a sharp hiss as though she expected to surprise the intruder doing a dance, or, even more disquieting, in some sort of awful *flagrante delicto* with her own toothbrush. For in the mind of Mrs Blishen the thing was now developing a character all of its own, the tough head of bristles and the blue of the handle (that of her own was white), speaking very clearly of masculinity; of hairy chests and swelling biceps.

It was on the following Friday morning when Mrs Ouse came slowly downstairs with the red leather slippers in her hand.

'What do you want me to do with these?'

Mrs Blishen, who was about to go shopping, paused by the front door. 'What is it?'

'A pair of bedroom slippers,' Mrs Ouse said patiently. 'Men's.'

'Men's?' Mrs Blishen dropped her car keys with a sharp little crash. 'Where did you find them?'

'Under the spare-room bed.'

They are not Bernard's, Mrs Blishen thought for the tenth time. Bernard never wore red slippers. The last pair he had were brown suede and I gave them to Oxfam, together with his other personal effects. As for his toothbrush, face flannel and shaving equipment, I distinctly remember putting them in a polythene bag and then throwing them away.

She was sitting, late that same evening, in the lamplit drawing room with a small gin and tonic close at hand. The house was very quiet and her gaze returned broodingly to the red leather slippers on the floor by the sofa. She had examined them several times, turning them this way and that while she scrutinised the soles, the tartan linings and the red leather uppers. The toes were slightly scuffed, one heel worn down a little more than the other and the size she judged to be in the region of 9½ or 10. Like the toothbrush they were quite unexceptional, in their way, yet they too spoke of masculinity: of strong ankles and large bold toes.

Someone was playing a joke on her, but who? Again and again she ran through her list of friends and acquaintances and was unable to name one even possible suspect. Mrs Ouse? Why should she? Briskly Mrs Blishen brushed aside any notion that it might be Bernard making some kind of silly supernatural nuisance of himself; Bernard, poor darling, was dead and cremated and scattered at his own request over the municipal golf course, and that—as every sensible person knew— was that. Tossing down the last of her gin and tonic, Mrs Blishen switched out the lamps and, ignoring the slippers down by the sofa, retired resolutely to bed.

But her dreams were uneasy. Doors opened and closed, and footsteps (slippered footsteps) padded across the carpets. She sighed and shifted in her sleep and was only roused to consciousness by a loud knocking on the door.

'You haven't half overslept,' Mrs Ouse said, bearing a cup of tea and two ginger biscuits. 'It's gone half past nine.'

Struggling to a sitting position, Mrs Blishen noticed her gaze become riveted to a point on the floor at the foot of her bed.

'How kind of you,' she said, holding out a grateful hand for the tea while with the other she sought to establish some semblance of order among the tangled bedclothes. 'Dear me, I seem to have had rather a hectic night.'

'Yes . . . I dare say.'

Mrs Ouse removed her gaze from the front of the bed with an obvious effort, handed over the cup and saucer and then retired, tight-lipped.

As Mrs Blishen got out of bed, her bare toes suddenly encountered something alien, something dreadfully alien, and with a little scream she discovered that the pair of red slippers which she had left down by the drawing-room sofa were now lying in close and loving proximity to her own little soft feathered mules.

'Are you trying to say that you've been interfered with, madam?'

Removing his helmet, the police constable placed it down by the side of his chair and gazed respectfully at Mrs Blishen. He took out a small notebook and a ballpoint pen.

'No. I don't know. Well, I suppose I could have been, unobtrusively . . . .'

'Sorry, I don't quite get your meaning.'

'I haven't been unless it was in my sleep,' said Mrs Blishen and turned a deep, embarrassed pink.

'But you heard or saw nothing to arouse your suspicion that there was an intruder in the house at any time before these items appeared?'

Mrs Blishen shook her head.

'And where did you say you found the trousers?'

'On the chair in my bedroom. They were not there when I went out to play bridge, but they were there when I came back.'

'And there's no possibility of confusing them with, say, a pair of your own?'

'In my time,' replied Mrs Blishen, recovering a little of her old spirit, 'I have worn harem pants, cocktail pyjamas and ladies' slacks, but never have I contemplated dressing up in a pair of men's corduroy trousers with a patch on one knee and a hole in the pocket.'

'Ah—so you've examined the contents of the pockets, madam?'

'There were no contents.'

'A maker's name, or a dry-cleaning tag?'

'Nothing whatever,' said Mrs Blishen.

'And you yourself, madam, have no suspicions about his or her identity?'

'If I had,' replied Mrs Blishen tartly, 'I would not be enlisting the aid of the police.'

It was now ten days since the appearance of the toothbrush, and Mrs Blishen had fallen into the habit of standing on the threshold of each room and raking it with anxious eyes before entering. Now squeamish to the point of nausea, her principal torment was that she would find sundry articles of male underwear scattered among her own personal things. Her lingerie drawer she kept locked, and every morning she hid her nightgown between the base and the mattress of her bed, hoping to foil any possible arrival of alien pyjamas in its vicinity. And to calm herself further she telephoned the police station and asked the duty sergeant whether they had made any progress with their enquiries into her case. The sergeant asked her what case, and when she explained, told her to hold the line. When he came back again he said no, but they had the matter in hand. Demanding, in a rising voice, to know what steps were being taken to ensure her protection, she was told to hold the line again and when the sergeant returned he said it had been arranged that a plain-clothes man would call on her.

Replacing the receiver Mrs Blishen patted her neat hair, and, since it was almost mid-day, poured herself a small gin and tonic.

There came a ring at the front doorbell.

'Ah-ha,' said Mrs Blishen, opening the door, 'at last we're getting somewhere.'

The man in plain clothes smiled politely and stepped inside the hall.

'I have to admit that I'm relieved to see you,' went on Mrs Blishen, indicating that he should follow her into the drawing-room. 'After the useless bit of shillyshally with your predecessor it's high time we got down to business.'

The man repeated his polite smile.

'Is it in order that I should offer you a drink, Mr er*?' Mrs Blishen realised that she was unfamiliar with the correct mode of address for a detective in plain clothes.

'Palfreyman,' said the man. 'Edward Palfreyman, and a small sherry would be nice.'

She poured it, handed it to him and told him to sit down. He did so, perching a little uncertainly on the edge of the chair. Mrs Blishen seated herself opposite.

'Now,' she said briskly, 'about all these men's things that keep appearing in my house. Who is responsible?'

The man in plain clothes took a sip of sherry then sat revolving the glass on his knee.

'Well, I am,' he said matter-of-factly. 'That's why I've come.'

Seldom in her life had Mrs Blishen been rendered totally incapable of speech. She tried unsuccessfully to rise from her chair.

'I was in two minds whether to come round,' the man said diffidently.

'Come round . . . ? Do you mean that you are not a detective?'
'Oh no—I'm in wholesale pharmacy.'
'But how—why in the name of God . . . ?'
Striving to assimilate the actual presence of her tormentor,
Mrs Blishen's glazed eyes beheld neat grey hair and a small clipped
moustache set above a hovering smile.

'How is the easy way to answer,' he said. 'The lock on your utility
room door is the same as mine, and the same key fits. All I did was
walk in. The why part takes a little longer to explain.'

'You have already explained enough,' Mrs Blishen said, recovering
and beginning to shake with anger. 'You are a trespasser—self-
confessed and evidently unrepentant since you appear happy to sit in
my chair and drink my sherry—you are a picklock and a predator, a
common sneak thief and—'

'I don't see how I can be a thief,' the man said mildly, 'when I
haven't taken anything from your house. On the contrary, I've put
one or two things in—'

'And the sooner you remove them from my house the better!' cried
Mrs Blishen in a high voice.

'Listen to me, ' the man said. 'Please, please listen to me. I realised
that I was probably making difficulties for myself, but you see I had this
idea that since you've never noticed me during the fifteen years you've
lived here—it was terribly sad about Mr Blishen, by the way—it might
work better·if I sort of insinuated myself into your life by way of
intimate objects. Personal objects that might puzzle you a bit at first
but which gradually become familiar, and then acceptable. In time, I
hoped they'd even offer you a sort of quiet reassurance, until in the
end you felt that you could tolerate the presence of their owner in your
life. In other words, it was rather a foolish and roundabout way of
courting you and asking you to marry me.'

'Marry you?' repeated Mrs Blishen, astounded. 'But we've never
even met!'

'We've been introduced four times,' the man said. 'Once at the
Rawlinsons' Christmas do, once in the post office and twice at bridge
parties. I came to Mr Blishen's funeral and you shook my hand and
thanked me for my condolences—'

'I don't—'

'I live at The Chestnuts, only five houses away, and whenever we
meet I always pass the time of day.'

'And what do I do?' asked Mrs Blishen involuntarily.

'You smile,' said the man, 'And you walk on without seeing me.'

Mrs Blishen sat blinking rapidly. 'Drink your sherry,' she said finally. 'I think it's time for another.'

'Glenda—my late wife—was rather similar in her outlook,' the man went on. 'I mean, she also tended to notice things rather than people. She never knew the colour of anyone's eyes, but was marvellous at spotting missing buttons or dust on the mantelpiece.'

'But why a *toothbrush?*' Mrs Blishen demanded.

'I gave it a lot of thought,' the man confessed, 'and at first I was more in favour of something like my copy of Omar Khayyam or some fresh spinach from the garden. Then I realised that it had to be much more personal than that, because remembering back to when I first lost poor Glenda, it was always the little personal things which caused me the most pain. No more pink toothbrush standing next to mine, no more little feathery slippers under the bed. . . .' He seemed to choke for a moment and Mrs Blishen waited for him to recover. 'And I felt sure that you must have gone through the same thing only much, much worse, as you—like Glenda—didn't seem to notice *people* all that much—'

'In other words,' said Mrs Blishen, 'you imagined that you could insinuate yourself into my house and remain unobserved. Well, I suppose no-one could accuse you of overwhelming egoism.'

'Glenda was an assertive woman,' the man said. 'Which must be why I feel so lost without her.'

'Nevertheless—' Mrs Blishen drained her glass and stood up— 'it won't do. It simply won't do. The whole idea is ludicrous.'

Hastily, Mrs Blishen left the room and returned with the man's trousers folded over her arm and the toothbrush sticking out of the pocket. In the other hand she carried his slippers. Sadly, mutely he took them from her and then the front doorbell rang again.

He was young, bulky, and he flicked an identity card before Mrs Blishen's eyes and announced himself as Detective Sergeant Willis.

'I understand you've been troubled by an unwelcome intruder, madam,' he said and walked through the open drawing-room door.

Mrs Blishen agreed that this was so.

'Sundry articles of clothing, namely one pair men's bedroom slippers, one pair pants, brown corduroy—' continued Detective Sergeant Willis, reading from a slip of paper—'plus one toothbrush, all of which are reported to have appeared unexplained on your private premises. Is that correct?'

Mrs Blishen nodded, and watched the Detective Sergeant's busy little eyes taking in the room with its gracious furniture, its flowers and lamps and silver drinks tray, and, on the oriental hearthrug, the tall elderly man clutching a pair of trousers and two slippers.

'One pair of corduroy pants, one pair men's slippers,' repeated the Detective Sergeant thoughtfully.

'This,' said Mrs Blishen, drawing a deep decisive breath, 'is Colonel Smollett, to whom I was just showing the—the articles in the hope that he may be able to throw some light on them.'

'And can you, sir?'

'Well, as it happens. . . .?' The man gave a small desperate smile.

'As it happens, he has never seen them before,' said Mrs Blishen. 'And because I now have things of greater importance on my mind. I should be grateful if I might withdraw my complaint and consider the whole matter closed.'

Detective Sergeant Willis eyed her narrowly. 'I'm afraid it's not always as simple as that. Having been notified of a complaint by a member of the public we must satisfy ourselves that the reason for it is no longer viable.'

'Speaking as the complainant,' said Mrs Blishen rather grandly, 'I presume that I may be regarded as the person most suitable to judge whether it is still viable or not. And I am giving you formal notice to the effect that since my last telephone call to the police station Colonel Smollett has persuaded me that the ridiculous behaviour of some poor contemptible idiot is best ignored and I therefore withdraw my complaint with apologies for wasting your time. And as a token of gratitude for any help you and your colleagues may have inadvertently rendered—' Airily she twitched the trousers and slippers from the arms of the man on the hearthrug and deposited them in those of the Detective Sergeant. 'I should be grateful if you would donate the objects to your favourite charity.'

'Are you quite sure about this?' the Detective Sergeant said, wearily.

'I have never been more sure about anything in my life,' said Mrs Blishen, 'Good morning.'

'I was fond of those trousers,' the man said as he and Mrs Blishen stood at the drawing-room window watching them being tossed into the back of the police car.

'Serve you right.' She dropped the curtain back in place. 'And now if you will be good enough to excuse me, I'm already late for my hair appointment.'

'Still, thank you for telling fibs on my behalf.'

'I don't suppose I shall lose any sleep over them. But I must make a note to have my utility room lock changed.'

'Forgive me for making such a hash of it.' He stood by the open front door; lonely, looming, yet somehow quite nice.

'If I may make a suggestion,' Mrs Blishen said, looking up at him, 'I would be inclined to try the Omar Khayyam next time.'

Comrades in Arms

George Gissing

L uncheon hour was past, and the tide of guests had begun to ebb.
From his cushioned corner, his familiar seat in the restaurant,
Wilfrid Langley kept an observant eye upon chatting groups and
silent solitaries who still lingered at the tables near him. In this quiet
half-hour, whilst smoking a cigarette and enjoying his modest claret,
he caught the flitting suggestion of many a story, sketch, gossipy
paper. A woman's laugh, a man's surly visage, couples oddly assorted,
scraps of dialogue heard amid the confused noises—everywhere the
elements of drama, to be fused and united in his brain. Success had
multiplied his powers a hundredfold; success and the comforts that
came with it—savoury meats, wine, companionship. No one was
dependent upon him; no one restrained his liberty; he lived where he
chose, and how he chose. And for all that—his age fell short of
thirty—something seemed to him amiss in the bounty of the gods.

A figure was moving in his direction; he looked up from a moment's
reverie, to see a woman seat herself at the opposite side of his table.
A laugh of pleased recognition; a clasp of hands.

'Thought I might find you here,' said Miss Childerstone. She turned
to the waiter. 'Roast mutton—potatoes—bread. And—soda-water.'

'Soda!' Langley exclaimed in surprise. 'That's where you women
make a mistake. You need a stimulant.'

'Thanks, old man; I am better acquainted with my needs than you
are. Here's something for you.'

She threw an evening paper at him saying, 'Page seven.' Langley
opened it, and his eyes sparkled with pleasure. A notice of his
new book; three-quarters of a column; high laudation, as he saw
immediately.

'Yours?' he asked.

'Take it without questions, and be thankful you're not slated.'

'It *is* yours. Don't I know the fine Roman hand? Irony in the first sentence.' He read in silence for a few minutes, then gave his companion a look of warm gratitude. 'You're a good sort.'

Miss Childerstone was drinking deep of her soda-water. Neither plain nor pretty, she had noticeable features, a keen good-humoured eye, an air of self-possession and alertness. She dressed well, with a view to the fitness of things. Her years were in the fourth decade.

She began to eat, but, it seemed, with little appetite.

'I've had a headache since yesterday. I should like to go to bed and lie there for a week. But there's my stuff for Tomlinson. Don't feel like it, I tell you.'

'I see now that you look out of sorts. Yes, you look bad. I tell you what—couldn't I scrawl something that would do for Tomlinson?'

She looked at him, and smiled.

'I dare say you could. Any rubbish you wanted to shoot somewhere. The truth is, I don't think I'm equal to it.—No, I can't eat. Thump! thump! on the back of the head.'

They discussed the literary business in question, and Langley undertook to supply the article due from his friend to a weekly paper. It must be posted tonight. Miss Childerstone, abandoning the scarcely touched food, rested her head upon her hands for a few moments.

'I've done something I'm proud of,' she said at length, 'and I may as well have the satisfaction of telling you. My sister has just gone off to Natal, to be married there. I provided her outfit, paid her passage, and gave her fifty pounds. All off my own bat, old boy! Not bad, is it?'

'Your sister? Why, you never told me she was going to be married.'

'No. It wasn't quite certain—all along. Two years ago she engaged herself to a man who was going out yonder—a man of no means, and not quite up to her mark, I thought. (I must eat something; I'll try the potatoes.) A very decent sort of fellow—handsome, honest. Well, she's been in doubt, off and on. (Are these potatoes bad? Or is it my taste that's out of order?) She stuck to her teaching, poor girl, and had a pretty dull time of it. In the end, I made up my mind that she'd better go and get married. There couldn't be any doubt about the man's making her a good husband; I read his letters, and liked them. Good, plodding, soft-hearted sort of creature; not at all a bad husband for Cissy. Better than the beastly teaching, anyway. So she's gone.'

'That's a disappointment to me,' said Langley. 'I hoped to meet her some day. And you promised I should.'

'Yes—but I altered my mind.'

'What do you mean? You didn't wish me to meet her?'

'The probability was you'd have unsettled her. She never knew a man of your sort. She might have fallen in love with you.'

Miss Childerstone spoke in a matter-of-fact voice; her smile could not have been less ambiguous. Langley, gazing at her with surprise, exclaimed at length:

'Well? And why not?'

'Why not? Oh, my dear boy, I would do a good deal for you, but I couldn't indulge your vanity in that direction. I'm fond of my little sister.'

'Of course you are. And why shouldn't I have been? Describe her to me.'

'Fair—pretty—five-and-twenty. An old-fashioned girl, with all sorts of beliefs that would exasperate you. The gentlest creature! Vastly too patient, too good. Will make an ideal housewife and mother.'

Langley smote the table with his fist.

'But you're describing the very girl I want to find, and can't! How absurdly you have behaved! And she's gone to the end of the earth to marry a man she doesn't care about—this is too ridiculous! Why, I want to marry, and the difficulty is to find such a girl as this. I shall never forgive you.'

His companion looked searchingly at him, with mocking lips.

'Bosh!' she replied.

'It isn't! I'm desperately serious.'

'In any case, I wouldn't have let her marry you. You've been too frank with me. I know you too well. Of course, I like you, because you're likeable—as a comrade-in-arms. We've fought the battle together, and done each other a good turn now and then. But you're very young, you know. You have money in your pocket for the first time, and—by-the-bye, I heard about that supper at Romano's. How much did it cost you?'

'Oh, ten or fifteen pounds—I've forgotten.'

He said it with a touch of bravado, his smile betraying pleasure that the exploit had become known.

'Precisely. And your Dulcinea of the footlights—Totty, Lotty—what's her name?—was there. My dear boy, you mustn't marry for another ten years. It would spoil you. You're only just beginning to look round the world. Go ahead; enjoy yourself; see things; but don't think of marrying.'

'I think of it perpetually.'

The other moved an impatient hand.

'I can't talk. My head is terrible. I must go home.'

'You've been working yourself to death to provide for your sister. And very likely made her miserable after all.'

'Mind your own business. Where's the waiter? Call him, will you? I'm turning blind and deaf, and I don't know what.'

'I shall take you home,' said Langley, rising.

'You can put me in a cab, if you like.'

She looked very ill, and Langley kept glancing at her with uneasiness as they went together from the restaurant. His resolve to see her safely home was not opposed. In the hansom they exchanged few words, but Langley repeated his promise to do the bit of literary work for her editor. 'Tomorrow morning,' he added, 'I shall come and ask how you are. Send for a doctor if you're no better by night.'

His own rooms were in the same district, that of Regent's Park, and after leaving Miss Childerstone he went off to perform the task he had undertaken—no difficult matter. Though it was holiday time with him just now, he spent the whole evening in solitude, more discontented than usual. The post brought him news that the first edition of his book was sold out. Satisfactory, but it gave him no particular delight. He had grown used to think of himself as one of the young men whom the public run after, and his rooted contempt for the public made him suspicious of his own merits. Was he not becoming vulgarised, even personally? That supper the other night, in honour of the third-rate actress, when everyone got more or less drunk—pah! These dreary lodgings, which no expenditure could make homelike. A home—that was what he wanted. Confound Miss Childerstone! That sister of hers, now steaming away to Natal—

At twelve o'clock next day he called on his friend, and was asked to wait in her sitting-room. He had been here only once or twice; today the room seemed more uncomfortable than on former occasions, and Langley wondered how a woman could live amid such surroundings. But was Miss Childerstone to be judged as a woman? For seven or eight years she had battled in the world of journalism, and with a kind of success which seemed to argue manlike qualities. Since he had known her, these last three years, she seemed to have been growing less feminine At first he had thought of her with the special interest which arises from difference of sex; now he rarely, if ever, did so.

He liked her, admired her, and could imagine her, in more natural circumstances, a charming woman. If, as was probable, her sister resembled her in all the good points—

She came in, and her appearance startled him. She wore a dressing-gown; her hair was tossed into some sort of order; illness unmistakably blanched her face. Without offering to shake hands, she tumbled on to the nearest chair.

'Why on earth did you get up?' Langley exclaimed. 'Have you seen a doctor?'

'No; but I think you shall go and fetch someone,' she answered, hoarsely and faintly. 'Did you send the stuff to Tomlinson?'

'Oh yes, and forged your signature. Go back to bed; I'll—'

'Wait a minute. I want to ask you—I haven't any money—'

The change from her wonted vigour of speech and bearing was very painful to the young man. Money. Why, his purse was hers. In his pocket he had only a few sovereigns, but he would go to the bank straightway.

'Three or four pounds will do,' she replied. 'I don't know anyone else I care to ask. Borrowing isn't in my line, you know. I could sell or pawn some things—but I haven't the strength to get about.'

Langley stepped towards her and put coins into her hand.

'What is it?' he asked, gravely. 'A fever of some kind?'

'I'm not feverish—at least I don't think so. Fearful head. Look chalky, don't I?'

'You do. Go back to bed at once, and leave things to me.'

'You're a good fellow, Wilfrid.'

'Pooh!'

'I feel so wretchedly weak—and I *hate* to feel weak—I—'

She suddenly turned her head away; and Langley was horrified to hear her sob. He moved for a moment about the room, as if in search of something; but it only served to hide his embarrassment. Then Miss Childerstone stood up, and went quickly away.

In half an hour's time the necessary assistance had been procured. Nervous collapse, said the man of medicine; overwork, and so on. Langley, finding that no one in the house could act as bedside attendant, obtained the services of a nurse. He did not see his friend again, but had a message from her that she was 'all right'; he might call the next day if he liked.

He paid the call as early as ten o'clock, and had a talk with the nurse, who could give but an indifferent report.

'If I write a few lines for her, can she read them?' he asked.

Yes, she could read a letter. So Langley sat down at the table, and tried to find something to say. To his surprise, he wrote with the utmost difficulty; words would not come. 'Dear Miss Childerstone—I feel sure that a little rest and nursing will soon—' Oh, that was insufferably childish. He bit his pen, and stared at the books before him: novels and plays, heaped newspapers, a volume or two of an encyclopædia, annuals, and dictionaries. She had no instinct of order; she lived from day to day, from hand to mouth. Her education must be very defective. On the moral side, no doubt, she was sound enough, but a woman should have domestic virtues.

What was he doing? Abusing his friend just when she lay helpless, and this defeat of her splendid strength the result of toil on a sister's behalf! He tore the sheet of paper and began anew. 'Dear Bertha'— why not? She now and then called him 'Wilfrid'—'don't trouble your head about anything. I have nothing to do, and to look after you will give me pleasure. Is there anyone you would like to communicate with? Consider me absolutely at your service—time, money, anything. I will call morning and evening. Cheer up, dear old chum! You must go away as soon as possible; I'll get lodgings for you.'

And so on, over another page, in the hearty comrade tone which they always used to each other. The nurse, summoned by a light tap, handed this note to her patient, and in a few minutes she brought back a scrap of paper, on which was feebly scrawled in pencil, 'Good old boy. All right.'

It was the last he saw of Bertha Childerstone's handwriting for more than a month. Daily he called twice. What the nurse, doctor, and landlady thought of his relations with the invalid he would not trouble to conjecture. He met all current expenses, which amounted to not very much. And the result of it was that the sick woman became an almost exclusive subject of his thoughts; his longing to speak again with her grew immense.

One day in July, as he stepped as usual into the parlour, thinking to wait there for the nurse, his eye fell upon a figure sitting in the sunlight. A pale, thin face, which he scarcely recognised, greeted him with a smile, and a meagre hand was held out to him.

'Up? Oh, that's brave!'

He hurried forward and clasped her hand tightly. They gazed at each other. Langley felt a thrill in his blood, a dimness about his eyes, and before he knew what he was doing he had given and received a kiss.

'No harm,' said Miss Childerstone, laughing with a look of confusion. '*Honi soit qui mal y pense!*'

But the young man could not recover himself. He was kneeling by the chair in which she reclined, and still kept her hand, whilst he quivered as if with fever.

'I'm so glad—I wanted so to see you—Bertha—'

'Hush! Don't be sentimental, old man. It's all right.'

He pressed her hand to his lips. She abandoned it for a moment, then firmly drew it back.

'Tell me all the news.'

'I know of nothing, except that I—'

He had lost his head. Bertha seemed to him now not only a woman, but beautiful and sweet and an object of passionate desire. He touched her hair, and stammered incoherencies.

'Wilfrid'—she spoke in the old blunt way—'don't make a fool of yourself. Go a yard or two away, there's a good boy. If not, I hobble back into the other room. Remember that I can't stand excitement.'

Eyes averted, he moved away from her.

'I had a letter from Cissy this morning—'

'I don't want to hear of it,' he interrupted pettishly. 'She was the cause of your illness.'

Miss Childerstone pursued in the same tone.

'—Posted at Cape Town. Very cheerful. She was enjoying the voyage, and looking forward to its end in a reasonable and happy way. We did the right thing. There's a letter, too, from the expectant lover; a good letter; you may see it if you like.'

Common-sense came at length to Wilfrid's support. He sat down, crossed his legs, and talked, but without looking at his companion.

'I owe you a lot of money,' said Bertha.

'Rubbish! When can you go away? And what place would you prefer?'

'I shall go next week to the seaside. Anywhere near. Some place where there are lots of people. I was dead, and am alive again; I want to feel the world buzzing round.'

'Very well. Choose a place, and I'll go after rooms for you.'

'No, no. I can do all that by letter. By-the-bye, I've been hearing from Tomlinson. He's a better sort of fellow than I supposed. What do you think? He sent me a cheque for five-and-twenty pounds—on account, he says.'

Langley kept his head down, and muttered something.

'I suppose somebody or other has been pitching him a doleful story about me. It took a long time before people missed me; now they're beginning to write and call.'

'Yes—you have a great many friends—'

'Heaps of them! Now, goosey, don't hang your head. The fact of the matter is, we oughtn't to have met just yet. There's an artificial atmosphere about an invalid. You're not to come again till I send for you—you hear that?'

'As you please,' answered Langley, shamefaced, but no longer petulant. And he stayed only a few minutes after this. At parting, their eyes did not meet.

That night he wrote a letter, the inevitable letter, page upon page, strictly according to precedent. When two days had brought no answer, he wrote again, and this time elicited a short scrawl.

'Goosey, goosey gander! I don't like the style of these compositions; it isn't up to your later mark. Go and see Totty—Lotty—what's her name? I mean it; you want the tonic of such society. And pray, what work are you doing? Come tomorrow at three and tell me.'

He would have liked to refuse the invitation, but had fallen into so limp a state that there was no choice save to go and be tortured. Miss Childerstone looked better.

'I pick up very quickly,' she said. 'In the early days, before I knew you, I had a worse floorer than this, and astonished everyone by the way I came round. Well, what are you doing?'

'Nothing much,' the young man replied carelessly.

She pondered a little, then laughed.

'Now isn't it an odd thing, how far we were from knowing each other? I misunderstood you; I did indeed; as it goes without saying that you quite misunderstood me. I didn't think you could have written those letters.'

'I'm not ashamed of them.'

A certain quiet manliness in the words had its effect upon Miss Childerstone. She smiled, and regarded him kindly.

'Nor need you be, my dear boy. For my part, I'm considerably proud of them; I shall store them up and read them in years to come when they have a value as autographs. But I suppose you had purposely misled me, with your random talk. If I had known—yes, if I had known—I don't think I should have let Cissy go to Natal.'

'Stop that nonsense,' said Langley, 'and answer me a plain question.

Is it hopeless?—or can't you make up your mind yet?'

'I *have* made up my mind—since receiving your letters.'

'Before, you were in doubt?'

'Just a wee bit. Partly, I suppose, because of my weakness. I like you so much, and I have such hopes of your future—it was tempting. But—No!'

Langley looked at her with eyes of thwarted passion.

'What do you mean? Just because I have really and honestly fallen in love with you—'

'Just so,' she interrupted, 'and shown yourself as I didn't know you. I like you as much as ever—more, perhaps. I more than half wish I could bring Cissy back again. You would have suited each other very well. And yet, it would have been an unkindness to *you*, however kind to *her*. It would have meant, for you, a sinking into the comfortable commonplace. You are too young for marriage. I had rather see you in any kind of entanglement. That longing for domesticity gave me a shudder. It's admirable, but it's the part of you that must be outgrown. Oh, you are so much more respectable than I thought.'

She broke off, laughing.

'And you mean to say,' exclaimed Wilfrid, 'that if I could have given proof of blackguardism you might have been inclined to marry me?'

Miss Childerstone laughed uncontrollably.

'Oh, how young you are! No, I shouldn't have married you in any case. I might have promised to think about it. I might have promised to do it; but when the time came—*via*! Dear boy, I don't want to marry. Look at this room, dirty and disorderly. This is all the home I care for. Conceivably, I might marry a man with a big income, just for the sake of a large life. But it's only just conceivable. In poverty—and anything you or I can count upon would be poverty—I prefer the freedom of loneliness.'

'You imagine I should lay any restraint upon you?'

Again she broke into laughter.

'I have a pretty good theoretical knowledge of what marriage means. Unfortunately, one can't experiment.'

Langley turned from her, and stared gloomily.

'Look here,' said his companion. 'In a few days I think I shall be strong enough to go away, and I shall not tell you where I'm going. Let us say good-bye, and see each other again when we're both recovered. In the meantime, live and work. Give fifteen-pound suppers, if you like. Anything to keep your thoughts off domesticity. Cultivate blackguardism'—her voice rang mirthfully. 'Then we shall get back to the old footing.'

'Never!'

'Well, that's as you please. I should like it, though.'

He left her, and determined neither to write nor to call again. In a day or two the former resolve was broken; he wrote at greater length than ever. When the silence that followed became unendurable, he went to the house, but only to learn that Miss Childerstone had left that morning.

For the mere sake of talking about her, he spent the evening with people who had known his friend for a long time. They, it appeared, were ignorant of her movements.

'Gone as war correspondent, I shouldn't wonder,' said a young man; and the laughter of the company appreciated his joke.

'Oh, she really is too mannish,' remarked a young matron. 'I suppose you study her as a curiosity, Mr. Langley?'

'We're great chums,' Wilfrid answered with a laugh.

'Well, at all events we needn't bid *you* beware,' jested the lady.

On reaching home, late, he found in his sitting-room an object which greatly puzzled him; it was a large and handsome travelling-bag, new from some shop. By what mistake had it got here? He examined it, and found a ticket bearing his name and address. Then, turning to the table, he saw a letter, the address in a well-known hand.

'DEAR OLD MAN,—I shall not offer to pay back the money you have spent upon me, but I'm sending a present, one of the useful order.

'Yours in *camaraderie*,

'B.C.'

After a day or two of brooding he saw the use of Bertha's gift, and for a month the travelling-bag did him good service.

He and she had long been back in town, and were again tugging hard at the collar, before they met. It was a miserable day of November, and amid sleet, fog, slush, they came face to face on the pavement of the roaring Strand. Their umbrellas had collided, and as they shook hands the hurrying pedestrians bumped them this way and that.

'All right again?' asked Bertha merrily.

'Quite,' was the stalwart reply. 'Come somewhere and talk.'

'Can't. Appointment in ten minutes.'

'Move on, please!' shouted a policeman. 'Mustn't stop the way.'

'Lunch at the old place tomorrow?' said Wilfrid hurriedly.

'Yes. Two o'clock.'

Each plodded on, and Langley had no cardiac tremor as he thought of Miss Childerstone. For all that—for all that—he could not forget that he had kissed her lips.

The Needlecase
Elizabeth Bowen

The car was sent to the train—along the straight road between dykes in the late spring dusk—to bring back Miss Fox, who was coming to sew for a week. Frank, the second son of the house, had come suddenly back from town; he was pleased to find the car there, which was more than he hoped, but appalled to see Miss Fox, in black, like a jointed image, stepping in at the back. Frank had, and wished to have, no idea who she was. So he sat in front with the chauffeur, looking glumly left at the willows and dykes flitting by, while Miss Fox, from the back, looked as fixedly out at willows and dykes at the other side of the road. No one spoke. They turned in at the lodge gates and the avenue trees closed in.

When the car drew up at the hall door, Frank got out and shouted. It embarrassed him having come home, and he did not want to explain. His sister Angela, sitting up at her window, heard, shot downstairs, and flung her arms round his neck, nearly knocking him over, like far too big a dog, as though he had been away two years instead of two days. This pleasure she over-expressed was perfectly genuine; Angela was effusive because she was often depressed; she could not be bothered being subtle with Frank, whom she knew far too well, and whose chagrins she often shared. So she kept up this rowdy pretence that everything was for the best.

'Had-a-good-time?' she said.

'No.'

'I'm sure you did really,' said Angela.

'No doubt you know best,' said Frank. 'Who in God's name's that in there?'

'Oh, that's Miss Fox,' explained Angela, peering into the car, where Miss Fox sat like an image, waiting to be let out. Angela rang the bell wildly for someone to come and cope. The chauffeur carried

Frank's bag and the sewing-woman's strapped-up brown paper suitcase up the wide steps. The front of the house loomed over them, massive and dark and cold: it was the kind of house that easily looks shut up, and, when shut up, looks derelict. Angela took Frank's arm and they went indoors, into the billiard-room, the only place they could be certain of meeting nobody else. The room had a dank, baizey smell, and a smell of cold anthracite from the unlit stove: four battered green shades hung low over the sheeted table. It was not cheery in here. Frank sat on the fender-stool with his shoulders up and stared through his sister Angela heavily, uninvitingly. Had he wished to be quite alone he would not, however, have shouted.

'What did you do?' said Angela.

'Nothing special,' Frank said. He had been up to London to meet a man who might get him a job if he liked the looks of him, and the man clearly had not. The man had seen Frank to do Arthur a good turn: unfortunately the brothers did not resemble each other. Everyone liked Arthur. And Frank had stayed up in London, and had hoped to stay longer, because of a girl, but that had been a flop too: he had run through his money; that was why he was home. Angela had the good sense to ask no more. Leaning against the table and screwing her left-hand white coral ear-ring tighter (she always looked rather well) she said nonchalantly: 'The Applebys have been over. Hermione's after Arthur. They want us for tennis on Monday. The vet came about Reno; he says it's nothing—oh, and Mother has heard from Arthur; he's coming down Friday week and bringing his new girl. So then Mother wired to hurry on Miss Fox. She's going to make us all over— first the drawing-room covers, then Mother's black lace, and then do up Toddy and me—cut some dresses and run up some tennis frocks. She's our one hope for the summer. No doubt she sews like hell, but we really couldn't look worse. Could we, Frank? I mean, could we?'

'Yes,' said Frank. 'I mean no.'

'We heard of her through Aunt Doris,' said Angela, chatting away. 'She's one of the wonderfully brave—she's got a child to support that she shouldn't have. She trained somewhere or other, so I suppose she *can* make. She's been on these rounds for years, going down in the world a bit. She seems dirt cheap, so there must be something fishy. She used to work, years ago, for the Fotheringhams, but Aunt Doris only got on to her after she fell.'

'You surprise me,' said Frank, yawning drearily, wanting a drink more than anything in the world.

Miss Fox's arrival, though perfectly unassuming, had left quite a wake of noise: she had been taken up and put somewhere, but doors went on opening and shutting, Frank's mother stood out in the hall giving directions, and his elder sister Toddy began shouting for Angela. As Frank crossed the hall his mother broke off to give him her vivid mechanical smile and say, 'Oh you're *back*.' The house—far too big but kept on for Arthur, who was almost always away but liked to think of it there—had many high windows and a white stone well staircase that went, under a skylight, up and up and up. This would have been an excellent house for someone else to have lived in, and heated; Frank and Angela could then have visited comfortably there. As it was, it was like a disheartened edition of Mansfield Park. The country around was far too empty and flat.

Miss Fox was not to work tonight; they left her to settle in. But Toddy was in such a hurry to get in first with her things that she slipped upstairs, unobtrusively, as soon as dinner was over. She found Miss Fox still smoking over her supper tray. She was of that difficult class that has to have trays all the time. Too grand for the servants, she had to be fed in her room—one of those top bedrooms in any Georgian house with high ceilings and windows down by the floor. It looked rather bleak in the light of two hanging bulbs. A massive cheval glass, brought from downstairs today, reflected Miss Fox's figure sitting upright at the table. Deal presses stood round the walls, dress-boxes tottered in stacks and two dressmaker's dummies—one stout and one slimmer—protruded their glazed black busts. A sewing-machine with a treadle awaited the dressmaker's onslaught. In the grate, a thin fire rather uncertainly flapped. What should be done had been done to acclimatize Miss Fox. But her purpose here could be never far from her mind, for she rigidly sat at the table where she would work. A folded-back magazine was propped on the coffee-pot: when Toddy came in she lifted her eyes from this slowly, but did not attempt to rise.

Her meek, strong, narrow, expressionless face, with heavy eyelids, high cheekbones and secretive mouth, framed in dusty fair hair brushed flat and knotted behind, looked carven under the bleak overhead light. Its immobile shadows were startling. Toddy thought: 'She's important'. But this was absurd.

Toddy kicked the door to behind her and stood stock still, a cascade of tired dance dresses flung over one arm, two bales of gingham for tennis frocks balanced under the other. Success this forthcoming summer was deadly important, for Toddy was now twenty-four. She felt Miss Fox held her fate in the palm of her hand. So she stood stock still and did not know how to begin. She had quieter manners, a subtler air than Angela, but was in fact a rather one-idea girl.

'I hope you have all you want,' she said helplessly.

'Yes, thank you, Miss Forrester.'

'I mustn't disturb you tonight. But I thought you might like some idea—'

'Show me,' said Miss Fox politely, and pushed her chair back from the table.

'My red tulle is ripped right round. It caught on a spur—'

She stopped, for Miss Fox was looking at her so oddly, as though she were a ghost, as though it were terror and pleasure to see her face. Toddy's looks were not startling, but were, like her brother Arthur's, pleasant enough. No one, no man, had been startled this way before.

'It caught on a spur,' she said, on a rising note.

Miss Fox's eyes went quite blank. 'Tch-tch-tch,' she said, and bent quickly over the stuff. She had unpacked and settled in—Toddy saw, looking round—screens hid her bed and washstand, the facts of her life, away, but one or two objects had appeared on the mantelpiece, and a fine, imposing work-basket stood at her elbow. Toddy, who loved work-baskets, had a touch of the jackdaw, so, while Miss Fox was examining the martyred red dress, she flicked back the hinged lid of the basket and with innocent, bird-like impertinence routed through its contents. All sorts of treasures were here: 'souvenir' tape-measures, tight velvet emery bags, button-bags, a pin-cushion inside a shell, scissors of all sorts in scabbards—and oh, such a needle-case! 'As large as a family Bible,' said Toddy, opening it, pleased. And, like a family Bible, it had a photo stuck inside. 'Oh, what a nice little boy!'—'*Thank you*,' exclaimed Miss Fox, and with irresistible quickness, a snatch, had the needlecase back. The movement was so surprising, it seemed not to have happened.

'That looked such a dear little boy,' Toddy went on, impenitent.

'My little nephew,' Miss Fox said impenetrably.

It was odd to think she had a child, for with such a nun-like face she had looked all wrong, somehow, smoking a cigarette. The dusty look of her hair must be the effect of light, for Toddy, standing above her, looked down and saw how well brushed her hair was. Her fingers looked as though they would always be cold, and Toddy dreaded their touch on her naked spine when the time would come to try on her evening dresses. And felt frightened alone with her, at the top of this dark, echoing house. They saved light everywhere, you had to grope up the stairs, for this well of a house drank money. So its daughters, likely to wither, had few 'advantages'. Everyone knew, Arthur knew, that Arthur must marry money. Toddy was sick of the sacrifice. She was in love this year, baulked all the time, and her serene, squarish face concealed a constant, pricking anxiety.

'I've *got* to look nice,' she said suddenly.

'I'll do all I can,' said Miss Fox, flashing up once again that odd, reminiscent look.

'How *like* you, Toddy,' Angela cried at breakfast.

'What was like Toddy?' Frank asked, scrawling a maze among the crumbs by his plate. He seldom listened to what his sisters were saying, but sat on at table with them because he had nowhere special to go next.

'Creeping up there, then poking about in her things. You really might give the poor old creature a break.'

'She's not so old,' said Toddy, serene. 'And the child looked about seven.'

'What was it like?'

'I only saw curls and a collar—I tell you, she snatched it away.'

'What child?' said Frank. He pushed his cup across vaguely and Angela gave him more coffee, but it was cold.

'The child she had,' said Toddy.

'Oh God,' said Frank, 'is she fallen?' But he did not care in the least.

'I told you she was, last night,' said Angela, hurt.

That morning, Miss Fox was put in the drawing-room to work. Bales of chintz were unrolled and she cut out the new covers, shaping them over the backs of the chairs with pins. In cold, windy April sunlight she crawled round and round the floor, with pins in her mouth. The glazed chintz looked horribly cold. Frank, kept so short of money, not only thought the rosy-and-scrolly pattern itself obscene, but found these new covers a frenzied extravagance. But now Arthur's most promising girl was coming to stay, and must at all costs be impressed. If she did marry Arthur, she'd scrap these covers first thing. Any bride would. Frank leaned in the doorway, letting a draught in that rustled under the chintz, to watch Miss Fox at work on her thankless task. She magnetized his idleness. Their silence was fascinating, for if he spoke she would have to spit out those pins.

The drawing-room was full of tables covered with photographs: Arthur at every age. He watched Miss Fox dodge the tables and drag her lengths of chintz clear.

Then she sat back on her heels. 'How fast you get on,' Frank said.

'I give my whole mind to it.'

'Don't your hands get cold, touching that stuff?'

'They may do; I'm not particular.'

She put pins in her mouth and Frank wondered how she had ever been seduced. He picked up her big scissors idly and snipped at the air with them. 'This house is like ice,' he said. 'Do you know this part of the world?'

She was round at the back of the sofa and nothing came for some time; she must be eyeing the pattern and chewing the pins. Then her voice came over the top. 'I've heard speak of it. It seems very quiet round here.'

'*Quiet*—' began Frank.

But, hearing his voice, his mother looked in and said with her ready smile: 'Come, Frank, I want you a moment. We musn't disturb Miss Fox.'

That same afternoon, the sun went in. Sharp dark clouds with steely white edges began bowling over the sky and their passing made the whole landscape anxious and taut. Frank went out riding with Angela; the wind, coming up and up, whistled among the willows; the dykes cut the country up with uneasy gleams. The grass was still fawn-coloured; only their own restlessness told them that it was spring. It *was* quiet round here. They jogged tamely along, and Angla said she saw no reason why things should ever happen, and yet they did. She wished they saw more of life. Even Miss Fox in the house was *something*, she said, something to talk about, something going on. 'And of course I do need those clothes. But when we *are* all dressed up, I don't know where we're to go. Oh hell, Frank. I mean, really.' She rode hatless, the wind stung her cheeks pink: Frank bitterly thought that she looked like some Academy picture about the Morning of Life.

'Do you think Arthur'll marry that girl?'

'I daresay he'll try,' said Frank.

'Oh, come. You know, Frank, our Arthur's a big success. . . . It's terrible how we wonder about Miss Fox. Do you think we are getting prurient minds? But the idea's fantastic.'

'Fantastic,' Frank agreed, feeling his own despondency ironed into him. Angela shot off and galloped across the field.

That night, in a wind direct from the Ural mountains, the house began to creak and strain like a ship. The family sat downstairs with as few lights as possible. It was Angela who slipped up to talk to Miss Fox. The handsome work-basket was present but hasped shut, and Angela, honourably, turned her eyes from it. She really did not want to talk. She sat on the rug by the grate; the wind puffed down the chimney occasional gusts of smoke that made her eyes smart. Miss Fox sat at the table, puffing away at a cigarette with precision. Perhaps she was glad of company. Nothing showed she was not. Her head, sculptured by shadows, was one of the finest heads that Angela had ever seen.

'You must see a lot of funny things, going from house to house.'

'Well yes, I do. I do see some funny things.'

'Of course, so do hospital nurses. But people must be much funnier trying on clothes. And some families are mares' nests. I wish you'd tell me. . . .'

'Oh well, that would hardly do.'

'You know nurses aren't discreet. . . . My brother Frank thinks you're a witch.'

'Gentlemen will have their fun,' said Miss Fox, with an odd inflection, as though she were quoting. Meeting Angela's eye, she smiled her held-in, rigid smile. Angela thought with impatience of gentlemen's fun that they must have—and, in this connection, of Arthur, who had his share. She heard the wind gnaw at the corners of this great tomb of a house that he wouldn't let them give up.

'It's all right for Arthur,' she said.

'Those photographs in the drawing-room—they are all your Arthur?'

'Of course,' said Angela crossly.

'Miss Toddy favours him, doesn't she?'

Angela hugged her knees and Miss Fox got no answer to this. So the sewing-woman reached out her cold hand across the table, shook out of the packet and lit with precision another thin cigarette. Then: 'I've seen Mr Arthur,' she said.

'Oh yes, I've seen Mr Arthur. He was staying one time in a lady's house where I worked. There were several young gentlemen there, and I wasn't, of course, in the way of hearing their names. They were a big party, ever so gay and high-spirited, dodging all over the house, they used to be, every night, and in and out of my workroom playing some game. I used to be sitting alone, like I sit here, and they used to stop for a word as they went through, or sometimes get me to hide them. Pleasant, they all were. But I never did catch any names. Mr Arthur took a particular fancy to one of my dummies, and asked me to lend it him to dress up for some game. I should have known better; I ought to have known my place.

'But it was eight years ago. The last night, I let him take the dummy away. They did laugh, I heard. But there was an accident and Mr Arthur let it drop on the stairs. The pedestal broke and some of the skirt-wires bent. He came back, later, to tell me how sorry he was. He *was* sorry, too. He said he'd make it all right. But he went off next day, and I suppose something happened to put it / out of his head. My lady was not at all pleased, as she had had the dummy made to her own figure, and her figure was difficult. I didn't work there again.'

'How like him!' exclaimed his sister, savagely reclasping her hands round her knees.

Miss Fox, immensely collected, let out a cloud of smoke. 'He meant no harm,' she said stonily.

Frank came upstairs in the dark, feeling his way by the handrail and calling, 'Angela?' It gave him the creeps when anyone disappeared. And downstairs Toddy was fumbling on the piano. 'Here,' called Angela. Frank knocked once, and came in. 'You look very snug,' he said, rather resentfully. This room's being inhabited gave the house a new focus. Soon they would all be up here. He came and stood by the fire and watched his sister rocking and hugging her knees. He saw by her face that he had cut in on a talk. His own superfluity bit him.

'Miss Fox once knew Arthur, Frank.'

'A ladder's run right down your stocking,' said Frank with angry irrelevance.

'Damn,' said Angela vaguely.

'Best catch it up,' said Miss Fox.

She looked from Frank to Angela. There was a pause. Then, in the most businesslike way, she put down her cigarette, opened her work-basket, glanced at Angela's stocking and, matching it with her eye, drew a strand from a mixed plait of darning silks. Then she took out the big black needlecase. 'Mr Frank . . .' she said. He went over and, taking the case, brought it across to Angela. She knelt upon the hearthrug; he rested a hand on her shoulder and felt the shoulder go stiff. 'What a lot of needles,' she said mechanically. She and Frank both stared at the photograph of the child. They saw, as Toddy had seen, its curls and its collar. Like Arthur's collar and curls in old photographs downstairs. And between the collar and curls, Arthur's face stared back again at the uncle and aunt.

'I should take a number five needle,' said Miss Fox calmly.

'I have,' said Angela, closing the needlecase.

'Ladders down stockings break one's heart,' said Miss Fox.

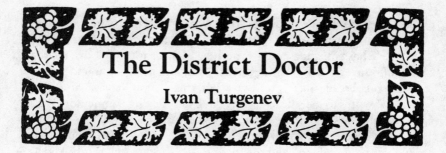

The District Doctor

Ivan Turgenev

One day in autumn on my way back from a remote part of the country I caught cold and fell ill. Fortunately the fever attacked me in the district town at the inn; I sent for the doctor. In half-an-hour the district doctor appeared, a thin, dark-haired man of middle height. He prescribed me the usual sudorific, ordered a mustard-plaster to be put on, very deftly slid a five-rouble note up his sleeve, coughing drily and looking away as he did so, and then was getting up to go home, but somehow fell into talk and remained. I was exhausted with feverishness; I foresaw a sleepless night, and was glad of a little chat with a pleasant companion. Tea was served. My doctor began to converse freely. He was a sensible fellow, and expressed himself with vigour and some humour. Queer things happen in the world: you may live a long while with some people, and be on friendly terms with them, and never once speak openly with them from your soul; with others you have scarcely time to get acquainted, and all at once you are pouring out to him—or he to you—all your secrets, as though you were at confession. I don't know how I gained the confidence of my new friend—any way, with nothing to lead up to it, he told me a rather curious incident; and here I will report his tale for the information of the indulgent reader. I will try to tell it in the doctor's own words.

'You don't happen to know,' he began in a weak and quavering voice (the common result of the use of unmixed Berezov snuff); 'you don't happen to know the judge here, Mylov, Pavel Lukitch?. . . You don't know him?. . . Well, it's all the same.' (He cleared his throat and rubbed his eyes.) 'Well, you see, the thing happened, to tell you exactly without mistake, in Lent, at the very time of the thaws. I was sitting at his house—our judge's, you know—playing preference. Our judge is a good fellow, and fond of playing preference. Suddenly' (the

[233]

doctor made frequent use of this word, suddenly) 'they tell me, "There's a servant asking for you." I say, "What does he want?" They say, "He has brought a note—it must be from a patient." "Give me the note," I say. So it is from a patient—well and good—you understand —it's our bread and butter. . . . But this is how it was: a lady, a widow, writes to me; she says, "My daughter is dying. Come, for God's sake!" she says; "and the horses have been sent for you." . . . Well, that's all right. But she was twenty miles from the town, and it was midnight out of doors, and the roads in such a state, my word! And as she was poor herself, one could not expect more than two silver roubles, and even that problematic; and perhaps it might only be a matter of a roll of linen and a sack of oatmeal in payment. However, duty, you know, before everything: a fellow-creature may be dying. I hand over my cards at once to Kalliopin, the member of the provincial commission, and return home. I look; a wretched little trap was standing at the steps, with peasant's horses, fat—too fat—and their coat as shaggy as felt; and the coachman sitting with his cap off out of respect. Well, I think to myself, "It's clear, my friend, these patients aren't rolling in riches." . . . You smile; but I tell you, a poor man like me has to take everything into consideration. . . . If the coachman sits like a prince, and doesn't touch his cap, and even sneers at you behind his beard, and flicks his whip—then you may bet on six roubles. But this case, I saw, had a very different air. However, I think there's no help for it; duty before everything. I snatch up the most neeessary drugs, and set off. Will you believe it? I only just managed to get there at all. The road was infernal: streams, snow, watercourses, and the dyke had suddenly burst there—that was the worst of it! However, I arrived at last. It was a little thatched house. There was a light in the windows; that meant they expected me. I was met by an old lady, very venerable, in a cap. "Save her!" she says; "she is dying." I say, "Pray don't distress yourself—Where is the invalid?" "Come this way." I see a clean little room, a lamp in the corner; on the bed a girl of twenty, unconscious. She was in a burning heat, and breathing heavily—it was fever. There were two other girls, her sisters, scared and in tears. "Yesterday," they tell me, "she was perfectly well and had a good appetite; this morning she complained of her head, and this evening, suddenly, you see, like this." I say again: "Pray don't be uneasy." It's a doctor's duty, you know—and I went up to her and bled her, told them to put on a mustard-plaster, and prescribed a mixture. Meantime I looked at her; I looked at her, you know—there, by God! I had never seen such a face!—she was a beauty, in a word! I felt quite shaken with pity. Such lovely features; such eyes! . . . But, thank God! she became easier; she fell into a perspiration, seemed to come to her senses, looked round, smiled, and passed her hand over her face. . . . Her sisters bent over her. They ask, "How are you?" "All right," she says, and turns away. I looked at her; she had fallen asleep. "Well," I say, "now the patient should be left alone." So we all went out on tiptoe; only a maid remained, in case she was wanted. In the parlour there was a samovar standing on the table, and a bottle of rum; in our profession one can't get on without it. They gave me tea; asked me to stop the night. . . . I consented: where could I go, indeed, at that time of night? The old lady kept groaning. "What is it?" I say; "she will live; don't worry yourself; you had better take a little rest yourself; it is about two o'clock." "But will you send to wake me if anything happens?" "Yes, yes." The old lady went away, and the girls too went to their own room; they made up a bed for me in the parlour. Well, I went to bed—but I could not get to sleep, for a wonder! for in reality I was very tired. I could not get my patient out of my head. At last I could not put up with it any longer; I got up suddenly; I think to myself, "I will go and see how the patient is getting on." Her bedroom was next to the parlour. Well, I got up, and gently opened the door—how my heart beat! I looked in: the servant was asleep, her mouth wide open, and even snoring, the wretch! but the patient lay with her face towards me, and her arms flung wide apart, poor girl! I went up to her . . . when suddenly she opened her eyes and stared at me! "Who is it? Who is it?" I was in confusion. "Don't be alarmed, madam," I say; "I am the doctor; I have come to see how you feel." "You are the doctor?" "Yes, the doctor; your mother sent for me from the town; we have bled you, madam; now pray go to sleep, and in a day or two, please God! we will set you on your feet again." "Ah, yes, yes, doctor, don't let me die. . . . please, please." "Why do you talk like that? God bless you!" She is in a fever again, I think to myself; I felt her pulse; yes, she was feverish. She looked at me, and then took me by the hand. "I will tell you why I don't want to die; I will tell you. . . . Now we are alone; and only, please don't you . . . not to anyone . . . Listen. . . ." I bent down; she moved her lips quite to my ear; she touched my cheek with her hair—I confess my head went round—and began to whisper. . . . I could make out nothing of it. . . . Ah, she was delirious! . . . She whispered and whispered, but so quickly, and as if it were not in

Russian; at last she finished, and shivering dropped her head on the pillow, and threatened me with her finger: "Remember, doctor, to no one." I calmed her somehow, gave her something to drink, waked the servant, and went away.'

At this point the doctor again took snuff with exasperated energy, and for a moment seemed stupefied by its effects.

'However,' he continued, 'the next day, contrary to my expectations, the patient was no better. I thought and thought, and suddenly decided to remain there, even though my other patients were expecting me. . . . And you know one can't afford to disregard that; one's practice suffers if one does. But, in the first place, the patient was really in danger; and secondly, to tell the truth, I felt strongly drawn to her. Besides, I liked the whole family. Though they were really badly off, they were singularly, I may say, cultivated people. . . . Their father had been a learned man, an author; he died, of course, in poverty, but he had managed before he died to give his children an excellent education; he left a lot of books too. Either because I looked after the invalid very carefully, or for some other reason; any way, I can venture to say all the household loved me as if I were one of the family. . . . Meantime the roads were in a worse state than ever; all communications, so to say, were cut off completely; even medicine could only with difficulty be got from the town. . . . The sick girl was not getting better. . . . Day after day, and day after day . . . but . . . here. . . .' (The doctor made a brief pause.) 'I declare I don't know how to tell you.' . . . (He again took snuff, coughed, and swallowed a little tea.) 'I will tell you without beating about the bush. My patient . . . how should I say? . . . Well, she.had fallen in love with me . . . or, no, it was not that she was in love . . . however . . . really, how should one say?' (The doctor looked down and grew red.) 'No,' he went on quickly, 'in love, indeed! A man should not over-estimate himself. She was an educated girl, clever and well-read, and I had even forgotten my Latin, one may say, completely. As to appearance' (the doctor looked himself over with a smile) 'I am nothing to boast of there either. But God Almighty did not make me a fool; I don't take black for white; I know a thing or two; I could see very clearly, for instance, that Alexandra Andreevna—that was her name—did not feel love for me, but had a friendly, so to say, inclination—a respect or something for me. Though she herself perhaps mistook this sentiment, any way this was her attitude; you may form your own judgment of it. But,' added the doctor, who had brought out all these disconnected sentences without taking breath, and with obvious embarrassment, 'I seem to be wandering rather—you won't understand anything like this . . . There, with your leave, I will relate it all in order.'

He drank off a glass of tea, and began in a calmer voice.

'Well, then. My patient kept getting worse and worse. You are not a doctor, my good sir; you cannot understand what passes in a poor fellow's heart, especially at first, when he begins to suspect that the disease is getting the upper hand of him. What becomes of his belief in himself? You suddenly grow so timid; it's indescribable. You fancy then that you have forgotten everything you knew, and that the patient has no faith in you, and that other people begin to notice how distracted you are, and tell you the symptoms with reluctance; that they are looking at you suspiciously, whispering . . . Ah! it's horrid! There must be a remedy, you think, for this disease, if one could find it. Isn't this it? You try—no, that's not it! You don't allow the medicine the necessary time to do good . . . You clutch at one thing, then at another. Sometimes you take up a book of medical prescriptions—here it is, you think! Sometimes, by Jove, you pick one out by chance, thinking to leave it to fate. . . . But meantime a fellow-creature's dying, and another doctor would have saved him. "We must have a consultation," you say; "I will not take the responsibility on myself." And what a fool you look at such times! Well, in time you learn to bear it; it's nothing to you. A man has died—but it's not your fault; you treated him by the rules. But what's still more torture to you is to see blind faith in you, and to feel yourself that you are not able to be of use. Well, it was just this blind faith that the whole of Alexandra Andreevna's family had in me; they had forgotten to think that their daughter was in danger. I, too, on my side assure them that it's nothing, but meantime my heart sinks into my boots. To add to our troubles, the roads were in such a state that the coachman was gone for whole days together to get medicine. And I never left the patient's room; I could not tear myself away; I tell her amusing stories, you know, and play cards with her. I watch by her side at night. The old mother thanks me with tears in her eyes; but I think to myself, "I don't deserve your gratitude." I frankly confess to you—there is no object in concealing it now—I was in love with my patient. And Alexandra Andreevna had grown fond of me; she would not sometimes let anyone be in her room but me. She began to talk to me, to ask me questions; where I had studied, how I lived, who are my people, whom I go to see. I feel that she ought not to talk; but to forbid her to—to forbid her resolutely, you know—I could not. Sometimes I held my head in my hands, and asked myself, "What are you doing, villain?" . . . And she would take my hand and hold it, give me a long, long look, and turn away, sigh, and say, "How good you are!" Her hands were so feverish, her eyes so large and languid. . . . "Yes," she says, "you are a good, kind man; you are not like our neighbours . . . No, you are not like that. . . . Why did I not know you till now!" "Alexandra Andreevna, calm yourself," I say. . . . "I feel, believe me, I don't know how I have gained . . . but there, calm yourself . . . All will be right; you will be well again." And meanwhile I must tell you,' continued the doctor, bending forward and raising his eyebrows, 'that they associated very little with the neighbours, because the smaller people were not on their level, and pride hindered them from being friendly with the rich. I tell you, they were an exceptionally cultivated family; so you know it was gratifying for me. She would only take her medicine from my hands . . . she would lift herself up, poor girl, with my aid, take it, and gaze at me . . . My heart felt as if it were bursting. And meanwhile she was growing worse and worse, worse and worse, all the time; she will die, I think to myself; she must die. Believe me, I would sooner have gone to the grave myself; and here were her mother and sisters watching me, looking into my eyes . . . and their faith in me was wearing away. "Well? How is she?" "Oh, all right, all right!" All right, indeed! My mind was failing me. Well, I was sitting one night alone again by my patient. The maid was sitting there too, and snoring away in full swing; I can't find fault with the poor girl, though; she was worn out too. Alexandra Andreevna had felt very unwell all the evening; she was very feverish. Until midnight she kept tossing about; at last she seemed to fall asleep; at least, she lay still without stirring. The lamp was burning in the corner before the holy image. I sat there, you know, with my head bent; I even dozed a little. Suddenly it seemed as though someone touched me in the side; I turned round. . . . Good God! Alexandra Andreevna was gazing with intent eyes at me . . . her lips parted, her cheeks seemed burning. "What is it?" "Doctor, shall I die?" "Merciful Heavens!" "No, doctor, no; please don't tell me I shall live . . . don't say so . . . If you knew. . . . Listen! for God's sake don't conceal my real position," and her breath came so fast. "If I can know for certain that I must die . . . then I will tell you all—all!" "Alexandra Andreevna, I beg!" "Listen; I have not been asleep at all

[238]

. . . I have been looking at you a long while. . . . For God's sake! . . . I believe in you; you are a good man, an honest man; I entreat you by all that is sacred in the world—tell me the truth! If you knew how important it is for me. . . . Doctor, for God's sake tell me. . . . Am I in danger?" "What can I tell you, Alexandra Andreevna, pray?" "For God's sake, I beseech you!" "I can't disguise from you," I say, "Alexandra Andreevna; you are certainly in danger; but God is merciful." "I shall die, I shall die." And it seemed as though she were pleased; her face grew so bright, I was alarmed. "Don't be afraid, don't be afraid! I am not frightened of death at all." She suddenly sat up and leaned on her elbow. "Now . . . yes, now I can tell you that I thank you with my whole heart . . . that you are kind and good—that I love you!" I stare at her, like one possessed; it was terrible for me, you know. "Do you hear, I love you!" "Alexandra Andreevna, how have I deserved—" "No, no, you don't—you don't understand me." . . . And suddenly she stretched out her arms, and taking my head in her hands, she kissed it. . . . Believe me, I almost screamed aloud. . . . I threw myself on my knees, and buried my head in the pillow. She did not speak; her fingers trembled in my hair; I listen; she is weeping. I began to soothe her, to assure her. . . . I really don't know what I did say to her. "You will wake up the girl," I say to her; "Alexandra Andreevna, I thank you . . . believe me . . . calm yourself." "Enough, enough!" she persisted; "never mind all of them; let them wake, then; let them come in—it does not matter; I am dying, you see. . . . And what do you fear? Why are you afraid? Lift up your head. . . . Or, perhaps, you don't love me; perhaps I am wrong. . . . In that case, forgive me." "Alexandra Andreevna, what are you saying! . . . I love you, Alexandra Andreevna." She looked straight into my eyes, and opened her arms wide. "Then take me in your arms." I tell you frankly, I don't know how it was I did not go mad that night. I feel that my patient is killing herself; I see that she is not fully herself; I understand, too, that if she did not consider herself on the point of death, she would never have thought of me; and, indeed, say what you will, it's hard to die at twenty without having known love; this was what was torturing her; this was why, in despair, she caught at me—do you understand now? But she held me in her arms, and would not let me go. "Have pity on me, Alexandra Andreevna, and have pity on yourself," I say. "Why," she says; "what is there to think of? You know I must die." . . . This she repeated incessantly. . . . "If I knew that I should return to life, and be a proper young lady again, I should be ashamed . . . of course,

ashamed . . . but why now?" "But who has said you will die?" "Oh,
no, leave off! you will not deceive me; you don't know how to lie—
look at your face." . . . "You shall live, Alexandra Andreevna; I will
cure you; we will ask your mother's blessing . . . we will be united—
we will be happy." "No, no, I have your word; I must die . . . you have
promised me . . . you have told me." . . . It was cruel for me—cruel
for many reasons. And see what trifling things can do sometimes; it
seems nothing at all, but it's painful. It occurred to her to ask me,
what is my name; not my surname, but my first name. I must needs be
so unlucky as to be called Trifon. Yes, indeed; Trifon Ivanitch. Every
one in the house called me doctor. However, there's no help for it. I
say, "Trifon, madam." She frowned, shook her head, and muttered
something in French—ah, something unpleasant, of course!—and
then she laughed—disagreeably too. Well, I spent the whole night
with her in this way. Before morning I went away, feeling as though I
were mad. When I went again into her room it was daytime, after
morning tea. Good God! I could scarcely recognise her; people are laid
in their grave looking better than that. I swear to you, on my honour,
I don't understand—I absolutely don't understand—now, how I lived
through that experience. Three days and nights my patient still
lingered on. And what nights! What things she said to me! And on
the last night—only imagine to yourself—I was sitting near her, and
kept praying to God for one thing only: "Take her," I said, "quickly,
and me with her." Suddenly the old mother comes unexpectedly into
the room. I had already the evening before told her—the mother—
there was little hope, and it would be well to send for a priest. When
the sick girl saw her mother she said: "It's very well you have come;
look at us, we love one another—we have given each other our word."
"What does she say, doctor? What does she say?" I turned livid.
"She is wandering," I say; "the fever." But she: "Hush, hush; you told
me something quite different just now, and have taken my ring. Why
do you pretend? My mother is good—she will forgive—she will
understand—and I am dying. . . . I have no need to tell lies; give me
your hand." I jumped up and ran out of the room. The old lady, of
course, guessed how it was.

'I will not, however, weary you any longer, and to me too, of
course, it's painful to recall all this. My patient passed away the next
day. God rest her soul!' the doctor added, speaking quickly and with a
sigh. 'Before her death she asked her family to go out and leave me
alone with her.

' "Forgive me," she said; "I am perhaps to blame towards you . . . my illness . . . but believe me, I have loved no one more than you . . . do not forget me . . . keep my ring." '

The doctor turned away; I took his hand.

'Ah!' he said, 'let us talk of something else, or would you care to play preference for a small stake? It is not for people like me to give way to exalted emotions. There's only one thing for me to think of; how to keep the children from crying and the wife from scolding. Since then, you know, I have had time to enter into lawful wedlock, as they say. . . . Oh . . . I took a merchant's daughter—seven thousand for her dowry. Her name's Akulina; it goes well with Trifon. She is an ill-tempered woman, I must tell you, but luckily she's asleep all day. . . . Well, shall it be preference?'

We sat down to preference for halfpenny points. Trifon Ivanitch won two roubles and a half from me, and went home late, well pleased with his success.

Lalla

Rosamunde Pilcher

There was a Before and After. Before was before our father died, when we lived in London, in a tall narrow house with a little garden at the back. When we went on family ski-ing holidays every winter and attended suitable—and probably very expensive—day schools.

Our father was a big man, outgoing and immensely active. We thought he was immortal, but then most children think that about their father. The worst thing was that Mother thought he was immortal too, and when he died, keeling over on the pavement between the insurance offices where he worked, and the company car into which he was just about to climb, there followed a period of ghastly limbo. Bereft, uncertain, lost, none of us knew what to do next. But after the funeral and a little talk with the family lawyer, Mother quietly pulled herself together and told us.

At first we were horrified. 'Leave London? Leave school?' Lalla could not believe it. 'But I'm starting 'O' levels next year.'

'There are other schools,' Mother told her.

'And what about Jane's music lessons?'

'We'll find another teacher.'

'I don't mind about leaving school,' said Barney. 'I don't much like my school anyway.'

Mother gave him a smile, but Lalla persisted in her inquisition. 'But where are we going to *live*?'

'We're going to Cornwall.'

And so it was After. Mother sold the lease of the London house and a removals firm came and packed up all the furniture and we travelled, each silently thoughtful, by car to Cornwall. It was spring, and because Mother had not realised how long the journey would take, it was dark by the time we found the village and, finally, the house.

It stood just inside a pair of large gates, backed by tall trees. When we got out of the car, stiff and tired, we could smell the sea and feel the cold wind.

'There's a light in the window,' observed Lalla.

'That'll be Mrs. Bristow,' said Mother, and I knew she was making a big effort to keep her voice cheerful. She went up the little path and knocked at the door, and then, perhaps realising it was ludicrous to be knocking at her own door, opened it. We saw someone coming down the narrow hallway towards us—a fat and bustling lady with grey hair and a hectically flowered pinafore.

'Well, my dear life,' she said, 'what a journey you must have had. I'm all ready for you. There's a kettle on the hob and a pie in the oven.'

The house was tiny compared to the one we had left in London, but we all had rooms to ourselves, as well as an attic for the dolls' house, the books, bricks, model cars and paint-boxes we had refused to abandon, and a ramshackle shed alongside the garage where we could keep our bicycles. The garden was even smaller than the London garden, but this didn't matter because now we were living in the country and there were no boundaries to our new territory.

We explored, finding a wooded lane which led down to a huge inland estuary where it was possible to fish for flounder from the old sea wall. In the other direction, a sandy right-of-way led past the church and over the golf links and the dunes to another beach—a wide and empty shore where the ebb tide took the ocean out half a mile or more.

The Roystons, father, mother and two sons, lived in the big house and were our landlords. We hadn't seen them yet, though Mother had walked, in some trepidation, up the drive to make the acquaintance of Mrs. Royston, and to thank her for letting us have the house. But Mrs. Royston hadn't been in, and poor Mother had had to walk all the way down the drive again with nothing accomplished.

'How old are the Royston boys?' Barney asked Mrs. Bristow.

'I suppose David's thirteen and Paul's about eleven.' She looked at us. 'I don't know how old you lot are.'

'I'm seven,' said Barney, 'and Jane's twelve and Lalla's fourteen.'

'Well,' said Mrs. Bristow. 'That's nice. Fit in nicely, you would.'

'They're far too young for me,' said Lalla. 'Anyway, I've seen them. I was hanging out the washing for Mother and they came down the drive and out of the gate on their bicycles. They didn't even look my way.'

'Come now,' said Mrs. Bristow, 'they're probably shy as you are.'

'We don't particularly want to know them,' said Lalla.

'But . . .' I started, and then stopped. I wasn't like Lalla. I wanted to make friends. It would be nice to know the Royston boys. They had a tennis court; I had caught a glimpse of it through the trees. I wouldn't mind being asked to play tennis.

But for Lalla, of course, it was different. Fourteen was a funny age, neither one thing nor the other. And as for the way that Lalla looked! Sometimes I thought that if I didn't love her, and she wasn't my sister, I should hate her for her long, cloudy brown hair, the tilt of her nose, the amazing blue of her eyes, the curve of her pale mouth. During the last six months she seemed to have grown six inches.

I was short and square and my hair was too curly and horribly tangly. The awful bit was, I couldn't remember Lalla ever looking the way I looked, which made it fairly unlikely that I should end up looking like her.

A few days later Mother came back from shopping in the village to say that she had met Mrs. Royston in the grocer's and we had all been asked for tea.

Lalla said, 'I don't want to go.'

'Why not?' asked Mother.

'They're just little boys. Let Jane and Barney go.'

'It's just for tea,' pleaded Mother.

She looked so anxious that Lalla gave in. She shrugged and sighed, her face closed in resignation.

We went, and it was a failure. The boys didn't want to meet us any more than Lalla wanted to meet them. Lalla was at her coolest, her most remote. I knocked over my teacup, and Barney, who usually chatted to everybody, was silenced by the superiority of his hosts. When tea was over Lalla stayed with the grown-ups, but Barney and I were sent off with the boys.

'Show Jane and Barney your tree-house,' Mrs. Royston told them as we trailed out of the door.

They took us out into the garden and showed us the tree-house. It was a marvellous piece of construction, strong and roomy. Barney's face was filled with longing. 'Who built it?' he asked.

'Our cousin Godfrey. He's eighteen. He can build anything. It's our club, and you're not members.'

They whispered together and went off, leaving us standing beneath the forbidden tree-house.

When the summer holidays came, Mother appeared to have forgotten about our social debt to the Royston boys and we were careful not to remind her. So their names were never raised, and we never saw them except at a distance, cycling off to the village or down to the beach. Sometimes on Sunday afternoons they had guests and played tennis on their court. I longed to be included, but Lalla, deep in a book, behaved as though the Roystons didn't exist. Barney had taken up gardening, and, with his usual single-mindedness, was concentrating on digging himself a vegetable patch. He said he was going to sell lettuces, and Mother said that maybe he was the one who was going to make our fortune.

It was a hot summer, made for swimming. Lalla had grown out of her old swimsuit, so Mother made her a cotton bikini out of scraps. It was pale blue, just right for her tan and her long, pale hair. She looked beautiful in it, and I longed to look just like her. We went to the beach most days, and often saw the Royston boys there. But the beach was so vast that there was no necessity for social contact, and we all avoided each other.

Until one Sunday. The tide came in during the afternoon that day, and Mother packed us a picnic so we could set off after lunch. When we got to the beach, Lalla said she was going to swim right away, but Barney and I decided we would wait. We took our spades and went down to where the outgoing tide had left shallow pools in the sand. There we started the construction of a large and complicated harbour. Absorbed in our task, we lost track of time, and never noticed the stranger approaching. Suddenly a long shadow fell across the sparkling water.

I looked up, shading my eyes against the sun. He said 'Hello', and squatted down to our level.

'Who are you?' I asked.

'I'm Godfrey Howard, the Roystons' cousin. I'm staying with them.'

Barney suddenly found his tongue. 'Did you build the tree-house?'

'That's right.'

'How *did* you do it?'

Godfrey began to tell him. I listened and wondered how any person apparently so nice could have anything to do with those hateful Royston boys. It wasn't that he was particularly good-looking. His hair was mousey, his nose too big and he wore spectacles. He wasn't even very tall. But there was something warm and friendly about his deep voice and his smile.

'Did you go up and look at it?'

Barney went back to his digging. Godfrey looked at me. I said, 'They wouldn't let us. They said it was a club. They didn't like us.'

'They think you don't like them. They think you come from London and that you're very grand.'

This was astonishing. 'Grand? *Us?*' I said indignantly. 'We never even pretended to be grand.' And then I remembered Lalla's coolness, her pale, unsmiling lips. 'I mean—Lalla's older—it's different for her.' His silence at this was encouraging. 'I wanted to make friends,' I admitted.

He was sympathetic. 'It's difficult sometimes. People are shy.' All at once he stopped, and looked over my shoulder. I turned to see what had caught his attention, and saw Lalla coming towards us across the sand. Her hair lay like wet silk over her shoulders, and she had knotted her red towel around her hips like a sarong. As she approached, Godfrey stood up. I said, introducing them the way Mother introduced people, 'This is Lalla.'

'Hello, Lalla,' said Godfrey.

'He's the Roystons' cousin,' I went on quickly. 'He's staying with them.'

'Hello,' said Lalla.

Godfrey said, 'David and Paul are wanting to play cricket. It's not much good playing cricket with just three people and I wondered if you'd come and join us?'

'Lalla won't want to play cricket,' I told myself. 'She'll snub him and then we'll never be asked again.'

But she didn't snub him. She said, uncertainly, 'I don't think I'm much good at cricket.'

'But you could always try?'

'Yes.' She began to smile. 'I suppose I could always try.'

And so we all finally got together. We played a strange form of beach cricket invented by Godfrey, which involved much lashing out at the ball and hysterical running. When we were too hot to play any longer, we swam. The Roystons had a couple of wooden surf boards and they let us have turns, riding in on our stomachs on the long, warm breakers of the flood tide. By five o'clock we were ready for tea, and we collected our various baskets and haversacks and sat around in a circle on the sand. Other people's picnics are always much nicer than one's own, so we ate the Royston sandwiches and chocolate biscuits, and they ate Mother's scones with loganberry jam in the middle.

We had a last swim before the tide turned, and then gathered up our belongings and walked slowly home together. Barney and the two Roystons led the way, planning the next day's activities, and I walked with Godfrey and Lalla. But gradually, in the natural manner of events, they fell behind me. Plodding up and over the springy turf of the golf course, I listened to their voices.

'Do you like living here?'

'It's different from London.'

'That's where you lived before?'

'Yes, but my father died and we couldn't afford to live there any more.'

'I'm sorry, I didn't know. Of course, I envy your living here. I'd rather be at Carwheal than anywhere else in the world.'

'Where do you live?'

'In Bristol.'

'Are you at school there?'

'I've finished with school. I'm starting college in September. I'm going to be a vet.'

'A vet?' Lalla considered this. 'I've never met a vet before.'

He laughed. 'You haven't actually met one yet.'

I smiled to myself in satisfaction. They sounded like two grown-ups talking. Perhaps a grown-up friend of her own was all that Lalla had needed. I had a feeling that we had crossed another watershed. After today, things would be different.

The Roystons were now our friends. Our relieved mothers—for Mrs. Royston, faced with our unrelenting enmity, had been just as concerned and conscience-stricken as Mother—took advantage of the truce, and after that Sunday we were never out of each other's houses. Through the good offices of the Roystons, our social life widened, and Mother found herself driving us all over the county to attend various beach picnics, barbecues, sailing parties and teenage dances. By the end of the summer we had been accepted. We had dug ourselves in. Carwheal was home. And Lalla grew up.

She and Godfrey wrote to each other. I knew this because I would see his letters to her lying on the table in the hall. She would take them upstairs to read them in secret in her room, and we were all too great respecters of privacy ever to mention them. When he came to Carwheal, which he did every holiday, to stay with the Roystons, he was always around first thing in the morning on the first day.

He said it was to see us all, but we knew it was Lalla he had come to see.

He now owned a battered second-hand car. A lesser man might have scooped Lalla up and taken her off on her own, but Godfrey was far too kind, and he would drive for miles, to distant coves and hill-tops, with the whole lot of us packed into his long-suffering car, and the boot filled with food and towels and snorkels and other assorted clobber.

But he was only human, and often they would drift off on their own, and walk away from us. We would watch their progress and let them go, knowing that in an hour or two they would be back—Lalla with a bunch of wild flowers or some shells in her hand, Godfrey sunburned and tousled—both of them smiling and content in a way that we found reassuring and yet did not wholly understand.

Lalla had always been such a certain person, so positive, so unveering from a chosen course, that we were all taken by surprise by her vacillating indecision as to what she was going to do with her life. She was nearly eighteen, with her final exams over and her future spread before her like a new country observed from the peak of some painfully climbed hill.

Mother wanted her to go to university.

'Isn't it rather a waste of time if I don't know what I'm going to do at the end of it? How can I decide now what I'm going to do with the rest of my life? It's inhuman. Impossible.'

'But darling, what do you want to do?'

'I don't know. Travel, I suppose. Of course, I could be really original and take a typing course.'

'It might at least give you time to think things over.'

This conversation took place at breakfast. It might have continued forever, reaching no satisfactory conclusion, but the post arrived as we sat there over our empty coffee cups. There was the usual dull bundle of envelopes, but, as well, a large square envelope for Lalla. She opened it idly, read the card inside and made a face. 'Goodness, how grand, a proper invitation to a proper dance.'

'How nice,' said Mother, trying to decipher the butcher's bill. 'Who from?'

'Mrs. Menheniot,' said Lalla.

We were all instantly agog, grabbing at the invitation in order to gloat over it. We had once been to lunch with Mrs. Menheniot, who lived with Mr. Menheniot and a tribe of junior Menheniots in a beautiful house on the Fal. For some unspecified reason they were very rich, and their house was vast and white with a pillared portico and green lawns which sloped down to the tidal inlets of the river.

'Are you going to go?' I asked.

Lalla shrugged. 'I don't know.'

'It's in August. Perhaps Godfrey will be here and you can go with him.'

'He's not coming down this summer. He has to earn money to pay his way through college.'

She would not make up her mind whether or not she would go to Mrs. Menheniot's party, and probably never would have come to any decision if it had not been for the fact that, before very long, I had been invited too. I was really too young, as Mrs. Menheniot's booming voice pointed out over the telephone when she rang Mother, but they were short of girls and it would be a blessing if I could be there to swell the numbers. When Lalla knew that I had been asked as well, she said of course we would go. She had passed her driving test and we would borrow Mother's car.

We were then faced with the problem of what we should wear, as Mother could not begin to afford to buy us the sort of evening dresses we wanted. In the end she sent away to Liberty's for yards of material, and she made them for us, beautifully, on her sewing machine. Lalla's was pale blue lawn and in it she looked like a goddess—Diana the Huntress perhaps. Mine was a sort of tawny-gold and I looked quite presentable in it, but of course not a patch on Lalla.

When the night of the dance came, we put on our dresses and set off together in Mother's Mini, giggling slightly with nerves. But when we reached the Menheniots' house, we stopped giggling because the whole affair was so grand as to be awesome. There were floodlights and car parks and hundreds of sophisticated-looking people all making their way towards the front door.

Indoors, we stood at the foot of the crowded staircase and I was filled with panic. We knew nobody. There was not a single familiar face. Lalla whisked a couple of glasses of champagne from a passing tray and gave me one. I took a sip, and at that very moment a voice rang out above the hubbub. 'Lalla!' A girl was coming down the stairs, a dark girl in a strapless satin dress that had very obviously not been made on her mother's sewing machine.

Lalla looked up. 'Rosemary!'

She was Rosemary Sutton from London. She and Lalla had been at school together in the old days. They fell into each other's arms and embraced as though this was all either of them had been waiting for. 'What are you doing? I never thought I'd see you here. How marvellous. Come and meet Allan. You remember my brother Allan, don't you? Oh, this is exciting.'

Allan was so good-looking as to be almost unreal. Fair as his sister was dark, impeccably turned out. Lalla was tall but he was taller. He looked down at her, and his rather wooden features were filled with both surprise and obvious pleasure. He said, 'But of course I remember.' He smiled and laid down his glass. 'How could I forget?' Come and dance.'

I scarcely saw her again all evening. He took her away from me and I was bereft, as though I had lost my sister for ever. At one point I was rescued by Mrs. Menheniot herself, who dragooned some young man into taking me to supper, but after supper even he melted away. I found an empty sofa in a deserted sitting-out room, and collapsed into it. It was half-past-twelve and I longed for my bed. I wondered what people would think if I put up my feet and had a little snooze.

Somebody came into the room, and then withdrew again. I looked up and saw his retreating back view. I said, 'Godfrey.' He turned back. I got up off the sofa, back on to my aching feet.

'What are you doing here? Lalla said you were working.'

'I am, but I wanted to come. I drove down from Bristol. That's why I'm so late.' I knew why he had wanted to come. To see Lalla. 'I didn't expect to see you.'

'They were short of girls, so I got included.'

We gazed glumly at each other, and my heart felt very heavy. Godfrey's dinner jacket looked as though he had borrowed it from some larger person, and his bow tie was crooked. I said, 'I think Lalla's dancing.'

'Why don't you come and dance with me, and we'll see.'

I thought this a rotten idea, but didn't like to say so. Together we made our way towards the ballroom. The ceiling lights had been turned off and the disco lights now flashed red and green and blue across the smoky darkness. Music thumped and rocked an assault on our ears, and the floor seemed to be filled with an unidentifiable confusion of people, of flying hair and arms and legs. Godfrey and I joined in at the edge, but I could tell that his heart wasn't in it. I wished that he had never come. I prayed that he would not find Lalla.

But of course, he saw her, because it was impossible not to. It was impossible to miss Allan Sutton as well. They were both so tall, so beautiful. Godfrey's face seemed to close up.

'Who's she with?' he asked.

'Allan Sutton. He and his sister have come down from London. Lalla used to know them.'

I couldn't say any more. I couldn't tell Godfrey to go and claim her for himself. I wasn't even certain by then what sort of a reception she would have given him. And anyway, as we watched them, Allan stopped dancing and put his arm around Lalla, drawing her towards him, whispering something into her ear. She slipped her hand into his, and they moved away towards the open french window. The next moment they were lost to view, swallowed into the darkness of the garden beyond.

At four o'clock in the morning Lalla and I drove home in silence. We were not giggling now. I wondered sadly if we would ever giggle together again. I ached with exhaustion and I was out of sympathy with her. Godfrey had never even spoken to her. Soon after our dance he had said goodbye and disappeared, presumably to make the long, lonely journey back to Bristol.

She, on the other hand, had an aura of happiness about her that was almost tangible. I glanced at her and saw her peaceful, smiling profile. It was hard to think of anything to say.

It was Lalla who finally broke the silence. 'I know what I'm going to do. I mean, I know what I'm going to do with my life. I'm going back to London. Rosemary says I can live with her. I'll take a secretarial course or something, then get a job.'

'Mother will be disappointed.'

'She'll understand. It's what I've always wanted. We're buried down here. And there's another thing; I'm tired of being poor. I'm tired of home-made dresses and never having a new car. We've always talked about making our fortunes, and as I'm the eldest I might as well make a start. If I don't do it now, I never will.'

I said, 'Godfrey was there this evening.'

'Godfrey?'

'He drove down from Bristol.'

She did not say anything and I was angry. I wanted to hurt her and make her feel as bad as I felt. 'He came because he wanted to see you. But you didn't even notice him.'

'You can scarcely blame me,' said Lalla, 'for that.'

And so she went back to London, lived with Rosemary, and took a secretarial course, just as she said she would. Later, she got a job on the editorial staff of a fashionable magazine, but it was not long before one of the photographers spied her potential, seduced her from her typewriter, and started taking pictures of her. Soon her lovely face smiled at us from the cover of the magazine.

'How does it feel to have a famous daughter?' people asked Mother, but she never quite accepted Lalla's success, just as she never quite accepted Allan Sutton. Allan's devotion to Lalla had proved unswerving and he was her constant companion.

'Let's hope he doesn't marry her,' said Barney, but of course eventually, inevitably, they decided to do just that. 'We're engaged!' Lalla rang up from London to tell us. Her voice sounded, unnervingly, as though she was calling from the next room.

'Darling!' said Mother, faintly.

'Oh, do be pleased. Please be pleased. I'm so happy and I couldn't bear it if you weren't happy, too.'

So of course Mother said that she was pleased, but the truth was that none of us really liked Allan very much. He was—well—spoilt. He was conceited. He was too rich. I said as much to Mother, but Mother was loyal to Lalla. She said, 'Things mean a lot to Lalla. I think they always have. I mean, possessions and security. And perhaps someone who truly loves her.'

I said, 'Godfrey truly loved her.'

'But that was when they were young. And perhaps Godfrey couldn't give her love.'

'He could make her laugh. Allan never makes her laugh.'

'Perhaps,' said Mother sadly, 'she's grown out of laughter.'

And then it was Easter. We hadn't heard from Lalla for a bit, and didn't expect her to come to Carwheal for the spring holiday. But she rang up, out of the blue, and said that she hadn't been well and was taking a couple of weeks off. Mother was delighted, of course, but concerned about her health.

By now we were all more or less grown-up. David was studying to be a doctor, and Paul had a job on the local newspaper. I had achieved a place at the Guildhall School of Music, and Barney was no longer a little boy but a gangling teenager with an insatiable appetite. Still, however, we gathered for the holidays, and that Easter Godfrey abandoned his sick dogs and ailing cows to the ministrations of his partner and joined us.

It was lovely weather, almost as warm as summer. The sort of weather that makes one feel young again—a child. There was scented thyme on the golf links and the cliff walks were starred with primroses and wild violets. In the Roystons' garden the daffodils blew in the long grass beneath the tree-house, and Mrs. Royston put up the tennis net and swept the cobwebs out of the summer house.

It was during one of these sessions that Godfrey and I talked about Lalla. We were in the summer house together, sitting out while the others played a set.

'Tell me about Lalla.'

'She's engaged.'

'I know. I saw it in the paper.' I could think of nothing to say. 'Do you like him, Allan Sutton, I mean.'

I said 'Yes', but I was never much good at lying.

Godfrey turned his head and looked at me. He was wearing old jeans and a white shirt, and I thought that he had grown older in a subtle way. He was more sure of himself, and somehow more attractive.

He said, 'That night of the Menheniots' dance, I was going to ask her to marry me.'

'Oh, Godfrey.'

'I hadn't even finished my training, but I thought perhaps we'd manage. And when I saw her, I knew that I had lost her. I'd left it too late.'

On the day that Lalla was due to arrive, I took Mother's old car into the neighbouring town to do some shopping. When the time came to return home, the engine refused to start. After struggling for a bit, I walked to the nearest garage and persuaded a kindly, oily man to come and help me. But he told me it was hopeless.

We walked back to the garage and I telephoned home. But it wasn't Mother who answered the call, it was Godfrey.

I explained what had happened. 'Lalla's train is due at the junction in about half-an-hour and we said someone would meet her.'

There was a momentary hesitation, then Godfrey said, 'I'll go. I'll take my car.'

When I finally reached home, exhausted from carrying the laden grocery bags from the bus stop, Godfrey's car was nowhere to be seen.

A short time later the telephone rang. But it wasn't Lalla, explaining where they were, it was a call from London and it was Allan Sutton.

'I have to speak to Lalla.'

His voice sounded frantic. I said cautiously, 'Is anything wrong?'

'She's broken off our engagement. I got back from the office and found a letter from her and my ring. She said she was coming home. She doesn't want to get married.'

I found it in my heart to be very sorry for him. 'But Allan, you must have had *some* idea.'

'None. Absolutely none. It's just a bolt from the blue. I know she's been a bit off-colour lately, but I thought she was just tired.'

'She must have her reasons, Allan,' I told him, as gently as I could.

'Talk to her, Jane. Try to make her see sense.'

He rang off at last. I put the receiver back on the hook and stood for a moment, gathering my wits about me and assessing this new and startling turn of events. I found myself caught up in a tangle of conflicting emotions. Enormous sympathy for Allan; a reluctant admiration for Lalla who had had the courage to take this shattering decision; but, as well, a sort of rising excitement.

Godfrey. Godfrey and Lalla. Where were they? I knew then that I could not face Mother and Barney before I had found out what was going on. Quietly, I opened the door and went out of the house, through the gates, down the lane. As soon as I turned the corner at the end of the lane, I saw Godfrey's car parked on the patch of grass outside the church.

It was a marvellously warm, benign sort of evening. I took the path that led past the church and towards the beach. Before I had gone very far, I saw them, walking up over the golf links towards me. The wind blew Lalla's hair over her face. She was wearing her London high-heeled boots so was taller than Godfrey. They should have appeared ill-assorted, but there was something about them that was totally right. They were a couple, holding hands, walking up from the beach as they had walked innumerable times, together.

I stopped, suddenly reluctant to disturb their intimacy. But Lalla had seen me. She waved, and then let go of Godfrey's hand and began to run towards me, her arms flailing like windmills. 'Jane!' I had never seen her so exuberant. 'Oh, Jane.' I ran to meet her. We hugged each other, and for some stupid reason my eyes were full of tears.

'Oh, darling Jane . . .'

'I had to come and find you.'

'Did you wonder where we were? We went for a walk. I had to talk to Godfrey. He was the one person I could talk to.'

'Lalla, Allan's been on the phone.'

'I had to do it. It was all a ghastly mistake.'

'But you found out in time. That's all that matters.'

'I thought I was going after what I wanted. I thought I had what I wanted, and then I found out that I didn't want it at all. Oh, I've missed you all so much. There wasn't anybody I could talk to.'

Over her shoulder I saw Godfrey coming, tranquilly, to join us. I let go of Lalla and went to give him a kiss. I didn't know what they had been discussing as they paced the lonely beach, and I knew that I never would. But still, I had the feeling that the outcome could be nothing but good for all of us.

I said, 'We must go back. Mother and Barney don't know about anything. They'll be thinking that I've dissolved into thin air, as well as the pair of you.'

'In that case,' said Godfrey, and he took Lalla's hand in his own once more, 'perhaps we'd better go and tell them.'

And so we walked home; the three of us. In the warm evening, in the sunshine, in the fresh wind.

Acknowledgements

The Publisher has made every effort to contact the Copyright holders, but wishes to apologise to those he has been unable to trace. Grateful acknowledgement is made for permission to reprint the following:

'Miss Geraldine Parkington' by Catherine Cookson. Copyright © Catherine Cookson 1984. Reproduced by permission of Anthony Sheil Associates Limited.

'A Constellation of Events' by John Updike. Reprinted by permission of André Deutsch Limited and Alfred A. Knopf, Inc., New York.

'The Square Peg' by Jilly Cooper. Reproduced by permission of Desmond Elliott.

'Kiss Me Again, Stranger' by Daphne du Maurier. From *The Birds and Other Stories* © Daphne du Maurier 1952. Reproduced by permission of Curtis Brown Limited, London.

'When Love Isn't Enough' by Stella Whitelaw. Reprinted by permission of Rupert Crew Limited.

"A Girl I Used to Know," as "The Valiant Heart," in *Good Housekeeping*, March 1988. Reprinted by permission of Rosamunde Pilcher.

'Joe Johnson' by H.E. Bates. From *Colonel Julian and Other Stories*. Reproduced by permission of Laurence Pollinger Limited; courtesy the Estate of H.E. Bates.

'Snow Storm' by Jean Stubbs. Reproduced by permission of Macmillan Limited.

'The Letters' by Edith Wharton. From *The Stories of Edith Wharton, Vol. 1*. Edited and introduced by Anita Brookner, Simon & Schuster 1989. Reproduced by permission of Watkins/Loomis Agency Inc., New York.

'Ethel Crowther' by Audrie Manley-Tucker. Reprinted by permission of Rupert Crew Limited.

'The Curious Courtship of Mrs Blishen' by Judy Gardiner. Reprinted by permission of Rupert Crew Limited.

'The Needlecase' by Elizabeth Bowen. From *The Collected Stories of Elizabeth Bowen*. Copyright © 1981 by Curtis Brown Limited, London, Literary Executors of the Estate of Elizabeth Bowen. Reproduced by permission of Curtis Brown Limited, London and Alfred A. Knopf, Inc., New York.

'Lalla' by Rosamunde Pilcher. Reprinted by permission of Felicity Bryan, Oxford.